SCORNED

and

Craved

THE FRENCHMAN'S LIONHEARTED WIFE

BY
BREE WOLF

Scorned & Craved-The Frenchman's Lionhearted Wife

by Bree Wolf

Cover Art by Victoria Cooper
Copyright © 2021 Bree Wolf
E-Book ISBN: 978-3-96482-066-2
Paperback ISN: 978-3-96482-067-9
Hardcover ISBN: 978-3-96482-068-6

www.breewolf.com

Acknowledgement

A great big thank-you to all those who aided me in finishing this book and made it the wonderful story it has become. First and foremost, of course, there is my family, who inspires me on a daily basis, giving me the enthusiasm and encouragement I need to type away at my computer day after day. Thank you so much!

Then there are my proofreaders, beta readers and readers who write to me out of the blue with wonderful ideas and thoughts. Jillian, my most critical reader, who often provides feedback I don't want to hear, but which then makes the book a lot more fun to write and read. Thank you for your honest words! Jodi, Dara and Monique comb through my manuscripts in an utterly diligent way that allows me to smooth off the rough edges and make it shine. Thank you so much for your dedication to my stories! Brie, Carol, Zan-Mari, Kim, Martha and Mary are my hawks, their eyes sweeping over the words to spot those pesky errors I seem to be absolutely blind to. Thank you so much for aiding me with your keen eyesight!

SCORNED

and

Craved

Prologue

London, 1808 (or a variation thereof)

Four Years Earlier

Lady Juliet, daughter to the late Earl of Goswick, did not dare believe her eyes. She tried not to stare but to keep her gaze averted and merely glance at the stranger through lowered lashes.

Yet...

Was it possible? A pirate! He had the look of a pirate, did he not? Not that Juliet had ever laid eyes on a pirate before. Considering the sheltered life she had lived, she knew next to nothing of the world.

Yet...

The man's dark green eyes seemed to spark with something almost devilish, matching that sinfully wicked smile that curled up his lips as he shifted his attention from Juliet's newly discovered stepsister Violet to her.

Juliet immediately dropped her gaze and retreated another step toward the window, dabbing a handkerchief to her eyes. If only there was a way to hide from the man's inquisitive gaze, for the way his eyes swept over her made her feel...

...vulnerable,

...lightheaded,

...and strangely out of breath.

"Lady Silcox, may I speak to you?" Violet addressed Juliet's mother, urging her as well as her husband Lord Cullingwood out of the drawing room...

...leaving Juliet alone with...

...the pirate!

Juliet knew she ought to protest. After all, the door had yet to close. Violet still stood upon its threshold, exchanging a few whispered words with her cousin.

Her cousin, the pirate!

Who pronounced her stepsister's name *Violette*!

Juliet shook her head as bright spots began to dance in front of her eyes. None of what had happened today made any sense, and a part of her wondered if perhaps she was still asleep, lost in a dream that felt... too real.

Again, Juliet dared a peek at the tall, dark-haired stranger with the roguish smile. He wore his hair unfashionably long and tied at the nape of his neck, his chin covered in a mild stubble that gave him a most dangerous allure. He stood tall with broad shoulders and large hands, and the way he moved made Juliet think of a feline she had once seen in a zoological garden.

Yes, he was no doubt a dangerous man, and she ought to object to being left alone with him.

Yet, she did not, for a traitorous part of her wanted to know more about this pirate—this Frenchman!—who had so unexpectedly found his way to London and into her life.

And then the door did close, and they were alone.

Juliet felt ready to faint on the spot, and she pinched her eyes shut against the bright spots that returned with full force, their light almost blinding. Was her new-found stepsister mad? Why would she leave her alone with a man like that, cousin or not?

For a long moment, silence lingered as she fought to regain her composure, her thoughts focused inward so that she did not even hear him approach.

"Will you not look at me, *Cherie?*" he asked in a deeply tantalizing voice.

Instantly, Juliet's eyes flew open.

Shocked to find him so close, no more than a few steps from where she stood, she stumbled backward until her back hit the window, her breath coming fast as she stared up into his face.

The corners of his mouth curled upward. "Do I frighten you?"

Juliet swallowed. "N-No, s-sir," she stammered before reminding herself that she *was* a lady and ought to hold her head high. "I...I am merely surprised that my sister—stepsister — deemed it right to leave us alone together." Her face felt as though it were on fire, and it was a considerable effort for her not to drop her gaze.

Instead of being offended as a true gentleman would be, the Frenchman chuckled. "Violette knows that I would never lay a hand on you...without your permission." The dark look in his eyes whispered of daring and temptation, and Juliet could not help but wonder what he would do if she were...to give her permission.

Not knowing how to reply, Juliet drew in an unsteady breath, her mouth opening and closing as she desperately searched for something to say.

A half-sided grin came to his face before he took yet another step closer. "I hear you're about to be married, *non?*" His brows rose in a challenging gesture.

Juliet felt her hands begin to tremble for the mere thought of her impending nuptials never failed to make her feel sick to her stomach.

"I hear you are to marry an old man," he continued, measured steps moving him ever closer, his dark gaze never once leaving her face.

Juliet bit her lower lip, aware that she simply ought to step around him and leave. Why then could she not bring herself to move?

Barely an arm's length in front of her, the French rogue lowered his head down to hers and whispered, "Do you think your future husband will honor your wishes and not lay a hand on you without your permission?"

Feeling the faint brush of his warm breath against her lips, Juliet felt herself begin to sway. Her knees threatened to buckle at any moment, and those dreaded bright spots once again hindered her vision. "You are...not to speak of such things," she managed to say, doing her utmost to hide her mortification, her temptation even, behind righteous indignation. "A gentleman would never address a lady thus, and we are not even acquainted in the least." She lifted her chin a fraction. "I do not even know your name."

The rogue grinned then dipped his head in a greeting gesture. "Henri Duret, *Mademoiselle*, at your service. You may call me Henri."

Juliet barely kept herself from curtseying. "You're French?"

Again, he grinned. "What gave me away?" he asked, his French accent now thicker than before.

Juliet tried her best to ignore his mocking tone. "And you're...a pirate?"

"A privateer," he corrected, a touch of pride in his voice that surprised her. "For God and country and above all my family."

His words pleased her; although, she knew they ought not. "You're Violet's cousin?"

He nodded. "Not by blood." Something warm and deeply affectionate came to his green eyes. "But she is like a sister to me, and I would give my life to see her safe."

Juliet swallowed; her throat dry as she tried her hardest not to allow his words to weaken her resolve. "Is that why you're here? To protect her?"

His eyes searched hers, and then he inched closer, and for a shocking moment, his gaze dropped to her lips. "Here in London? Or here in this room?"

Her breath lodged in Juliet's throat as she felt the tips of his fingers touch her arms, then trail lower, running along the fabric of her sleeves.

"*Ma chère cousine* asked me to speak to you," he whispered in that voice of his that never failed to send unfamiliar sensations dancing across Juliet's skin. "She asked me to give you a reason to choose differently." His gaze held hers, teasing, daring, challenging, as his hands moved from her arms and reached for her waist.

Juliet drew in a sharp breath. "I am betrothed," she defended herself. "My stepfather arranged this match for me and—"

"Though he did not ask your opinion, *n'est-ce pas?*" Henri whispered as his hands settled more firmly upon her waist.

"He did not," she managed to reply and then surprised herself by tilting up her head to meet his eyes more fully. All of a sudden, she could not seem to look away as though those green eyes of his were a beacon she did not dare let out of her sight.

"Do you wish to marry the man he chose for you?" Henri questioned her as his hands slid farther onto her back. "Perhaps as an innocent lady you're not aware of the intimacies shared between husband and wife." A dark chuckle rumbled deep in his throat as he urged her closer, urged her to bridge that last bit of distance between them. "Would you care for me to enlighten you, *Cherie?*"

Warning bells went off in Juliet's head. Innocent or not, she knew very well that this was her last chance to escape the drawing room unscathed.

To escape *Henri Duret* unscathed.

And then the moment passed, and instead of rushing out the door, Juliet found herself taking that last step...closer.

A wickedly triumphant smile curled up Henri's lips before he slowly lowered his head to hers. "You are a rare treasure, *Cherie.* Any man would enjoy kissing you." His lips brushed against hers in a feather-light touch, and Juliet felt herself respond in a way she would never have expected. Her eyes closed, and her hands came to rest upon his broad chest. "But would you enjoy every kiss bestowed upon you?"

Again, his lips returned to brush against hers. Only this time, they lingered, their touch no longer feather-light but with a tentative depth. "Be warned," he whispered against her mouth, "for an arranged match is rarely of a passionate nature." One hand grasped her chin before he nipped her lower lip.

Juliet gasped at the sensation, and heat shot into her cheeks.

"Be certain of what you want, *Cherie.* Be very certain," Henri whispered huskily before words became obsolete and his mouth claimed hers without consideration for her innocence or any measure of restraint.

Juliet completely lost herself in his kiss. It was wild and passionate and dangerous like the man himself. She knew next to nothing about him, and yet, she felt oddly complete and almost at peace in his arms.

For the first time in her recent memory, Juliet felt her heart beat not with dread or apprehension or a sense of foreboding, her impending nuptials to her stepfather's oldest friend a constant threat looming upon the horizon.

No, for the first time, the rapid thud against her ribcage made her feel strong and daring and...

...hopeful.

Henri's left hand moved into her hair, and she could feel pins come loose before they fell to the floor. He grasped a fistful of her tresses and gave a soft tug, tilting her head back.

Then he deepened his kiss, his other arm slung around her, holding her pressed to his body so she could feel his heartbeat as though it were her own.

Perhaps in this short, precious moment, it was.

It was also in this very moment that Juliet realized that she had to accept Violet's daring offer to escape the match her stepfather had arranged for her. There had to be more to life than duty and sacrifice, didn't there?

Juliet desperately hoped that it was so.

Chapter One

STUCK

London, 1812 (or a variation thereof)

Four Years Later

All of London seemed present at tonight's ball. Lights sparkled everywhere, and the delicate notes of the orchestra mingled with the soft swaying of the many couples determined to dance the night away. Joy rested upon their features as they laughed and smiled and chatted animatedly. Ladies batted their eyelashes, bestowing precious smiles upon gentlemen, who bowed gracefully and offered their arms to the ladies of their choice.

Happiness and delight lingered in the air as well as the hope and promise of a future most desired.

Standing on the edge of the ballroom, Juliet heaved a deep sigh, wishing she could be one of them, wishing she still had a future.

Four years ago, she had agreed to her stepsister's daring plan, and, yes, it had freed her of the threat of marriage.

Marriage to an older man.

Marriage to someone she had not wanted.

Marriage to...anyone.

"Are you unwell tonight, my dear?" her mother asked, a concerned look upon her face. Kindness and understanding rested in her eyes as she placed a gentle hand upon Juliet's arm. "You seem distraught."

Again, Juliet heaved a deep sigh. What was she to say? "I am well, Mother. Please do not worry." She tried to smile but could see that her mother was wise to it.

"Is there no one you would consider marrying?" her mother inquired, her hands grasping Juliet's and holding them tightly. "Yes, a love match is something every woman desires; however, other joys can be found in marriage." Her hands held Juliet's tighter, and a wide smile came to her face. "You could be a mother. Motherhood is such a joy. Will you truly deny yourself the experience?"

Once, Juliet had hoped that perhaps despite everything, she might still find love or at least affection in marriage. However, that dream had left her long ago. "Do not pretend, Mother, that I could simply choose a husband." She sighed and glanced around the large ballroom. "You know as well as I do that very few men would consider marrying me after what happened, and those that would..."

Four years ago, her stepsister Violet had used her husband's influence to force Juliet's fiancé, Lord Dowling, to accept her decision to change her mind. Juliet had cried off, and her stepfather's oldest friend had gritted his teeth and not said a bad word about her as he bowed his head in defeat. Others had seen to it that he would comply, for Violet's husband, Lord Cullingwood, was an influential man and he had threatened Lord Dowling with severe repercussions should he not oblige.

At first, everything had seemed so promising. Freed from her impending marriage, Juliet had been able to breathe again. Hope had returned to her heart...until reality had caught up with her.

Despite Lord Dowling's courteous acceptance of her change of heart, the *ton* did not forgive those who broke the rules. To break a marriage agreement was something that was simply not done, or if it was, those involved would never be able to recover fully.

A mark remained.

Something that tainted Juliet.

Something that made her undesirable to most.

"What about Lord Hastings?" her mother suggested as she turned to look at the man in question, who was presently guiding Miss Hawthorne across the dance floor. "Did you not dance with him a fortnight ago? Did you not find him amiable?" Her mother's gaze returned to her, a pleading look in her eyes.

Juliet knew that her lack of happiness weighed heavily upon her mother's heart. Yet, what could be achieved by pretending? "He spoke kindly to me, yes, but that was all. I have no way of knowing if he would even want to marry me."

More importantly, Juliet did not wish to marry him.

With her reputation far from sparkling, the only men who seemed to show a small measure of interest in her were not unlike her former fiancé. They were either of advanced age or possessed some other quality or lack thereof that hindered their chances of a fortunate match. In the end, it meant that she was no one's first choice.

Perhaps not even their second.

"I do not wish for a husband who only marries me because he has no other option," Juliet told her mother, lifting her chin with the last bit of pride she had left. "You, yourself, know what marriage to an uncaring man is like, Mother."

Sadness and regret lingered in her mother's eyes as she nodded. "Of course, my dear." She patted Juliet's hand and cast her a warm smile. "Of course, I would not want that for you."

While her mother had been married twice, she had not found love in either union. Not with Juliet's late father, Lord Goswick, nor with Violet's late father, Lord Silcox.

Yes, she had become a mother and always loved her children—Juliet as well as her younger half-brother Jacob—with all her heart. Still...

Her mother heaved a deep sigh, and Juliet could all but see her mother's thoughts, those she did not dare voice. If not marriage, what other option was there for Juliet? Would she remain unmarried for good? Would she never have love and family? Children?

Juliet knew that she had very few options. Yes, she could agree to marry an older gentleman and hope that he would be kind to her, that she would not suffer overly in that marriage, that she would at least become a mother. Yet, whenever Juliet considered that option, her heart drew her back to that day four years ago.

When Henri Duret had come into her life.

Four years had passed since she had last seen him, since he had left England and sailed away. After all, he had only come in order to protect her stepsister, his cousin, and after doing so, he had returned to his life of privateering.

Was that another option? Juliet wondered, had wondered more than once. She often thought of her stepsister's life, out there on the open seas.

Although Violet had grown up as the adopted daughter of a French privateer, she had been born to English aristocracy, the daughter of Viscount Silcox. Her life had started out the same as Juliet's, only it had taken a drastic turn. That turn had made Violet strong and daring and brave, and it had given her the courage to return to England when Juliet had been on the cusp of marriage.

Cherishing her own freedom, Violet had felt determined to offer the same freedom to Juliet.

Only things had not turned out as they had hoped. While Violet had found love with an English Lord, his own heart as adventurous as her own, Juliet had not been so fortunate. Still, she cherished every letter from her stepsister as well as every visit from Violet and Oliver, who now commanded their own ship and were rarely in England these days.

English privateers in contrast to the French family Violet still called her own.

In many ways, Juliet envied her sister. Yet, she knew she did not possess the strength and daring that seemed to come so natural to Violet. No, Juliet was timid and hesitant and fearful. As much as she sometimes dreamed of running off and leaving this life behind, she knew that she would never survive out there in the world.

What then?

Unbidden, Juliet's thoughts returned to the one other option she currently possessed. About a fortnight ago, a letter had arrived. A letter from an old friend. A friend who was now offering her a choice.

After crying off, Juliet had found herself on the outskirts of society.

She was still a lady by birth, and yet, the friends she had once thought to have had slowly, one by one, deserted her.

And then she had met Miss Clarissa Kingston.

Since Clarissa's father was a merchant and had made his fortunes with ships carrying goods back and forth between England and India, the *crème de la crème* of London society tended to look down upon them. After all, there was nothing worse than those who obtained their fortune through honest work.

Juliet sighed at the silly notions of her peers. Yes, in recent years she had come to see many things in a different light, many things she had not even noticed before or paid much attention to. Now, she knew better.

In the end, Juliet and Clarissa had formed a bond together they faced all those who would deem them unworthy. They had become fast friends, and Juliet had been relieved to have at least one friendly face to look upon, one soul to confide in.

Until Clarissa had left England as well, accompanying her father to India.

Two years had passed since, and now Clarissa was on the brink of marriage. She was happy and in love, and every letter from her made Juliet yearn to find something, something...

...anything.

Juliet's mind drifted back to Clarissa's letter. She had read it countless times and had all but committed it to memory, for it never failed to make her heart beat faster in her chest.

...Please, Juliet, consider this. My uncle travels on one of my father's ships to India on the 19th. Please, will you not accompany him? Come to India and begin a new life here. I cannot bear to think of you so sad and forlorn back in England. Please, come. What do you have to lose?...

Indeed, what did she have to lose?

It was the one question that continued to echo in Juliet's head day and night. Ought she to risk it all and leave everything behind? Or remain in England forever and continue to sleepwalk from day to day with nothing to hope for?

Yes, these were her options, and Juliet wished that her heart knew which one to choose. She wished that there was one that was clearly meant for her.

But there was not.

Still, the thought of going to India was perhaps the one most appealing. As much as Juliet wanted love and marriage, she knew that the only marriage open to her would be one absent of love. And ever since...

A deep sigh left her lips as it never failed to do whenever her thoughts drifted back to that day four years ago.

No, she could not marry without love and affection, without passion and temptation. Ever since Henri Duret had kissed her, Juliet knew that she could not deny her heart.

Unfortunately, it seemed that her heart was rather steadfast, for it continued to hold to the thought of Henri, to the few moments they had shared, to that one kiss.

That one kiss that had changed everything.

At least, for her.

Countless times over the past four years, Juliet had wondered if he even still remembered her. Had she merely been one among many? Had his heart not been touched by her as hers had been touched by him?

Of course, it was foolish to think that an adventurous soul such as his would ever attach itself to a timid, little mouse like Juliet. Yet, every once in a while, she allowed herself to dream.

To imagine what it would be like to see him again.

To pretend that at least, every once in a while, he still thought of her as well.

Of course, it was a lie, but it was a lie that brought a smile to Juliet's face.

What was she to do?

Chapter Two

A MEMORY

1812 Off the coast of France

With his legs braced, Henri Duret stood on the quarterdeck of the *Voile Noire*, the Black Sail, his own ship, his pride and joy. Lifting his head, he gazed up at the dark sail billowing in the strong wind, pushing the *Voile Noire* through the churning waves. His crew worked seamlessly as one, some up in the rigging while others manned the lower deck. He saw determined faces, eyes focused on tasks assigned, their minds in concentration as they all worked together to bring the ship about.

Slowly, the *Voile Noire* turned into the wind.

Toward France.

Toward home.

Long months had passed since Henri had last seen his family. His father Alain as well as his uncle Antoine. Privateering was a family business for the Durets. It had begun with Henri's grandfather, Hubert Duret, decades ago before he had passed the torch after many years at sea to Antoine. Now, he spent his days at home in *La Roche-sur-Mer*, rarely leaving his wife's side. Unfortunately, Henri's own father, Alain, suffered from severe seasickness and always tended to business from the safety of France.

Thus, the two brothers had always worked as one. Henri had known from the first that he, too, belonged out on the open sea. He had set sail with his uncle when he had been all but seven years of age, his eagerness for adventure unmatched and impossible to deny.

To this day, Henri cherished the feeling of the sea air whipping into his face, tugging upon his shirt as the *Voile Noire* surged through the waves, the sky filled with dark clouds as the wind howled around them. He loved the up and down of his ship, the way it threatened to toss him overboard as the sea rolled almost violently across the globe.

This was life!

This was freedom!

There was nothing like it.

"Back to France!" Henri called as he stepped up to the helm where his first mate stood with his hands tightly wrapped about the ship's wheel, his flaxen hair whipping in the wind as much as Henri's raven-black hair.

"Aye, Capt'n!" the man called, his Scottish accent revealing more about him than the few words the taciturn man ever spoke.

As many burdened by their past, Ian Stewart—if indeed that was his real name!—kept to himself. The only companion to never leave his side was a wolf, a large beast with a torn right ear and a long scar on his left flank.

As far as Henri knew, the man had been pulled out of the waters near the Scottish coast by a fisherman roughly three years ago.

As had the wolf.

No one knew what had happened, and Ian never volunteered any details about his life before. It seemed he had been all but reborn that day, a new man struggling to forget the life he had left behind.

To Henri, Ian's past did not matter. What mattered was the man's dedication to the ship, its crew and their captain. He never complained or argued, never gambled or ended up in brawls. He pulled his weight upon the ship, always there when needed, and over the years, Henri had come to place his trust in the silent Scot.

Moving his gaze to the horizon, Henri inhaled a deep breath of sea air. He could all but smell the soft scents of France, the mild hints of vegetation as they drew closer to the coast, and he felt a slow smile claim his face.

It had been too long!

"Do you not long to see your family, Ian?" Henri asked his first mate with a sideways glance. He did not truly expect an answer and was, therefore, not surprised to hear the man merely grumble something unintelligible under his breath.

Chuckling, Henri strode forward then climbed down onto the main deck, his watchful eyes sweeping over his crew as they secured the lines. "Home to France!" he called, and a joyous cheer went up around him.

"Home to France!" his crew echoed, pumping their fists up into the air, wide smiles upon their faces.

Henri stepped up to the bowsprit, his gaze fixed on the distant horizon as he thought of those he had left behind but would see again soon.

His early years had been spent in the one village the Durets had always called home, *La Roche-sur-Mer*. It lay situated in a small cove where only his family's ships docked. It was a close neighborhood where people knew one another, where people *cared* about one another.

Even beyond the bonds of family.

Still, Henri longed most to see his father and uncle as he had been closest to them all his life. Antoine had been the one to teach him how to sail, how to navigate, how to be a privateer. To this day, Antoine Duret was the man Henri admired most.

Only Antoine's life had changed the night he had stumbled upon the love of his life on a beach in Norfolk, England, and had whisked her and her little daughter—Violette!—away with him to France, leaving Viscount Silcox under the impression that his wife and child were dead.

After more than fifteen years of wedded bliss and four more children, Antoine and Alexandra were still as much in love as they had been that very first day.

Henri remembered it well.

He equally well remembered meeting his new cousin.

Within moments, six-year-old Violette had snatched the spyglass out of his hands because she had wanted to watch her old life disappear upon the horizon. Back then, Henri had not yet known what a fierce daredevil she was.

Today, the thought of her dauntless courage never failed to make him chuckle. Yes, he missed her, now that she was married to an English lord, a mother herself, and captian of her own ship—under an English flag, no less!

Still, she often visited home for at heart she was still a daughter of France.

More importantly, she was still a Duret.

And family was forever.

As strong winds pushed the *Voile Noire* toward home, Henri found himself wondering if he would see his beloved cousin upon reaching France. Would she be there? She and her family? It had been too long since he had seen little Antoinette? Would the little girl even still remember him?

Running a hand through his tousled hair, Henri felt his thoughts stray to another face he had not seen in a long time.

In four years, to be exact.

Henri felt his teeth grit together as her face slowly took shape against his will, her shy green eyes framed by thick lashes that constantly seemed to sweep downward as though trying to hide her. Her dark auburn hair had glistened in the sun, and his right hand closed involuntarily as though he could still feel those soft, thick curls against his skin. He remembered running his fingers through them before grabbing a fistful to urge her head back and allow him to deepen his kiss.

A dark growl rose from Henri's throat as he remembered that one unburdened moment with her. Four years had passed since, and yet, he still remembered it as though it had been no more than four minutes.

"*Merde!*" The curse flew from his lips as his hand once more rose to rake through his wind-swept hair. Why could he not simply forget her? Why?

She was like a plague upon his soul, always there, always reminding him of something he could never have.

Something he did not even *want* to have.

She was an English lady, delicate and shy, and he was a French privateer, adventurous and dauntless. Their lives were vastly different, their countries were at war, and yet...the same had been true for Antoine and Alexandra.

Once.

Henri hung his head as his grandfather's voice echoed in his head. Often had Hubert Duret spoken to him of love and family, the same as he had spoken to Antoine when he had taken over command of his father's ship years ago.

Once, Antoine had been a carefree young man, his only love the sea, his eyes fixed upon the horizon. Henri remembered how, as a boy, he had once overheard a similar conversation when his grandfather had urged Antoine to keep an open mind, promising him that love would eventually find him, urging him to heed its call.

Antoine had laughed at the notion.

And then, one night, *something* had made him turn his ship into the wind and head toward an English beach in the middle of a storm.

Alexandra.

It had taken no more than a single glimpse, and Antoine's life had come undone. Henri had seen his uncle's face the moment his gaze had fallen upon Alexandra.

He had been thirteen years old at the time, but he remembered it well. He remembered the look of utter shock upon his uncle's face as well as that sense of awe that had illuminated his eyes from within.

The look upon Alexandra's face had been the same.

Everything had changed that night.

Strangers—enemies, for all intents and purposes!—had become a family. It was a thought that constantly lingered in Henri's mind, refusing to release him no matter how hard he fought to banish it.

Fate had guided Antoine that night.

Would it ever guide him, Henri? Or had it already and he had merely refused to listen?

Chapter Three

A LEAP OF FAITH

Port of London, 1812

The stench that lingered in the air urged Juliet to breathe through her mouth. She did not even dare analyze what it was made of, but kept her attention focused on the tall-masted ship in front of her. She craned her neck and allowed her eyes to run ever higher, along the rigging to the crow's nest. It seemed to almost touch the sky.

"It is quite impressive, is it not?" Mr. Kingston, Clarissa's uncle, asked with a chuckle. "I do remember the first time in my life that I saw such a ship." Heaving a deep sigh, he shook his head, a small smile playing over his face at the memory. "It was a magnificent moment; one I shall never forget."

Juliet smiled at him. "I only ever heard them described, but I never once saw one in person." She once again allowed her gaze to sweep over the tall masts. "I never imagined they could be this big." It was another testimony to the sheltered life she had led, and it sent a pang of fear through her heart. What was she doing here? This was madness!

"Ah!" Mr. Kingston exclaimed, as his gaze moved past her to something beyond her shoulder. "Here comes Miss Smith." He waved a hand, then looked down at Juliet. "I've hired her to see to you during our voyage."

Juliet sighed in relief. Of course, she had wondered about daily life on a ship without a lady's maid around to assist her. Yet, she had not dared bring her own, uncertain if Martha would have even agreed. After all, who would leave England behind, her entire family, and venture out into the world to an unknown place, far, far away?

Only a fool would, was that not so?

Or someone desperate.

The thought of her own family threatened to bring tears to Juliet's eyes. She thought of her mother and her little brother Jacob, and she quickly turned around to greet Miss Smith, hoping to distract herself and prevent her thoughts from dwelling on the significance of what she was about to do.

Miss Smith had a pleasant face, her blue eyes wide as they drifted to the tall-masted ship again and again. She gave a small curtsey the moment she stopped in front of them, a kind smile coming to her face. "Good day, my lady. Mr. Kingston."

"Good day, Miss Smith," Mr. Kingston greeted the young woman before he gestured toward Juliet. "May I introduce the Lady Juliet Edwards? My lady, this is Miss Elizabeth Smith."

Juliet smiled at her, and Miss Smith curtsied again. "It's a pleasure to make your acquaintance, Miss Smith."

"Oh, please call me Elizabeth, my lady. Or Betsy, if you prefer." A shy smile lingered upon her face.

Juliet nodded, relieved to find a kindred spirit in the young woman. "Very well then, Elizabeth."

"Shall we?" Mr. Kingston asked, looking from Elizabeth to Juliet before his gaze moved to his brother's vessel once more. "As this is a cargo ship, we will be the only passengers on board. There will be ample space on deck, however, not much company for a young lady such as yourself." He grinned at her kindly as they moved toward the gangway to board the ship. "I do hope you'll find a good companion in Miss Smith."

Juliet was fairly certain that she would, for she had liked the young woman instantly. However, the moment her feet stepped on deck of the large ship, her thoughts once more turned to the daring endeavor she was about to undertake.

Her hands began to tremble, and she had trouble drawing breath into her lungs. It seemed every muscle tensed under the enormity of what lay ahead, and she barely heard Mr. Kingston continue to speak and explain the layout of the vessel.

Walking about, he pointed out various areas, explained where the cargo hold was as well as the captain's quarters. He introduced them to Captain Sanders and then showed them to their cabins. While Elizabeth immediately busied herself with unpacking the few belongings they had brought, Juliet could not bring herself to remain inside. She followed Mr. Kingston back out on deck where the sailors were readying the ship for departure.

With her hands gripping the rail tightly, Juliet stood next to Mr. Kingston and watched as the ship slowly pulled out of the harbor. Tears shot to her eyes as she thought of her mother and wondered if she had already found the letter Juliet had left behind.

Would she be angry? Or saddened that Juliet had not said a word but had all but left in the night?

Yet, Juliet knew that if she had spoken to her mother, she would never have been able to leave. Her mother would no doubt have convinced her to stay. After all, this was madness, was it not?

No, Juliet had not dared to say goodbye to her mother for fear she would break down and stay.

Stay in England for the rest of her life.

A life that was becoming a torment with each day that passed.

A life that seemed to stand still.

A life that would not see her happy.

Out here, in the world, she might have a chance. It was not a big chance, but it was a chance, nonetheless. Out there, Juliet had hope.

Something to cling to.

Something to keep her sane.

As the coast slowly fell away, Juliet wondered what lay ahead. She felt a brief moment of panic, and her gaze darted down to the dark waters, her hands clutching the rail even more tightly than before.

"Breathe," Juliet whispered to herself silently. "Breathe."

The salty sea air chilled her skin but felt invigorating as it seemed to surge through her body. She breathed in and out a few times and slowly felt herself begin to calm. Of course, she was far from at peace, her nerves still frayed. Yet, the panic had receded and her head cleared.

Never in her life had Juliet done anything that could be described as daring. Her life had always been predictable, following the steps every young woman of her position would follow. No decision had ever been hers, her life always directed by others.

First, by her father, Lord Goswick, and then, by her stepfather, Lord Silcox.

Until the day, her stepsister had returned to England and provided her with a choice.

Despite everything that had happened in the past four years, Juliet still could not bring herself to regret the decision she had made that day. Every time she had seen Lord Dowling at an event, she had known that she did not want to be his wife. He was a man like her late stepfather.

A man who considered women his property.

A man who would never care for his wife's heart.

A man who would ignore his wife's objections.

Do you think your future husband will honor your wishes and not lay a hand on you without your permission?

Henri's voice echoed in her ears as it often did. As much as she tried to forget the audacious Frenchman, she could not.

He was still there.

In her head.

And her heart.

What had it been that had endeared him to her? Juliet had asked herself that question countless times. Had it been the wicked glimmer in those green eyes of his? Or that sinfully tempting smile? The way he had kissed her? The affection with which he had spoken of his family? Of her stepsister? The risk to his life he had accepted without hesitation in order to see Violet safe?

Juliet did not know.

But it did not matter, did it?

In the end, all that mattered was that he was still on her mind, preventing her from ever truly considering another for a husband. Yes, once or twice, she had found a potential suitor amiable, but she had nonetheless shied back from the idea of marriage because...

...because of Henri.

Curse her heart! For a reason she could not name, the dreaded thing still clung to him, to the memory of him, to the sliver of hope that perhaps one day she might see him again.

Perhaps that was why Juliet had finally decided to go to India, to rid herself of Henri's hold on her. So long as she remained in England, a place Violet also called home, there was always the chance of seeing him again. Violet was family to him, and he would never be far. Juliet knew that. And although she had not seen him once in the past four years, that small sliver of hope had remained.

Perhaps one day.

Perhaps.

It was a dangerous train of thought because it kept her from moving forward. But no longer! Now, she was taking charge of her own life. She had boarded the ship, and now, she was on her way to India, a different place far, far away. Juliet did not know what the future had in store for her, but it would be a future without Henri.

Half the world would be between them, ensuring that they would never cross paths again.

The thought brought utter sadness to Juliet's heart, and yet, she knew it was for the best. Somehow, she needed to find her own place in this world. And perhaps India was the place to do it. Perhaps with Clarissa's help, she would find a way to be happy.

Perhaps even fall in love.

As unlikely as that seemed at the moment.

Juliet's gaze swept over the receding coast of England as it slowly disappeared from view, and she heaved a deep sigh. "Farewell," she whispered to the wind and allowed one last tear to fall. "Farewell."

Then she loosened her hold on the rail and took a step back. Her feet moved and turned her around. Step by step, she moved away, England now behind her, and stepped up to the other side of the ship, her gaze moving to the horizon.

A small smile appeared on Juliet's face as she contemplated all that awaited her. Of course, she was not the woman Violet was. She was not daring and adventurous. She could never be a privateer and sail the seas, a sword strapped to her hip and her hair billowing in the wind, her heart full of joy. After all, they were only stepsisters. They did not share the same blood.

Still, the thought that Violet was somewhere out there was comforting as though, despite everything, Juliet was not alone after all. If only she could have seen her stepsister one last time because, unlike Juliet's mother, Violet would have understood, would she not have?

"Will I ever see you again?" Juliet whispered to the wind, trying to picture her stepsister's face. Indeed, she was leaving everything behind, not only her mother and brother here in England, but also her stepsister and...

...Henri.

Always did her thoughts circle back to him. As much as she tried to direct them elsewhere, they would not listen. And yet, how could she not think of him now? Here she was leaving England for good, leaving Europe for good. Never again would she lay eyes on him.

This was it.

This was goodbye.

One last and final goodbye.

"Farewell, Henri," she whispered as the wind tossed her auburn curls about, tugging her onward. "Thank you for everything. I shall never forget you. Never."

Lifting her chin, Juliet willed a smile onto her face.

One day she would be happy again.

One day.

Chapter Four

LA ROCHE-SUR-MER

France, 1812

As the *Voile Noire* neared the small pier of the cove, Henri let his gaze sweep over the many people assembled there, waving their arms, bright smiles upon their faces. Most of them were family and friends come to greet the returning sailors, overjoyed to have their sons and fathers and brothers and husbands back for at least a few days before the *Voile Noire* would set sail once again.

Henri spotted his own father, Alain, walking down from the village proper, as always, a ledger tucked beneath his arm. A thick beard covered the lower half of his face, and yet, Henri could see the wide smile that lingered beneath.

Children dashed here and there, jumping up and down to see better as they waved their little hands and called out to those of his crew they held close to heart. Many of the sailors waved back, joy written all over their faces as they spotted their children and wives, the families they had not seen in months.

Four of those young faces called to Henri, and he turned toward them, lifting his hand in greeting. They were Antoine's and Alexandra's four children: Victor and Vincent, aged fourteen and twelve, as well as Aime and Aurelie, aged ten and eight. While Vincent and Aime greatly resembled their mother as well as their half-sister Violette, with their golden hair and sparkling blue eyes, Victor and Aurelie had inherited Antoine's dark locks.

Everyone on deck rushed to bring the ship into port and secure it. Sails were packed away and lines tied before the gangplank was lowered and the sailors all but jumped off board and into their families' arms.

"Henri! Henri!" The four rascals called to him before the youngest Aurelie threw herself into his arms. "Did you bring me anything?" she asked, that familiar mischievous gleam in her eyes.

Henri knew he should not but he could not help but admire her for it. "*Ma chère cousine*, what do you think of me? I've always brought you something, *non?*" He pulled a small doll from his pocket, and Aurelie shrieked with joy.

"Did you see any pirates?" came Victor's excited question, his dark brows drawn down in anticipation of new adventure stories. "Was there a battle?"

Henri laughed, ruffling his cousin's hair. He could see that Victor disliked being treated like a child; after all, at fourteen years of age he was already much older than Henri had been when he had first set sail. Henri could see that his young cousin was becoming impatient. Yet, Antoine and Alexandra were still reluctant to let him go.

Handing out small trinkets to all of them, Henri delighted in their excitement as they showed each other what they had received, small gifts from places far away, places they could only dream of. Their pure, innocent delight never failed to amaze Henri.

"So, you found your way back here," came his father's deep voice a moment before a familiar hand clasped his shoulder. "I was beginning to doubt you ever would." His father chuckled warmly, then he embraced his son. "It is good to see you." Then he pulled back, and Henri noticed his father's gaze sweep over him the way it always did after he returned following a long absence. It was as though his father needed to ensure that his son was still in one piece, safe and sound.

"*Papa!*" Henri grasped his father's shoulders and gave them a squeeze. "You know me."

His father laughed. "That is why I was worried."

Again, they embraced, slapping each other's back, both relieved to be granted this reunion. After all, privateering was a dangerous business, and they both knew that.

"Is all well here?" Henri asked as his gaze moved from his father to the village. He could not say what it was, but an odd feeling settled over him.

His father's face darkened before he turned to the children. "Go on! Rush ahead and tell your mother that Henri has returned!"

In an instant, the four children dashed off, laughing and talking as they went, their little feet carrying them through the village and then up the slope to where the Durets' home had always been, overlooking the cove.

"What is it, *Papa?*" Henri asked as he fell into step beside his father. "Is Antoine here?" Indeed, if he was, his ship would be moored at the dock.

His father shook his head. "He is not, but we are expecting him back soon."

"Have you heard from Violette?" Henri asked, unable to shake the feeling that something was indeed wrong.

Again, his father shook his head. "Not in weeks. But as far as we can tell, she's well."

Henri stopped in his tracks. "Then what is it, *Papa?*" He was about to say more, when he suddenly paused and his head rose, his gaze moving along the houses set neatly side-by-side along the road.

His heart constricted painfully when his eyes fell upon the charred remains farther up the road, closer to the woods. It was a place he had known well, a place he had visited frequently not too long ago. "Noële?" he choked out, then he turned pleading eyes to his father. "Is she well? What happened?"

His father bowed his head. "We do not know. There was a fire one night, but we are uncertain what caused it. It must've raged inside for quite some time before anyone took notice." He looked up into

Henri's face, and placed a hand upon his arm. "She's gone, Henri. I'm so very sorry."

Henri gritted his teeth against the onslaught of sadness and guilt that rushed over him. He had not known Noèle for long as she had not grown up in *La Roche-sur-Mer*. Yet, she had been all but family when she had married Étienne Clément, Henri's childhood friend.

And then Étienne had died, swept away in an angry storm aboard the *Voile Noire*. Henri had never forgotten that night nor had he ever forgiven himself for failing his friend.

And now, he had failed him again.

"We believe it might have been an accident," his father said gently. "She'd kept to herself since losing Étienne. She rarely left the house or spoke to anyone." A heavy sigh left his lips. "We tried, but..." Sadly, he shook his head.

Henri felt his hands curl into fists as a paralyzing anger seized him. Why was it that he was never there when it mattered?

"That is not all," his father said gently.

Henri closed his eyes, then he turned around to look at his father. "What else?" he gritted out, uncertain he even wanted to know.

His father inhaled a deep breath. "A letter arrived from England."

Sudden fear froze the blood in Henri's veins. "Violette?"

His father shook his head. "No, it is from Lady Silcox. Alexandra has it. She bade me fetch you as soon as you arrived. She says it is urgent."

Without another thought, Henri rushed up the small slope toward the house. He did not know what to expect; however, the look upon his father's face as well as Alexandra's instructions meant something horrible had happened. But what? And to whom? If Violette was well, then why had Lady Silcox written?

Juliette, a voice deep down whispered, and a crippling pain shot through Henri's heart, almost stilling it in his chest as he burst through the door and into the hall. "Alexandra!"

Halfway up the stairs, his grandmother paused, a wide smile coming to her face as she beheld him. "Ah, *bienvenue*, Henri!" Then she saw the tension upon his face, and before Henri could say a word, she gestured toward the salon.

"Henri?" came Alexandra's voice a second later as she stepped out of the salon on the right.

Instantly, his uncle's wife came hastening toward him, relief in her wide blue eyes. Nevertheless, the look upon her face remained tense in a way Henri had rarely seen it. "I'm so glad you've returned." She quickly embraced him, her right hand cupping his cheek as a mother would, a soft smile coming to her face as her eyes swept over him in much the same way his father's had earlier. Then she sighed, and the expression upon her face grew serious again. "I need to speak with you. Come." She gestured him forward the moment his father stepped through the door behind him. "Alain, you as well."

Together, they stepped into the library, its walls covered in maps showing different routes all originating in France. "What is this about?" Henri inquired. "My father said you received a letter from Lady Silcox. What happened?"

Alexandra quickly crossed the room and stepped up to the fireplace on its opposite end. Upon its mantle sat a small wooden box, from which she retrieved a letter. Turning around, she heaved a deep sigh, a hint of hesitation in her eyes, before she held it out to him. "Here. Read it yourself." Her gaze moved to Alain.

Henri swallowed then stepped forward. He grasped the letter and unfolded the parchment.

Dearest Violet,

As I have no notion of your current whereabouts, I have dispatched several letters to several locations, hoping and praying that at least one will reach you.

"If you were wondering," Alexandra said suddenly, wringing her hands as she took a step toward him. "Violet gave us permission to open her letters in her absence."

Henri nodded, touched by Alexandra's concern. Yet, he would not have expected it to be any different. There were no secrets in their family, and yet, each family member's privacy was upheld with the utmost respect. It was the way it ought to be, granting everyone the freedom they desired while never leaving anyone to stand alone.

Juliet has left England! A part of me still cannot believe it to be true!

Without a word, she left in the night, leaving behind nothing more than a note to explain her decision. As far as I can tell, she boarded a ship to India.

Henri felt the shock of those words slam into him, almost making him rock back on his heels. "*Merde!*" What foolishness was this? What madness?

Perhaps you are aware that a friend of hers, Miss Clarissa Kingston, accompanied her father to India about two years ago. As I understand it, it was Clarissa who offered Juliet passage on one of her father's ships traveling from England to India.

I am unaware why Juliet suddenly decided to leave England. I cannot recall her ever speaking of India nor contemplating the idea of traveling there.

I beg you, if there is anything you can do. I am utterly terrified of what might happen to her on such a voyage. You know best all the dangers that might befall her out there at sea. Bring her back home or if need be, see her safely to the Kingstons in India.

I pray for you and yours are well.

Elaine Winters, Viscountess Silcox

Without thought, Henri spun around and rushed back out into the hall, the letter still clutched in his hand. "Ian!" As the silent, tall Scot had no family of his own, he generally stayed with the Durets whenever they docked in *La Roche-sur-Mer*.

Barely a moment later, the front door flew open and Ian strode in, the wolf upon his heel. "Capt'n?"

Henri willed himself to calm the rapid beating of his heart as he looked at his first mate. "Gather the crew and prepare the ship! We'll leave with the next tide!"

The Scotsman's brows drew down in confusion; yet, he did not ask any questions nor voice any objections. "Aye, Capt'n!" With a quick nod of his head, he turned around and left, the large beast following him like a lapdog.

Henri turned around to face his father. "Do you have any information on cargo ships traveling between England and India?"

His father scoffed. "Are you serious?" His brows drew down. Slowly, he took a step toward his son. "We are at war, Henri! England and France are at war! Have you forgotten that?"

Henri's jaw clenched painfully as his gaze once more dropped down to the crumpled letter in his hand. How could she have done this? Never had she struck him as foolish! What had happened to make her act in such an irresponsible way?

Alexandra stepped forward, and he felt her soft hands upon his arm. "What will you do?" she asked gently, those wide blue eyes of hers shining with understanding.

Henri swallowed, then turned to meet her gaze. "I will find her, and I will take her back home. Where she belongs."

A bit of an indulgent smile came to Alexandra's face. "What if she does not wish to return? After all, no one would upend their life without a very good reason."

Henri could see the memory of that night over fifteen years ago flash across his aunt's face. The night she had stumbled upon a French privateer on the beach below Silcox Manor. The night she had decided to risk it all, leave her old life behind and begin again.

Had something similar urged Juliette onto the ship to India? Henri wondered, feeling every muscle in his body tense at the thought that perhaps she had acted out of love. Had she boarded the ship alone? Or did a young gentleman travel by her side? Or possibly await her arrival in India?

Neither option appealed to Henri; however, Juliette's motivation did not matter at this point. What mattered was that he found her as quickly as possible. After all, what other choice did he have? He could not simply remain here and do nothing!

He simply could not!

As expected, the news of their immediate departure did not sit well with his crew. Although they were all accounted for and on deck when Henri arrived, he could see their displeasure upon their faces. After all, they had only just arrived home after months at sea without their families.

Ian stepped up to him, his face taut. "The men have asked why we're leaving so soon." He spoke calmly, and Henri could not shake the feeling that unlike the rest of the men the Scotsman did not care whether he received an answer to that question or not.

Although Ian never failed to obey a command, his diligence to the ship and its crew beyond reproach, the man never truly seemed to care.

Or allow himself to care.

He took one day at a time, keeping himself apart from all those around him, never showing any emotions, good or bad.

Sometimes Henri wondered if Ian truly never felt anything.

Facing his crew, Henri cleared his throat, trying his best to remain calm despite the way his pulse was pounding in his ears. "I apologize for this abrupt change of plans; however, an emergency has arisen that does not allow for time."

The dark expressions upon his men's faces changed from displeasure to concern as all eyes turned to him, asking for more information.

Henri swallowed, uncertain how much to say. "We are to retrieve a young woman who boarded a merchant ship to India some time ago. Further details are unclear."

Deep frowns drew down his men's brows. "Who is the woman?" Jacques asked, scratching his chin.

The others grumbled in agreement.

Henri knew that he needed to give them a good reason to undertake this endeavor. Yes, he was their captain. Still, if he were to lose his crew's respect, he would not remain the captain for long. After all, there was nothing worse than a leader who made decisions on a whim, endangering those he was responsible for.

Running a hand through his hair, he straightened and met their eyes one by one. "The woman is an English lady," he told them honestly.

Confused grumbling echoed to his ears for his words did not answer their questions but posed new ones. Still, his crew needed to know. After all, once they retrieved Juliette, one word out of her mouth would reveal the truth about her origin.

Henri inhaled another deep breath, his shoulders squared, and his gaze slightly narrowed as he faced his men. "She is to be my wife," he lied, shocking himself as much as his crew, "and I want her back." Oddly enough, that last bit did not quite feel like a lie.

For a moment, silence lingered as his men absorbed all he had said. Then, heads began to nod, and Henri could see that they would stand with him. Most of them had wives they loved and would defend until their last breath.

Fortunately, the fact that Alexandra and Violette as well hailed from England had helped many in *La Roche-sur-Mer* to look at the English as people not unlike themselves instead of seeing a faceless enemy at the mere mention of them.

Henri paused, wondering why he had not simply told them that it was Violette's sister they were to retrieve. If only he had thought of that before!

It would have been by far the simpler reason. It also would have been the truth.

As his crew readied the *Voile Noire* for her next adventure, Henri stepped up onto the quarterdeck. His gaze swept over the far horizon, and he wondered where out there Juliette was. What ship had she boarded? And where was it now?

His teeth gritted together painfully as anger began to stir in his blood. How could she have done this? In times of war no less! Anything could happen to her out there on the open seas!

It was that thought that caused something inside Henri to constrict painfully. If she were to come to harm, what...?

Striding up to the rail, Henri grasped the smooth wood with tight hands, unable to finish the thought. Yet, it seemed that words were not needed, were all but oblivious, when it came to describing the painful ache in his chest. No matter where he tried to place his focus, Henri found every fiber of his being return to the brief moments he had shared with her. Whether he kept his eyes open or closed did not matter either.

Her green eyes shone in front of him like two beacons, beckoning him onward.

Henri cursed under his breath, upset with himself for responding in such a highly emotional way. Always had he prided himself on his ability to keep a clear head, to act with thought and consider everything rationally. Yes, he knew that his family often described him as a bit of a hothead. He enjoyed being impulsive and carefree, yet, when it mattered, he always did what was right.

Was it right to go after her? Or ought he simply try to find Violette and leave this up to her? He knew she was more than capable! After all, Lady Silcox's letter had been addressed to her. This was not *his* concern. Juliette was not *his* responsibility.

Henri knew that, and yet...

He ran a hand through his tousled hair, disbelief filling him as his gaze moved to the unfurling sails above. Slowly, the *Voile Noire* pulled away from the pier, his men rushing to tighten the lines.

Four years.

Four years had passed since he had last seen her, and yet, the memory of her in his arms had never abated. Why that was he did not know!

In the end, it did not matter. The truth was that whether or not she was his responsibility, Henri could not simply stand by and wait and do nothing. That odd feeling in his chest, strangely intense and overwhelming, urged him to go after her.

Now.

Again, Henri saw her soft features before his inner eye as though she were standing right in front of him, her shy, green eyes slightly lowered as she peeked up at him, not certain if she should dare.

A smile came to his face, and he had to fight the urge to reach out a hand and try and touch her. What would it feel like to see her again after all this time? What would he do once she was again within arm's reach?

Henri could not deny that he longed to find out.

Chapter Five

TRAPPED

In utter disbelief, Juliet stared down at the young, dark-haired woman upon the cot. Burn marks were visible on her arms and legs, even her face, the ends of her dark hair singed. The scent of smoke still lingered about her, and Juliet cringed at the thought of what had happened.

"Make yourself useful," a harsh, terrifying voice ordered, "and see to her!"

Juliet blinked, then turned her head and all but gaped at the tall, grim-looking stranger, who stood in the doorway, unable to make sense of what he was saying.

Nothing seemed real.

Everything had happened as though in a bad dream.

A nightmare.

A dark sneer came to the man's face before he stepped away and then slammed the door shut, locking her in.

Locking *them* in.

Juliet's gaze once more moved to the woman upon the cot. Whoever she was, the woman did not move, and her breathing was faint. Where her skin had been burned, her flesh was an angry red whereas other parts seemed frighteningly pale.

See to her! The man's words once more echoed in Juliet's head; yet, she could not for the life of her think of anything to do. How was she to see to her? Never had she tended to anyone. What was she to do?

As her gaze swept over the cabin, Juliet's mind drifted back to earlier that day and her hands began to tremble.

The day had started like any other, exciting and full of new experiences. Despite having left behind her home, Juliet had begun to enjoy herself, determined to focus on the many wonderful things she was granted instead of on the sadness that lived in her heart.

They had sat at breakfast when the first cannon had been fired.

She remembered voices, so many voices, yelling. She had heard Captain Sanders' voice as well as many others she had not been able to identify. Commands had been shouted, and the almost deafening sound of running feet still echoed in her ears as the sailors had rushed toward their stations.

Mr. Kingston had tried to remain calm, but Juliet had seen the terror in his eyes. He had ushered her out of the room and instructed her to head to her cabin and bar the door.

Juliet had followed him blindly down the companionway until they had come around a corner and found Elizabeth, her maid, rushing toward them with wide, panicked eyes.

How much time had passed since the first cannon shot, Juliet could not say. Everything had seemed to happen so quickly while at the same time lasting much longer than she would have expected. She had not been aware that they had been boarded until the sound of French shouts had echoed to her ears.

Of course, as an accomplished young lady, Juliet was fluent enough in French to hold a civilized conversation. However, the words that had reached her ears had been ones she had never encountered before.

Terrified, they had huddled in her cabin, the door locked. Yet, at the same time, none of them had been under any illusion that the lock held the power to protect them. Elizabeth had all but lost her mind, unable to sit still, panic in her wide-open eyes. At some point, she had bolted toward the door, unlocked it and thrown herself out into the companionway.

Mr. Kingston had immediately rushed after her. When Juliet had stepped into the doorway, she had spotted Elizabeth halfway down the companionway, nearing the corner from where voices were approaching.

French voices.

We are at war, Juliet had thought in that moment. Of course, she had known so before even setting foot on the merchant vessel. Yet, the reality of that fact had escaped her until that very moment.

Exhausted, Juliet sank down onto the floor beside the cot. Her knees no longer had the strength to hold her upright as the memory of the past few hours replayed before her inner eye. Had this truly happened? Had Captain Sanders' ship truly been boarded by a French privateer? Had she truly been taken onto an enemy vessel?

Indeed, it all seemed like a horrible nightmare, yet, when Juliet looked down at her hands, she still saw them stained with Elizabeth's blood.

Never had she seen someone die. Especially not in a violent manner. When her own father had passed on, it had been from overindulgence and she had not been in the room when he had drawn his last breath.

Now, all Juliet could think of were the thundering footsteps as Elizabeth had fled blindly down the companionway. She had been frantic...

...and then she had been still.

A deafening shot had rung out, and in the next instant, Elizabeth had screamed and gone down. Blood had pooled around her, and all too swiftly her eyes had closed for good.

Juliet pinched her eyes shut against the memory as tears collected. She felt them roll down her cheeks as she wrapped her arms around her knees in a desperate attempt to still the trembling that seized her limbs.

How could this have happened?

It was a futile question, but it was one that lingered upon Juliet's mind. She dimly remembered Mr. Kingston telling her that merchant ships rarely sailed alone as there was strength in numbers. Unfortunately, Captain Sanders' ship had been delayed in London, but they had been hoping to catch up with a number of other merchant vessels once they had left England well behind.

Juliet had not paid close attention at the time; yet, now, here, she could not help but think that perhaps they had been delayed because of her. Had *she* been the reason this had happened? After all, she had been a last-minute passenger. Arrangements had needed to be made and...

The woman upon the cot moaned in pain, and Juliet shot to her feet, a part of her grateful for the distraction.

Frantic, she looked about herself. "What can I do?" Her gaze fell on a bowl of water and some linen cloths. She also found a jar with a salve in it that smelled like herbs. Of course, Juliet had no knowledge of what they were or what could be done for burns. Still, she could smell the faint remnants of the same salve upon the woman's skin.

For a moment, Juliet hesitated, wishing the woman could tell her if that was what she needed. Yet, it was clear that the woman was far from awake. No doubt it had been the pain that had roused her to movement. Her eyes, however, remained closed and her mind absent.

Inhaling a deep breath, Juliet carefully spread some of the salve onto the woman's burns. At first, the woman flinched at the touch but then after a while began to calm. It seemed the salve had a cooling or soothing effect; perhaps it even numbed the pain, judging from the slight tingling sensation coming to Juliet's fingertips. She quickly grabbed the small cloth and wiped the remnants of the salve off her hand.

For a few more heartbeats, Juliet continued to stare down at the sleeping woman. Then she once again lowered herself to the floor, leaning her back against the cot and resting her forehead upon her bent knees. Her eyes began to close of their own accord as exhaustion washed over her. Yet, Juliet was afraid to give in.

Gritting her teeth, she forced her head back up, blinking her eyes rapidly, trying to stay awake. Her gaze swept over the cabin, and she felt oddly reminded of the *Chevalier Noir*, the ship of Antoine Duret, Violet's stepfather.

Only once had Juliet been aboard. It had been the day Captain Duret had married his beloved stepdaughter to Lord Cullingwood. It had been a happy day, and Juliet remembered the many nautical instruments she had seen upon his table. The same nautical instruments she now saw upon this one.

Not if her life depended upon it could she have named any of them. Yet, they looked familiar.

Those few moments aboard the *Chevalier Noir* also belonged to those precious ones she treasured beyond most others. Moments she had spent in Henri's presence.

They had both stood on deck and watched as Violet and Lord Cullingwood had become husband and wife. Juliet remembered well the way she had carefully lifted her gaze to look upon Henri, the way he had looked back at her.

He had still been angry.

Angry with her.

Of course, he had had every right to be. She had made a mistake. Because of her, her stepfather, Lord Silcox, had learned of his daughter's whereabouts in London. He had wasted no time and instantly abducted Violet, threatening her life in order to protect his own lineage.

After all, the first Lady Silcox had not died as he had thought. Instead, she had sailed away with a French privateer and begun a new life.

To this day, only a few people knew the truth of what had happened that night. Society remained ignorant of the fact that Juliet's half-brother Jacob, the new Lord Silcox after her stepfather's death, was illegitimate or would be considered illegitimate if anyone should ever learn the truth and make it known.

With the first Lady Silcox still alive, Juliet's mother's marriage had never been valid!

Henri had been furious when he had learned of what Juliet had done. He had been out of his mind with fear for his beloved cousin, and it had only been thanks to him and Lord Cullingwood as well as Violet's daring spirit that none had died that night with the exception of Juliet's stepfather, Lord Silcox.

Henri had left England upon his uncle's ship the very next day. He had refused to speak to her when she had tried to apologize, and over the past four years, Juliet had wondered more than once whether he was still angry with her, whether he still blamed her.

Juliet's gaze moved to the three windows that opened up the cabin to the outside world. The sun was beginning to slip past the horizon, casting its soft glow over the wide, seemingly unending waters. It was a beautiful view, and it was that stark contrast to the fear that had taken up root in Juliet's heart that brought fresh tears to her eyes.

How had this happened? And why had she been brought to the captain's quarters? To tend to the young woman? Was she the captain's wife?

Another moan from the cot drew Juliet's attention. She scooted closer on her knees and was surprised to see the woman's eyes begin to flutter. "Hello?" Juliet began tentatively, not certain how to address this unknown woman. "Is there anything you need?"

The woman's pale blue eyes slowly focused upon Juliet's face. Then her lips parted as though she wished to speak, but no more than a puff of air escaped. Still, a hint of confusion seemed to linger upon her face as her eyes swept over Juliet's. After an agonizingly long moment, she finally managed to say, *"Ex-Excusez-moi?"*

"Oh!" Juliet shook her head when she realized her mistake. Of course, the woman was French and would not understand a word of English.

Closing her eyes, Juliet did her best to recall her own French lessons, her tutor's many instructions. The words left her lips in a somewhat stuttering fashion; yet, she could see the woman's eyes light up with understanding. It was a relief to be able to speak to someone.

Anyone.

Unfortunately, the woman was far too weak to hold a conversation. Her eyes were already beginning to close again, and Juliet could see unconsciousness tugging upon her mind. "Do you know this ship?" she asked quickly, searching the woman's face. "Who is its captain? We were on our way—"

"Dubois." The name left the woman's tongue on a weak breath. Still, Juliet shuddered at the way her lips seemed to thin in disgust. "Beware. He...He's the devil," were the last words to drift to Juliet's ears before the woman's eyes closed once more, slumber granting her a reprieve from the harsh reality of life.

Juliet sank back down onto the floor, her limbs weak and her heart almost paralyzed with fear. Her gaze moved to the door through which the tall, grim stranger had left hours ago.

Captain Dubois.

Who was he? And what would he do with them? With *her*?

Closing her eyes, Juliet once again wrapped her arms tightly around her bent knees. "I should never have left," she whispered into the stillness. "I should never have left."

Chapter Six

CONSEQUENCES

The two vessels drifted lazily upon the open waters, side by side as though holding a conversation. Fortunately, the sun shone and only a mild breeze stirred the air. The sails had been taken down, and thick ropes kept the two ships from drifting apart.

The moment Henri's feet landed upon the deck of the *Chevalier Noir*, Antoine's ship, his uncle came rushing forward. The easy smile Henri had seen upon his face before was now gone, replaced by a tense look of apprehension. "Henri, what is wrong?" Antoine asked, his dark gaze searching his nephew's face. "Is it Alexandra? Violette or the chil—?"

Henri quickly held up a hand. "They are all well," he assured him, giving a quick nod for emphasis. "Your family is well."

Antoine inhaled a deep breath, and his features relaxed. "Still, something is on your mind, *n'est-ce pas?* What happened?"

Henri gritted his teeth, the odd pressure in his chest becoming more unbearable with each moment that passed. "A letter arrived from England," he said without preamble and then in as few words as possible explained what had happened in Antoine's absence.

"We need to find Violette," his uncle stated immediately. "I expect her to be farther north. We should—"

Henri shook his head. "There is no time for that," he gritted out, and the pressure in his chest increased.

Antoine's gaze narrowed. "What is it? Something's happened. Tell me."

Henri squared his shoulders, the words almost stuck in his throat. "The merchant vessel she boarded was taken by Dubois." That name never failed to tighten his muscles. He had known Dubois for years, not well, but well enough.

The man had a reputation that far exceeded that of any honorable privateer. He was ruthless and did what he did not out of honor or duty or obligation. As he followed rules only as far as they served him, one could never truly be certain of his allegiance.

Antoine's jaw tightened. "Did you see her on board?"

Henri shook his head. "I did not encounter Dubois's ship, but the merchant vessel Dubois's crew was sailing back to France to be sold."

A dark look fell over Antoine's face. "And the prisoners? Were they not on board?"

Henri scoffed, a dark sound if ever there was one. "As far as I know, they were."

"But she was not among them?"

Henri's teeth ground together painfully. "Dubois's crew was not all that forthcoming; however, it seems that an English lady had been taken onto his ship." Henri felt an almost desperate need to plant his fist in someone's face, preferably Dubois's.

A groan rose from Antoine's throat as he turned away and ran a hand through his hair. "Do you know where he is headed?" His dark gaze returned to meet Henri's.

"South," he replied, his feet already carrying him back to the rail. "From the way his crew spoke, I suspect he will return to his home port, to *Monpont*." He reached for the rope that would carry him back onto the *Voile Noire*. A hand on his shoulder, however, stopped him. He turned to look back at his uncle. "Antoine, you know Dubois. You know the kind of man he is. There is no time to lose."

43

Antoine's hand upon his shoulder remained, holding him back. "What do you intend to do, Henri? You know you cannot attack his ship." His brows rose, and Henri could read doubt upon his uncle's face.

He scoffed. "I'm not a fool."

"I did not mean to say that you were," Antoine pointed out. "However, we need to think before we act. This is a most delicate situation. If you attack Dubois, a fellow privateer, a countryman, it is treason. We need—"

"I know that!" Henri growled.

Antoine's hand upon his shoulder tightened further. "We need Violette! She and Oliver sail under an English flag. If anyone can justly attack Dubois and retrieve Juliette, it is her." A frown came to his uncle's face as his gaze searched Henri's. "But you know that," he mumbled thoughtfully. "Yet, you're out here. You were not looking for Violette or even me. The only reason we are having this conversation is because I happened upon you, *vraiment?*"

Henri turned back to face his uncle more fully. "As I said before, there is no time to lose. If we wait for Violette..." He could not bring himself to finish the thought. Indeed, this was worse than what he had imagined! Why on earth had Dubois kept Juliette with him? Why was she not being taken to France with the other prisoners to be ransomed back to England? What did he want with her?

Henri did not dare contemplate this question further!

"Then what do you intend to do when you catch up to him?" Antoine demanded. "What will you do?" He huffed out a deep breath, a hint of resignation coming to his eyes. "Do not let him see that you care for her. As soon as—"

Henri opened his mouth to protest, but Antoine stopped him, his hand upon Henri's shoulder tightening further. "As soon as he realizes that you came for her, he will not give her up. He will keep her from you out of spite." He shook his head, deep contemplation marking his features; yet, Henri could read the hopelessness of their situation upon his uncle's face. "Go," Antoine finally said, "but promise me you will not do anything rash. Her life as much as yours depends on you keeping a clear head."

Henri nodded. "I will do what I can. I cannot promise you

anything beyond that." Even now, Henri could feel something almost savage bubbling in his veins.

Antoine heaved a disapproving sigh. "I will go and find Violette, and we will follow you as soon as possible. If you can, wait for us."

Henri gripped the rope tightly and stepped up onto the rail. "You know as well as I do that I might not have a choice. Dubois is the kind of man who simply takes what he wants. He—"

"We all take what we want," Antoine interrupted him. "We are privateers. It's our business."

Henri shook his head. "It might be for you and me, but Dubois has his own reasons. You know that."

The look upon Antoine's face told Henri that his uncle agreed. "Be careful, Henri."

Henri held his uncle's gaze and then nodded. "I will do what I can. Hurry!" Then he turned his gaze back to the *Voile Noire* and jumped off the rail. His hands grasped the rope tightly, and he felt the wind tug upon his shirt as he swung through the air. He landed with a thud upon his own vessel and quickly called orders to continue their journey.

Looking over his shoulder, Henri saw his uncle's ship head north. He could only hope that Violette was nearby, that she could be found quickly, that...

Striding across the deck, Henri watched the sails unfurl above him. The winds were not in their favor; however, the *Voile Noire* slowly picked up speed. He moved to stand at the bowsprit and gazed down into the churning waters before he moved his eyes to the far horizon.

Always had the sea had a calming effect upon him. Always had he felt at peace out here. Now, however, the need to move burned in his veins. He felt restless and agitated, and it took all his willpower to maintain an outward appearance of calm. It would not serve him if his crew began to doubt his authority. He needed to remain in control of his vessel as much as of himself.

As the sun slowly went down, the wind began to pick up. Henri could feel the change, and his heart felt a little lighter. They were in pursuit. Finally, they were in pursuit again.

Staring out at the slowly darkening world, Henri felt himself reminded of that day four years ago when he had last left England. He had seen his beloved cousin married, and then he and Antoine had returned to the *Chevalier Noir* and headed out to sea, leaving her behind.

Her...and Juliette.

Henri still remembered how furious he had been with her on that last day. He had blamed her for what her stepfather had done. Yes, she had made a mistake informing him of Violette's whereabouts. Yet, Henri had known from the start that she had not acted with malicious intent. Juliette had simply been an innocent, young woman, unaware of the evils that lurked in this world. She had not known to be on her guard.

He sighed. Did she now? He did not dare picture what she might be going through upon Dubois's ship. Still, he knew that Juliette would never again be that young, innocent woman, who knew nothing of the world.

It had taken days, weeks even, for Henri to realize that he had never truly been furious with her. There had been something special about her. Even after only such a short acquaintance, he had known that, and deep down, he had come to realize it would be hard for him to leave her.

It had been a thought that had unsettled him, and he had counteracted it in the only way he knew how...by pushing her away.

By blaming her.

By feeling anger instead of...

Henri drew in a deep breath as one of the last moments they had spent together resurfaced in his mind. Four years had passed since, and yet, it remained crystal clear to him.

"Henri! Please!" came Juliette's pleading voice as she raced after him down a corridor at Silcox Manor. "Please, wait!"

Despite knowing that he ought not, that any word from her might prove a danger to his resolve, Henri did stop and turned to face her. His jaw clenched as he stared down at her, his eyes hard. "What is it you wish to say?"

Her green eyes were wide, and she almost shrank back at the harshness in his voice. "Please, you must believe me. I never meant for any of this to happen. I never meant for Violet to be hurt." Tears glistened in her eyes, and Henri knew that she spoke truthfully.

His insides tensed, and he could feel the sudden urge to reach out and cup his hand to her cheek. Instead, he pulled back his shoulders and linked his hands behind his back. "Whether you intended it or not does not matter," he told her, his eyes hard on hers. "Yet, it happened. Violette was almost killed because of you." His lips clamped shut. "It is not something easily forgiven."

Her eyes closed, and she bowed her head, anguish written all over her face. "What can I do?"

Henri knew that Violette did not blame Juliette for what had happened. He had overheard their conversation and knew that the two stepsisters had taken the first steps toward a deeper familial bond. They did not share the same blood, but then again, neither did he and Violette. Yet, she was his cousin, felt like a sister in many ways, and he could not imagine a life without her.

She was family.

And Juliette's foolish words had almost taken Violette from him. From all of them. No, it was not something easily forgiven.

A sob left her lips, and to his surprise, Juliette took a step closer. He would have expected her to turn and walk away, but she did not. Instead, she slowly lifted her head and looked up at him. She stood so close that he could feel the faint brush of her breath upon his skin. The scent of the sea seemed to linger upon hers, and he breathed in deeply, savoring that inconveniently intoxicating scent of her.

"When will you leave?" she asked, and unwittingly, his gaze strayed to her lips, tracing the soft movement as she spoke.

A quiet moment lingered between them before Henri swallowed, calling himself to reason. "Today. After they've been married."

Her eyes widened slightly. "So soon?"

He nodded. "Why would I linger? Have you forgotten that England and France are at war?" Holding her gaze, he leaned closer, curious if he could make her turn and run. "We are enemies," he snarled, his eyes hard as they held hers.

Juliette drew in a shuddering breath; yet, she did not move. Only her eyes widened and grew sad in a way that Henri felt his heart squeeze in a way he had not encountered before. He felt the sudden urge to reach for her, to comfort her, to brush away those tears that still lingered.

Involuntarily, he felt the tight clasp of his hands behind his back loosen. He felt his arms move forward as though intending to give in to that urge. It was almost too late when Henri finally recalled his senses.

His shoulders snapped back, and he lifted his chin, his gaze veering from hers.

Never before had Henri Duret felt vulnerable.

"Will you come back?" Juliette asked, a pleading note in her voice that surprised him.

Henri's gaze lowered back down to hers, and he felt the need to move closer grow with each second that passed. "Why would I come back?" he forced himself to ask, steeling his voice against the traitorous emotions that welled up in his chest.

Juliette swallowed. "To...To see Violet. You will come back to see her, won't you?"

Holding her gaze, Henri slowly shook his head. "Non, I shall never set foot on English soil again. More than ever, I know where I belong, as does Violette. Married to an Englishman or not, she is still a daughter of France, and we will see each other again out there at sea...where we belong."

A slight quiver gripped Juliette's jaw as she nodded her head. "I see." Her eyes fell from his, and once again, she bowed her head. "Then I wish you well," she whispered before lifting her eyes to his once more. "Henri."

Almost mesmerized, Henri stared down at her. Her eyes shone in the deepest, most sparkling green he had ever seen as she suddenly moved closer and her hand reached out to touch his.

It was no more but a fleeting brush of her skin against his; yet, Henri knew that he would never forget it.

And he never had.

Standing at the bowsprit, Henri looked down at his hand, his skin still tingling with the memory of her touch. It had been the last time they had stood close, had spoken.

Moments after, they had all ventured out to the *Chevalier Noir* to see Violette and Oliver married. Immediately following the short ceremony, those that were to remain in England had left the ship and returned to Silcox Manor while Antoine and Henri had set sail for France.

For home.

Four years had passed since then, and yet, Henri still remembered her touch. Remembered her. He had done his utmost to banish her from his thoughts, but he had failed. Still, he had never expected to ever see her again, had he?

Again, his heart tightened in his chest at the thought of all that stood between them.

At the thought of Dubois.

If only the winds would pick up and hasten their journey! Henri's patience was wearing thin!

Very thin!

Countryman or not, he knew he would do everything within his power to retrieve her...and hang the consequences!

Chapter Seven
THE DUBOIS

J uliet could not say how many days had passed since she had been brought onto Dubois's ship. Time seemed to pass agonizingly slowly, and her mind was in no position to keep track of anything beyond her immediate surroundings. She did not dare dwell upon where they were headed or what would happen to her once they reached their destination. No, Juliet did her best to focus her thoughts on the immediate here and now.

Most days, she slept little, curled into a ball on the floor, her head sometimes resting upon the cot upon which Noèle slept.

Every few hours, the pain from her burns would wake the young woman, drawing tortured moans from her lips. Fortunately, the salve provided relief, soothing the pain and allowing her head to clear. Still, Noèle was weak and exhausted and rarely managed to say more than a few words.

"*De l'eau, s'il vous plaît*," she whispered through cracked lips.

Juliet immediately reached for the pitcher and poured the young woman a cup of water. Then she helped her sit up and held it to her lips.

Noèle drank greedily, coughing in between big gulps, before she sank back onto the cot, looking even more exhausted than before. "*Merci*."

"How did you come to be on this ship?" Juliet asked quietly as she glanced at the door.

To her great relief, Captain Dubois seemed to have made other living arrangements for himself. These were clearly his quarters, and yet, he never lingered for long. Every other day, he would stop by, rifle through some of his belongings and then leave once again. Still, the way he sometimes looked at Noèle never failed to send a cold chill down Juliet's back.

There was no kindness in his gaze.

No compassion.

But instead, something calculating as though he did not yet quite know what to make of the injured young woman nor what to do with her.

Captain Dubois rarely looked at Juliet, and when he did, it was mostly to bark another order at her. He told her to keep her head down and see to Noèle.

That was all.

Noèle's gaze moved to meet Juliet's; yet the woman did not say a word. Still, Juliet could not help but think that in that moment Noèle chose to remain quiet. How on earth had the woman gotten onto the ship? Where had she received these burns? And who was she?

"How do you know the captain?" Juliet tried again, remembering the words of warning Noèle had whispered to her on her first day aboard. "What do you know of him?"

Noèle's eyes closed, and a single tear ran out of one corner.

Juliet gritted her teeth, torn between compassion and a most urgent desire to shake the woman and receive some answers. "Did he do this to you? The burns?"

In that moment, the door opened and a young man stepped over the threshold.

At first glimpse, Juliet thought it was Captain Dubois for their features seemed so similar. Then, however, she noticed that this man was a good deal shorter than the captain and that he walked with a slight limp. A bandage had been wrapped around his left leg, suggesting that he had recently been injured.

Perhaps in the confrontation with the merchant vessel.

The moment his eyes fell upon Noële, they filled with deepest compassion. His mouth dropped open in shock as his eyes swept over her injuries. Slowly, he moved closer, his face paling with each step he took. "Oh, *mon dieu!*"

Juliet remained where she was, seated at the foot of the cot, her gaze trained upon their visitor. He seemed all but oblivious to her, his full attention focused on Noële. "I'm so sorry this happened," he stammered as tears filled his eyes. "I'm so sorry I could not get to you sooner." His gaze strayed to his bandaged leg. "Thank God for my brother. If he had not come along, I—"

"Your brother?" Juliet asked without thought, only realizing what she had done as the man's gaze finally turned to her.

He blinked, clearly only now becoming aware of her presence.

"I'm sorry," Juliet mumbled. "I did not mean to—" She broke off, relieved not to see anything hostile in his gaze. "Who are you?"

The man's lips parted; yet, before he could say a word, Captain Dubois appeared in the doorframe. "What are you doing here, Brother? Did I not tell you to remain where you were? You need to heal before strutting around the ship once more."

Juliet stared in shock at the captain. *Brother?* Of course, it was true. They looked so much alike, and yet, the difference in their demeanor set them apart so markedly that Juliet experienced a moment of disbelief.

"I'm sorry, Bastien," the young man replied. "I simply had to see her. It's been days, and..." His voice trailed off, and he shrugged. "I simply had to see her."

Juliet's gaze drifted to Noële, surprised to see the woman's face rather tense as she watched the exchange with apprehension. The way the captain's brother had spoken *to* her and *about* her suggested some kind of emotional attachment. Noële's reaction, on the other hand, proved otherwise. How did she know the captain and his brother? How had she come to be here?

Captain Dubois stepped forward, an unusually kind look upon his face. "I understand, Benoît." Juliet almost flinched as his gaze drifted to her. "As you can see, I procured this lovely English lady to see to her." A sickening grin spread across his face as he looked at her, his eyes drifting over her from head to toe.

Never before in her life had Juliet felt worse. A cold shiver ran down her back, and she could feel every muscle in her body tensing. The way he looked at her felt like an attack or at least the threat of one.

"Thank you, Bastien," the younger brother replied, gratitude in his voice. "Thank you for saving her life," he sighed, and a smile came to his face as he looked at the captain, "and mine. We both would have died if you hadn't come along. Thank you."

Captain Dubois clasped a hand on his brother's shoulder, a companionable smile upon his face. "You are most welcome, Benoît. Now, please return to your quarters and rest. You've seen for yourself that everything that can be done for her is being done. You will serve her best if you recover your own strength as soon as possible."

Benoît Dubois nodded. "*Bien sûr. C'est vrai.*" His gaze returned to Noèle, and he inhaled a deep breath. "Be well. I shall come and visit you again soon." Then he limped out of the cabin and down the companionway.

To Juliet's great shock, Captain Dubois did not follow his brother. Instead, he closed the door and then turned around to look at Noèle. "I see that you're awake, *ma cherie.* How convenient."

Juliet's gaze flew to Noèle, and she could see the terror upon the young woman's face. Despite her exhaustion, her burned limbs worked to push her closer to the wall and away from the approaching captain.

The devil, as Noèle had called him.

Juliet felt the urge to step forward and into the captain's path to protect Noèle. Yet, her body seemed frozen with terror, the same kind of terror she could see upon Noèle's face. She did not know what had happened between the young woman and the captain, but the terrified look in Noèle's widened eyes suggested that it had been hell on earth.

Coming to stand beside the cot, Captain Dubois leaned down to Noèle. His right hand reached out, and his fingers grasped her chin tightly. Juliet could not see into his face from where she sat; however, she saw the corner of his mouth curl up into a vindictive sneer. Then he leaned closer and whispered something to Noèle that had her eyes going even wider than before. A violent shudder shook her, and a moment later, she pinched her eyes shut, her face contorting in anguish.

"Stop it!" Only belatedly did Juliet realize that these two brave words had left her own lips. She had not meant to surge to her feet nor to speak out in defense of the other woman.

Yet, it seemed she had done both.

Perhaps it was wrong to call it bravery. Perhaps foolishness was a more accurate term because the moment her voice, sharp and commanding, echoed through the stillness of the cabin, Captain Dubois lifted his head and turned to look at her.

Juliet almost fainted on the spot.

"*Excusez-moi?*" Captain Dubois demanded in a cold, almost icy voice. He straightened, his attention now fully settling upon her as he turned away from Noèle.

On instinct, Juliet backed away, her breath coming fast as she stared at him in utter panic. "I'm... I'm sorry. I didn't mean to—" Her back collided with the wall, cutting off her retreat.

Captain Dubois's eyes were hard as he stared at her, a sneer upon his face. "You forget your place, *mademoiselle*." Slow, measured steps carried him closer while those hard eyes of his trailed over her as though taking stock. Then they returned to meet hers once more, all but pinning her to the wall.

With every fiber of her being, Juliet wished she would faint. In that very moment, she desired nothing more but to be far, far away from here...even if only in her mind. "Please, I'm sorry. I—"

"*Mais, oui*, you are," Captain Dubois snarled as he crossed those last few steps toward her. "You will be even more sorry if you do not remember to keep your head down." He stood so close that Juliet could smell his foul breath as he leaned forward and braced his hands upon the wall beside her head. "Do you understand?"

Dropping her gaze, Juliet nodded. "Yes, I do." She could almost feel his gaze trailing over her, and she wished he would step away.

Yet, he remained, not a word leaving his lips as though he knew how torturous this silence was for her.

Juliet's mind frantically searched for something to say, something that might appease him. Unfortunately, her thoughts ran all but rampant, unable to focus on anything.

And then, as she closed her eyes, Henri's face appeared in front of her. Why she had not thought of him before, she did not know. After all, the situation she found herself in ought to have reminded her of the other French privateers she had known long ago. Perhaps she had simply not allowed herself to think of him.

"Are you...Are you acquainted with the Durets?" she asked, her voice no more than a whisper. She was afraid to say the wrong thing but equally afraid to remain silent. The stillness in the cabin was unnerving, urging her to break it.

Captain Dubois drew in a slow breath, and Juliet carefully raised her eyes. "The Durets?" he snarled, his brows knitting together, giving his face a most menacing expression. "Are *you* acquainted with them?" Suspicion resonated in his voice as he watched her through narrowed eyes.

Juliet bit her lower lip, for she had clearly said the wrong thing. In her panic, she had foolishly assumed that as privateers serving the same country her association with the Durets might aid her.

Unfortunately, it seemed the opposite was the case.

"Answer me!" he snapped, his large hands gripping her shoulders and shoving her hard against the wall.

Juliet gasped. "My...My stepsister Violet, she—"

Captain Dubois's eyes widened with a hint of recognition. "Violette Duret? She is your stepsister?"

Gritting her teeth against the shivers that shook her, Juliet nodded.

Captain Dubois's gaze held hers, something contemplative in it before a sickening smile came to his face. "Well, well, well, the fair Violette." He chuckled darkly. "Who would've thought? I heard she now commands her own ship." His gaze narrowed once more. "An English ship."

Juliet did not know if he wanted her to give a reply, but she chose to remain quiet, hoping not to draw his anger.

"Is she the only Duret you are acquainted with?" he asked quietly, suspicion resting in his dark eyes as they held hers, daring her not to lie to him.

Juliet swallowed. "She's not," she stammered, balling her hands into fists in a desperate attempt to hold onto her wits. "Of course, I've met her father Antoine as well as—"

"Her cousin," Captain Dubois snarled, his eyes now narrowed into slits, open hostility in his voice. "Henri Duret." Again, his hands tightened upon her shoulders. "You know Henri Duret?"

Hearing his name sent a shiver of a different kind through Juliet. Her breath hitched, and she could not help that spark of delight that ignited in her heart.

A knowing look came to Captain Dubois's face. "Ah, I see," he sneered, no small measure of satisfaction in the way he spoke, in the way he looked at her. "And I assume you are more to him than a mere acquaintance, n'est-ce pas?"

Juliet felt her cheeks flush as treasured memories unwittingly resurfaced. Yes, she had lost her heart to Henri long ago; he, however, had walked away without a moment's hesitation. In all likelihood, he had never once thought of her since they had last bid each other farewell. "I...I have not seen him in four years," Juliet told the captain truthfully, and yet, saying so out loud broke her heart.

A growl rose from Captain Dubois's throat, and he grasped her chin painfully, yanking up her head to make her look at him. "Do not play games with me! Are you his?"

Again, Juliet's heart skipped a beat at the mere thought of it, and tears shot to her eyes as she fought against the tremble in her knees. "I am not," she willed herself to say, knowing that it was the truth. "I am nothing to him."

The captain gritted his teeth, open displeasure in his eyes as they lingered upon hers a moment longer. "We shall see," he snarled into her face, then abruptly released her chin and took a step back.

Juliet almost crumpled to the floor, her breath coming in rapid gasps as she rubbed her chin, trying to banish the feel of his hand upon her.

For a reason she did not know, it seemed that Captain Dubois detested Henri. Something had to have happened in their past to explain this animosity. Juliet had been a fool to mention the Durets, to think that simply because they were all French privateers some sense of loyalty or companionship existed between them.

"See to her," Captain Dubois snarled with a sideways glance at Noèle. "We shall see if you mean nothing to him," he then added with a contemplative look in his eyes before turning away and striding out of the cabin, locking the door behind him

Relief flooded Juliet, and she sank to the floor when her knees finally gave in. Loud sobs tore from her throat, and she closed her eyes, resting her head against the wall.

Never before, not even when she had been forced into the betrothal to Lord Dowling, had Juliet felt so powerless, so much at the mercy of another. There was nothing she could do but remain here and wait. There was no one who would stand with her. No one who would come for her.

Yes, her mother knew by now that Juliet had left England. Yet, she could not know what had happened since, that their ship had been attacked by a French vessel and that Juliet had been taken onto that vessel and was now being held prisoner.

For a reason she did not know. Was it merely to see to the woman Noèle? It was the only thing that made sense. After all, Captain Dubois had not initially known of her association with the Durets. However, now that he did, what would he do? Would he harm her, thinking that any injury done to her would be one felt by Henri as well?

If only someone knew where she was. If only Violet knew. She was the only one who would come for her, would she not? After all, she had before. Despite all the risks to her own life, Violet had ventured into England four years ago in order to protect Juliet.

A young woman she had never even met before.

A stepsister she had not even known of.

Only Violet was somewhere out at sea, with no knowledge of what had happened to Juliet. No one knew. Even if the Durets somehow were to find out, would they care? At least for Violet's sake?

Tears squeezed out of Juliet's eyes as the hopelessness of her situation washed over her. She was alone.

Completely and utterly alone.

"I should never have left," she whispered as tears streamed down her face. "If only I'd never left."

Chapter Eight
NOÉLE

"Would you like to try and get up?" Juliet asked the young woman, now sitting upright upon the cot.

Noèle inhaled a deep breath, looking down upon her arms and legs, the skin there still bright red and painful to the touch. Yet, over the past sennight, she had slowly begun to heal and gain strength. "*Oui*, I think I would." A tentative smile came to her face as she looked at Juliet. "*Merci*."

Stepping closer, Juliet carefully pulled the woman to her feet, always watchful not to touch the burned skin in any way. Noèle placed an arm over Juliet's shoulder, and Juliet wrapped one of hers around her lower back. "All right?"

After a couple of deep breaths, Noèle nodded. "*Oui*." Then, step by step, they began to make their way around the cabin. At first, it was slow and painful, judging from the grimace that occasionally came to Noèle's face. After a while, however, the woman seemed to move with more ease.

Both of them tensed, stopping in their tracks, when the sound of approaching footsteps drifted to their ears. They looked at one another, their eyes widening, their breaths lodging in their throats.

And then the door opened, and Benoît Dubois stepped into the cabin, his left leg still bandaged. The moment his eyes fell upon Noële, his whole face lit up. "You're on your feet," he exclaimed, joy in his voice as he stepped forward. "Are you feeling any better?"

Juliet stared at the young man, his kind smile and gentle manners almost shocking after Captain Dubois's harsh treatment of them.

With her arm still wrapped around Noële, Juliet felt the young woman tense. "I am better," she whispered. "*Merci.*"

Benoît exhaled in relief. "That is good to hear, but please do not overexert yourself."

Feeling Noële weaken in her arms, Juliet urged the young woman back to the cot and eased her down. However, the moment she looked up, she all but flinched for her eyes fell upon Captain Dubois standing leisurely in the doorway.

The captain's eyes remained upon his brother before they drifted to Noële and then to her. A warning rested in his dark gaze for as long as his brother's back remained turned to him. However, the moment Benoît spotted him, the captain's expression changed. A friendly smile came to his face, and he looked at his brother with eyes that almost shone with affection.

Juliet swallowed hard. Never had she seen such different faces on one and the same person. Was it truly possible that Captain Dubois loved his brother? Was he capable of such emotions when he showed no mercy and compassion in the treatment of others?

"Do you see, Brother?" Benoît exclaimed, his right hand gesturing toward Noële. "She's gaining strength. She even managed to walk around the cabin." Pride and joy rang in his voice, and yet again, Juliet wondered how Noële and the captain's brother knew one another. While he seemed utterly familiar with her, speaking to her as though they were family, Noële remained distant.

"I am glad to see it," Captain Dubois replied before his gaze wandered to Noële. "I am certain her health will continue to improve so long as she remembers to heed my words of caution." A hidden warning lingered behind those words; his gaze fixed upon Noële in a way that made the young woman shudder.

Completely unaware of his brother's hidden message, Benoît

nodded. "*Oui*, please, Noële, take good care of yourself." He heaved a deep sigh. "Would you like some company?"

He was about to seat himself in one of the chairs when Noële spoke up. "That is very kind of you; however, I am terribly fatigued and would rather sleep."

A hint of disappointment came to the young man's face, but he nodded. "Of course, I shall come and visit you again soon."

Juliet tried her hardest not to look directly at Captain Dubois. Still, she, too, had seen the look of warning he had cast in Noële's direction, prompting her to refuse his brother's offer of company. It seemed the captain did not wish for his brother to remain in Noële's presence without his supervision. Juliet wondered why that was. Was there a secret he was trying to keep from his brother? A secret Noële knew about?

With a last look over his shoulder, Benoît left the cabin and continued down the companionway. The captain, however, once more stepped inside and closed the door. "I see you've learned your lesson, *Cherie*," he sneered, his dark gaze fixed upon Noële.

No doubt feeling the full force of his gaze upon her, Noële seemed to shrink back, unable to look at him, her face once again pale.

Captain Dubois laughed, then turned toward the door, but he paused as his eyes fell upon Juliet. "*Et toi?*" Slowly, he moved toward her, his gaze watchful. "Have you learned your lesson as well? Or is there something on your mind? Something...you wish to say? Or ask?"

Once again, Juliet took a step back and instantly came up upon the wall. She kept her head lowered but could all but feel the captain's gaze upon her. She was not certain what he wished to hear, and so she remained quiet.

The tips of his boots appeared in her field of vision as he stepped closer until barely an arm's length separated them. "I can all but hear your thoughts, *Cherie*," he whispered in a sickeningly sweet voice. Then his hand moved toward her and once again grasped her chin, forcing her head up.

Juliet wanted to close her eyes but was afraid of what he might do should she do so.

"What is it you wish to know?" Captain Dubois asked as the pad of his thumb brushed over her chin in a sickeningly intimate way that sent a wave of nausea through Juliet.

Gritting her teeth, she fought to keep it from showing upon her face. "What happened to the others?" she finally asked, remembering how her maid Elizabeth had died upon the merchant vessel. "Captain Sanders and Mr. Kingston and all the others?"

"They will be ransomed back to England," the captain told her with a smug smile.

Juliet nodded, relieved to hear it. "And me?"

The captain's smile grew wider as he lowered his head to hers. "I believe I shall keep you, *Cherie*." His gaze darted to her mouth, and another wave of nausea rolled through Juliet. "I have no doubt I will be able to think of something amusing to do with you once we have this cabin to ourselves." A dark chuckle left his lips, and he pushed closer, his mouth closing in on hers.

Panic clawed at Juliet's heart, and she balled her hands into fists to remain calm. She told herself that it would only be a kiss and nothing more. After all, they were not alone...yet.

Noèle sat right there on the cot behind him.

Yet, the moment, Juliet felt the brush of his lips against hers, she could not help but jerk her head sideways, unable to bear the intimate contact.

It made her long for Henri with a desperate ache. A desire that was irrational and futile, but her heart still clung to him.

Again, a dark chuckle rose from Captain Dubois's lips. "Play coy if you like, *Cherie*," he whispered in her ear, then stood back and looked down at her. "But soon we will make port, and once my brother and his future wife," he glanced over his shoulder at Noèle, "are settled," his grin deepened as he leaned closer once more, "you'll be mine." He pinched her chin, then turned and with another dark laugh strode from the cabin.

Closing her eyes, Juliet rested her head against the wall. "This cannot be happening," she mumbled to herself. "This cannot be happening."

"There is no escape," came Noèle's voice from the cot. "He is the devil."

Opening her eyes, Juliet looked at the young woman, whose gaze was distant as she stared into nothing. Her face was pale, and dark memories lingered in her eyes.

Juliet buried her face in her hands. "There has to be something we can do," she mumbled to herself, unable to give up all hope just yet. "What do you know of him?" she asked looking up at Noële.

The young woman blinked, and slowly turned her head until her eyes met Juliet's. "He takes what he wants," she whispered as tears came to her eyes. "If you defy him, he will punish you for it."

Cold shivers went down Juliet's back. "And what of his brother? He seems to care for you." Tentatively, Juliet moved closer and then came to sit upon the cot next to Noële. "Please, tell me how you know them."

Noële swallowed hard, the look upon her face one of utter despair. "Benoît Dubois has always fancied me," she whispered, her gaze distant, fixed upon the past. "Even before my husband died, I often felt his gaze upon me. Once I was a widow, he sought me out and asked for my hand in marriage." She blinked and looked up at Juliet. "I refused him because my heart was not free to love again." Her lips pressed into a thin line.

Carefully, Juliet reached out to grasp the young woman's hand, mindful of her injuries. "What happened then? Did he get angry?"

Sighing, Noële shook her head. "He was...disappointed. I could see it upon his face, but he accepted my refusal and left." A tear rolled down her cheek. "His brother was a different matter."

Juliet could hear the revulsion Noële felt toward Captain Dubois in the young woman's voice. A part of her did not want to hear more, and yet, she knew that she needed to be prepared as best she could. "What did he do?"

Noële's hand tensed upon Juliet's. "He lashed out at me, slapped me hard across the face. I fell, and before I could get up, he was upon me. He held me down and..." Noële's eyes closed, and she bowed her head. "He told me to reconsider, to think things through." Slowly, she shook her head and looked up at Juliet. "If I'd had anywhere to go, I would have left." She shrugged. "Weeks passed, and then months. I told myself that it had been nothing more but a nightmare." She swallowed hard. "Until the day he did return."

Juliet stared at the young woman, her eyes sweeping over her burned skin before returning to look into her tear-misted eyes. "Did he do this to you? Because you would not marry his brother?" The thought was too awful to even consider, yet, remembering the cold look in Captain Dubois's eyes told Juliet that it was possible, nonetheless.

"I do not remember much," Noèle whispered, a new sadness coming to her eyes before she once more dropped her gaze. "He was angry with me. I remember his fist colliding with my jaw. For a moment, I thought my head would explode. I barely remember falling to the floor. I think I knocked over a table because I have the faintest memory of a lit candle rolling across the rug right in front of me." She blinked, and her gaze moved to Juliet's. "The next thing I remember is waking up on this ship."

"Did you agree to marry his brother?" Juliet asked, trying her best not to think of the horrors Noèle had lived through. "The way Captain Dubois spoke, it seemed as though—"

"I did not," Noèle insisted, anger in her voice as she gritted her teeth. "I know that he cares for me and I know him to be a decent man, especially compared to his brother," vehemently, she shook her head, "but I will not marry him."

Juliet nodded, grateful despite everything to have Noèle here with her. "We need to find a way out of this cabin," she suddenly heard herself say, an odd surge of energy pulsing through her veins.

Noèle's head snapped up. "How? We are on the open seas." Her gaze drifted to the tall windows in the back, allowing them a view of the wide blue ocean. "There's nowhere to go."

"But not for long," Juliet reminded the young woman beside her. "I don't know if you heard, but Captain Dubois just told me that we would soon be making berth in his home port."

Noèle nodded. "Yes, I heard." Her gaze met Juliet's, anguish in her eyes. "I am to marry his brother, and you..." Her voice trailed off.

Juliet did her best to suppress the shudder that gripped her. "Do you believe Benoît Dubois would harm you? Perhaps once you are at his family's home with him, there will be a way for you to flee. He seemed so taken with you, do you think we should speak to him?"

Noèle shook her head. "He would never believe us. His trust in his brother is infallible." She swallowed hard. "Also, Dubois would know. He warned me not to say a word. He said he would—" she gritted her teeth, then once again shook her head. "No, we must not say a word to Benoît."

Juliet inhaled a deep breath as that last shred of hope drifted away. "Then we must find a way to escape," she told Noèle insistently. "Once this ship makes berth, we need to find a way off it."

Looking defeated, Noèle shook her head. "How?"

Juliet shrugged. "I don't know, but we must think of something. Perhaps we can create a distraction." She heaved a deep sigh. "I do not know what happens when a ship makes berth. What does the crew do?"

"They see to the ship and its cargo," Noèle explained, the look in her eyes that of one who had seen it many times. "When all tasks are completed those that have loved ones nearby will seek them out whereas the others can usually be seen heading straight to the next tavern."

"Will that not give us a chance?" Juliet asked, trying not to get her hopes up too early. "Of course, Captain Dubois will not leave his ship unattended, will he? However, with fewer sailors on board, we might be able to sneak away." She grasped Noèle's hands tightly. "We have to try. What do we have to lose?"

For a long moment, Noèle held her gaze before Juliet thought she saw a spark of hope, of determination, of something other than resignation come to the young woman's eyes. "*Oui*, we must try."

Juliet exhaled a breath of relief. Perhaps, just perhaps, not all hope was lost after all.

Chapter Nine
ONCE UPON A PLAN

Holding a spyglass to his left eye, Henri surveyed Dubois's home port as the *Voile Noire* drifted lazily in the open waters near the coast. He spotted the two-masted ship immediately, moored at the docks, sailors unloading the cargo as the sun upon the horizon slowly went down.

"What are yer orders, Captain?" his first mate asked beside him, the expression upon his face squinted as he looked out at the coastline.

Henri inhaled a deep breath, trying his best to think this through calmly. His blood was all but boiling in his veins, urging him to surge forward and attack Dubois's ship with everything he had. It was an uncivilized impulse, and Henri knew that it would not serve him. Not only would he be committing treason against his country, but he would also be endangering Juliette's life.

No, the situation called for a covert approach. After all, Dubois could not possibly know that Henri had come, let alone why. "I need five men to accompany me into port," Henri finally said as his mind pieced together a plan with the greatest likelihood of success.

"Five?" Ian inquired with a sideways glance.

Henri nodded. "*Oui*, the *Voile Noire* will remain behind. The men must have her ready though to make way upon our return."

The Scotsman nodded. "I shall speak to them and have the dinghy readied." His gaze moved to the setting sun. "By nightfall then."

Henri looked at his first mate, relieved to see that the taciturn Scotsman understood him without much explanation. "Will you accompany me?" Henri inquired, knowing that he would have a greater chance of success with Ian by his side. "You and your friend?"

Ian leaned down and patted the wolf's head, a contemplative look upon his face. Then he turned and looked at Henri. "We shall come with you."

Henri nodded, grateful to have his first mate's support. "No matter what happens," he instructed, a stern look in his eyes, "she must reach the *Voile Noire*, am I understood?"

The Scotsman nodded solemnly, a flicker of something, some deep emotion in his pale eyes that made Henri wonder.

"Should I fall," Henri continued, "you are to take her to *La Roche-sur-Mer*, understood? Violette or my uncle will find a way to see her back home."

Again, Ian nodded, not a word leaving his lips. Then he turned to go and to carry out his orders, the furry beast by his side as always.

Henri turned back toward the coast; his eyes once more sweeping over the harbor. He wished he knew where she was. Probably under deck. The captain's quarters? His teeth gritted together painfully at the thought. Why had Dubois held onto her? Why had she not been ransomed back with the other prisoners?

Thus far, Henri had not seen her being taken off the ship. Whatever Dubois's plan, it seemed that Juliette would accompany him further.

Slowly, night fell over the land, and Henri left the quarterdeck, grateful to see all of his men in position, each one tending to the task assigned to him. The dinghy had been readied and four other volunteers had been found, who would join him and Ian on this endeavor.

"Good luck, Capt'n," Jacques mumbled, dipping his head as Henri strode past him. The rest of his crew nodded, a fierceness in their eyes that made Henri proud. "Bring us back the lady."

Chuckles drifted to his ears, and he could see wide grins coming to their faces.

Henri swallowed. After all, his crew believed him to be going after Juliette because she was to be his wife. It had been a necessary lie in order to secure their support; however, Henri felt a deep sense of unease because of this deception.

Finally seated in the dinghy, he and the others waited as it was lowered down to the water. A low whine drifted from the wolf's muzzle as the dinghy began to sway softly across the rolling waves. Still, a pat of Ian's hand instantly reassured the beast, and it settled down quietly.

With six men at the oars, it did not take long for them to row toward the harbor. They kept close to the rocky cliff face, heading north, slowly inching closer to land until they found a spot where they could climb ashore. "Wait here," Henri instructed the other four men of his crew, "and keep a wary eye. We might have to leave at a moment's notice. Approach the port when you see us coming."

Not for a second did Henri expect their endeavor to go unnoticed, not even in the dark. Yet, without involving the *Voile Noire*, it might simply be considered a quarrel among men about a woman.

Instead of treason.

With a last look at Dubois's ship moored at the dock, Henri gestured Ian forward, and together, they walked closer inland, circling back around toward the harbor. "You know what to do?"

The silent Scotsman nodded, the large beast trotting by his side, ears alert as they drew closer.

"Good." Inhaling a deep breath, Henri fixed his gaze on Dubois's ship when he felt a sudden sharp tug upon his heart that almost made him falter in his step.

She was here!

He was certain of it.

It was as though he could feel her. Was this how Antoine had felt the night he had found Alexandra?

Henri did not dare dwell on the thought. There would be time for that later. Now, however, he needed to remain focused.

For her.

∼

"Are you ready?" Juliet asked, looking at Noële over her shoulder. She had gathered together a few rolled-up maps as well as some rags she had found and then placed them all atop the small table.

Noèle's eyes were wide as she stared at the candle in Juliet's hand. Fear lurked in her gaze, and yet, she nodded her head. "*Oui.*"

After being burned so recently, Noèle watched in terror as Juliet held the candle's flame to the items upon the table.

Instantly, they caught fire, and she could hear Noèle draw in a sharp breath. Juliet hated doing this to her; however, a fire was the only distraction they had managed to come up with. There simply was no other way.

The captain as well as the crew had been busy these past few hours, tending to the ship and seeing to the cargo as it was being unloaded. Benoît had meant to take Noèle off the ship earlier; however, she had feigned sleep while Juliet had urged him to allow her some more rest. Of course, the concerned, young man had complied, requesting that Juliet see to Noèle while he prepared for her arrival at his family home. After that, a flurry of activity had kept the two women on edge as they had waited for night to fall. Eventually, the sound of rushing footsteps up on deck had receded, and grunts and groans had been replaced by cheers and bellows as sailors had disembarked from the ship, relieved to look toward more enjoyable pursuits.

Now, silence lay over the ship, and Juliet worried that Captain Dubois would come for them soon.

It was now or never.

Helping Noèle onto a chair near the door, Juliet then turned toward the wooden barrier blocking their way out. She drew in a deep breath and then began banging her fists against it. "Fire! Fire! Help us! Please!"

The table now stood fully engulfed by flames, and for a moment, Juliet feared that no one would come. What would they do then? Perhaps this had been a foolish idea after all.

Continuing her efforts, Juliet almost slumped down in relief when she finally heard voices drawing closer. Footsteps came running along the companionway and toward them. She stepped back when someone tried to pull open the door and then cursed when he found it locked.

"Only the captain has the key," she heard a sailor mutter to his companion, a moment before someone threw himself against the door with a loud *thud*.

"I'll go fetch him!" another yelled.

"He's at the tavern! It'll be too late by the time he returns!" the first man objected. "Do you not see the smoke under the door?" Again, he threw himself against the wooden barrier.

Behind Juliet, Noële was beginning to cough despite the wet cloth she was holding to her face. Juliet, too, felt the smoke curl down into her lungs, the need to cough becoming stronger and stronger with each moment that passed. "Please! Help us!" she tried to call out again, but her voice choked and she had to lean forward, bracing her hand against the wall as she tried to draw in another breath.

Again and again, the sailor threw himself against the door before it finally gave in.

With a loud crash, the wood splintered and the man all but shot into the room, closely followed by his companion. The other man took one look at them and gestured toward the companionway. "Out! Head up on deck!"

Juliet did not wait to be told twice. She quickly gathered Noële into her arms, helping the young woman to remain on her feet, before she all but dragged her out of the captain's quarters and along the companionway. Step by slow step, the two women moved onward until they reached a ladder leading upward.

Together, they climbed rung for rung, Juliet holding on tightly to Noële, who seemed at the end of her strength. And then finally, they were out on deck, and the fresh night air filled their lungs.

Still coughing, Juliet sank to her knees and tried her best to draw in one breath after another. Noële could no longer hold herself up, lying flat on deck as she too tried her best to breathe.

Juliet barely noticed as two other sailors came running. They rushed past them and down the ladder. "We need water! In the galley!" And then their voices were gone.

"We need to move," Juliet gasped, her voice sounding rough as she staggered toward Noële. "Please, you have to help me." She tried to pull the young woman up but knew she could never support her by herself. "Noèle, please."

Slowly, Noèle pushed herself upward, her face pale as Juliet pulled her onto her feet. The young woman's knees almost buckled, and she moaned as Juliet accidentally grasped her burnt arm.

With her eyes fixed on the gangplank, Juliet pulled Noèle forward. "We're almost there," she whispered, uncertain where they would go from there. However, she pushed that thought away, knowing she could not focus on it right now.

One step at a time.

Noèle's knees gave out, and she sank down. "I can't," she gasped, her eyes closing as every last bit of strength left her. "Go on without me. I can't."

"No!" Juliet insisted, pushing her hands under Noèle's shoulders and dragging her across the deck toward the gangplank. "We're doing this together," she gritted out against the exhaustion that washed over her. "I'm not leaving you behind."

Noèle's eyes closed, and Juliet could tell that the young woman had lost consciousness.

Panic surged through her, but she did her best to tamp it down, her eyes fixed upon the gangplank. "Almost there," she mumbled to herself. "Almost there."

Turning around, Juliet made to walk down the gangplank backward, dragging Noèle behind her, when rough hands seized her out of nowhere. "Who have we here?"

Terror gripped Juliet's heart as she was spun around and found herself face to face with Captain Dubois.

Chapter Ten

AFTER FOUR YEARS

Even from a distance, Henri could see the warm glow of the fire. It shone like a beacon, its bright shine lighting up the windows of the captain's quarters. "*Merde!*"

Gesturing to Ian, he took off running, crouched low so as not to draw attention. He could barely hear the Scotsman as well as the wolf behind him, but he did not stop to look, his gaze fixed upon Dubois's ship.

The moment he stepped onto the docks, Henri spotted two figures staggering out of the hatch. They did not walk upright but stumbled along before sinking to their knees.

Juliette!

Henri rushed onward, not daring to believe that it was truly her. Her and...? Who was with her? Had she boarded the ship with a man after all?

The thought tensed his muscles as he charged down toward Dubois's ship. He could see one of the two figures stumble to her feet, her skirts billowing in the mild breeze. Then she bent low and tried to pull the other up but to no avail.

Finally nearing the ship, Henri saw her head toward the gangplank, dragging something heavy behind her—probably whoever was with her. However, the moment she set a foot onto the wooden plank, a dark figure separated from the shadows and stepped toward her.

Dubois!

Henri's insides clenched painfully as he forced himself to slow down and retreat into the shadows alongside the ship. He could no longer see on deck but heard Dubois's voice say, "Who have we here?"

A startled yelp escaped the young woman, and Henri could all but picture Juliette, her green eyes wide with terror as she struggled against Dubois.

Forcing himself to stop, Henri gestured to Ian, who quickly lit the small torch they had brought along and waved it from side to side in front of him.

In the distance, another small torch lit up but only for a moment before it was tossed into the sea. Immediately, Ian extinguished his own.

Fortunately, the docks lay deserted, only a handful of ships moored here and there. Loud voices and singing though drifted to their ears from a nearby tavern. Henri hoped that the sailors would remain occupied and not come rushing out into the night.

Inhaling a deep breath, Henri gestured for Ian to follow him and then move forward silently. He headed toward the gangplank, still crouched low so as not to be spotted. As he proceeded higher up, his gaze fell on Dubois.

Fortunately, the man stood with his back to him.

Behind Dubois, Henri could no more but sense Juliette for she was all but dwarfed by Dubois's tall stature.

"Please," Juliette pleaded, her voice full of fear. "Please, let us go."

Dubois laughed in a way that made Henri want to rip his head off. "*Cherie*, why would I do that? After all, we haven't even had the chance to get better acquainted with one another."

Inching closer, Henri spotted another young woman lying by the gangplank, her dark hair covering her face as she lay on her side, clearly unconscious. Who was she? He wondered briefly before his gaze moved back to Dubois.

A whimper left Juliette's lips as the man shoved her against the ladder leading up to the quarterdeck. "You set fire to my ship," he growled all of a sudden, leaning into her face. "Be assured that I shall make you pay for that." Then he shifted on his feet and called down the hatch, "Is the fire out?"

Calls of affirmation echoed up to them, and Henri could all but picture Dubois grinning that evil grin of his. The man sickened him!

Nevertheless, time was running out.

Any moment now, the sailors below deck would return to report to their captain, and Henri did not like those odds. They needed to act fast!

Looking over his shoulder, he met Ian's steady gaze, then gestured at the young woman still lying unconscious upon deck. He did not know who she was, but they could not leave her behind.

Not with Dubois!

Ian gave a quick nod as he and the wolf moved silently toward her. She looked frail and thin, and the Scotsman would have no trouble carrying her down to the dinghy.

Henri could only hope his men would be here soon to pick them up.

Turning back to Dubois, Henri felt the desire to shoot the man here and now rush up and down his arm, and his hand tensed upon the pistol he held. Yet, it would be far from wise, and he could all but picture his uncle's stern look, urging him to think first.

Henri almost grinned at the thought. Yes, he was the impulsive sort, but he was no fool.

As Dubois once again turned his attention to Juliette, Henri rushed closer. The shadows hid his approach as he moved silently across the deck, eyes fixed upon the man he loathed like no other.

Especially now.

Especially after he had taken Juliette.

Henri could hear footsteps below as well as voices echoing upward through the open hatch. They were almost out of time!

It was now or never!

A few more steps separated Henri from Dubois, his eyes straining to see around the man, his heart longing to glimpse Juliette's face. Yet, he reined in that desire and focused.

Dubois chuckled darkly. "You're a little spitfire, *n'est-ce pas?* I know I shall greatly enjoy—"

Henri did not care to hear the rest of that sentence, and he brought down the butt of his pistol upon Dubois's head with a swift swing.

With a groan, the tall man went down and lay slumped upon the deck of his own ship a second later.

Then Henri turned to look upon Juliette for the first time in four years.

She looked as she always had, as he remembered her. Her auburn hair seemed almost black in the dim light of the night. Only now it was not styled elaborately but looked rather tousled, a simple braid lying draped over her shoulder. Her chest rose and fell with each rapid breath, and her eyes were wide as she stared up at him.

For a moment, she seemed to sway upon her feet before one hand reached back and grasped the ladder Dubois had pushed her against. Terror rested in her wide eyes, and yet, Henri thought to see a sense of disbelief as she continued to stare at him.

Knowing that time was of the essence, Henri held out his hand to her. "Come! We have to leave!"

Despair settled in Juliet's heart as Dubois shoved her against the ladder leading up to the quarterdeck. His hands gripped her upper arms tightly as he snarled into her face, the look in his eyes chilling her to her bones.

This was it, she thought. All was lost. There would be no escape.

And then, from one second to the next, everything changed. Captain Dubois's eyes suddenly rolled back, his hands upon her arms slackened and, in the next second, he dropped down to the deck, lying sprawled at her feet.

For a seemingly endless moment, Juliet felt thunderstruck, unable to cope with what had just happened. Indeed, what *had* just happened?

And then something moved at the edge of her vision, and she lifted her head.

Once again, Juliet felt shaken to her core because the man who suddenly stood in front of her was no other but Henri Duret.

Juliet felt her eyes widen as she stared at him, stared at his familiar face. For although four years had passed since they had last stood this close, she had seen his face in her dreams countless times. Those green eyes of his, always teasing, always challenging, pushing her to the edge, daring her to respond. Never had he acted like a gentleman, for he was anything but. Something dangerous constantly lurked in his eyes, a dark allure that had fascinated her from the first. Yet, gentleman or not, he had always been kind and respectful...

...and she had always trusted him.

Of course, her head would conjure him in such a moment when all hope was lost. She ought to have expected this. Still, blinking her eyes, Juliet could not help but gawk at him. She knew he was not truly here; he could not be.

And then he suddenly moved toward her, holding out his hand. "Come! We have to leave!"

Juliet flinched, fearing the moment he would disappear into thin air and she would be alone again.

Alone to face Captain Dubois.

"This cannot be," she whispered, still staring at him, terrified of what would happen if she did not. "You're not here. Not truly." Tears shot to her eyes for she had never thought she would ever see him again.

And he looked so real.

So very real.

A hint of urgency came to Henri's eyes before he glanced over his shoulder and down the hatch.

Juliet exhaled a shuddering breath, wishing that this could be true. That he was truly here! That—

In the next instant, Henri stood right in front of her. His hands reached out and grasped her, pulling her against him. "Are you all right?"

Juliet gasped at the feel of his hands, wondering how her mind managed to conjure such a lifelike hallucination. She felt like closing her eyes and leaning into him. If only he were made of more than thin air!

"Are you hurt?" Henri asked, the same urgency in his voice she had seen in his eyes. "Juliette!" He grasped her chin when she failed to answer, his eyes drilling down into hers. "Answer me! Are you hurt?"

Feeling his fingers upon her chin, Juliet shook her head as she continued to stare at him. "You're not here. You cannot—"

"We need to go!" He grasped her by the arm and pulled her along. "Now!" Again, he glanced over his shoulder.

Afraid to give in, Juliet dug in her heels. "No, I will not go with you." Who knew who this man was! Was she truly hallucinating? Was this Dubois who was leading her away to—? She did not even dare finish that thought.

Again, Henri—or whoever he was!—grasped her by the arms, pulling her closer. "Juliette, listen to me. We need to—"

"No!" Juliet tried to free herself from his embrace. "No, you can't be here. You're not!" She felt tears shoot to her eyes, his face blurring slightly as despair swept through her anew. "You're not here. You're not. You can't be. It's not you. You—"

Without warning, he yanked her closer and his mouth claimed hers in a frighteningly familiar kiss.

Juliet stilled instantly, shocked out of her wits as he held her crushed in his arms, his kiss urgent and echoing with the same desperate longing she felt pulsing in her own veins.

"It is me, *Cherie*," Henri whispered a bit breathlessly as he lifted his head. "You better believe it, or they'll catch us."

Juliet blinked and her teeth dug into her lower lip as happiness swept through her like a tidal wave. "Henri?"

He nodded. "*Oui.*" He stepped back, his gaze yet again drifting to the hatch. Voices were moving closer, and she could hear footsteps approaching. "We need to leave! Now!" He grasped her by the arm and pulled her along and toward the gangplank.

This time, Juliet followed, unable to look at anything but him. Was it truly him? It could not be, and yet, his kiss had... "How is this possible?" she stammered. "Why... Why are you here?"

With one foot on the gangplank, Henri stopped and looked at her.

"For you," he stated simply as though she truly ought to know. Then he pushed her ahead of him down toward the dock, his hands upon her shoulders, keeping her moving.

Juliet tried her best to keep her feet under her as the shock of Henri's presence continued to make her head spin. Her limbs felt heavy, and every once in a while, her eyelids closed and she found it an effort to open them once again.

"This way!" Down on the boards of the pier, Henri once again took her arm and pulled her along—not land inward but down toward the sea.

Behind them, Juliet could hear voices and footsteps, both growing louder, a note of alarm in them.

"They've found Dubois," Henri muttered beside her as they hurried along. "Faster!"

At the end of the pier, Juliet spotted a dinghy, gently bobbing upon the waters of the bay. She saw the shadowed outlines of four or five men seated inside. "Who—?"

The moment they reached the small boat, Henri picked her up and deposited her inside. Juliet felt roughened hands grasp her around the middle before she was seated on a wooden bench. Her eyes moved back to the tall-masted ship that had been her prison these past few weeks, and she saw men rushing across the deck and then down the gangplank, angry voices shouting words she could not make out.

Still, they sent a shiver down her back that had nothing to do with the chilling night air. If they were to catch up with them...

Juliet's eyes went wide. "Noële," she mumbled under her breath as Henri pushed the boat away from the pier and then jumped inside, making it sway dangerously.

As the men began to row, Juliet's hands clamped down on the side of the boat, afraid she might tumble into the black sea. "Henri," she exclaimed the moment he came to sit beside her and lowered another oar into the water. "There was another woman on board. I cannot leave without her. She—"

"She's safe," Henri told her with a look over his shoulder. "My first mate brought her down while I went after you."

Following his gaze, Juliet spotted a fair-haired man seated in the back of the dinghy, his hands wrapped tightly around another oar as he rowed in tandem with the others. In front of the bench beside him lay a dark figure. Juliet could not see her face, and so she reached out a hand to place upon her head, relieved to find her warm and breathing.

In the next moment, a deafening sound echoed to her ears, and Juliet jerked back around. "What was that?"

The men seemed to be rowing with more determination, their faces concentrated, their jaws tight as they strained to move the dinghy through the water, away from the coast and out to sea. "Someone took a shot at us," Henri gritted out beside her, his dark eyes fixed upon the moored ship in the harbor.

Juliet followed his gaze and saw men standing at the pier's end. She assumed they were Captain Dubois's men, furious to have found their captain unconscious and their captives stolen. A shudder went down her back at the thought of what else might have happened to her aboard that ship...

...had Henri not come...

...for her.

A part of Juliet still could not believe that he was truly here. That he was sitting right beside her. That she could simply reach out a hand and touch him.

For so long he had been nothing more than a thought and a memory, and now, he was here. Flesh and blood. Warm and alive, instead of the hollow dream she had clung to.

Another shot rang out, and Juliet flinched yet again.

"Do not worry, *Cherie*," Henri said with a sideways look at her. "We're far out of reach."

Juliet nodded, surprised to feel herself relax. Although they had not seen each other in years, although she knew nothing about his capabilities as a privateer, it seemed that she truly did trust him. Trusted him without hesitation or doubt, and it felt good.

Before long, a large, dark shadow loomed in front of them, and Juliet felt a sense of awe wash over her at the sight of the enormous ship sitting upon the black waters. Ropes were lowered and attached to the front and back of the small dinghy. Then she could hear the soft creaking of metal before they were silently lifted out of the water.

Up and up, the dinghy went as Juliet craned her neck to see.

A part of her wanted nothing more but to feel land under her feet. She had had enough of ships for a lifetime and could not help but feel reluctant to board another one. Yet, this, here, now was different, was it not?

The moment the dinghy was secured on deck, Henri rose to his feet and jumped out. Then he held out his hands to her, his green eyes holding hers. "Come."

Still a bit unsteady upon her feet, Juliet complied, allowing him to grasp her by the waist and lift her out as though she weighed nothing. Her eyes were still wide as she looked up into his, and she felt her insides flutter in a way they had only once before.

Four years ago, in London.

Henri kept an arm wrapped around her as he turned to face his crew. "I want four men up on deck at all times," he instructed, then turned to look at the tall, fair-haired man, who was lifting Noële out of the dinghy. "Take the girl to François."

The fair-haired man nodded. "Aye, Capt'n." Juliet frowned for she thought to hear the hint of a Scottish accent.

"François?" she asked, looking at Henri.

"The ship's surgeon," he told her before redirecting his gaze to the tall, fair-haired man. "Ian, then I want you at the helm. You know what to do." He turned to look at his crew. "Everyone to their stations. Remain alert."

Juliet could not help but notice the way Henri's crew was eyeing her. It was a far cry from the way Captain Dubois's men had looked at her upon occasion. While their gazes had been either hostile or filled with lust, Henri's crew was looking at her with almost glowing eyes, smiles upon their faces. Juliet had never seen these men in her life, and yet, they seemed overjoyed to have her with them. Why? It made no sense.

Henri's hand grasped her by the arm and pulled her closer, his gaze lowering to fall upon hers. "*You*," he whispered in a low voice that sent a shiver down Juliet's back, "are coming with me."

A moment later, he propelled her across the deck and then down the hatch. She heard footsteps moving up on deck and voices as men called to one another, readying the ship to get it underway. All the while, Henri said not a single word, his hand still upon her arm, guiding her along the companionway and to the captain's quarters.

An eerie sense of familiarity fell over Juliet; yet one look at the dark-haired man by her side was enough to chase it away.

"In here." Pushing open the door, Henri led her through.

Juliet's eyes fell upon a cabin that looked not unlike the one that had been her prison cell these past few weeks. Still, it *felt* different, and she turned to look at a man who was nothing like Captain Dubois.

Holding her gaze, Henri stepped inside, then closed the door with a kick of his boot, his eyes never leaving hers. His breath came fast as did her own, and she could not help but think that their reunion had shaken him as much as it had shaken her.

"Why are you here?" Juliet whispered as bright spots began to dance in front of her eyes. She could not help that feeling of lightheadedness that fell over her as those daring, green eyes looked into hers. "Why?"

Certain she would pass out at any moment, Juliet dug her nails into her palms, willing herself to stay awake. She needed an answer.

Now.

Chapter Eleven

AN UNEXPECTED ENCOUNTER

Henri knew that he was staring at her like a foolish youth;
yet, it had been four years since he had last laid eyes upon
her, and...

He gritted his teeth. *Merde*, but he had missed her!

He barely knew her. They had spent no more than a handful of
days in each other's company, and yet, something about her had always
thrown him off balance. What was it about her?

Was it those wide, innocent eyes that looked at him as though he
held a place in her heart? Was it that slight tremor that seized her
every time he stepped close? Was it the way she fought to hold her
head high despite the alarm he often thought to see in her eyes?

With his gaze fixed upon her, Henri kicked the door closed. He
knew he ought to head on deck; yet, Ian would alert him if something
was amiss. The silent Scot was more than capable, and right here, right
now, Henri had other matters on his mind.

"Why are you here?" Juliette asked in a feeble voice. She seemed
close to fainting, her eyelids drooping every so often. Yet, determination sparked in her eyes as she faced him. "Why?"

Henri swallowed as he moved closer as though drawn to her by an invisible force. For so long, they had been miles apart, separated by enemy lines, and now?

Now, Juliette was right here in front of him. He could simply reach out and kiss her if he wanted to, and...

...*merde*, but he wanted to!

The feel of her had seared itself into his being, and yet, it was not enough. It had never been enough.

When she had looked at him with utter disbelief earlier this night on Dubois's ship, Henri had welcomed the excuse to snatch her close and claim a kiss. He could still feel her lips beneath his and wondered how soon he would lose this battle with himself and reach for her once more.

"Why are you here?" Juliette demanded yet again, her voice a bit more forceful as she stared at him, her head shaking from side to side as though a part of her still doubted him. Still, she looked exhausted, all but swaying on her feet.

"You need rest," Henri growled, his hands balling into fists as he resisted the urge to pull her close. "We can talk tomorrow." He walked past her to the bed in the corner, trying his best to keep his distance. "You can sleep—"

"No!" Juliette snapped as she whipped around. "We will—" Her words broke off as she began to sway, her eyes all but rolling backward.

On instinct, Henri seized her, his hands grasping her arms before she could slump to the floor. "You need sleep," he insisted as he gathered her in his arms.

Her wide, green eyes looked up at him as her fingers curled into his shirt, holding on tightly. "You kissed me," she whispered then her teeth dug into her lower lip, her eyes closing and opening.

Henri chuckled, finding himself mesmerized by her. "*Oui*," he whispered, gently lifting her into his arms. "You needed it."

Her head came to rest against his shoulder, and she closed her eyes, a deep sigh leaving her lips. "I suppose I did."

Carefully, Henri laid her down upon the bed then began unlacing her boots. "You were looking at me as though you thought me a ghost," he remarked, tossing her boots aside before pulling the blanket up and over her. "Or a hallucination perhaps."

Curled on her side, Juliette snuggled deeper into the pillow, a contented sigh leaving her lips. "A dream," she whispered, before her breathing evened and slumber claimed her.

Henri swallowed as he stared down at her. *A dream?* He could not deny that her words affected him, and although he knew he ought to see to things up on deck, Henri found himself sinking down on the bed beside her.

For a long moment, he simply watched her sleep, his gaze tracing the curved line of her closed eyes. Her skin was pale, and she looked utterly exhausted; yet the rhythm of her breathing spoke of deep, contented slumber.

Unable not to, Henri reached out a hand and tugged a loose curl back behind her ear. The tips of his fingers grazed her soft skin, and he felt a jolt shoot up his arm as though lightning had struck him in that moment.

Oddly enough, it was in this rather innocent moment that Henri Duret finally realized that somehow this timid yet bewitching English lady had come to mean more to him than he would ever have thought possible. He had done all he could to keep her at arm's length, to banish her from his mind and heart, and yet, here he was, still drawn to her like a moth to the flame.

In truth, he all but craved her, and had all this time without realizing it. It had been the very reason he had never allowed himself to think of her, knowing that once he gave in, he would be lost.

And now, she was here.

On his ship.

In his cabin.

In his bed.

Finally.

After all this time.

Henri swallowed and quickly pushed to his feet, aware of the weakened state of his resolve to stay away. He had promised himself that there was no other reason for why he had gone after her but to see her safely returned home.

Yet, deep inside, a most insistent voice was calling him a liar.

A fool, even.

84

Gritting his teeth, Henri spun around and strode from the cabin. He needed to clear his head, and so, he marched up on deck. The sea air welcomed him, and he breathed in deeply, his hands wrapping tightly around the railing as he looked down into the black waters.

He had been a fool to go after her, thinking he would be able to maintain his distance once she was within arm's length. He had never been able to, not even when he had first laid eyes upon her that day long ago in London.

Oui, Violette had asked him to give her sister a reason to choose differently. She had asked him to make Juliette realize what she would be missing out on if she refused to break her betrothal to old Lord Dowling.

Yet, it had been Henri's choice to kiss her the way he had. And he had, simply because he had wanted to. Because he had needed to. Because he had not been able to help himself.

Even then.

What was he to do now?

Lifting his head, Henri strode across the deck and then climbed up to the quarterdeck, relieved to see Ian at the helm. "Anything to report?" he asked the Scotsman as he came to stand beside him, his gaze moving to the horizon.

Night had long since fallen, and the world was dark. The moon hung as a slim sliver in the sky, twinkling stars surrounding it, casting a faint light across the world. Out here at sea, especially at night, every-thing seemed utterly peaceful; yet, the winds blew strong, pushing them onward.

Toward home.

Toward *La Roche-sur-Mer*.

"All is well, Capt'n," Ian replied, his hand steady and his gaze watchful. "So far, no ship appears to be in pursuit." He glanced up to the crow's nest and then across the deck to the men keeping a watchful eye upon the horizon.

"The woman?" Henri asked, remembering the other captive they had snatched from Dubois.

Ian's jaw tightened, and Henri was surprised to see an emotional reaction from the silent Scotsman. "She's been burnt," he gritted out, his gaze never veering from the horizon. "She's weak. Ye better go speak to François."

Henri nodded, then turned to go, but he paused when he reached the ladder. "Thank you for your help today," he said, then looked back over his shoulder at Ian.

The Scotsman met his eyes and gave a quick nod before his gaze resettled on something in the distance.

Inhaling a deep breath, Henri made his way below deck. While a few men kept watch, the rest of his crew was asleep. They could not know what lay ahead, and so they needed to be alert and ready to fight at any moment. While Henri doubted that Dubois would openly attack him, he was certain that the man would not simply let such an affront go. After all, one privateer could not simply take the bounty of another.

Walking along the companionway, Henri gritted his teeth at the thought of Juliette as bounty. Still, it was common practice during times of war. Why then had Dubois not ransomed Juliette back to England? Why had he held onto her? It was a question that still haunted him, one that he would have to address at some point. He needed to know what had happened to her on Dubois's ship.

Or he would go mad.

"François," Henri addressed the short, bearded man as he stepped into the small sick bay. "How is she?" His gaze moved to the small cot in the corner, next to which François stood, a deep frown line upon his face.

The ship's surgeon turned to Henri and then stepped toward him, an odd look in his eyes. It made the hairs on the back of Henri's neck stand on end as though the words François was about to speak held some deeper meaning for him. "Have you looked at her yet?" François asked, his chin slightly lifted to be able to meet Henri's eyes. "Have you seen her face?"

Henri frowned. "*Non*," he replied with a slight shake of his head. "Why? How bad is it?"

François inhaled a deep breath, something hesitant in the way he paused before speaking. "It looks as though she suffered severe burns quite recently. They've begun to heal, but she still has a long way to go until recovery." His chest rose and fell with a deep breath, and once again reluctance stood in his eyes.

"What is it?" Henri pressed, hating the feeling that there was something he did not know but ought to. "There is clearly something on your mind, so say it!"

François reached out a hand and placed it upon Henri's shoulder. "It's Noèle."

For a brief moment, Henri felt confused. However, it only lasted for a second before shock slammed into him. "Noèle? But..." He shook his head as though it might help clear his thoughts. "It cannot be her! She is..." He broke off, then swallowed. "She died in a fire. My father told me so upon our return to *La Roche-sur-Mer*."

François shrugged. "I do not know what to tell you," he replied, then he stepped aside, his right hand gesturing toward the cot. "Have a look for yourself if you do not believe me. I, too, felt stunned when I saw her face. She has some burns, but...it is her."

Carefully, slowly, somewhat apprehensively, Henri put one foot in front of the other, his gaze fixed upon the cot and the woman lying upon it. The blanket was pulled up to her shoulders, her arms resting upon it, both of them bandaged. Patches of red, almost raw skin were visible upon her face and neck. Her black hair was tousled, and looked uneven, as well as singed here and there.

Henri cringed at the thought of what had happened to her, but it was her! It was Noèle. Noèle Clément, his late friend's widow.

Étienne.

A deep breath rushed from Henri's lungs, and he sank down to sit beside her. He almost reached out to grasp her hand, but then he stopped, remembering her injuries. "How did she end up on Dubois' ship?" he mumbled more to himself than to anyone else. "Her house burned down, and yet..." He shook his head, unable to make sense of all this. "She clearly was inside when it burned." He looked over his shoulder at François. "What happened to her?"

The ship's surgeon shrugged. "That I cannot say. She regained consciousness briefly but not for long enough to say anything. She was in great pain, and I was relieved when her eyes closed again soon after. She needs rest and nourishment." He placed a hand upon Henri's shoulder. "I know what she means to you, but I'm afraid it will take some time before you will get answers from her."

Henri nodded, knowing that François was right. Still, it was torture not knowing, sitting here and looking down at her, seeing her misery and her pain, and not being able to do anything about it.

Yet, she was alive, and Henri promised her silently that he would do all in his power to ensure that one day she would be well again.

And happy.

Even without Étienne.

His friend would have wanted that.

Chapter Twelve

SWEPT AWAY INTO A DREAM

The scent of smoke still lingered, and Juliet pinched her eyes shut when her mind involuntarily filled with images of a burning cabin. Deep-seated panic stood on Noèle's face, and Juliet felt her skin almost scraped raw as her hands continued to pound against the locked door.

"Help! Please!" Her body moved as she tried to get away from the heat and the smoke...

...until warm hands settled upon her shoulders.

Juliet stilled instantly, her thoughts drifting to a man with cold, merciless eyes.

Dubois.

"Juliette," a voice called, its tone urgent, yet warm and reassuring. "Juliette, wake up."

Was she dreaming? Juliet wondered as her mind tried to place everything that had happened. *Where was she?*

Blinking, her eyes opened slowly and her body tensed, for she expected to see what she had seen for the past few weeks whenever she had woken from slumber. She expected to see the captain's quarters upon Dubois's ship, Noèle lying on the cot, the sea outside the tall windows.

Her prison cell.

A part of Juliet did not want to open her eyes. Yet, it seemed her dreams were even less appealing than reality.

"Juliette," that familiar voice said again, and Juliet found herself once again wondering if she was dreaming. Was it possible to dream of two things at once? To travel back and forth between two different dreams? One horrific and the other...?

A soft smile came to her face. She could feel it tug upon her lips, and without thought, her eyes fluttered open...

...and she found herself looking at Henri Duret!

Instantly, Juliet's heart slammed to a halt and her breath lodged in her throat. "Am I still dreaming?" she gasped as the feel of his hands upon her shoulders made her head spin. Bright spots once more danced in front of her eyes as her breathing quickened and a deep desire to remain in this wonderful dream spread through her.

Henri grinned down at her in the way he often did in her memories. "Do you often dream of me, *Cherie?*" he asked teasingly, his hands still upon her shoulders, a soft pressure, but insistent, nonetheless.

Juliet blinked, trying to rid herself of these bright spots that kept blurring her vision; yet, her head still seemed to be spinning, for she could not make sense of anything. "What happened?"

"Do you not remember?" Henri asked as his right hand moved from her shoulder to touch her cheek, his fingers trailing along the line of her jaw. Concern rested in his eyes in a way she had never seen before, and it touched her deeply.

Tears came to Juliet's eyes. "You are truly here?" she whispered, afraid to give into that feeling of joy and relief lest it be snatched away again. "Did you truly come for me? Was it not just a dream?"

His fingers tensed upon her chin, the expression on his face hard and unyielding. "*Non, Cherie,* it was not a dream. You're safe. I promise."

In that moment, something snapped inside of her. Without thought, Juliet surged upward, her hands reaching for him as she flung herself into his arms. She buried her face in his shoulder and wept.

Juliet did not know at what point his arms moved to enfold her in his embrace, but they did. He held her as she cried, his hands running over her back as well as her arms before they slipped into her hair. She could feel the pads of his fingers tracing the hard contours of her skull, and then down her neck. The soft pressure felt reassuring. It grounded her to the here and now, kept her from slipping away, and slowly her sobs quietened.

Still, she kept holding on to him, unable to let go, to be alone and apart from him. He had come for her! Juliet kept repeating those words in her head, and yet, part of her still did not believe them. Never would she have thought he would. Never would she have thought to see him again.

Yet, he was here, and so was she.

In each other's arms.

"I missed you," she whispered into the folds of his shirt. She knew she ought not to, but she could not help herself. This was a dream come true, and her heart would not be silenced, foolishly daring to express what it wanted.

What it had been wanting for a long time.

No matter the consequences.

Even if Henri were to turn away from her now, she would cherish this moment until her last breath.

A low growl rumbled in his throat, and she felt his right hand reach up once more and grasp a fistful of her hair. A swift tug urged her head back until her eyes were looking up into his.

The expression upon his face was tense, almost thunderous, as though he, too, felt more than he had expected. As though his world, too, had been turned upside down. As though he, too, felt as though he were drowning and she the only one who could hold him above the churning waters.

Juliet's breath quickened as he stared down into her eyes, a muscle in his jaw pulsing with some deep emotion. His green eyes were dark, wild and untamed as they had always been. Juliet remembered them. She remembered that he had looked at her like this before. It had spoken to something deep inside her, and barely a second had passed before he had—

His lips claimed hers in an overpowering kiss that would have knocked her legs out from under her if she had been standing.

Indeed, there was nothing gentle or sweet about Henri Duret. There never had been. He held nothing back but gave as much as he took.

His hand was still curled into her hair, holding her close, urging her closer. She could feel his heart beat as fast as her own, the pulse in his neck hammering against the tips of her fingers. It terrified her, and yet, it did not.

Her need for him made no sense. She ought to be frightened by the way he seemed to crave her, his mouth on hers demanding and force-ful, urging her lips apart.

But she was not.

The moment she complied, he deepened the kiss, his tongue meeting hers as he pushed her back down onto the bed.

A sharp knock on the door shocked them both.

Henri stilled as though someone had dumped a bucket of cold water on him. Yet, his mouth remained on hers, a sound of deepest displeasure rumbling deep in his throat.

The knock came again. "Capt'n?"

Henri's hand in her hair tensed before he slowly loosened his hold, and she felt his fingers trail down along the column of her neck.

Juliet was reluctant to let him go, and her fingers curled into the front of his shirt, holding on.

Henri smiled against her lips, then he stole another kiss before finally pulling away. His green eyes were dark and almost feverish as he stared down at her for a moment longer. Then his throat worked and he swallowed before he tore himself away and rose from the bed.

For one last moment, his gaze swept over her before he turned toward the door. "Enter."

Juliet pushed herself upright as she moved to smooth her tangled curls. Her face felt flushed, and she could hardly bring herself to look upon Henri. Had this truly just happened? Had she—? Had they—?

"*Bonjour, Captaine*," a tall, rather lanky young man greeted as he strode into the cabin, a tray with food upon it in his hands. "*Mademoi-selle*," he added with a wide smile as his gaze strayed to her. "I hope you slept well." His grin widened even more before his eyes moved back to Henri.

Henri tensed at the young man's words; still, a good-natured smile played over his lips. "*Merci*, Pierre." He shook his head, chuckling.

Pierre set down the tray upon the small table in the center of the cabin, stealing curious glances at her. "If there is anything else you requi—"

"*Merci*, Pierre," Henri repeated, something insistent, but still humorous in his voice. He moved to open the door, the look in his eyes clearly *inviting* Pierre to take his leave.

All but walking backward, Pierre retrieved his steps until he bumped into the doorframe. A chuckle left his lips, and Juliet saw a hint of red come to his cheeks before Henri shut the door in his face.

Then they were alone again.

Inhaling a deep breath, Juliet lifted her gaze, her heart beating frantically against her ribcage. The moment their eyes met, she could have sworn her heart was about to jump from her chest. It felt like a shock wave of awareness that rocked against her, bringing with it those blasted bright spots that swirled in her head and made her feel unsteady and lightheaded.

"Are you all right?" Henri asked, his voice rough and tense as though he too was battling emotions he had not seen coming. The look in his dark eyes was intense, and for a moment, Juliet thought that at any moment now he would return to the bed and—

Her stomach rumbled loudly as the aroma of warm food drifted to her nostrils.

Instantly, a deep flush shot into her cheeks, and Juliet dropped her gaze. She pulled up her knees and hugged them to her chest, unable to look at him.

An amused chuckle drifted to her ears before she heard footsteps moving over to the table. "I suppose you should eat, *Cherie*."

Juliet chanced a look at him and watched as he set the table for the two of them, his green eyes every so often straying to her, that wicked gleam in them she had come to love all those years ago.

Wishing she could do something about her flushed cheeks, Juliet inhaled a deep breath, then pushed away the blanket and slowly rose to her feet. She felt a bit unsteady but kept her balance as the floorboards swayed beneath her feet. Again, her stomach protested against the lack of food and she bit her lower lip, embarrassed.

Henri moved to stand in front of her, and his right hand once more settled on her chin, urging her to look up at him. "Do not apologize for being hungry," he whispered, that amused chuckle still rumbling in his throat. "Only a fool would." His gaze swept over her face, something deeply sincere in his green eyes. "And you are anything but."

Again, Juliet felt her breath catch in her throat as he looked at her in the way he did. Temptation once again swept over her, and she felt herself leaning closer.

Instantly, his gaze started to drift lower, and she could see his jaw tightening as his heart and mind warred with what to do. Then he suddenly straightened, and his gaze returned to hers. "Sit," he instructed, taking a few steps backward and gesturing toward one of the two chairs, "and eat."

Smiling at him, Juliet complied, and the moment she began to eat, she finally realized how famished she was. She barely noticed what she put in her mouth but chewed quickly and swallowed, eager for more.

All the while, Henri sat across from her, eating from his own plate. His gaze, however, seemed distracted, straying to her time and time again. "You should change," he suddenly said, his nose crinkling slightly. "Or those nightmares will return, for the smell of smoke still lingers upon your dress."

Juliet paused and looked down at her wrinkled and stained dress. She had done her best to keep it clean and tried to wash herself daily at least a little with what Captain Dubois had provided; still, it was true, she was in desperate need of a bath.

Especially after the fire. Indeed, even now, she could smell the soft aroma of burnt wood, and it sent a shudder down her skin.

Yet...

Her gaze flitted to his. "I cannot," she whispered, feeling that flush return with full force. "These are all the clothes I have." Inhaling a deep breath, Juliet slowly lifted her gaze.

The look in Henri's eyes told her that he was thinking along the same lines as she was, recalling the intimate moment they had shared earlier. He cleared his throat then sat back in his chair. "I can give you a shirt and some breeches." He swallowed, and she could feel his gaze sweep over her slowly, lingering every now and then.

Juliet bit her lower lip, willing her mind to remain focused and not be led astray. "I cannot," she replied, softly shaking her head. "A lady is not supposed to w—"

A wide grin stretched across Henri's face.

Juliet frowned. "What?"

He shook his head, still grinning. "Even out here, you insist on etiquette?" His brows rose challengingly. "Are there other rules I should be aware of?" A wicked gleam came to his eyes as his gaze strayed from hers to linger upon the bed behind her.

Juliet closed her eyes, wanting to sink into a hole in the ground.

"Would it make you feel better," Henri asked teasingly, "if I reminded you that your own sister stands at the bow of her ship not in a fancy gown but instead in a shirt and a pair of breeches?" His brows rose in question.

Juliet sighed. "I am not Violet, and I never shall be." She could not help but wonder if perhaps Henri disliked her ladylike sensibilities; yet, what was she to do about them. It was the way she had been raised, and it was not an easy thing to have one's life turned upside down.

A slow smile spread over Henri's face. "I'm aware of that," he whispered in a husky voice that did not speak of disappointment or displeasure at all. "Believe me." Then he rose to his feet and walked over to a small trunk in the corner. Opening it, he retrieved what looked like a shirt and a pair of breeches before he turned back to look at her. "Finish your food," he instructed, tossing the clothes onto the bed behind her. "I shall have a bath drawn for you." He grinned. "It is a luxury few are afforded out at sea."

His gaze continued to hold hers for another long, seemingly endless moment before he finally stepped back and then walked out the door, gently closing it behind him.

Juliet exhaled a deep breath as she did not hear a key turn in the lock. Of course, he would not lock her in. Yet, it had been a sound she had come to expect over the past few weeks.

A shiver went through her as the memories resurfaced, and yet, she felt a smile tug upon the corners of her mouth as a deep sense of safety welled up in her chest. She was safe!

Finally!

With him!

Truly, this was a dream come true in more ways than one, and deep down, Juliet wished it did not have to end.

Chapter Thirteen

MA PETITE LIONNE

"Inform me the moment you spot anyone's approach," Henri instructed, his gaze fixed upon the distant horizon. "No matter who it is, understood?"

Ian gave a quick nod, and Henri stepped away, making his way down the ladder to the hatch.

Roughly an hour ago, he had left Juliette to her bath, stepping up on deck to see to everything. Fortunately, nothing unexpected had occurred during the night, and even this morning, no sails could be spotted upon the horizon. Perhaps Dubois would not pursue them. Perhaps the man had not yet recovered consciousness. Henri supposed his crew would not act without command, unaware of what precisely had happened that night. All they could be certain of was that their prisoners had been stolen from them. Apart from that, they could not know who was responsible, could they? Or was it possible that one of them had spotted the *Voile Noire?*

As Henri stepped toward the hatch, Pierre looked up from where he sat, tending to a rip in a sail. "You look happy, *Capitaine*," the youth grinned, "if I might say so."

Henri paused and then turned to look at him. "You may not," he told Pierre with feigned sternness in his voice. "I suggest you keep your mind on your task." He fixed the young man with a pointed look.

Pierre nodded, the smile upon his face lessening. Still, Henri could all but see the young man's thoughts continue to linger upon Juliette. "Congratulations, *Capitaine*. She's something, *n'est-ce pas?*"

Henri swallowed hard, remembering what he had told his crew about Juliette, about who she was, about who she was *to him*. Indeed, now, they all believed that she was his bride and would soon be his wife. No wonder the smiles that kept following him, the smiles that he had seen upon his men's faces all morning. "That she is, Pierre." Unable to hide a grin, Henri then finally turned toward the hatch and went below.

Outside the door to his cabin, he stopped and then knocked. Only when her voice bade him to enter, did he open the door and step inside.

A small tub stood on one side of the room, filled halfway with water his men had heated in the galley and brought up. Unfortunately, it was empty—of course, Henri had not expected it to be any different.

Juliette stood in the back by the windows, her auburn hair gleaming in the soft sunlight. She had braided it down her back, and only a few damp tendrils had escaped near her temples. Her skin glowed in a rosy red as though she had scrubbed it most thoroughly in order to rid herself of the lingering scent of smoke. She had donned his breeches and shirt, both items far too big on her.

As she met his gaze, she shifted uncomfortably, tugging upon the shirt here and there as though trying to make it fit right. "This must look awful," she muttered, looking down at herself, then bit her lower lip as her gaze fell upon her bare feet.

"Awful is not the word I'd use," Henri mumbled, transfixed by the sight of her. Indeed, his shirt was too wide, and yet, the way she had used a ribbon to fit it in place just below her breast gave it the impression of a dress.

A very short dress!

Of course, her legs peeked out, wrapped in his breeches that hung all the way down to her feet. Truthfully, Henri would have preferred her without breeches!

The red lingering upon her cheeks darkened when she realized the direction of his thoughts. Again, her gaze fell from his, only to return a moment later, curiously peeking up at him.

Henri chuckled. "Did you wash your clothes? Your dress and..." He trailed off, lifting his brows meaningfully.

Another flush shot to her cheeks, and he laughed, enjoying her bashful ways. She was utterly endearing, and he could see himself spending all day teasing her in this manner. She was truly innocent, and yet, somehow, she had survived upon Dubois's ship.

The thought still turned his stomach, and he gritted his teeth against the images that his mind conjured. He still did not know what had happened to her.

Juliette nodded, pointing toward a small stack of wet clothing. "But I don't know how to dry them. I wrung them out as best as I could, but..." She looked around the cabin. "Do you suppose we could hang them up?"

"It might make more sense to hang them up on deck," Henri replied with a wide grin.

As expected, another flush crept up her cheeks as she stared at him in shock, clearly scandalized.

Henri held up his hands and laughed. "I was merely jesting, *Cherie*." Rummaging through another chest, Henri procured a bit of string, which he hung up on one side of the cabin. "Would you like me to help you or...?" His gaze drifted to her wet clothes before returning to her, his brows raised.

Indeed, he could do this all day!

Juliette jumped forward, shaking her head. "No, that will not be necessary. I can do it." Careful to keep her gaze away from him, she proceeded to hang up her dress and shift and stays, her cheeks darkening with each item that went up on the line.

When she was finished, she glanced up at him and then turned away, a few quick steps carrying her over to the windows, her gaze directed outside at the sea. There she stood for a long moment without saying a word, and Henri watched as her shoulders rose and fell with each deep breath.

This was it, he thought. The moment he had dreaded. Thus far, they had lived in a somewhat suspended world outside of reality where neither past nor future existed. However, now it was time to let them back in and discuss all that had happened and would happen in the days to come.

"What do you know about the other woman who was with you upon Dubois's ship?" Henri asked, deciding against a direct approach. Perhaps it would be better to start with something less emotional between them.

Turning around, Juliette looked up at him. "Not much," she replied, and he could see her thoughts traveling backward to the moments that had changed her life. "She was already on board when," she heaved a shuddering breath, "Captain Dubois brought me there."

Henri felt his teeth grit together. He wanted to ask for further details but held himself back.

"She had these burns," Juliette continued, frown lines creasing her forehead. "At first, she only slept. She barely even woke, and...he instructed me to see to her." She shrugged, a helpless look in her eyes as she looked at him. "I've never taken care of anyone. I didn't know what to do. I tried to make her drink whenever she woke and put salve on her burns that seemed to ease the pain. Apart from that, there was nothing I *could* do."

Stepping closer, Henri reached out to take her hands. Her skin was cool to the touch, and he felt a slight tremble as her hands held his tighter. "Did you ever speak to her?"

Juliette nodded. "After a while, she came to. At first, she didn't say much. She was not strong enough." She looked up at him. "Her name is Noèle, but that is all I know about her." The moment the last word left her lips, her gaze dropped from his, and Henri could see that there was more.

"Juliette," Henri pressed, his hand tensing upon hers. "Tell me."

Her gaze did not rise to meet his; instead, she kept her head bowed. "She feared Dubois, feared him in a way that..." Her jaw gritted together, and Henri felt every muscle in his own body tense. "She told me that his brother asked her to marry him, but that she refused him. Although disappointed, he accepted her refusal. Dubois, however, he..." Her eyes rose and finally met his, tears brimming in them. "Oh, Henri, he did something awful to her."

Releasing her hands, Henri took a step back, afraid he would crush her delicate bones as red-hot fury chased itself through his veins. "The burns?" he gritted out, running a hand through his hair.

Biting her lower lip, she nodded. "Yes, she told me so," she whispered, something thoughtful and contemplative lingering in her gaze. "Of course, the burns happened perhaps only days before she was brought onto the ship, before I met her." Her teeth sank into her lower lip as thoughts continued to swirl in her head. "But there was more, long before that." Blinking, she looked up at him. "She did not tell me everything. I could see her pain and fear, and I didn't push her. But I'm sure that there's something she's holding back." Abruptly, she stepped forward and placed a hand upon his arm. "Perhaps now that she is safe from Dubois, she will talk to me. How is she?"

Henri swallowed, trying not to remember the burns upon Noële's face. "François said that she will live," he finally said, uncertain if Noële would consider that good news considering what she had undoubtedly been through. "But she needs time to heal. Your escape weakened her, and she has barely regained consciousness since."

Tears spilled over and ran down Juliette's cheek. "I'm so sorry for what happened. I knew she wasn't strong enough, but..."

Henri stepped forward and placed his hands upon her shoulders. "You did nothing wrong. You could not leave her behind." He smiled at her. "You're a brave little lioness."

Juliette scoffed, and her eyes closed. "I'm anything but brave. I've been a fool to do what I did. I should've known..." She shook her head. "I should never have left."

Henri tensed at the thought that if she had never left England, she would not be here with him right now. Yet, it would also mean that she would never have had to suffer what she had. *Oui*, perhaps she ought never have left. Perhaps she was right.

"Then why did you?" Henri growled, surprised at the anger he heard in his voice.

Anger at her for endangering herself.

Anger at himself for succumbing to the temptation she presented.

If she had never come, he would not be forced to bid her farewell again. Now, it was inevitable.

And would be harder than before.

Juliette's eyes flew open at the harsh tone in his voice, and she stared up at him.

For a long moment, they simply looked at one another, each entertaining thoughts of their own before Juliette took a step back, thus removing his hands from her shoulders. "That is none of your concern," she finally said, her voice feeble, but the look in her eyes was hard and unyielding.

Henri frowned. Never had he seen her like this before. "It *is* my concern," he insisted, his gaze as hard as her own as he took a step toward her. "You became my concern the moment your mother's letter arrived."

Her eyes widened. "My mother? She...She sent a letter?" A hint of understanding came to her eyes.

"She did," Henri confirmed, remembering the day he had returned to *La Roche-sur-Mer* and learned of Juliette's disappearance. "She tried to reach Violette, but, of course, did not know where she would be. So, she sent a letter to France as well."

Her mouth opened and closed as she stared at him. "And then you came after me?"

Henri nodded. "I found out what happened with the merchant vessel you boarded and then went in pursuit of Dubois."

A shuddering breath left her lips. "Thank you," she whispered breathlessly. "Thank you, Henri." Her whole body began to tremble, and she clamped her lips together, her jaw tensing as though she bit down hard, willing away memories that refused to leave her.

Henri swallowed as he saw deep fear linger in her eyes. "What happened...to you...aboard his ship?" He hated asking that question as well as the thought of learning its answer; yet, he needed to know.

He needed to know how badly she had been hurt.

At his question, her gaze immediately dropped from his and she stepped away.

Henri felt his insides twist and turn painfully as he forced himself to remain where he was. Patience had never been his strong suit!

"He yelled at me," Juliette whispered as she stepped up to the windows, the calm sea stretching out in front of her. "He didn't like it when I spoke. A few times, he grabbed me and all but snarled into my face." She inhaled a fortifying breath. "Once he tried to kiss me."

Henri stepped up behind her, his hands balled into fists at his sides. "He tried?" he asked through clenched teeth.

Juliette turned to look at him, her green eyes wide. "I...I thought I could simply pretend that..." Her lips clamped shut. "But then I couldn't, and so I turned my head away before he could..."

Henri exhaled the breath he had been holding before a frown came to his face. "And he did not...?" His brows rose meaningfully.

Juliette swallowed. "He said he would keep me around, and once we had his cabin to ourselves, he would..."

All but surging away from her, Henri swung his fist, desperate to sink it into something.

Anything.

Preferably Dubois' face.

With his current lack of options, however, he made do with the cabin wall. The moment his fist connected with the sturdy wood, pain shot up his arm and he groaned.

Still, it served as a momentary distraction from the anger that tore at his insides. Indeed, he hardly felt it, and within moments, the pain went away as though it had never been. Outrage still pulsed in his veins, and yet he could not deny that measure of relief he felt that Juliette had not suffered worse, that she had not been raped. Fear and pain stood in her eyes as she spoke of her ordeal, *oui*, but he could tell from the tilt of her head that Dubois had not broken her spirit.

"Are you mad?" came Juliette's aghast voice before her hands grasped his arm and pulled him around to face her. "Why did you do that?" Her eyes were wide as she looked up at him. Then her gaze moved to his hand, his knuckles slightly bloodied from the blow.

"It is nothing," Henri shot back, flexing his fingers to shake off the lingering tension. Still, he could not deny that her soft touch, her hands upon his, felt...good.

Soothing.

Yet, also stirring.

Reaching for a small cloth, Juliette swiftly cleaned and then bandaged his hand, her face in a slight frown as she concentrated on the task.

Henri watched her carefully, surprised to see her so self-assured, so competent. *Oui*, most of the time she appeared like an innocent, young miss; yet, there was a depth in her eyes that whispered of a strong heart and an unyielding will.

"Why did you board that ship?" Henri demanded, waiting until her gaze rose to meet his. "Back in London, why did you board the merchant vessel?"

A deep sigh left her lips, and he could see that she was torn about whether or not to speak to him about her motivation. "I simply wanted to get away," she finally said before tying a small knot with the ends of the cloth and then stepping away.

"Why?" Henri pressed, his eyes fixed upon her as she tried to evade him, her back once more turned as she gazed out at the open sea.

Juliette shrugged. "You wouldn't understand." She glanced at him over her shoulder. "I had my reasons. Be assured of that."

Henri huffed out a deep breath. "You were acting like a foolish, spoiled, young miss," he snarled, still overcome by the thought of what could have happened to her out here.

At his words, Juliette whipped around, her gaze wide. Yet, anger curved her lips in a most enticing way. "How dare you say that? You know nothing of my life!" When Henri opened his mouth to speak, to object, her right hand snapped up to stop him. "No, you will listen to me now." Straightening, she inhaled a deep breath. "You have a life you love, is that not true?" Henri gave a quick nod. "I do not." She swallowed hard, deep longing in those green eyes of hers. "I wish I had something, anything that would give my life meaning, that would give it joy. Yes, I am grateful for what you did, you and Violet. You saved me from a marriage that would have been awful to endure." Slowly, she shook her hand. "But ever since then, I've been standing still."

Henri frowned. "What do you mean?"

A slightly hysterical chuckle left her lips as she threw up her hands. "Four years have passed since I broke my betrothal, and I am still unwed and without a family of my own." She took a daring step toward him. "You might think it foolish, but I always dreamed of love and children; however, after my broken engagement, most of the men who dared come near me were men like Lord Dowling." Spinning around, she began to pace in front of the windows, words pouring from her lips in a way Henri would not have expected.

"I attended ball after ball, and yet, nothing changed. My life stood still." She huffed out a deep breath. "And even when the unthinkable happened, when on one of those endless days a young lord finally asked me to dance, I could not bring myself to look at him and...see someone I could spend my future with." She stopped pacing and turned to look at him, her jaw tight and her eyes hard.

Juliette was radiant in her fury, and Henri could not help but stare at her. The way she finally let go and allowed herself to be honest about how she felt and what she wanted changed his image of her completely. She was no longer the delicate, innocent, young lady with no notion of the world and the way it worked.

"It is your fault!" she suddenly snapped; her right forefinger pointed at him accusingly. "I was perfectly fine before you came along. I was content with the life I was offered, but then you had to come to London and change everything." Glaring at him, she shook her head. "I tried! Truly, I tried to move on, to find a life I could be happy with. That's why I boarded the ship! Because I was hoping for a new beginning in India. Because it was a chance after four long years of nothing."

Henri could see the rapid beating of the pulse in her neck, and it was as though it bridged the gap between them and sneaked into his own veins. He could feel his own heartbeat quicken as he watched her, listened to her, heard her words. They urged him closer, urged him to reach for her. That craving for her once more pulsed in his veins, and he saw no one and nothing but her.

It was a curse!

A sickness!

And he was helpless against it!

Tears clung to her eyelashes, and yet, she still stood tall before him. "I was tired of it. I was tired of merely existing, of watching others find happiness, knowing it would forever be denied me." She swallowed. "I haven't felt alive since the day you—" She broke off, and her gaze fell from his. She took a step backward until her back came to rest against the glass of the window, then her head rolled back, and she closed her eyes.

Henri stared at her, his body tense with the need to move, to be closer, to reach for her. He knew he ought not. He knew he was to return her home. He knew she could not stay.

And yet...

I haven't felt alive since the day you—

Without another thought, Henri moved toward her, his fingers grasping her chin. At the sudden contact, her eyes flew open and she stared up at him, something deeply vulnerable in her gaze once more.

Henri lifted his brows, pressing her to finish her thought, his breath lodged in his throat as he waited. He knew it was dangerous to press her for an answer for it would be nigh on impossible to let her go if she—

"Since the day you left England," Juliette whispered, telling him what he wanted to hear, what he dreaded to hear. "I've missed you, and I've dreamed of you." A tear rolled down her cheek. "For so long."

The air rushed from Henri's lungs as he stared down at her, disbelief mingling with something deeply intoxicating, and for the first time in his life, Henri Duret acted against his better judgement. "As have I," he whispered as they all but drifted toward one another.

A slow smile claimed her lips, and he could see the same sense of disbelief swirling in her eyes. "You thought of me every once in a while?"

His thumb brushed over her chin. "Whenever I could not prevent it," he growled, still at war with himself. "You were like a plague, always on my mind. No matter what I did I could not rid myself of the memory of you, *ma petite lionne.*"

Another tear spilled over and snaked its way down her cheek; still, a small chuckle escaped her lips.

"From the first moment I saw you," he told her as he pushed closer, "I knew I wanted to kiss you."

A terribly endearing blush darkened her cheeks.

"Did you know?" he asked, settling his other hand upon her waist. "Could you see it upon my face?"

Juliette swallowed. "I didn't know what to make of you. I was... overwhelmed, but I knew I wanted..."

"What?" he whispered against her lips.

Her breath came fast. "A part of me was terrified, and yet, I knew I wanted to kiss you. I knew I would regret it if I didn't."

"Have you been kissed since?" Henri whispered before softly brushing his lips against hers. "By one of those stuffed English shirts?"

A tremor snaked down her back, and she lifted her hands and placed them upon his arms, her fingers digging into his flesh for balance. "Not once."

"Did you want to?"

"Not once," she replied, her teeth once more sinking into her lower lip. "I only ever dreamed of kissing you." She licked her lips. "I still do."

If Henri had been in danger of losing himself to her allure before, he was now completely and utterly lost. He still did not know what it was about her that made her stand out, that made her special, that made him look at her in a way he had never looked at another before.

It did not matter though. Nothing mattered. Nothing but the fact that she was right here with him.

In his arms.

And if he wanted to, he could bridge the remaining gap between them and kiss her...

...and, *merde*, he wanted to!

Juliette gasped when his mouth closed over hers. He could feel the tension in her limbs fall away, and she all but sank into his arms.

Henri held her tightly as he continued what they had begun earlier that morning. He wanted her, and she wanted him, and that was all that mattered.

Tomorrow needed to wait.

Henri's hand curled into her thick hair as he kissed her, one arm slung around her small waist. Then he moved her away from the window and toward the bed in the corner. Together, they all but tumbled onto the mattress.

Her hands reached up to pull him closer, and her lips parted beneath his. He could feel her heart beating wildly as he undid the ribbon she had tied to hold his shirt in place. Then his hands moved to undo the buttons, and before long the floorboards in front of the bed were littered with discarded clothes.

Henri closed his eyes the moment he felt her warm skin against his and knew that no matter what tomorrow would bring, this moment...

...here...

...now...

...with her...

...was heartbreakingly perfect!

Chapter Fourteen
A PERFECT MOMENT

When Juliet's eyes opened, the world around her was dark. Only a soft silvery glimmer shone in through the windows, casting shadows over the cabin. The sea was still, the soft sound of waves rolling gently across the globe mixing with the faint creaking of wood from the ship as it cut through the water.

The moment was utterly peaceful, and Juliet breathed in deeply, feeling a slow smile tug upon the corners of her mouth. Warmth lingered in her heart, and she could feel it spread through her body. It was contentedness, that deep sense of being exactly where one was meant to be.

Turning her head, Juliet could not help the smile that spread over her face as her eyes fell on Henri. He lay on his back beside her, his eyes closed and his chest rising and falling with the deep breath of slumber. Never before had she seen him look so peaceful, his forehead smooth and free of concern and worry, the corners of his mouth for once not quirking upward with one devilish thought or another.

More than anything, Juliet wanted to reach out and touch him, feel his warm skin under the tips of her fingers. Still, she did not wish to disturb his sleep. Nevertheless, with each passing moment, her own mind grew more restless, and so she carefully slid out of bed and reached for the discarded shirt she had worn earlier.

Fortunately, Henri did not wake as she slipped it on, her feet still bare as she moved over to stand by the window.

On Dubois's ship, she had been too frightened to realize how utterly breathtaking the view from the captain's quarters was. It looked as though the sea was right below her feet. All she needed to do was take one single step, and a second later, she would find herself disappearing within it.

The soft silvery light of the moon reflected upon the rolling waves, casting a most precious light across the world below her feet. Everything seemed so dark, and yet, deeply peaceful. Was this why people like Henri and his uncle and Violet went out to sea? Not because of the adventure, but because of moments like this one?

Breathing in deeply, cherishing the sensation of that breath traveling down into her body, Juliet smiled. Every muscle in her body felt so wonderfully loose and relaxed and at peace.

Over the past few weeks, nothing had happened without thought, without careful consideration, without concern for what the consequences might be. Upon Dubois's ship, every wrong step, every wrong word could have cost her. The constant threat of his forced attentions had hung over her head, keeping her on edge during every waking hour and even infiltrating her dreams. Every time he had drawn near, she had been terrified that...that...

Pinching her eyes shut, Juliet willed the memories away, reminding her heart that it was finally safe. A deeply heartfelt smile claimed her lips, and she looked over her shoulder, her eyes returning to the man who had liberated her from that life, from that existence.

As her eyes swept over his bare chest, remembering the intimacies they had shared, Juliet could not help but blush yet again. A part of her could not believe that she had acted with no regard for society's rules, for the way she had been raised. Yet she felt no regret, knowing that she would cherish the memory of their shared night for all the days to come. Society would condemn her if it ever became known what she had done, but Juliet could not care less. She would sink into Henri's arms again in a heartbeat. The truth was that she ought never have boarded the merchant vessel in the first place. Yes, that choice had forced something deeply challenging upon her, and yet, it had also brought her right here to this moment.

Before, Juliet had always lived her life according to the way she had been raised. She had never once dared to take one step beyond the boundaries of that life.

Not until Henri had come to London four years ago. The moment he had stepped into her life, she had felt as though she was awakening from a deep slumber. All of a sudden, she had felt more than the normal steady pitter-patter of her heart as life continued from one day to the next. All of a sudden, there had been more.

She had wanted more. Foolishly, she had not realized how much more in that very moment.

After breaking her betrothal, after acting out against everything she had been raised to be, Juliet had once again gone back to following the rules. And what had that brought her?

Closing her eyes, she leaned her forehead against the cool window-pane. *Nothing*, was the simple answer. Indeed, her life had come to a halt, not moving forward or backward, but standing still.

Utterly still.

Lifting her head, Juliet looked back out at the sea, feeling a slight quirk in the corners of her mouth as another smile slowly fought to the surface. Yes, she had stood still, but then she had once more dared to make a bold choice.

A bold choice that had looked like a mistake at first. Now, however, she was not so certain of that.

Again, her gaze traveled back to the man still sleeping in the bed behind her. What if this had not been a mistake after all? What if she had been meant to be with him all along?

Indeed, there was more than passion between them, was there not? He cared for her as she cared for him. At least, Juliet dared to believe it was so. The words he had spoken to her had been as though out of a dream. Always had she believed herself to be the only one to long for a reunion, to have her thoughts act against her will and stray to him despite her better judgment, thinking that she had already been erased from his memory.

Only it was not so, was it? Yet, would Henri dare admit that he wanted her in his life? Had he said what he had simply been inspired by the moment they had shared? Would he come to regret his words?

Juliet heaved a deep sigh, well aware that Henri Duret was a man who liked his freedom. He felt most alive out at sea, adventures ahead of him, waiting for him beyond the horizon. Did he even wish for a wife? Could she live such a life?

Of course, Juliet could not know for sure. Still, she could not help but realize that every time she had broken the rules, her life had taken a most wonderful turn. Indeed, she was not married to Lord Dowling, forced to share his bed and live a dull life free of love and affection, the only joy found in motherhood. No, indeed, she was not.

Instead, she was on a French privateer, sailing across the open seas, with a man who held her heart sleeping only a few steps away from where she stood. Most importantly, she was happy, was she not? Was it not happiness that odd, unfamiliar feeling in her chest? That feeling that made her feel warm and excited all over? That feeling that made her pulse beat faster and her skin hum? That brought a smile to her face again and again?

It had to be.

According to society's opinion, she was now ruined beyond even the slightest hope of redemption; and yet, she had never felt so alive.

Moving back over to the bed, Juliet sat down upon the edge and let her gaze sweep over Henri's face. Again, she marveled at how peaceful he looked, wondering what dreams lingered upon his mind. Was she in them?

"I cannot be certain of anything," Juliet whispered as she reached out a hand and gently placed it on his chest, feeling his heart beat underneath, "but I will not let you go without a fight."

Another one of those deliciously intoxicating smiles spread over her face, and Juliet slipped back under the blanket, snuggling close to him, to his warmth. Even in his sleep, Henri moved toward her, cradling her to his side, holding her close.

Closing her eyes, Juliet allowed herself to drift back off to sleep. Never before had sleeping felt so exceptionally wonderful.

Chapter Fifteen
NO TIME AT ALL

The moment Henri woke, he could feel Juliette stir beside him. Instinctively, his arm tightened around her, holding on to her. His eyes blinked open, and he squinted them for a moment against the stark sunlight shining in through the windows. Slowly, his vision cleared, and as he turned his head, Henri found himself looking into two sparkling green eyes.

A slight blush came to her cheeks as she found him looking at her. "Good morning," she whispered, her teeth once more digging into her lower lip. "How did you sleep?"

Trailing the tips of his fingers along her arm, Henri grinned when he felt her tremble. "Most wonderfully, *Cherie*."

"I did as well."

"In fact," Henri continued, longing to tease her yet again, "I had the most exceptional dream." His eyes settled upon hers. "You were in it."

Her eyes seemed to glow. "I was?"

He feigned a slight frown, still watching her most carefully. "Come to think of it, it might not have been a dream after all." A wicked grin came to his face, and he waited patiently until he could see understanding dawn upon her face. Then he moved swiftly, pulling her closer before rolling on top of her.

Juliette gasped, yet the look upon her face was not one of displeasure.

Not wasting another moment, Henri lowered his head and claimed her mouth as he had the day before, as he intended to do until—

Cringing away from that direction of his thoughts, Henri deepened the kiss, desperate to forget the farewell that loomed upon the horizon. His hands moved into her hair before trailing down the slim column of her neck. He felt her pulse beat wildly against the tips of his fingers before he suddenly paused.

Frowning slightly, he lifted his head and looked down at her. "I thought I'd taken that off last night," he remarked, fingering the collar of her shirt, his brows rising in question. Had their shared night been a mere dream after all?

Juliette licked her lips. "You did, but I put it back on."

"Why on earth would you do that?"

Laughing, she reached up to touch his face. "I woke and I did not wish to wake you as well. So, I got up and looked out at the water." She sighed. "It's so peaceful."

Trailing kisses down her temple, Henri murmured, "Not always." His hand moved to once again remove her shirt when a knock sounded on the door. "*Merde!*" he growled, casting Juliette a questioning look when she laughed as though delighted with his irritation. "If that is Pierre—"

"He seems like a sweet lad," Juliette chuckled, pulling the blanket back over her when Henri rose from the bed and reached for his breeches. "Was it not kind of him to bring us breakfast?"

"It is his job," Henri shot back with a chuckle, wondering about himself, about this odd lightheartedness that seemed to linger...

...so long as she was close.

Pulling his shirt over his head, Henri stalked to the door and then pulled it open. Indeed, it was Pierre; yet, the look upon his face did not resemble the one of the day before.

"François asks you to come," he said in a quiet voice, the look in his eyes one of deepest sadness.

Henri tensed, his hands balling into fists. "Is she...?"

Pierre's eyes widened, and he quickly shook his head. "No, she is awake. That is why François bade me to fetch you." He swallowed hard. "I've never seen..." He shook his head, disillusionment in his eyes as he no doubt remembered Noële's burns. "Why would anyone...?"

Henri inhaled a deep breath, then he placed a comforting hand on the boy's shoulder. "Some questions we will never see answered," he told Pierre, knowing that sooner or later the young man would have to face that fact. "Tell François that I will be there shortly."

Pierre nodded and then turned away and left.

Henri closed the door, resting his forehead against the rough wood. Then he breathed in deeply and turned to look upon Juliette.

Scrambling out of bed, she moved over to her dress, which was still hanging up on the line on the other side of the cabin. Her hands grasped the fabric, feeling the hem, before she looked over her shoulder at him. "I will go with you," she said, urgency in her voice as she gathered together her clothes. "I need to see how she is."

Henri nodded, disappointed that reality had caught up to them so soon. Deep down, he had hoped for a little more time with her. For a little more time with her in that place where nothing mattered but the two of them. "So, you intend to change?" Henri asked teasingly, unable to let go quite so soon.

Juliette's gaze met his. "I could not walk around outside in a shirt and breeches, now, could I?"

Grinning, he moved over to her. "Of course, you could; however, I admit it would cause quite a stir." He took her clothes from her and set them down upon the table. "Let me help you." He reached out to pull the shirt up and over her head. Before he could, though, Juliette shrank back, that fetching blush once again blossoming upon her cheeks.

Henri laughed. "Surely, you're not shy now," he remarked, reaching out to grasp her chin so she would look at him. "After all, last night was not a dream, was it?"

Even though Juliette could not bow her head for his fingers upon her chin kept her from doing so, her eyes turned downward, refusing to hold his. "That is different," she mumbled, her voice no more than a hesitant whisper.

"How so?" Henri pressed, enjoying seeing her so flustered. How was it that she could be bold one moment and then terribly shy the next? "Only moments ago, I rose from the bed and dressed in front of you."

Her flush worsened if that was even possible. "I-I didn't l-look," she stammered.

Henri's heart stumbled in his chest. Indeed, what was it about her that so easily got under his skin? "Oh, you should have," he told her, his voice serious.

Her eyes, wide and unblinking, snapped up to meet his.

Henri laughed, then he reached out and pulled her against him, his mouth claiming hers the moment her lips parted on a surprised gasp.

Her hesitation, though, melted away quickly, and before long, Henri felt her hands curl into his hair, urging him to deepen their kiss.

He smiled against her lips, then he did as she asked, kissing her thoroughly until they were both out of breath. "You confuse me, *ma petite lionne*."

Panting slightly, she smiled up at him, a hint of shyness back in her eyes. "I'm confusing myself."

Giving her chin another affectionate pinch, Henri stepped back. "Very well. Is it enough if I turn my back?" he asked her with raised brows. "Or do you insist I leave?"

Her mouth opened to reply before she paused, eyeing him with indecision. "Can I trust you not to peek?"

"No!" The word shot out of his mouth without thought, and he laughed, seeing the shocked look upon her face.

"Henri!"

Lifting his hands in surrender, Henri stepped back. "Very well. I give you my word that I will not peek. There? Happy?"

Biting her lip, Juliette nodded, then waved her hand at him, urging him to comply. "Turn around."

Henri did as he was bid; yet the temptation to steal a glance at her was torture. He heard the shirt rustle as she pulled it over her head and then let it drift to the floor. "Changed yet?" he dared her.

"No!" came her instant reply, a hint of panic in her voice. "Don't turn around!"

Henri chuckled. "Are you certain?"

"Yes!"

"You don't know what you're missing."

A few more torturous moments ticked by, moments that fueled his imagination, before he heard a muttered curse fly from her lips.

"Is something wrong?" Henri asked, awfully tempted to glance over his shoulder.

"It's nothing," she muttered, her voice a bit strained, before another grumbled complaint left her lips.

"If you don't tell me, I'll simply turn around and see for myself," Henri threatened, wondering what was going on. "Which is it going to be?"

After a moment of silence, Juliette huffed out a deep breath, one that sounded awfully like resignation. "Oh, very well. Turn around."

Henri did not hesitate. "What is it?" His gaze swept over her, standing there in her shift and stays.

Tentatively, her gaze rose to meet his. "I could use your help." Then she turned her back to him, and he could see that the laces still hung loosely down her back.

Henri chuckled and stepped forward to assist her. Teasingly, he trailed the tips of his fingers over her skin before reaching for the laces and pulling them tight. "Like this? Or is that too loose?"

"It's fine," Juliette replied, her limbs still trembling with something Henri liked to believe was temptation. "Thank you." The moment his hands fell away, she stepped forward and reached for her dress, quickly pulling it over her head.

Henri continued to watch her, all but mesmerized by these simple movements, the way she kept glancing up at him, her eyes more expressive than he had ever seen them. "Here." She stepped toward him, holding his neatly folded shirt and breeches out to him. "Thank you."

The look upon her face held such a serious note that Henri merely nodded. "You're welcome." Then he placed the clothes back in his trunk and held out his hand to her. "Ready?"

Inhaling a deep breath, Juliette stepped forward and took his hand. "I think so," she mumbled, then paused, something deeply hesitant in her eyes. "A part of me does not want to go," she told him, her gaze meeting his. "Part of me does not want to know what happened to her."

Henri nodded. "I know," was all he said, knowing that it was enough. After all, he felt the very same way. He kept picturing Étienne in his mind, remembering his friend's laughing face as well as the moment he had disappeared beneath the waves. The memory still sent a deep sense of powerlessness through him, one Henri knew would remain with him until the end of his days. A whole year had passed since. More than a year. Yet, it had *only* been a year.

Oddly enough, it still felt as though it had been yesterday.

Chapter Sixteen
NOÈLE'S STORY

J uliet was glad for Henri's calm presence by her side as they
walked down the companionway to the sick bay. Her limbs trembled at the thought of what they might learn. Would Noèle now
tell them more about what had happened to her? Now that the
danger of Dubois was removed.

Juliet knew the young woman needed help. More than anything,
she probably needed to talk about what had happened, needed
someone to listen. Still, Juliet was not certain if she had the strength to
be that person for Noèle.

François, the ship's surgeon, was a middle-aged man with kind eyes
and a bushy beard. He greeted her with a polite nod then stepped aside
and allowed them to pass. "I'll be up on deck if you need me," he said
and then left.

Juliet took note of very little in that small cabin, her eyes fixed
upon Noèle as she lay in the corner upon a cot. A blanket was covering
her up to her shoulders; yet, her arms rested on top, bandages wrapped
around them. Only the burns upon her face and neck were still visible,
bright red and angry. Her face seemed pale, especially in contrast to
her dark hair.

The moment they stepped into the sick bay, Noèle's eyes blinked and then she turned her head toward them. Juliet drew in a sharp breath for she could feel the young woman's gaze like a weight in her chest.

And then Noèle's eyes moved from her and settled upon Henri's face. Instantly, her eyes widened and a sharp gasp left her lips.

Juliet stepped forward, intent to reassure the young woman. "Noèle, please do not worry. This is—"

"Henri!" Noèle gasped, a profound sense of disbelief in her voice. "Is this really you?"

Juliet stared as Henri stepped forward, a dark look upon his face. "*Oui*, it is me, Noèle." He moved to sit beside her on the cot, his hands slowly reaching out to grasp hers, careful not to hurt her.

Dumbfounded, Juliet looked back and forth between the two of them. Careful steps carried her closer, her mind unable to believe what her eyes were seeing.

Tears shot to Noèle's eyes, and she closed them, turning her head away. "I never wanted you to see me like this." A sob fell from her lips. "I'm so sorry."

Henri's jaw hardened, and for a moment, it seemed as though no words would ever make it past his clamped lips. His eyes closed briefly, and he inhaled a deep breath. Then, however, he forced his muscles to relax and turned to Noèle. "You have nothing to apologize for," he stated vehemently; yet there was a frown upon his face. "What happened to you? I thought you were dead. I thought you had died in the fire. My father told me that—" His voice broke off, and he shook his head, still staring at her.

Juliet could not believe what she was seeing. Quite obviously, Noèle and Henri knew one another. But how?

Gently, Henri reached out and touched his fingertips to her jaw, urging her to look at him. "How did this happen?" he asked, his gaze sweeping over her burns. "Was it the night your house burned down?"

Closing her eyes, Noèle nodded.

"Tell us how it happened," Henri said, his hand tensing upon hers. "Was it Dubois?" A muscle in his jaw twitched angrily.

For a long moment, Noèle remained quiet, tears silently falling from her eyes and running down her temples until they disappeared in her hair.

Juliet's heart broke seeing the young woman's misery. She could not deny that she disliked the closeness she had just witnessed between Noèle and Henri; however, it meant nothing compared to the deep empathy she felt when looking at Noèle. Something awful had happened to this young woman, and they needed to know what it was. They needed to know so they could help her.

Stepping forward, Juliet moved to Henri's side. "Noèle, please tell us," she whispered gently. "What happened to you?"

Henri's gaze rose and met Juliet's, and she could see that he, too, felt torn about this moment. They needed to know, and yet they did not wish to. Henri reached for her hand and then pulled her closer, urging her to sit down on the cot in front of him. It was a tight fit, but Juliet welcomed his warmth behind her, and she reached out to grasp Noèle's other hand.

The young woman heaved a fortifying breath before the first words tumbled from her lips. Slowly, she spoke of her husband's death, of her grief and of the day Dubois's younger brother had come to her, asking for her hand in marriage. She spoke of her surprise, for her heart was still so burdened by the loss of her husband that she had not yet considered the possibility of allowing it to turn toward another.

"And then?" Henri pressed, and Juliet could hear the tension in his voice.

Noèle's eyes pressed shut, and Juliet could see that Dubois's attack upon her remained a torturous memory to this day.

One Noèle could not put into words.

Not here.

Not in front of...Henri?

After all, on Dubois's ship, Noèle had all but confessed to Juliet that he had attacked her. Her words had been far from detailed, and yet their meaning had been crystal clear.

Suddenly, Noèle's eyes flew open. "I have a child," she whispered on a sob before fresh tears shot to her eyes and she wept with heart-breaking sorrow.

Juliet felt Henri freeze behind her. She looked at him over her shoulder and saw that his expression was one of utter shock. "You did not know?" she whispered, still wondering about the kind of relationship that connected them.

Henri's gaze moved to her, and he swallowed hard. "I did not." His voice was strained, and his hand tensed upon Noèle's, giving it a short tug. "You have a child?" he asked, incredulity in his voice. "A child? But Étienne, he died—"

"She's not his," Noèle whispered, her chest rising and falling with rapid breaths. She seemed exhausted and at the end of her rope. "She's not his." Her eyes closed, shame coming to her face.

A low growl rose from Henri's throat, and Noèle flinched. "Not his? What do you—?"

Juliet turned around and placed a hand upon Henri's arm. "Would you leave us please?" she said to him, holding his gaze as he opened his mouth to object. "Now!"

The look upon his face clearly told her that he was most reluctant to comply. Anger and confusion swirled in his dark gaze, something that Noèle need not be subjected to. The young woman had been through enough.

"Please," Juliet whispered, her gaze imploring as it held his. "Go up on deck and...see to things."

His jaw tightened, but after a moment, he finally nodded his head. "Very well." Then, he rose to his feet and with a last look over his shoulder left the sick bay.

"*Merci*," Noèle mumbled the moment the door closed behind him. "He and Étienne were such good friends. I..." She sighed deeply, her eyes closing once more.

Juliet could see how exhausted Noèle was, her body weakened not only by the burns but the torments upon her soul. How could one ever recover from such a thing?

"You have a daughter?" Juliet asked gently, her hand still holding onto Noèle's. "Does she have a name?" Juliet prayed with every fiber of her being that the child was still alive. So far, she could not be certain of what had happened; yet Noèle had said, *I have a child*.

A sad smile came to Noèle's face as her hand clamped down upon

Juliet's. "Ophélie," she whispered, a deep ache etched into her eyes. "Her name is Ophélie."

Juliet smiled at her. "It's a beautiful name." She swallowed hard, wishing there were no more questions she need ask. "Is she Dubois's?"

With tears in her eyes, Noële nodded. "Henri will hate me for it. He will say that I betrayed my husband. His memory."

Juliet froze. "Why would you think that? He would never—" She stopped, belatedly realizing how little she truly knew about Henri Duret. Yet her heart told her that Henri would never lay blame at a woman's feet for being—

"Dubois," Juliet whispered reluctantly, "He...He forced himself on you, did he not?"

Pressing her lips together, Noële nodded. "He was furious when I refused his brother. He came to see me one night. I did not want to let him in, but he pushed open the door." Her eyes became distant, drawn back to that day long ago. "He berated me for denying his brother what he wanted. I tried to explain...about my husband, about..." Her eyes closed, and she slowly shook her head. "But it was no use. He was furious, and the more I tried to explain, the more furious he became. He slapped me, and I fell to the floor. And then..."

Juliet nodded, remembering how Noële had spoken to her of that moment before. Only then, she had been unaware that a child had resulted from that night. "What about the fire? Henri said that your house burned down. What happened? Why did Dubois come back? Was it because of his brother? Clearly, he has not forgotten you."

Noële shrugged. "That, I cannot say. One night, he was simply there. In my house." She shook her head, a look of disbelief in her eyes as though a part of her still doubted what had happened.

"And what of your child? Your daughter?" Juliet asked, frowning as she realized something did not add up. "Why does Henri not know of her? I thought you lived in the same village, or did I misunderstand?"

Noële swallowed. "We do," she replied, a shiver racing itself down her limbs. "I...I never spoke to anyone about what Dubois did to me that night. And when I found out I was with child, I...I didn't want to believe it." Fresh tears rolled down her cheeks as Noële turned pleading eyes to Juliet. "Étienne and I always wanted children, but for some reason, we never had any." She pressed her lips together as another sob rose in her throat. "I didn't want to believe it. I couldn't. For a long time, I pretended that it wasn't true. I retreated from the world and spoke to no one. Everyone tried to help me with my grief, and I felt awful for deceiving them. Yes, I was still grieving my husband, but it was not grief that kept me locked away inside my house."

Juliet stared down at the young woman. "So, no one ever knew? But what happened when your daughter was born? Did you not call on a midwife or...?" She shrugged, uncertain who else might assist a young mother bring her child into the world.

Noèle shook her head. "She was born quickly, and it was over before I knew what was happening."

"How long ago was that?" Her gaze drifted over Noèle's face. "Your burns are beginning to heal, but the fire could not have been too long ago. When was your daughter born?" Juliet wanted to ask what had happened to the child. She clearly had not been upon Dubois's ship, and yet from what Henri had said no one in their home village knew of the child. What on earth had happened to the baby?

Noèle frowned. "I'm not quite certain. How long were we on Dubois's ship?" She shook her head, confusion drawing down her brows. "The night he came back, the night of the fire was no more than a fortnight after Ophélie had been born."

Juliet swallowed, scooting a little closer, holding Noèle's hand a little tighter. "Where is she?"

Noèle's eyes closed. "I don't know." Her jaw trembled, and she pressed her lips together against the emotional onslaught that was no doubt wreaking havoc upon her heart.

"When was the last time you saw her? The night of the fire?"

Noèle nodded. "I don't remember exactly what happened. At some point, I suppose I lost consciousness. When I woke, I was on Dubois's ship." She blinked, and her eyes focused upon Juliet's face. "And you were there."

"Do you think she...?" Juliet began, unable to finish the question. It was too horrifying.

Noèle gritted her teeth. "I cannot say for certain, but I believe

Dubois has her. Of course, he might be lying. She might be dead." Another sob rose from her lips.

"What did he say to you?" Juliet whispered, remembering a very specific moment. "He spoke to you once, whispered something. What was it? Was it about your daughter?"

Noèle nodded. "He warned me not to say anything to his brother about..." She swallowed, her wide eyes expressive enough. "He said if I ever wanted to see her again, I needed to keep quiet."

"Did he say where she was?"

Noèle shook her head. "He did not. I asked, but he just laughed." Tears filled her eyes. "Do you think I will ever see her again?"

Juliet felt tears well up in her own eyes as well, and she held Noèle's hand so tightly that for a moment she feared the young woman's bones might snap in half. "We will find her," Juliet promised solemnly, uncertain how she would ever keep such a vow; yet the sorrow in Noèle's eyes broke her heart. "We will find her. I promise you."

A hint of relief came to Noèle's face, and her eyes closed briefly before they opened again, but only with considerable effort. More than ever before, Noèle looked exhausted and once more close to slipping into unconsciousness.

"Sleep now," Juliet whispered, brushing a tear from Noèle's face. "You need your strength. I will speak to Henri, and we will find a way to get her back. I promise you."

A deep sigh left Noèle's lips, and her eyes closed for good. It took no more than a heartbeat or two before her breath evened out, and she was fast asleep, exhaustion still etched into her face.

Chapter Seventeen
A TOUCH OF JEALOUSY

S tanding at the bowsprit, Henri felt the wind whipping in his face. His skin burned, and his muscles ached with the need to strangle someone.

Dubois!

Tempted almost beyond his own willpower to resist, Henri was close to turning the *Voile Noire* around and head back south, praying to cross Dubois's path. Of course, he could not. He would never endanger Juliette nor Noèle. No, first he needed to take them both to safety before he went after Dubois.

"Henri?"

At the sound of Juliette's voice, Henri spun around. Her eyes were tear-stained, and she looked beyond miserable. Still, something hard and unyielding sparked in her eyes that made her seem strong and vulnerable at the same time. She was an eternal contradiction, and he loved that about her.

"How is she?" he asked, stepping toward her.

Her hands came into his as though they belonged there. "She's sleeping now," Juliette replied, her mouth opening and closing with more to say. Yet the words would not come. Her gaze swept over the deck from sailor to sailor, all of whom were looking at them most curiously, those blasted delighted smiles upon their faces yet again

"Perhaps we should head under deck," Henri suggested, and when she nodded her head, he took her by the elbow and guided her toward the hatch.

The moment the door to the captain's quarters closed behind him, Henri pulled her back, his eyes searching hers. "What did she tell you? About the child? About...Dubois?"

Hesitation rested in Juliette's eyes as they met his. "She's afraid you will hold what happened against her."

Frowning, Henri shook his head, a dull pain echoing through his heart. "Why would she think that?"

Juliette sighed. "Because of her husband. Because *she* is holding it against herself."

Henri's teeth ground together. "What happened? What did Dubois do to her?"

Juliette bowed her head. "I think you know."

Indeed, he did know. Not the details, of course, but he was certain that it was better he did not.

As his muscles tightened, Henri turned away and began to pace the small length of the cabin. Once again, he felt overwhelmed by the almost desperate need to plant his fist in Dubois's face. If only the man were within arm's reach!

"He took her child."

Rocking back on his heels, Henri whirled around to face her. "What?" Two large strides carried him closer before his hands grasped her by the arms, yanking her against him. "He did what?"

Juliette drew in a shuddering breath, and her palms came to rest against his chest. "It's a daughter," she whispered. "Ophélie."

Henri swallowed. "The name of Étienne's mother was Ophélie."

In a few simple words, Juliette informed him of what she had found out from Noèle. "We will find her," Henri gritted out, selfishly relieved that there was something for him to do.

When Étienne had been swept out to sea, there had been nothing Henri could have done. He had tried, but everything had happened so quickly. Within moments, his friend had been gone. And then, he had returned home only to learn that Noële had died in a fire. Again, everything had happened without a chance to change the outcome, to prevent the tragedy from occurring.

Now, here, this was different. There was still something that could be done. He could only hope that Dubois had not lied about the child. That the girl was still alive and could be returned to her mother.

Sighing, Juliette sank into his arms, and for a long time, they simply held one another. "I never knew, I never imagined that men like Dubois truly existed. How could he have done this to her?" She lifted her head and looked at him. "I saw him with his brother. It seemed that he truly cared for him. How can he love his brother but feel nothing when he hurts another? A mother and her child? His child!" Her eyes widened as realization dawned. She pulled back, her eyes blinking. "Do you think he knows? Do you think he intends perhaps to keep the baby for himself?"

Henri shook his head. "That, I cannot say. Except for his brother, I have never seen him show affection to anyone. He is a cold-hearted bastard!"

"I think he wanted to force Noële to marry his brother," Juliette mumbled, her eyes thoughtful. "Yet, it seemed that his brother knew nothing of it. He treated Noële with affection and kindness. Once, he mentioned that he had been the one to pull Noële from the fire, that he would have failed had his brother not come along and aided him."

In his mind's eye, Henri tried to picture the scene, Noële's little house at the edge of the village near the forest. He saw it go up in flames. Had Dubois left Noële there to die? Had the bastard's brother happened upon the scene by sheer happenstance?

Perhaps Benoît Dubois had intended to renew his proposal. Still, everything had to have happened fast for no one in *La Roche-sur-Mer* to have learned of the Dubois brothers' involvement in what happened that night. Everyone had believed Noële to be dead. But what of the child?

Henri shook his head; certain they would not get any answers until they caught up with Dubois.

"You've known her for a long time, have you not?"

Jarred from his thoughts, Henri looked down at her. "I have," he mumbled, remembering the wide-eyed, young woman his friend had brought back to *La Roche-sur-Mer* one day. "Ever since Étienne fell head over heels in love with her."

Juliette swallowed; her eyes hesitant as they met his. "And you are close?"

Henri frowned, watching her closely. "She is very dear to me, *oui.*" He waited, wondering what was going through her head.

Juliette's eyes fell from his before returning once more. "Like a dear friend?" she asked tentatively. "Or...?"

Henri could not help but grin, and the moment she saw it, heat shot to her cheeks and she stepped away. Her hands clamped together, and she walked over to the other side of the cabin, coming to stand by the window once again.

Henri chuckled. "What are you asking, *Cherie?*" Slowly he moved closer, and he could see her listening to each footfall upon the wooden floorboards. "Did she not tell you that she loved Étienne?"

Juliette cast him a chiding look over her shoulder. "She did."

"Then why would you assume that...?" He intentionally let his voice trail off, his hands falling onto her shoulders, urging her to turn around and face him.

Again, her eyes refused to meet his, and he reached out to grasp her chin, tilting her head upward. "Look at me," he whispered, waiting until her eyes rose to meet his. "What are you asking?"

A shuddering breath left Juliette's lips. "I...I am not asking anything. It is quite obvious that you care for her."

"Yet she loves her husband. Still." His brows rose in question.

Henri could feel that she wanted to evade him, to step away and escape this moment. Yet he held onto her, making it unmistakably clear that he would not let her, that he wanted an answer.

A moment passed and then another before some sense of determination sneaked into her eyes, the muscles in her jaw tensing as she made up her mind. Her eyes now looked into his without hesitation, and when she opened her mouth to speak, her voice did not tremble. "Not every heart finds its affections returned."

Henri all but stared at her, suddenly overwhelmed by the thought that she was not speaking of what he might feel for Noële. "Are you jealous, *ma petite lionne?*" His fingers on her jaw tightened, and he leaned closer, his eyes never leaving hers.

For a short moment, Juliette's lips pressed into a tight line. Then, however, they suddenly parted. "Yes!" There was no hesitation in her voice, and her gaze held his in a way that made him feel unable even to blink. "I know you're not mine," she said then, a hint of vulnerability coming to her tone once more, "but...but I want you to be."

Caught off guard, Henri stared down at her. Never would he have expected her to be so bold, so daring. Yes, last night, she had given herself to him, and he knew that it had been a life-changing decision for her, making a suitable marriage all but impossible. Still, to see her standing before him now, her eyes unwavering, her chin no longer held up by his grasp upon it, her words making her vulnerable beyond all measure, stole his breath.

She was magnificent!

From the look in her eyes, Henri knew that she was waiting for an answer. He saw uncertainty and hope but also fear. She was not certain of his heart as he had not been certain of hers. Indeed, allowing oneself to care for another was always a gamble.

In more ways than one.

No one knew that better than him, for he had watched his own father wither away for a long time after his mother's death. All his life, Henri had been surrounded by happy marriages, his grandparents', his uncle's and many others in *La Roche-sur-Mer*; and yet that empty space beside his father where his mother should have been had always been the one to draw his eyes most.

Henri knew that he ought to say something. Yet words often said too much. They only granted him the choice between reciprocating and seeing her heart broken...as well as his own.

Here, in this moment, Henri was ready to do neither.

And so, he chose option three and said nothing.

Instead, he dipped his head and kissed her.

His arms pulled her closer, held her to him until he could feel the beat of her heart against his own. Her hands touched his face as she returned his kiss, that daring side of her once more resurfacing.

How she did it, Henri did not know. Again, he marveled at those contradicting facets he often saw in her. She possessed a lion's heart, and yet she seemed delicate and fragile as a flower.

One of his hands curled into her hair while the other moved to the back of her dress, reaching for her laces. His mouth never left hers, and he was about to sweep her into his arms when a faint voice echoed to his ears from up on deck. "Sail ho!"

Henri froze, as did Juliette.

With wide eyes, she pulled back and stared up at him. "Was that—? Did that mean—?"

Grasping her hand, Henri pulled her toward the door. "Another ship," he confirmed as they hastened down the companionway.

"Dubois?" came Juliette's frightened voice from behind him.

Henri gritted his teeth. "I do not know yet." He rushed up the ladder and jumped out of the hatch and on deck. Juliette followed hesitantly.

"Capt'n!" his first mate called from the quarterdeck, then he tossed him a spyglass, his finger pointing due north.

Henri exhaled a breath of relief. North meant that it could not possibly be Dubois. Perhaps...

Squinting one eye shut, Henri looked through the spyglass. A tall two-masted ship appeared upon the horizon, its familiar sails billowing in the wind as it cut through the waters, heading straight toward them.

"Is it Dubois?" Juliette whispered beside him, her hand coming to rest upon his arm.

Henri turned to look at her, a wide grin coming to his face. "No, it's your sister."

Juliette's jaw dropped before her eyes lit up. "Violet," she breathed, her eyes turning toward the horizon.

It seemed Antoine had managed to locate her after all.

Chapter Eighteen

THE FREEDOM

J uliet felt her heartbeat quicken as she stared out to sea, her eyes fixed upon the small dot slowly coming closer.

Henri stood beside her, calling orders to change their course and meet the other ship. Sailors scrambled across the deck as they worked to adjust a sail. Only moments later, the *Voile Noire* changed course.

Excitement coursed through Juliet's veins at the thought of seeing her sister again. Almost a year had passed since they had last spoken. Although Violet was married to an English lord, her heart always drew her back home to France, to her parents and her four younger siblings.

And, of course, her daughter, Antoinette—named after her grandfather, Henri's uncle Antoine.

While the girl often accompanied her parents on short voyages that held little danger, Juliet knew that the girl often remained with her grandparents in *La Roche-sur-Mer*.

France and England; indeed, they were a family separated by state lines. And at present, France and England were at war.

As the *Freedom* drew closer, Juliet spotted her sister standing on the quarterdeck, her golden curls tied in the back; yet some had escaped and were billowing in the wind. She wore the same clothes Henri and

Antoine always wore out at sea, breeches and boots, a simple white shirt with a vest and a jacket. A sword dangled from her hip, and Juliet also spotted a pistol strapped to her chest.

Violet looked like a true privateer!

Like her father Antoine!

Like Henri!

Juliet stared at her sister in open-mouthed fascination. Indeed, she looked strong and capable and completely sure of herself and her place in this world. Always, from the first, had Juliet envied her sister that sense of certainty. Violet never appeared unsure in any way, knowing exactly where she was meant to be. She never hesitated, never feared.

To Juliet, she seemed dauntless. She was the kind of woman Juliet would never be. The kind of woman Juliet admired greatly.

The moment their eyes met across the shrinking distance between the two ships, Juliet saw her sister's face light up. "Juliet!" she called, waving her arm in greeting. Then she looked over her shoulder at the man at the helm and spoke to him.

Juliet squinted her eyes and she saw none other than her sister's husband, Lord Cullingwood. He was a tall man with the same sense of adventure in his eyes that Juliet always saw in her sister's. Indeed, they were a match made in heaven.

Both equally daring.

Both unable to stand still.

Both born to be out here at sea.

As the ships drew closer, the sails were pulled down to decrease speed. Fortunately, the sea was mostly calm today, and so, hooks were thrown to pull the ships closer to one another until they sat side-by-side, slowly bobbing atop the waves.

Sailors scrambled across the deck as Violet and her husband swiftly made their way down from the quarterdeck. Violet's eyes shone eagerly, fixed upon Juliet's face, and she moved to climb the railing without delay. The moment her feet landed upon the deck of the *Voile Noire*, Violet surged forward and pulled Juliet into her arms. "Oh, I am so very glad to see you. I feared for the worst when we received your mother's letter." She stood back and looked into Juliet's face. "Are you all right?"

Juliet felt tears burning in her eyes, but she nodded. "I am well, Sister. Thank you. I never would've thought that..."

Violet frowned. "That we would come for you?" A look of incredulity came to her eyes, and she shook her head. "Of course, we would! Of course, we did! You're family. We love you and would never let anything happen to you."

Sinking into her sister's arms once more, Juliet buried her face against her shoulder. The certainty with which her sister spoke warmed her heart, and yet she remembered well how alone she had felt upon Dubois's ship.

Indeed, it was the truth. While she had hoped that Violet might feel compelled to assist her, she had never believed that her sister's family would stand with her as well. Was it simply a sense of duty? Or was it possible that they truly cared for her?

Still, a part of Juliet did not dare believe; after all, over the past four years, she had not once encountered them. With Antoine and Henri sailing the seas, never once setting foot upon English soil, she had never expected see them again. Yes, upon occasion, she had seen her sister upon her return to England. Yet, those precious moments had been few and far between. And yet, when it had mattered most, they had come for her.

All of them.

A part of Juliet still could not believe it.

"*Bonjour, chère cousine,*" Henri greeted his beloved cousin, stepping forward and placing his hand upon her shoulder. His green eyes shone warmly, and yet that familiar, wicked smile once more tugged on his lips.

Violet stepped back and met his gaze. "Henri, I am glad to see you in one piece." She grinned at him before sweeping her eyes over his person. "I admit I was worried about what you might do. When *Papa* told me what had happened, I feared for the worst."

Henri chuckled. "Ah, you know me."

"That is precisely why I was worried," Violet insisted, turning toward him, a more serious expression coming to her face. "Why did you not wait for me? You know the kind of man Dubois is."

Juliet watched as Henri's brows drew down. A muscle in his jaw twitched, and she swallowed remembering the moment she had first seen him upon Dubois's ship. "That is precisely why I could not wait for you," Henri replied, his voice hard, "and I'm relieved I did not." His gaze moved to Juliet's, and she felt a shiver dance down her spine. Yes, the thought of Dubois made her feel sick to the stomach; and yet the way Henri was looking at her stole the breath from her lungs. He had been worried for her, afraid for her, and he had not hesitated to come to her aid.

If only she knew how he felt for her. It had not escaped her attention that he had failed to answer, to reciprocate when she had all but bared her heart to him. Was there any chance that his heart cared for her? Or had he merely been swept away by overpowering, but still fleeting, emotions in the aftermath of her rescue?

Was there a chance that they could find with one another what Violet had found with her husband?

Juliet's gaze moved to Lord Cullingwood, who stood silently behind his wife's right shoulder. His gaze was watchful, but he did not interfere in the moment between the two cousins.

Hearing Henri's words, Violet turned her attention back to Juliet, a question in her blue eyes that she held back. "I'm glad to see you all right," she said carefully, doubt and hesitation in her words as though she could not be quite certain. Her eyes swept over Juliet as though looking for something.

"A lot has happened," Henri interjected, his gaze still settled upon his cousin. "A lot we need to discuss."

Violet frowned. Then she looked over her shoulder at her husband, who took a step forward. He offered Henri a quick nod and then looked at Juliet. "Juliet, it is good to see you," he said with a soft smile.

Beside her, Juliet thought to hear an almost imperceptible growl rumbling in Henri's throat. She lifted her eyes to look at him and found his features tense as he all but glared at Lord Cullingwood. Indeed, she had known that the two men had always been at odd ends with one another. When Violet had fallen in love with Lord Culling-wood, Henri had opposed the match. Yet, ultimately, he had respected his cousin's decision.

"It is good to see you as well, my lord," Juliet replied, a deep smile coming to her face at seeing her sister so happy in her marriage. Indeed, the two of them looked perfect together.

Lord Cullingwood chuckled. "Oh, please call me Oliver. In fact, I must insist."

Before Juliet could reply, Henri moved closer, his arm coming around her and tugging her into his side. "There is no time for pleasantries," he said in a voice much harsher than Juliet would have expected. "Although I was able to recover Juliet, there is still a matter that remains unsolved."

Violet nodded, careful consideration in her eyes. "Shall we head below deck?" she asked, clearly sensing that what Henri needed to discuss was not something meant for everyone to overhear.

In silence, the four of them headed down the hatch and along the companionway until they all stepped into the captain's quarters. Henri then closed the door behind Oliver, casting the man another tense look before turning to face them all.

"Well?" Violet asked, her eyes moving from Juliet to Henri. "What is it you wish to discuss?" She frowned. "Quite honestly, I've never known you to be so tightlipped. Did something go wrong with Dubois?" She glanced at Juliet. "You did not fire upon him, did you? How did you retrieve her?"

Henri grinned, quite obviously enjoying his cousin's unease. "No, I did not fire upon him. It was not necessary." He lifted his brows in a show of triumph, and Oliver laughed, which in turn earned him a dark look from Henri. "Is there anything funny?"

Still grinning, Oliver shook his head. "Not at all," he assured his wife's cousin; the look in his eyes, however, stated otherwise.

Juliet saw Henri's jaw tighten and his hands ball into fists as he forced himself to remain where he was. Somehow, the two men always came close to exchanging blows. Why that was was beyond Juliet.

In a few quick words, Henri explained how he had saved her that night, and Juliet felt every word travel down her spine and send another shiver over her. She still did not like remembering that night nor those that came before while at the same time she could not help that feeling of awe that seized her whenever she thought of the moment her eyes had first fallen upon Henri after four long years.

A slight frown came to Violet's face. "Well, then all should be settled, should it not? Dubois might not even be aware that it was you who snatched her away." Her gaze moved from her cousin to Juliet and back again. "Which matter remains unresolved?"

Henri inhaled a slow breath. "Noèle," was all he said, and Juliet could see her sister's gaze widening as she too drew in a slow, shuddering breath.

"*Papa* said," Violet began, her throat working as she fought to say the words, "she was dead." Oliver stepped up from behind her, placing his hands upon her shoulders, and Violet leaned into him. "He said she died in a fire." Her brows drew down into a frown. "He said you told him so."

Henri nodded. "I did, but I was wrong. We were all wrong."

As Violet continued to stare at her cousin, Henri slowly told her all that had happened, all they had learned from Noèle. With each word, Violet's eyes grew rounder and her pulse in her neck began to beat more rapidly. "A daughter? She has a daughter?"

Juliet saw something cross her sister's face, an emotion she herself could not quite understand. Perhaps it was something only a mother could understand, for she was absolutely certain that in this moment Violet pictured her own daughter's little face.

Antoinette.

"We don't know where she is," Henri told them, his body rigid and his jaw clenched. "But I will find out, and I will bring her back."

Juliet could sense the turmoil within him, and so, she moved closer, her hands reaching out, slipping around his right arm, holding on. She looked up at him, and he turned his gaze down to her. She could feel him inhale a slow breath, and little by little, the hard muscles beneath her hands began to loosen.

"We all will go!" Violet insisted, anger burning in her voice. "We will be stronger together."

Henri shook his head. "No, I will go alone." Violet was about to protest when Henri lifted a hand to stop her. "We don't know what will happen, and I refuse to go after Dubois with both Noèle and Juliet on board. No, you need to take them home. What you do after that is up to you."

Juliet felt the breath catch in her throat at the thought of boarding her sister's ship and sailing away. Perhaps she ought to have seen it coming, but here in this moment when Henri suddenly spoke with such determination of sending her away, Juliet could not believe it. She had foolishly allowed herself to think that those few blissful moments they had had with one another would continue on forever. She had ignored that little voice that had whispered warnings into her ear, determined to make the most of the moments they had been granted.

Now, however, it seemed they were coming to an end. Shock froze Juliet's limbs, and she could do little else but stare at Henri as tears welled up in her eyes.

Violet gritted her teeth together. "Then you take them home, and I will go after Dubois." She held her cousin's gaze without flinching.

"I will not discuss this," Henri gritted out, his gaze narrowed as he stared down at Violet. "I have a score to settle. I will not turn back."

Violet scoffed. "A score to settle?" Staring at Henri, she shook her head, then she took a step closer, her eyes hard. "Why are you doing this? Who are you doing this for?"

Juliet tensed as the two cousins stood head to head. They were both insanely stubborn, both possessing a temper that easily flared to life. She knew that this was a situation that was emotional for the both of them, and because of that, it could easily get out of hand. She knew she had to interfere, yet —

"Enough," Oliver said in a calm but commanding voice. He stepped forward and placed a hand on each of the cousin's shoulders, urging them apart.

Looking up at him, Juliet tugged on Henri's arm, relieved when he complied and took a step backward.

Immediately, Oliver turned to his wife, his gaze seeking hers. "Go and see to Noèle," he told her calmly, his brows rising to convey the determination behind his words. "Go and see to her."

For a moment, Violet seemed hesitant, ready to argue. Then, however, she nodded. "Very well. Perhaps you're right."

Oliver leaned forward and placed a kiss upon her forehead. Then he turned to look at Juliet. "Will you show her the way?" he asked gently, the look in his eyes urging her to comply.

Juliet nodded, well aware that it was best to separate the two cousins at present. More than that, Juliet longed to speak to her sister. Her heart remained in turmoil, and she could use some help trying to sort through this mess she suddenly found herself in.

Would she truly be forced to leave Henri soon? Perhaps even today? Would she once again have to watch him sail away, uncertain if they would ever see each other again?

The thought alone nearly brought her to her knees.

Chapter Nineteen

BETWEEN MEN

H enri could not help but wonder at his cousin's sudden compliance with her husband's request. Generally, Violette was a no-nonsense kind of woman, who never feared to stand her ground, ready to argue until the end of time to make herself heard.

Now, however, she stepped back, casting him one last warning glance, before leaving the captain's quarters with Juliette.

The moment the door closed behind the two women, Henri turned to look upon his cousin-in-law, wondering what Oliver might hope to accomplish by sending the women away. Did he truly believe he could convince him?

If so, he would be severely disappointed.

"I thought it would be best for us to speak privately," Oliver said, the moment their gazes locked. "I—"

"I will not change my mind!" Henri interrupted, crossing his arms over his chest as he glared at his cousin-in-law. "You might as well save your breath."

A grin slowly stole onto Oliver's face, and he chuckled. "Believe me I am aware of that."

Henri frowned. "Then why?"

Oliver inhaled a deep breath, his gaze remaining upon Henri's face for a moment longer as though contemplating what to say. "Quite frankly, I do agree with you." Henri's frown deepened. "Don't look so surprised! My wife's safety is of the utmost concern to me, and, honestly, I'd like to keep her as far away from Dubois as possible."

Regarding his cousin-in-law, Henri nodded. "I'm glad to hear it." He paused, then asked, "Do you think she will agree?"

Oliver nodded. "Although it might not have seemed like it, I believe she agreed with you from the start."

Henri scoffed. "She hid it well!"

"She loves you, Henri," Oliver stated, a rather indulgent look in his eyes. "She loves you as much as you love her, and she worries about you." He took a step closer, his eyes watchful. "You have no idea how afraid she has been for you, for the both of you, ever since learning of what had happened. She feared you might do something—"

"Foolish?" Henri threw in helpfully.

Oliver grinned, then nodded. "Yes, something foolish." The expression upon his face sobered. "She was afraid she would lose you. Can you not understand that?"

Henri inhaled a slow breath, well aware how protective his little cousin was. It was an emotion they shared because they were family, because they loved each other beyond hope. "*Oui*," was all Henri said in reply.

Oliver nodded. "What do you intend to do?"

Henri shrugged. "I do not know yet. I found Dubois in his home port. Although I cannot know whether or not he is still there, I will first head south, trying to locate him."

"And then?" Oliver inquired. "I assume you don't intend to simply ask him where Noèle's daughter is."

Henri scoffed. "*Non.* That would be the definition of the futile attempt."

"Then how?"

Henri shrugged. "As I said, I do not know yet. I suppose I will follow him, see what he does, where he goes. If he truly took the child, perhaps someone in his crew knows, perhaps his brother. Should there be a chance to speak to one of them, I shall try;

however, if not, I will do whatever necessary to procure that information."

Straightening, Oliver nodded, his gaze suddenly seeking Henri's in a more insistent way. "And Juliet?" he asked all of a sudden.

Henri almost flinched, surprising himself. Indeed, over the course of the past half hour, he had done his utmost to banish the thought of leaving her behind from his mind. "What of her?" he replied, doing his utmost to appear unimpressed. "Violette will see her home."

Chuckling, Oliver shook his head. "You are as bad as she is; Violet, I mean."

Henri could not say he cared for his cousin-in-law's rather conde-scending tone nor that hint of amusement in his eyes. "I do not believe any of this is any of your con—"

"Whether you like it or not, we are family, Henri," Oliver inter-rupted, his gaze unflinching and his shoulders drawn back. "Was it not for the same reason that you came to London four years ago? To ensure Violet's safety?" He chuckled. "Do you not remember what you did when you found us together, her and me, out on the terrace?" His brows rose in challenge.

Henri's teeth ground together because he did remember. He remembered very well. "If I recall correctly, I planted you a facer and you went down like a ton of bricks." He grinned. "Was that not so?"

Still looking annoyingly amused, Oliver nodded. "You were furi-ous," he stated as though Henri's response fit perfectly in how he had planned this conversation. "When you learned that she and I had..." His voice trailed off, and he wiggled his brows meaningfully as an infu-riating grin came to his face. "Well, let's just say, you reacted in your usual, straightforward manner."

Henri felt tempted to grasp his cousin-in-law by the collar and punch him in the jaw once again. It certainly would serve him right! "You were supposed to *pretend* to be her husband," Henri snarled, his hands once more balling into fists at his sides. "I knew from the begin-ning that we could not trust you. That's why I came after her! I knew you would not keep your word!"

Frowning, Oliver shook his head. "You speak as though I acted against her wishes. We...We fell in love. Yes, I offered to pretend to be her husband in order to help her gain entrance into London society, to seek out her sister and offer Juliet her assistance. Yes, it was all meant to be a ruse, but along the way..." A deep sigh left his lips. "At some point, it simply stopped being a ruse. We fell in love, and as much as she tried to pretend that it wasn't true, she could not."

Still caught in his fury, Henri glared at him; a fury that in truth had very little to do with Violette and Oliver. "You had no right!" He took a step but kept himself from taking another. "You ought to have kept away from her!"

Oliver's gaze became contemplative. "Did you?" he asked calmly, his gaze slightly narrowing. "Did you keep away from Juliet?"

Henri felt that question hit him in the chest with such force that he almost stumbled backward. He stared at his cousin-in-law, unable to respond, unable to catch a clear thought.

The corners of Oliver's mouth quirked upward. "Something happened between the two of you, did it not?" he asked slowly, pronouncing each word carefully. "Something more than a kiss." He chuckled. "All of a sudden, it seems we find our roles strangely reversed." Breathing in deeply, Oliver sought his gaze, "Did you bed her?"

As though a shot had been fired, Henri flung himself toward his cousin-in-law, fist raised. Oliver, however, quickly danced out of the way, ducking as Henri's fist came flying toward his head.

"I must say, your response is quite telling, *dear cousin*," Oliver remarked, once more spinning sideways and out of reach as Henri came after him.

Somewhere in the back of his head, Henri was aware that he was acting like a fool, a lunatic even. Still, going after his cousin-in-law seemed like the far safer option than contemplating everything that had happened between him and Juliette. "This is not your concern!" he snarled, trying to round the table in order to get his hands on Oliver.

Sidestepping him yet again, Oliver moved to the other end of the cabin. "Well, Juliet has no cousin to come to her defense, to punch you in the face for taking liberties. Therefore, it falls to me." He stood with his back to the wall and did not even try to evade Henri as he stormed toward him.

Completely lost in this mindless fury, Henri grasped his cousin-in-law by the collar, shoving him hard against the wall. "I suggest you leave this instant," he snarled into his face.

Slowly, Oliver shook his head. "I cannot. Punch me if you like, but that won't change what happened between the two of you." He paused, waiting, and Henri could feel his anger slowly subside, overruled by something else. "You care for her."

Gritting his teeth, Henri released his cousin-in-law and stepped back. "I do not," he insisted like a child before he stepped over to the windows, raking his hands through his hair.

Behind him, he heard Oliver adjust his attire. "It is...terrifying," he said with a sigh, "when you first realize that your happiness suddenly depends on another. Believe me I felt much the same way. So did Violet. She was afraid to lose herself, her freedom if she were to acknowledge how she felt for me." Slow footsteps carried Oliver closer until he came to stand next to Henri, their eyes focused out the window at the open sea. "Ultimately, though, you do not have a choice." He turned to look at Henri. "You do not get to decide how you feel, and if you truly care for her, then nothing but misery will come from denying the truth."

Inhaling a deep breath, Henri turned to look upon his cousin-in-law. "What I feel does not matter. What matters right now is her safety." He straightened his shoulders, willing himself to hold onto that one thought that remained true no matter how he felt. "Violette needs to return her home."

"Why?" Oliver demanded.

Henri gritted his teeth. "Because I will not risk her life."

"Why?"

Henri stared at him incredulously. "Does there have to be a reason?"

"Yes, after all, you risked your own when you went after her." His brows rose in challenge. "Did you not?"

Henri did his best to chuckle as though he did not have a care in the world. "You underestimate me, my friend. I—"

"You went after her the moment you heard what had happened," Oliver continued. "You did not wait for Violet. You did not try to contact any of us. You met Antoine by chance alone." His gaze became more insistent. "You did not hesitate. Not for a moment. Not to contemplate the risk to yourself. Why?"

Henri swallowed hard. "Because—" Desperately, he searched his mind for something to say, but there was nothing. "Because—"

Inhaling a slow breath, Oliver reached out and placed a hand upon Henri's right shoulder. "That's what I thought."

Henri felt the sudden urge to shake off his cousin-in-law's hand, but he did not.

"All I'm saying," Oliver continued, "is that there is something between you. We knew it from the moment the two of you met."

Henri frowned. "We?"

"Violet and I," Oliver elaborated with a grin. "The day you sailed away and we stood up on the cliff watching, we wondered how long it might take for Fate to lead you and Juliet together again." Removing his hand from Henri's shoulder, he stood back. "It's been four years. Ask yourself: if you let her go now, how long will it take until your paths cross again. If ever."

Henri felt something cold spread through his being at the thought of never seeing Juliette again. Yet he knew he could not be selfish where she was concerned. The truth was that it did not matter what he wanted. What mattered was her safety.

Turning away, Henri moved toward the door, pulling it open. He paused in the doorway and looked back over his shoulder. "I will not risk her life," he said once again, and for a short moment, it seemed that Oliver understood.

Then Henri walked away.

Chapter Twenty

BETWEEN SISTERS

After Noèle had been settled comfortably in the sick bay of the *Freedom*, Juliet followed Violet to the captain's quarters, the place her sister and brother-in-law called home.

It was about as sparsely furnished as the other captain's quarters Juliet had laid eyes upon in her life; however, something about it made it seem warmer, more welcoming. Indeed, it felt like a home, a home upon the sea.

"I still cannot believe it," Violet muttered as she unstrapped her sword and removed the pistol, stashing them both in a trunk near the bed. "All the things she went through." With a deep sigh, Violet shook her head.

Juliet nodded. "We must find her daughter. I believe it is the only thing keeping her alive."

Together, the two sisters sat down at the small table. Violet moved aside a few maps, then offered Juliet some wine from a jug. "I cannot imagine...If Antoinette were ever..." She broke off, shaking her head against such an awful thought. Then she looked at Juliet. "What will you do?"

Frowning, Juliet looked at her sister. "What do you mean?"

A knowing smile came to Violet's face as she leaned forward, her blue eyes looking into Juliet's. "Will you do as he says? Or will you fight him?"

Juliet drew in a slow breath. She had never been one to fight for anything, not even herself. She had not even contemplated the possibility until Violet had come into her life. "It does not matter what I want. He will not change his mind." A slow smile came to her lips. "He is stubborn, like you."

Chuckling, Violet sat back. "Believe me I know. However, that does not mean that you have to give in."

Juliet sighed, wishing that there were a way.

"You care for him, do you not?" Violet asked, that knowing smile once more coming to her face.

Juliet closed her eyes. "I'm afraid so."

"I knew it!" Violet exclaimed, banging her fist on the table and making Juliet flinch. "He was the reason you changed your mind, was he not? You decided not to marry Lord Dowling because...?" She paused, her eyes directed at Juliet, watching her most curiously. "What happened between the two of you when we left you alone in the drawing room? I know it's been four years, and yet I've never once asked you. What did he do to change your mind?"

Juliet tried hard to keep a smile from showing upon her face, but to no avail.

Instantly, understanding lit up her sister's eyes, a slight chuckle rumbling in her throat. "I see," she mumbled. "It must've been one hell of a kiss."

Juliet buried her face in her hands. "What am I to do?" She shook her head then looked up at her sister once more. "I haven't been able to stop thinking about him since that day. Believe me I tried to, but..." She shrugged helplessly.

Violet reached out and grasped one of her hands. "Why did you never say a word? If you cared for him like this, why did you never speak to me? I could've...sent word to him, and..."

Juliet shook her head. "And? What difference would that have made? We both know that Henri never does anything he does not want. He left without a word, and that was message enough."

Violet heaved a bit of an exasperated sigh. "Oh, believe me I got his message loud and clear. Every time I returned from England, the first thing he would ask about...was you."

Juliet's heart stilled in her chest as she stared at her sister.

"Of course, he tried to hide it. He would ask about my time in London, about meeting friends and family. I could see it in his eyes though. He did not care about any of that, all he cared to learn about was you." Her hand tightened upon Juliet's. "What happened between the two of you? You've been on his ship together for the past few days..." Her brows rose in question.

Juliet felt that awful heat once more shoot up into her cheeks, and her eyes closed in embarrassment.

A delighted chuckle drifted from Violet's lips. "Oh, dear sister, you truly love him, do you not?"

"I wish I did not," Juliet exclaimed in agony. "Now, I will have to watch him sail away once more." She blinked her eyes as she felt tears well up. "I will never see him again, will I?"

Violet inhaled a deep breath. "Well, you have a choice to make. Your mother's letter said that I was to escort you safely home...or to India if you so choose."

Juliet's heart constricted at the thought of her mother, longing surging through her. "She would let me decide?"

Violet nodded. "She wants you to be happy, and she knows—as do we all—that these past few years were not filled with happiness, were they?"

Juliet shook her head. "That's why I left," she mumbled. "I could not bear that life a moment longer. I cannot imagine returning to it now." She shrugged. "Does that mean I shall go to India?" All of a sudden, that option no longer sounded appealing.

"That is not the only other option you have," Violet pointed out. "But you must be certain of what you want. Right now, here, you're standing at a fork in the road—so to speak." She squeezed Juliet's hand affectionately. "You need to decide what you want and what you're willing to risk in order to get it."

Juliet stared at her sister, her words echoing in her head. A fork in the road! Yes, Juliet could feel it. This was one of only a handful of moments in life that truly made a difference. But how was she to decide? What was it she wanted?

Juliet closed her eyes because that last question was the only one she could answer without thinking, without hesitating. Because she knew that what she wanted was Henri.

She had always wanted him.

From that very first moment.

Back then, she had not known it, at least not the way she did now. But even on the day of their first meeting, there had been something between them that had whispered to her, urging her toward him. She still felt it today; only it seemed to have grown stronger over the years.

Being apart these past four years had not lessened it. Juliet had feared that it had, but the truth was that nothing had changed for her since that very first day. And if that feeling deep inside her had survived those four lonely years, would it not also hold on for the next four? The next ten?

Juliet could not imagine ever being free of him. She could not imagine ever being free to give her heart to another. Ultimately, this was her chance.

Her only chance.

If she wanted to be happy, then she needed to be daring now!

Violet chuckled, and Juliet looked up at her sister, seeing a wide smile come to her face. "Well," Violet said, giving Juliet's hands another encouraging squeeze, "what did you decide?"

Juliet inhaled a deep breath. "I know what I want," she stated, shocked by how good it felt to say it out loud. "I want him. I do. It is the truth, and deep down, I have always known it." She heaved a deep sigh. "However, this is not only my decision. Henri made it unmistakably clear that he—"

Violet lifted a hand to stop her. "I know my cousin better than anyone," Violet stated, her blue eyes shining with determination and a certainty Juliet wished she felt herself. "He has always been one to shy away from *emotional entanglements* as he used to call them." She chuckled, shaking her head. "In short, he is afraid to love, to give his heart to another because he fears to see it broken...again."

Juliet felt a cold chill surge through her body. "Again?" Indeed, the thought that Henri had once loved another brought a most torturous pain to Juliet's heart.

Shaking her head, Violet smiled at her gently. "It is not what you think." She breathed in deeply, and for a moment, her gaze moved to something far away. "When I first met Henri, he was already thirteen years of age. I was six and I remember I adored him from the first moment we met. He has always been daring and adventurous, never hesitating, always so certain of himself. I admired him for a long time and tried my best to learn from him, to be like him, to do things the way he did them." She shrugged, a wistful smile upon her lips. "Of course, over time I learned that I needed to be myself."

Violet rose from her chair and walked over to the window, her gaze directed outside at the far horizon. "When I first met Oliver, I...I remember..." A deep sigh moved her shoulders before she turned around and met Juliet's gaze. "I think I knew from the first that he was the one. I could feel something deep in my heart awakening whenever he would look at me, and I tried to push those feelings away, afraid of what they might change for me."

Never before had Juliet seen her sister so contemplative. Yes, it was true, both—she and Henri—always seemed so self-assured as though nothing ever truly surprised them, as though they never felt uncertain about anything. Juliet had always envied them.

Perhaps, though, it was not entirely true.

"When my father came to the beach below Silcox Manor that night," Violet went on, "everything changed for my mother as well as for me. All of a sudden, I had this life ahead of me. A life full of choices. Freedom." A deep smile lit up her face. "I had never had that before; however, the moment I got my first taste of it, I knew I could never allow it to be snatched from me again. I coveted it like my most prized possession, always afraid someone might take it from me."

Juliet nodded, understanding what her sister wanted to say. "You were afraid to allow yourself to love him, were you not? You were worried that binding yourself to him would rob you of your freedom."

Sighing deeply, Violet nodded. "I fought against it for a long time, but ultimately, it was no use. Ultimately, it wasn't a choice I could make." Shrugging, she moved toward Juliet. "The truth is that some things are not within our power. Whether we like it or not, we cannot choose who we love. All we can do, all we can decide is how we react to that knowledge, to the truth."

Rising to her feet, Juliet nodded. "I understand what you're trying to tell me; however, before you mentioned something about Henri..." Her brows rose in question.

Violet nodded. "He feels the same," she finally said. "He's not worried about losing his freedom." She scoffed. "Of course, men generally aren't!" She stepped forward and reached for her sister's hands. "Has he ever spoken to you of his mother?"

Juliet shook her head. "No, not once. I assumed she...passed."

Violet nodded. "She died long before I met Henri. He was no older than six or seven when it happened. I look at my parents, and I know that it was the same for his. They were in love. They were everything to one another, and then she died and Alain was forced to continue on without her." Utter sadness rested in her blue eyes. "I've heard my grandfather as well as my father speak of her and of what it did to Alain to lose her. He broke down completely. It was at that time that they decided it would be best for Henri to join my father on his trips. He has been sailing ever since."

Juliet heaved a deep sigh, understanding perfectly what her sister was trying to tell her. Yes, Alain had been forced to continue on without his wife. He had been miserable, heartbroken, and Henri had been there to see it. He had not just lost his mother, but he had also seen the pain it had brought to his father.

"As daring as he is," Violet whispered, something sparking in her blue eyes, "I don't think he will ever find the courage to risk his heart... at least not on his own, not without help." She held Juliet's hands tighter. "If you want him, then you will need to risk yours first, and make him see that you will not walk away, that, no matter what you will be at his side."

Juliet stared at her sister. "I'm not certain I can do that. I am not like you. I'm not brave. I am not—"

Violet laughed. "Is that truly what you think?" She shook her head. "You, my dear sister, are braver than you will ever know. You came out here all by yourself and—"

Juliet scoffed. "I was a fool to do so! Look what happened!"

"You were right to do so," Violet insisted. "You realized that you weren't happy. You realized that nothing would ever change unless you took charge. And you did, and it has brought you here." She looked deep into her sister's eyes. "Now, you need to take charge again. You need to make a choice. What do you want?" She heaved a deep sigh. "And know that no matter what you decide, you will not stand alone. I will stand with you. You will always have my help should you wish for it."

Tears shot to Juliet's eyes before she suddenly flung herself into her sister's arms. Always had Juliet envied her sister, not only for the freedoms she possessed, but, most importantly, for the family that never once hesitated to stand with her. Antoine and Henri had both risked their lives in coming to London to protect Violet when she had needed them. Neither one of them had hesitated even a moment. Had they been found out they would have been imprisoned, perhaps even executed.

Yet, it had not mattered.

Not to them.

Family stood together. Always. It was the Duret motto, and now, here, in this moment, Juliet thought that perhaps they might consider her one of them.

Wiping tears from her eyes, Juliet looked at her sister. "I want him," she stated loud and clear, "and I will do whatever I must to convince him that we belong together, that he needs me by his side as much as I need him." She closed her eyes, and a liberating chuckle left her lips. "Although I admit, I have no clue how to go about it. He is as stubborn as they come, and if I speak to him, he will no doubt—"

Violet shook her head. "Oh, no, of course, you shouldn't speak to him. The man is worse than a mule. You will never move him in a direction he does not wish to go."

Juliet stared at her sister. "Then what am I to do?" She threw up her hands. "What other choices do I have? If I do not speak to him, then—"

"You need to force his hand," Violet insisted, nodding along to her words as a slow grin spread over her face. "Trust me, dear sister. I know just what to do."

An excited shiver danced down Juliet's back at the wicked gleam in her sister's eyes. Still, she could not deny that here in this moment she felt stronger and surer of herself than she ever had before. Yes, if she wanted something, then she needed to fight for it. The world would not fall into place simply because she wished it.

No, life was not that easy. Yet Juliet's life had never been easy, had it? In truth, she was used to hardship and fear and doubt. Her life had never been her own, but now it was.

Now, this was her choice.

Her decision.

And she knew that she had made it long ago.

Chapter Twenty-One
ANOTHER FAREWELL

Knowing that time was of the essence, Henri quickly made his way across to the *Freedom* to see to Noèle. He found her settled comfortably in the sick bay, her face still pale, in stark contrast to her dark tresses. She looked weak and vulnerable, and every glance at her angry, bright-red burns once again stirred anger in his heart.

"Noèle," he whispered gently, kneeling down by the side of the cot, his hand carefully reaching for one of hers. "Noèle."

After a long while, she began blinking open her eyes. At first, they seemed unfocused and confused as though she had forgotten where she was or what had happened. The moment they fell upon him though, he could see the knowledge return. Pain and anguish came to her gaze, and he almost groaned at the sight.

"Henri," she whispered, blinking her eyes as they began misting with tears. "Will you ever forgive me?"

Henri gritted his teeth. "There is nothing to forgive," he told her in a voice as hard as steel. "You've done nothing wrong, and if he were here, Étienne would tell you the same." He gently squeezed her hand. "Do you hear me? No one would lay blame at your feet, least of all him."

Her eyes closed; a deep sigh rushed from her lips.

After speaking to Juliette, Henri finally understood that Noële's fears had little to do with her trust in him and more with her own disappointment. She and Étienne had shared a rare love, and they had longed for a child. And now, that he was gone, she had given birth to a little girl.

It seemed wrong somehow. Henri understood that now. She felt guilty, unable to make her peace with the man she loved. He was no longer here to tell her that none of what happened had been her fault, that she need not feel guilty for loving her child.

But Henri could. He was here, now, and he would tell her all she needed to hear.

Her slim fingers curled around his, holding on, as her eyes began to close once more. She looked so weak, so incredibly weak. Looking at her, Henri could barely remember the vivacious, young girl Étienne had brought home one day.

"Violette will take you back home," he told her quietly. "You are one of us, and we will take care of you. You need to get better; you need to find a way to heal because your daughter will need you."

Her eyes began to flutter once more before they slowly opened and met his.

Henri nodded. "That's right," he said, determination in his voice for her to hear. "I will go, and I will find her. No matter what it takes, I will find her. I promise you."

Noële's eyes closed once more, and tears rolled out the corners. "I thank you, Henri."

Henri exhaled a deep breath, then he leaned forward and gently placed a kiss upon her forehead. "Be well. Until I see you again." Then he rose to his feet and left the sick bay, knowing that he could not fail.

Not her.

Nor her daughter.

Nor Étienne.

Stepping out onto the deck of the *Freedom*, Henri's gaze moved to Violette and her husband. They stood close together, their heads bent toward one another, whispered words passing to and fro. When they saw him coming, they broke off and turned to look at him. "How is she?" Violette asked, sadness clinging to her voice.

Running a hand through his hair, Henri shrugged. "I've never seen her so broken," he mumbled, his gaze drifting back along the way he had come. His mind pictured her pale face, and for a moment, he closed his eyes before shaking his head, hoping to rid himself of the image. "If she is to recover—"

"—she needs her daughter back," Violette finished for him, her jaw clenched in a way that made Henri think of Antoinette.

Oliver wrapped an arm around his wife's shoulders, his gaze coming to meet Henri's. "When will you leave?"

"Now," Henri replied without hesitation. "There's no time to lose. We do not know how soon Dubois will recover or when he will leave his home port. Once he does, it will be much harder to locate him."

Both, Violette and Oliver, nodded in agreement. "Please, Henri, be careful," Violette warned him sternly, her blue eyes hard as they held his. "I want you back in one piece, do you hear?"

Henri grinned at her, because it was simply what he did. "You know me, *chère cousine.*"

Violet rolled her eyes. "That is precisely why I'm telling you this." She stepped forward and poked a finger at his chest. "Don't make me come after you! I promise, you won't like it!"

Henri chuckled and pulled her into his arms. "I love you, too, *ma petite cousine.*"

Placing a kiss on the top of her head, he stepped back, his gaze sweeping over the deck. "Where is Juliette?" he asked, feeling a cold shiver rush down his back. He could not help but think that asking after her showed too much interest. After all, Violette had always looked at him in an odd way whenever she had spoken to him of her sister.

Still, Henri knew he could not leave without seeing her at least once more. Even now, he felt something deep inside tug him toward her. They had been apart for no more than an hour or two, and he already missed her. How was that possible?

He had gone four years without her, but now that she had come back into his life, the thought of being without her ever again felt utterly crippling.

Yet he knew he had no choice.

Violette cleared her throat, and for a brief moment, her gaze fell from his. "She is already below deck," she told him, something apologetic in her blue eyes. "She said she did not wish to bid you farewell."

Henri's teeth ground together as he stared at his cousin, willing himself not to utter a single word. He could feel his muscles twitch, urging him to rush below deck and seek her out. But what would that accomplish?

Nothing.

Absolutely nothing.

Perhaps Juliette was wise to avoid a farewell. Perhaps if they saw each other even one more time, he might not be able to leave. Even now, something deeply painful constricted in his chest, suddenly making it hard to breathe.

Henri cleared his throat. "Very well," was all he managed to say, two words gritted out through clenched teeth.

Oliver nodded. "Good luck then."

"*Merci*," Henri replied gruffly as he strode past them and quickly swung himself over the rails, his feet landing once more on the deck of the *Voile Noire*.

This was his ship, his home, the one place in the world where he had always felt at peace. Now, however, something felt...different. It was as though something was missing, something that had not been missing before.

Instantly, his mind conjured an image of Juliette, her bright green eyes looking up into his, that shy, yet daring smile playing over...

Henri shook his head, trying his best to banish the image. Then he lifted his hand in farewell. "I will return with news as soon as possible. Tell Noèle that I will not fail her."

Violette and Oliver nodded in affirmation. The ropes holding the two ships together loosened and ultimately fell away. Slowly, the waves carried them apart, the gap in between growing slowly but inevitably.

Never before had Henri experienced such a moment. It felt weighty and final, and he could hardly bear it.

Moving to stand upon the quarterdeck, Henri issued commands for the sails to be lowered, all the while keeping his gaze fixed upon the *Freedom*. Ian stood at the helm, his calm presence a reassurance. His eyes were wide and watchful as they swept over the crew, allowing Henri a moment of contemplation.

The winds picked up as though wishing to speed their journey, confirming the rightness of his decision. They caught in the sails, pushing the *Voile Noire* onward, away from the *Freedom*.

Away from Juliette.

As Henri stood up on deck, his eyes fixed upon his cousin's ship as it grew smaller and smaller, he could not help but wonder what Juliette might do next. He knew it was none of his concern, and yet the torturous thoughts came.

Would she remain in England? Would she eventually marry and have a family? Or would she decide to travel on to India after all?

Henri did not know which choice he preferred. Either one would ensure that they would never lay eyes upon one another again. His mind told him that it was for the best. Still, there was another part of him, a part he rarely allowed to speak freely that could not help but regret the choice he had been forced to make.

Still, it was for the best. He needed to remember that. He needed to remind himself of that. What mattered was her safety. Nothing else.

Only once the *Freedom* had completely vanished from sight did Henri move from his position upon the quarterdeck. He strode across his ship from stern to bow, then he decided to climb up the rigging, feeling a sudden, almost desperate need to feel the wind in his face.

As the *Voile Noire* cut through the waters, Henri stood high up above the deck, one foot upon a wrung, one hand wrapped tightly around the rope of the rigging. His gaze remained fixed upon the distant horizon, directed south where they were headed, his mind focused upon what was to come.

Upon Dubois.

Henri was under no illusions that the man would willingly give up the child's location. However, there were always ways. After all, everyone had a weakness.

Even a man like Dubois.

Henri closed his eyes when that voice deep inside him suddenly whispered, *And you as well.*

Cringing away from the thought, Henri all but flinched when a call from the crow's nest echo to his ears. "Sail ho!"

Instantly, his head flipped around, his eyes spotting wide sails upon the horizon. The sun was slowly setting, and yet its warm orange glow still lit up the world.

Henri's heart beat fast as he quickly made his way down to the deck below. He hastened up to the quarterdeck and Ian tossed him a spyglass. "Dubois?" he asked, his mind already arguing against it. Yet in that moment he wished for nothing more but a release for this pent-up frustration lingering deep inside him.

Ian shook his head. "Spanish, I'd say."

Looking through the spyglass, Henri focused his gaze. Then he nodded. "I concur."

"Do we pursue?" the Scotsman asked; however, Henri had no doubt that it was merely for clarification's sake.

"*Non*," Henri replied, knowing that he would have to address his crew once more.

Before, they had been willing to follow him in his quest to retrieve Juliette. Now, he had no doubt that they would once again join him in locating Noèle's daughter. After all, Noèle was one of them, and whatever other differences they might have, the residents of *La Roche-sur-Mer* had always stood together as one.

That was the meaning of loyalty, was it not? To know that one was not alone, that if need be, others would come and fight.

Heaving a deep breath, Henri once again turned to his crew, assembling them up on deck. He could see questions in their eyes, and so he told them honestly—or at least as honestly as he deemed appropriate —what had happened to Noèle and her daughter.

Anger and outrage followed swiftly, and he could see determination and the will to do whatever necessary upon his men's faces. Étienne had been well loved. He had been one of them as well, and even with him gone—perhaps especially with him gone—the crew of the *Voile Noire* would do everything within their power to reclaim his child and bring her back to her mother.

Only when night fell did Henri step below deck. The day had been long and trying, and he felt strangely exhausted, longing for sleep and the oblivion it promised.

Midnight came and went, and his frustration rose. He knew the days ahead would prove challenging. He knew he would need his wits about him. He knew he would need to be well rested.

That, however, seemed easier said than done.

For hours, he tossed and turned in his bed, memories of Juliette resurfacing whenever he closed his eyes. Had it only been the night before that she had been here with him in his arms? For a moment, he could all but feel her skin against his, her breath mingling with his own.

But then the sensation vanished.

A growl of frustration rose from his throat, and he once more pictured the moment the two ships had turned down different paths. Anger swept through him when he remembered his gaze sweeping over the *Freedom*'s deck. She had not been there. She had not even stepped on deck to wave to him as a last farewell.

After raking his hands through his hair, Henri buried his face in the pillow. Frustration tugged at him from all sides, and he knew not what to do, how to rid himself of this...this emotion. He was furious with himself for showing such weakness, remembering the way his father had fallen apart upon his mother's death.

Always had he promised himself never to allow anything like that to happen to him. Every time a friend of his had found love and got married, he had reminded himself of the day they had buried his mother. He barely remembered her. What he did remember was the look in his father's eyes in the years that had followed.

Every once in a while, he could still see it; proof that his father was still grieving.

And would be for all the days to come.

If only—

Henri stilled as a soft noise drifted to his ears. He could not quite say what it had been, only that it raised the hairs in the back of his neck. It had been more than the soft roll of the waves beneath his ship or the creaking of wood or even the wind pushing the *Voile Noire* closer to its destination.

It had been—

Footsteps, Henri thought, his right hand reaching for the knife under his pillow. Yet, at the same time, his mind reasoned that no one outside his crew could possibly be on his ship, and he trusted them all beyond the shadow of doubt.

Still, if someone from his crew had come to alert him to something, would they not have made their presence known by now?

After all, his men were not known to be delicate creatures, tiptoeing silently to his bed to give him a soft shake upon the shoulder!

Who then? And why?

Lying still, Henri waited as the footsteps slowly drew closer. He could feel his body tense, preparing for whatever would come. And then he felt the soft touch of another's hand on his bare shoulder.

Not hesitating, Henri spun around, his hands reaching for the intruder, before he propelled them both sideways. His hands grasped delicate arms, and as he shoved the intruder down onto the mattress, a soft gasp drifted to his ears.

A moment later, moonlight glittered in through the window and fell upon the intruder's face, lighting up her soft auburn curls as they lay splayed across his pillow.

Henri froze, blinking his eyes as he stared down at her. "Juliette?"

Chapter Twenty-Two

A STOWAWAY

T he sun had long since set when Juliet heard footsteps
approach the cargo hold of the *Voile Noire* where she was
hiding. She held her breath, her eyes peeking through a small
gap in between two large barrels. Seeing the small light heading toward
her, she felt her heart beat wildly in her chest and wondered for the
thousandth time if she would be found out now.

Violet had urged her to remain in hiding for as long as she could,
guaranteeing that by the time Henri learned of her presence upon his
ship, the two vessels would be far apart.

Too far apart to turn back.

"*Mademoiselle?*"

Juliet exhaled a deep breath at the sound of Pierre's voice, then she
rose to her feet. "I'm here," she called quietly.

Violet had promised her that she would speak to Pierre and ask for
his help. Her sister had known Henri's crew for a long time, and so,
Juliet had once again placed her trust in Violet.

She had done so before, and she had never regretted it.

Pierre stepped toward her, a wide smile upon his youthful face.
"The captain headed below deck a few hours ago," he told her in a
hushed tone. "Most of the crew are asleep as well."

Juliet exhaled a deep breath, knowing that the moment of truth was upon her. How would Henri react to finding her upon his vessel? Would he be furious?

Juliet almost laughed. Of course, he would be furious! After all, the man had a temper and he was not one to hold back.

"You think it's safe for me to come out?" Juliet asked tentatively. She had waited for so long, eager for this moment of truth; only now that the time had come, she could not help but tremble with nerves.

In the dim light of his lantern, Pierre nodded. "*Oui, mademoiselle.*"

Juliet stepped out of her hiding place. "*Merci, Pierre*," she whispered, giving him a warm smile.

Even in the near darkness of the cargo hold, Juliet could see the hint of a blush come to his cheeks before he turned away and gestured toward the door. "This way."

Together, they slowly made their way out of the cargo hold and toward the captain's quarters. Everything remained silent, the only sounds around them the soft creaking of wood as well as the waves churning on the other side of the wall.

And then, Juliet found herself back in the companionway, the door to Henri's cabin straight ahead. She stepped up to it and placed her hand upon the door handle. Then she turned back to Pierre. "Thank you."

The young man inclined his head to her and then vanished into the dark.

Inhaling a fortifying breath, Juliet slowly pushed the door open and stepped over the threshold. Then she swiftly closed it behind her and paused. After the pitch-black darkness in the cargo hold, the captain's quarters almost seemed as bright as day.

The full moon shone in through the windows, illuminating the rough outlines of trunks along one side of the wall, the table and two chairs in the center as well as the bed across from her.

Upon it, she could see Henri, his head buried in the pillow, a strangled groan drifting to her ears.

Her eyes narrowed, and for a moment, she worried that he might be injured or in pain somehow. Then, however, she realized that it was agony that held him in its clutches. Was it possible that leaving her behind tormented him in the same way as the thought of leaving him felt to her?

Whatever it was, there was no turning back now. Juliet knew she had made her decision, and now, she needed to see it through.

Slowly, she tiptoed toward the bed, careful not to make any noise. Why she did so she did not know. After all, in a matter of moments, he would be aware of her presence here.

There was no way around that. No way to prolong the inevitable. Nor did Juliet wish to do so; after all, she was here because she wanted to be.

Because she wanted *him*.

The only question was, would he ever dare admit that he wanted her as well?

Inching closer, Juliet reached out a hand and touched it to his bare shoulder. His skin felt warm against hers, and yet she only had a moment for that thought to register.

In the next, Henri suddenly spun around, his large hand grasping her by the upper arms, flinging her over him and then down onto the mattress. She felt his weight upon her, his hands like iron shackles upon her arms before he moved, pressing cold steel to her throat. A startled gasp escaped her lips despite the fact that every fiber of her being cheered with joy to be close to him once more.

And then his eyes settled upon hers, and she could see the expression upon his face change. The tense set of his jaw slowly melted away as stunned disbelief filled his eyes. "Juliette?" he whispered, his voice almost choked.

Juliet smiled up at him. "Hello, Henri."

Still staring at her, he breathed in and out a couple of times before his head began to shake from side to side ever so slowly. "This cannot be," he mumbled as his gaze lazily drifted over her features. "You're not here." His brows knitted together, and then his gaze fell upon the blade at her throat and he jerked it away. "Is this a dream?"

Juliet could feel her heart dance in her chest, for the awed look upon his face seemed to speak the very words he could not bring himself to say out loud. "Do you dream of me also?" she dared him.

At her words, something fierce and barely held at bay returned to his eyes as he stared down at her. She could read temptation upon his face as well as the need to resist it; still, with each breath to leave his lips, she could sense his resolve waning.

"Do you ever dream of me?" Juliet whispered into the stillness, issuing her own challenge and hoping that for once he would bow his head in defeat.

A muscle in his jaw twitched, and when she wet her lips, his gaze darted lower to follow the movement. "Always," he growled, then he surrendered, and his mouth came crashing down upon hers.

Yet, Juliet could not deny that this was her victory as much as his!

Like a man possessed, Henri kissed her, his hands sliding up her arms and into her hair. She could feel an almost desperate need in the way he touched her, held onto her, a need that lived in her own chest as well. Indeed, he had thought her lost to him, gone from his life for good and now that she had returned, he was afraid to allow as much as a breath of air to come between them.

Juliet knew how that felt.

For four years, she had longed for him with the same desperate need, always afraid to think of him, to remember the moments they had shared for fear it would make her loss even greater.

And now, she was here, back in his arms, and the thought of losing him once more felt like a crushing weight upon her chest! No, she would not let him sail away from her again! No, for once, she would stand and fight!

For him!

For herself!

For both of their sakes!

Because whether or not Henri was willing to admit it, he craved her as much as she craved him. If she allowed him to send her away now, they would both suffer for it.

His kiss softened, and she felt his hands cradle her face almost reverently as though she were the greatest treasure he had ever found. The tips of his fingers trailed along the line of her jaw and then down the column of her neck as he brushed his lips against hers in a feather-light touch that brought tears to Juliet's eyes.

He truly cared for her, did he not?

Then Henri lifted his head, and his dark eyes once more stared down at her, the same stunned disbelief etched into his features as before. "You're truly here," he whispered, and for a short, fleeting moment, Juliet watched the corners of his mouth quirk upward into a smile.

A smile of deepest longing and utter joy.

Then, however, his jaw suddenly hardened as though he only now realized that she was indeed right here with him.

That this was not a dream, but the truth.

Juliet inhaled a fortifying breath. Let the battle begin!

Chapter Twenty-Three
FRANCE & ENGLAND AT WAR

The moment Henri realized that the dream he had thought himself lost in was no dream, he felt like a battering ram hitting him square in the chest. He all but flew backward and off the bed, stumbling a few steps as he continued to stare at her.

Panting breaths left his lips, and he blinked his eyes, desperately hoping that this—she!—was nothing more than a mirage. She had to be! She could not possibly be here! Because if she were...

Swallowing, Henri raked his hands through his hair, then over his face as he closed his eyes, praying that despite everything he was mistaken.

However, the moment his eyes opened once more, he saw Juliette sitting upon his bed, her auburn hair undone and glistening in the silvery light of the moon. Her eyes were wide and dark as she looked at him, her teeth sinking into her lower lip as she slowly pushed to her feet and then step toward him.

"Henri," she began, tentatively moving toward him.

Henri flinched, then he squared his shoulders and met her eyes. "Why are you here?" he asked breathlessly, his mind still unable to believe what was right in front of his eyes. "You're supposed to be on the *Freedom*. Violette is supposed to take you home." He shook his head. "You cannot be here!"

Patiently waiting for him to finish, Juliette then lifted her chin, the look in her eyes one he would never forget. "But I am here." Although her voice trembled, it, nevertheless, had a steely edge to it.

Shaking his head, Henri stomped toward her. He felt tempted to reach out and touch her, a part of him still not convinced that this was truly happening. "We agreed," he snarled, feeling her soft breath fan against his lips. "You were to—"

Juliette scoffed. "We never agreed," she insisted, her hands rising to settle upon her hips in an utterly defiant gesture. "You decided! You did not even consult me. You did not ask what I wanted. You decided and expected me to go along with it." Pressing her lips together, she shook her head. "Well, I did not." Her brows rose in challenge.

Exasperated, Henri once again raked a hand through his hair. "There was nothing to discuss. The only sensible course of action was for you to return home. You cannot be out here...at sea." He lifted his hands, his eyes sweeping over the cabin, a gesture to encompass the life that was his, but could never be hers.

"Why?" Juliette demanded. "I do not see you insisting that Violet remain home where she would be safe."

Anger tensed every muscle in his body, and he spun away from her, stalking a few steps to the door before whirling around to face her once more. "That is different. *She* is different. Violette knows this life. She knows how to protect herself. You..." Slowly, he shook his head. "You saw what happened the moment you left London." Holding her gaze, he moved toward her, seeing the pulse beat rapidly in her neck. "What do you think would have happened to you if I had not come for you when I did?"

Juliette's lips pressed into a tight line, and he could see that she did not have a ready reply. Indeed, after speaking to Noèle, Juliette knew beyond a shadow of a doubt what would have awaited her upon Dubois's ship. "That is not the point," she insisted, her voice, though, sounded weak.

Not saying a word, Henri held her gaze. He could see how unnerved she was by the suggestion behind his objection. Whether she liked to admit it or not, she had not been born to this life and did not know how to live it. "Why did you do this?" he asked, fighting the urge to reach for her and offer comfort. "Violette will be frantic to find you gone. How could you put her through this?"

To his surprise, a slow smile curled up the corners of Juliette's mouth. "Who do you think helped me hide upon your ship?"

Henri stared at her dumbfounded.

"The moment you went to see Noële," Juliette continued on, "Oliver distracted your crew while Violet smuggled me on board." She inhaled a deep breath, the look upon her face relaxed as though all doubt had suddenly fled her mind. "She told me I had to make a choice, and so I did."

Still staring at her, Henri slowly shook his head. "I cannot believe she did that. Does she not care whether you—?" He clamped his lips shut, unable to even finish the thought.

Of course, deep down, Henri was not surprised that Violette had acted in the way she had. Always had she walked her own path, ignoring all those who would argue against it. It had been that spirit that had led her to London four years ago.

To Juliette.

Oui, back then, Henri had been furious with Violette. He had been terrified that something might happen to her. And yet if she had not, if he had stopped her...

Looking down at Juliette, Henri inhaled a deep breath. It was true that he could not imagine her not being in his life. He hated to think of her back in England, married to some stuffed shirt. The thought turned his stomach. And yet, there was one that was worse.

"I will take you back!" The moment he spun around to head toward the door, he felt Juliette's hands grasp his arms.

"No, you will not! By now, the *Freedom* is too far away. If you turn back now," she moved to step in front of him, her wide eyes seeking his, "you will lose your chance to find Noële's daughter."

Henri felt his teeth grit together painfully as he realized that she was right. Was that why she had only revealed her presence upon his ship to him now? So that he would have no choice but to take her along?

Squinting his eyes, Henri stared at her, unable to believe that she would force his hand like this. "How can you do this to Noèle? You've seen her despair." He shook his head, disappointment settling in his heart. "How can you take this chance from her?"

Juliette swallowed hard; yet the look in her eyes did not waver. "I did not," she insisted. "You are if you decide to turn back. What I did did not delay us in the least. We can still head back south, return to the port where—"

Henri's hands flew forward and grasped her upper arms. "Are you mad?" he snarled into her face as he jerked her toward him. "Have you forgotten who we are going after? I cannot take you along on such an endeavor."

"Why ever not?"

Henri inhaled a slow breath. "It would be too dangerous."

"It is dangerous for you as well," Juliette pressed, "yet I do not see you turning back, either."

"That is different!" Henri retorted, releasing her arms and striding past her toward the window. What on earth was he to do now?

"How?"

"It simply is."

"That is not an answer!" He could hear her approach despite the fact that her bare feet upon the wooden boards barely made a sound. It was as though a part of him could sense her moving closer. It was the warmth of her body that reached out to him, and he knew she was there long before she stepped around him, her eyes once more looking up into his. "Tell me why!"

When he remained silent, her hands flew up and grasped his face. She stared up at him, a fierce demand in her eyes. "How is it different? Tell me!"

Henri tried to pull away, but she would not let him, holding on with a determination that made him want to reach for her. Never before had anyone insisted to be in his life.

Not in such a way.

Nor had he ever wanted anyone to.

Not the way he wanted it now.

"Why!"

Henri inhaled a slow breath. "Because I cannot lose you," he whispered, then he reached up and placed his hands on top of hers. "I simply cannot." He swallowed and then removed her hands from his face. "I need to take you back." Turning away, Henri reached for his shirt, donning it quickly before striding toward the door.

"If you send me away," Juliette called after him, a slight quiver in her voice, "does that not also mean that you lose me?"

Stopping in front of the door, Henri heaved a deep sigh, then he closed his eyes and rested his forehead against the rough wood of the door. He knew he needed to leave. He needed to head up on deck and change course. Somehow, though, he found himself unable to move.

To take another step.

And then he heard her move toward him.

Chapter Twenty-Four

RISKS WORTH TAKING

J uliet's legs were trembling as she stepped away from the window, her eyes fixed upon Henri's back as he leaned against the door, his head bowed. He looked exhausted and vulnerable, and Juliet hated that she had done this to him. Still, there was no other way. She could not give up now.

I cannot lose you, Henri had whispered and he had meant it. She had seen it in his eyes. Those four little words had given her hope, had told her that she had touched him in the same way he had claimed a piece of her heart as well.

"Can you truly let me go," she asked, unsteady steps taking her closer, "and then continue on as though...as though we had never known each other?" Her voice faltered, for the thought alone brought agony to her heart.

Henri's shoulder seemed to slump even farther. "I never said that," he muttered, then he slowly lifted his head and turned around to face her. "However, I'd rather have you half a world away than lying dead at my feet."

Juliet frowned. "Do you truly believe that is the way the world works? The moment you reach for someone they are yanked out of your grasp?" She reached out her hands and placed them upon his chest, feeling his heart hammer beneath her palm.

Bowing his head, Henri heaved a deep sigh. "I simply cannot risk it."

Juliet swallowed. "Violet told me of your parents."

Henri's head snapped up, and his eyes met hers.

"Their story breaks my heart," she whispered, reaching out to cup a hand to his face. "Of course, it is a fate I would wish on no one. Still, at least, they had each other for a short while. Do you not think that was worth it? Do you truly believe that your father regrets having met her? Falling in love with her?" Gently, she smiled up at him. "If he had not, he wouldn't have you."

Henri's lips thinned, and she could feel him tensing, leaning away from her. "We never spoke of her," he suddenly said, his voice rough and burdened. "Yet I cannot imagine anyone would choose to go through that."

"Not everyone suffers such a fate; surely you know that?"

Henri scoffed. "Enough people do. Only look at Noèle and Étienne."

"And what about your grandparents?" Juliet counteracted, determined not to let him talk his way out of this. "Violet told me that they have been married for almost fifty years now." She moved closer, brushing the pad of her thumb over his cheek bone. "And what about Antoine and Alexandra? Violet and Oliver? Do they not count?"

Holding her gaze, Henri slowly shook his head. "There is always a risk, and—"

"Yes!" Juliet interrupted. "Of course, there's always a risk. Always! Yet, if you're truly so afraid to lose the people you love, then why are you still here? Why do you always return to *La Roche-sur-Mer*? Would it not be easier to simply sail away and never return home so that you could forever imagine everyone you love safe and sound?"

He blinked, and for a second, Juliet thought that a part of him had heard her.

Juliet heaved a deep breath, willing her courage not to falter now. "And what about me?" she asked quietly. "Do you truly not know that I'm in love with you?"

For a long moment, his eyes remained upon hers, his own widening ever so slightly as her words slowly sank in.

"I love you, Henri, and I cannot bear the thought of letting you sail away again. I did it once, and..." She shook her head, remembering those four long, lonely years. "I regretted not speaking up every day that followed. I will not make that mistake again." She swallowed, feeling suddenly vulnerable as though she stood out in a snowstorm in nothing more than a light summer dress.

No words left his lips, and yet he reached for her. His right hand settled upon her waist, then slid farther onto her back, urging her closer.

Juliet complied happily, her heart beating fiercely in her chest as she stepped into his embrace.

His eyes searched hers, and she could feel the soft brush of his knuckles against her skin before his hand slid back into her hair once again. "I cannot lose you," he whispered as he grasped a fistful of her hair, a possessive gesture as though he was afraid she might float away if he did not hold onto her.

"You already lost me once," Juliet whispered in reply, reminding him of the time they had spent apart. "Did you think of me in those four years? Or was it only me? Did you—?"

His head bent down to hers, cutting off her words. "If you make me regret this..." His dark eyes burnt into hers as he held her wrapped in his arms.

Juliet smiled up at him. "This?"

Slowly, with his eyes never leaving hers, Henri dipped his head and placed a tender, almost fearful kiss upon her lips. It spoke neither of passion nor desire but of the first tentative step toward risking his heart...despite his better judgement.

Returning his kiss with a feather-light one of her own, Juliet whispered, "Do you know what I realized hiding out in your cargo hold for all those hours?"

His brows knitted together, a bit of an incredulous look coming to his face. "The cargo hold?"

Juliet shrugged. "Violet said it would be my best chance."

A muscle in his jaw tensed, and she could see how hard he fought the urge to argue his case once again. "What did you realize?"

Juliet sighed. "I thought I'd boarded that ship to India because it promised a new life. I knew if I remained in London, either I would end up an old spinster or I'd eventually give in and marry a man like Lord Dowling." She felt his hand upon her back tense. "It seemed... reasonable to leave England, to begin again somewhere else."

Closing her eyes, Juliet thought back to those many sleepless nights after receiving Clarissa's letter. At first, her friend's offer to join her in India had shocked her, and she had been certain she would never accept it. Then, however, her thoughts had begun to circle, to consider her life as well as its future from every possible angle, and she had realized that she could not simply dismiss it.

Still, when thinking of boarding a ship and sailing to India, another thought had entered her mind. It had never quite formed, for she had not allowed it, leaving her almost completely unaware of its existence.

Yet it had been there, and it had been that thought alone that had made her board the ship to India.

That one thought and no other.

"I always knew you were somewhere out there," she whispered to him, "out at sea while I remained in England. Despite my efforts to banish you from my thoughts, I often found them straying to you, picturing you on deck or at the helm or up in the rigging." She smiled, shaking her head at all those years with nothing but memories of a man she had once known. "It felt as though we lived in two different worlds, and I knew that there was no chance that our paths would ever cross again." She heaved a deep sigh. "At least, not as long as I remained in England."

Henri stilled, a slight frown coming to his face. "Are you saying...?" His eyes searched hers. "You boarded that ship hoping...?"

Juliet nodded as tears began to prick the back of her eyes. "I missed you so desperately. I..." A trembling sigh left her lips. "I had to take a chance."

Staring at her, Henri shook his head. "You're mad," he mumbled, and yet a hint of awe rang in his voice.

Juliet chuckled. "Perhaps you're right." She shrugged. "But I do not regret my decision. Of course, I did not know it at the time. I did not know then what urged me onto the ship. Perhaps if I had, I would have talked myself out of it. After all, what were the odds of us meeting out here on the open sea?"

Henri drew in a deep breath.

"But we did," Juliet told him, unable to hide that feeling of triumph that swelled in her chest. "Perhaps not completely by chance. If my mother had not sent—"

Henri's head swooped down, and he captured her lips in a quick kiss.

Juliet felt her knees begin to tremble as she looked up at him, remembering the night Fate had allowed their paths to cross for the second time. "If you had not come for me..."

His jaw tightened. "I will always come for you. Always."

Pushing herself up onto her toes, Juliet kissed him as he had kissed her only a moment earlier. "Why?" she asked then. "Why did you come for me, Henri? The truth."

For a brief moment, his eyes closed. "I could not bear the thought of you coming to harm. The moment I learned what had happened, I knew I needed to find you, to keep you safe, to..."

"The truth, Henri," Juliet urged, knowing beyond the shadow of a doubt that there was more. Another reason; just like there had been another reason for her to board the ship to India.

"I ached for you," Henri gritted out, the look in his eyes almost feverish now. "As long as you were out of reach, I could..." His lips clamped shut, that muscle in his jaw pulsing with something barely held at bay. "All of a sudden, you were so close. All I had to do was sail down the coast and..." He closed his eyes and rested his forehead against hers, a deep breath leaving his lips. "The truth is that I've craved you for four years, and now that you're here," he lifted his head and looked into her eyes, "I'm afraid I won't be able to let you go again."

Juliet could have shouted with joy. "Is that why you pushed me away? Why you all but ran from me?"

Henri swallowed hard. "I still think you shouldn't—"

"Do you want me?" Juliet interrupted, unwilling to allow him to get lost in his fears again. "Do you want me? Not only for one moment, one night, but..."

The longing expressed upon his face answered her loud and clear; and yet the moment his lips parted to speak, she knew that he would offer objections. "The risks—"

"Hang the risks!" Juliet exclaimed, pushing herself out of his arms. She stepped away, needing a bit of distance between them; still, her gaze never left his. "There are always risks. You know that. You've always known that." Her brows rose, daring him to contradict her.

He did not.

"You cannot live your life always worrying about all the awful things that might happen." Swallowing, she shook her head. "You cannot. Believe me! It would be a life of regret." Oh, all the regrets she had collected in her life! But no more!

Heaving a deep sigh, Juliet gathered her courage. This was it, the moment of truth. "Forget the risks," she said gently, feeling her limbs begin to tremble. "Do you...Do you want me? Now and tomorrow and the day after that and the day—"

The rest of her words got stuck in her throat when Henri suddenly shot toward her. Juliet flinched, all but stumbling a step backward, when his hands closed around her arms, yanking her back into his embrace. His eyes were dark, but the silvery glow from the moon seemed to ignite something deep inside them.

She saw sparks where there had been none before, and the feeling of his thundering heartbeat below her palm made her feel dizzy.

Henri Duret was not a man of carefully chosen words and elaborate declarations of affection. Despite the deep emotions that lived in his chest, he knew how to lock away his heart and hide it from the world and the people in it. It was safer that way...

...but also lonelier.

Only now, Juliet could see that something had changed. In truth, it had changed the moment he had learned of her mother's letter, had it not? Indeed, he had not hesitated to go after her. He had come for her, risking his own life in order to save hers. And although he had never whispered words of love, he had held her in his arms in a way that spoke loud and clear of how he felt for her, did it not?

Juliet smiled, for she could see the truth in his eyes. She could feel it in the way he reached for her, unable to bear the distance between them.

Pushing closer, Juliet looked up at him, feeling his breath against her skin as he exhaled slowly.

A tentative smile came to his face as his gaze swept over her features. He grasped her chin, the pad of his thumb gently brushing over her skin. "My little lioness, I never knew you could be so brave."

Juliet could not help but chuckle. "Neither did I."

Henri's smile deepened. "It suits you."

Juliet drew in a shuddering breath, overwhelmed by that odd sensation of discovering a part of herself she had never known was missing.

Brushing a tender kiss against her lips, Henri then pulled her into his arms and held her tightly. He did not speak as she had known he would not, but he held her, his arms wrapped around her, stating without doubt that he never wanted to see her from them.

With a deep sigh, Juliet sank into him and rested her head against his shoulder.

This was where she was meant to be.

She was certain of it.

Chapter Twenty-Five
RETURN TO MONPONT

With great caution, the *Voile Noire* sailed along the coast closer to the bay and the home port of the Dubois family. Like the Durets, the Dubois family called a small village upon the coast their own, a village that flourished because of the family's business in privateering. Henri knew that most people in *Monpont* felt the same loyalty toward the Dubois family as the people of *La Roche-sur-Mer* held for the Durets. Therefore, it would be advisable to proceed with great caution. If people found out that they were going after Dubois, there would be trouble ahead.

More than they had time for.

Especially with Juliette on board.

"The harbor looks deserted," Henri mumbled, looking through a spyglass at the place they had only left a few days earlier. Only now, Dubois's ship was nowhere to be seen. Only a few fishermen moved in and out of the bay.

"How do ye intend to proceed, Capt'n?" Ian inquired as he stood beside Henri, hands linked behind his back. The large wolf lay on the deck beside him, its massive head rested upon its front paws.

Henri inhaled a deep breath, thinking of Juliette down in the captain's quarters. She had still been asleep when he had woken early that morning, and he had been unwilling to rouse her from her slumber. She had seemed so peaceful, a soft smile playing across her features.

He cleared his throat. "I'm not quite certain yet," he thought aloud, unconcerned to allow his first mate to know the uncertainties he felt. "Since Dubois is not here and we don't know where he went, we first need to find a way to locate him." He heaved a deep breath. "The man could be anywhere." Running a hand over his face, Henri tried his best to focus his thoughts.

"Perhaps there is someone we could ask," suggested Ian, one eyebrow cocked as he continued to gaze at the distant coast.

"Someone who would share such information," Henri mumbled as one thought turned into another and then another. "Or can be made to share that information."

Beside Henri, Ian tensed, something rigid coming to his shoulders. "The man's family?"

The darkened note to Ian's voice suggested clearly that he disliked his own suggestion. Henri did as well; however, there might not be another choice. "Perhaps," he replied thoughtfully.

As far as he knew, Dubois was married, and his wife lived not far from the village in a large house; the same house that had once belonged to his parents. After all, like for the Durets, privateering was a family business for the Dubois'.

"I wonder if his wife knows his whereabouts," Henri mumbled under his breath. "His brother might; however, if he, too, is on Dubois's ship, then..." He shrugged, running a hand through his hair.

It seemed their options were severely limited.

"Did ye not say he had been injured?" his first mate interjected, his blue eyes moving from the coast to settle upon Henri's face. His brows rose in question.

Slowly, Henri nodded, remembering what Juliette had told him. Indeed, she had spoken of a bandaged leg, a burn from the fire that had injured Noële. "Indeed," he mumbled, once more lifting the spyglass to his left eye. "Perhaps he did not leave with Dubois." He smiled and looked up at Ian. "I suppose there's only one way to find out."

The Scotsman nodded. "Do we approach then?"

Henri shook his head. "No, the Durets have never been welcome in *Monpont*. I believe it would be better to not approach openly." Especially since it remained unclear if they had been seen the night they had retrieved Juliette and Noële.

Ian gave a quick nod of acknowledgment. "The dinghy then."

"*Oui*, the dinghy." He looked at his first mate. "See to everything. We shall leave at nightfall." Again, he thought, hoping that as before they would be successful.

Turning away from the coastline, Henri paused when he spotted Juliette standing at the bowsprit. Her hands were wrapped around the railing as she leaned forward and peered down into the waters. The wind tossed her auburn hair about, making it swirl around her head like a separate being dancing upon the breeze.

A smile came to his face, and he stepped down from the quarterdeck and headed toward her. He moved quietly and knew that she could not hear his footfalls above the howling of the wind. Coming to stand behind her, his chest almost touching her back, he reached out and swiftly grasped her by the arms.

A shriek left Juliette's lips, and he could feel her heart hammering in her chest as she sank back against him. "How dare you scare me like this?" she gasped, turning in his arms to face him. "I felt as though my heart was about to jump from my chest."

Ignoring his crew's curious glances in their direction, Henri smiled at her. "I'm sorry, but I could not help it." He paused, his gaze seeking hers as all humor left his voice. "There are always dangers, especially upon the open sea. You might not see them, but they are there, and more often than not, they will come for you when you least expect it."

The look in her eyes became thoughtful. "You think too much," she whispered before a teasing smile claimed her lips.

Henri laughed. "I assure you I have never been accused of that." He caught an auburn curl between his fingers and gave it a soft tug.

Casting a glance over her shoulder, Juliette sighed. "Is this it? Are we here?"

Henri nodded.

A shuddering breath left her lips, and a shadow fell over her eyes. "What will we do now?"

Again, Henri felt the urge to take her far, far away from this place and anything or anyone who might pose a threat to her. Yet, selfishly, he could not. "*We* will do nothing," he told her sternly. "*You* will stay here aboard the *Voile Noire*, is that understood?"

Giving him a bit of an annoyed eye roll, Juliette huffed out a deep breath. "Aye, Capt'n."

Henri felt the urge to smile at her, amused by the way she teased him. Before, in London, he had not seen that side of her. "Good."

"And what will you do?" A slight tremble went through her, and Henri could not help that feeling of triumph, of delight that she would care for him in such a way.

In a few quick words, Henri told her what he hoped to accomplish. "Quite honestly, I do not believe Dubois's wife knows anything of value. Our only chance is his brother."

"And if he is not there? If he left with Dubois?"

Henri did not like that thought. "Then we will have to wait for their return."

~

Standing on deck of the *Voile Noire*, Juliet peered through the spyglass, trying to glimpse the small dinghy upon the waves carrying them closer to shore. Night had fallen and turned the world into an ink pot, only illuminated here and there by the moon high above.

"Is it not too dark to see?" Pierre asked beside her.

Juliet sighed, lowering the spyglass. "I'm afraid so. I cannot catch more than an occasional glimpse of them."

"But that is good, *n'est-ce pas?*" Pierre replied. "If we cannot see them, then neither can anyone else."

Juliet nodded, casting him a quick smile. "I suppose that is true." Still, she could not help but hold the spyglass to her eye once again. It was a connection to the man who held her heart, the man who once again was putting himself in danger for another. Juliet wished there was no need for that, but, of course, she understood.

Noële needed her daughter back, and she could not help but worry for the child. Was Ophélie even still alive? What had happened to the baby after the fire? What had Dubois done with her?

Whenever Juliet remembered the time she had spent upon the man's ship, she could not help but shiver. Always had he seemed cold and detached, deriving cruel delight from seeing others suffer. He had enjoyed the power he had held over Noële and her, and she wondered what thoughts had gone through Dubois's head the moment he had regained consciousness the night Henri had come for her.

Only too well did Juliet remember that she had foolishly mentioned the Durets that one time when Dubois had stepped dangerously close. She had hoped to...

Juliet shook her head, unable to put into words what she had thought at that point. It had been unreasonable. She had been out of her mind with fear, and she ought not have done so.

But she had, and now she could not help but wonder if Dubois knew that it had been Henri who had robbed him of his prisoners.

Are you his? Dubois had asked her, and although Juliet had denied his question, she knew he had not believed her.

If he knew, what would he do? Juliet could not imagine a man like Dubois letting such an affront slide. What she could well imagine was the man coming after them at some point, desiring revenge or retribution for something he no doubt considered a wrong done to him.

What if this was a trap?

A cold shiver gripped Juliet, and she knew she ought to have mentioned this to Henri. What if his life was now in danger because of her foolishness? If only she had kept her mouth shut! If only she had not said a word!

"Do not worry, *mademoiselle*," Pierre said softly. "The captain knows what he's doing." He chuckled. "I grew up hearing stories of the daring Durets. First, Hubert, then Antoine, and now Henri. This," his arm swept outwards to encompass the world itself as it seemed, "is in their blood."

Juliet heaved a deep sigh. "I hope you're right, Pierre. I truly hope so." Indeed, the thought of losing Henri was one she could not bear although it helped her understand the fear she had seen in his eyes when he worried about her safety. Yes, it was a heavy burden, something she would have to carry from now on if indeed their paths would not lead them down different directions. Still, would it not be worth it?

"You will see that all will be well," Pierre told her confidently, his belief in his captain unwavering. "They shall return shortly. We will discover the child's whereabouts and then return to *La Roche-sur-Mer* for your wedding."

Juliet nodded along to his words, hoping with every fiber of her being that they would come true, until she suddenly paused upon hearing the last word to leave young Pierre's mouth. "Wedding?" she repeated, a frown coming to her face as she turned to look at him. "What do you mean?" She could not help but think that she had misunderstood him, and yet what else could he have possibly meant?

His forehead creased as his eyes swept over hers. "Have you forgotten? I suppose the past few weeks have been quite an ordeal; however,..." He gave a quick laugh. "How can any bride forget her wedding day? The captain will not be pleased to hear it." He chuckled.

Juliet felt her head begin to swim, and her hand tensed up on the railing. "Henri—Captain Duret told you that we are to be married?"

Pierre nodded before he suddenly stilled. "Oh, was it supposed to be a secret?" He glanced out to sea where he no doubt supposed Henri and a few others from his crew were presently rowing toward shore in the dinghy. "He only told us after you had been taken. We had only just returned to *La Roche-sur-Mer*, and the men had expected a few days off to spend with their families. However, that very same day, the captain returned and ordered everyone back onto the *Voile Noire*."

Juliet stared at Pierre as he recounted in a few short words what had happened after Henri had no doubt read her mother's letter.

"Of course, the men were displeased to be leaving so soon yet again," Pierre continued, a bit of an apologetic look upon his face. "However, the moment the captain told us that it had been his bride that had been taken, everything changed. As always, we stood as one and immediately went in pursuit of you."

Feeling her heart beat wildly in her chest, Juliet did not quite know what to say or how to reply. "Even though I was English?" she asked, not knowing why.

Pierre grinned at her. "The English are people, too, *n'est-ce pas?*"

Juliet smiled at him, grateful that he was here with her. He had such a cheerful and kind disposition that she could feel her unease retreat.

"Perhaps you will want to lie down, *mademoiselle*," Pierre suggested. "It will be a while before they return." He cast her another kind smile and then he turned and walked down the deck, his gaze briefly drifting up toward the crow's nest.

Juliet knew that he was right, and yet she could not seem to tear herself away. Why had Henri told his crew that she was to be his bride? Had it merely been to gain their support? Or...?

Juliet wished she knew, for the thought of being his bride painted a smile on her face unlike any she had ever felt before.

Chapter Twenty-Six

A TRAP

After reaching the shore, Henri decided that the best course of action would be to seek out the local tavern. After all, men deep in their cups generally possessed a looser tongue. Leaving Ian and his wolf behind as lookouts—after all, the two of them would have a hard time blending in with the rest of them—Henri and four of his crew entered the tavern.

Singing loudly, they pretended to already have imbibed quite a lot, their gait unsteady, before they dropped down onto rather spindly-looking chairs and ordered another round. Henri felt the eyes of many move to them and linger. He saw suspicion but also a mixture of curiosity and simple surprise. Perhaps even a hint of envy as well.

For perhaps half an hour, they simply sat there, drinking and singing and cheering. Then, Henri raised his glass to Dubois, praising the man loudly, before ordering a round for everyone present.

As expected, loud cheers went up all around him, and before he knew it, words were exchanged, questions posed, and answers whispered.

Yes, it seemed that Dubois had left less than half a day after the *Voile Noire* had set sail and headed out to sea. And although none of the men knew where Dubois had taken his ship, they were quite certain that his brother had not accompanied him. According to many, Benoît Dubois was up at the house, recovering from some injury.

After ordering another round, Henri and his crew slowly slipped from the tavern one by one. They regrouped with Ian and his wolf and then slowly headed away from the harbor. Keeping to the shadows, they slipped past silent houses and toward the towering one at the end of a large market square. No lights burned in any of the windows, and they quietly entered through the garden gate.

Henri could not help but wonder where Dubois had gone. If only he knew, if Dubois had recognized him that night, or perhaps any of the other sailors that had rushed up on deck. Yes, it had been almost pitch-black, but just a glimpse might have offered Dubois information Henri did not wish for him to have. After all, he knew Dubois to be a vengeful man.

Slowly rounding the house, four of his crew took up positions along all four sides, keeping a wary eye on everything that might move closer and thus pose a threat. In the meantime, Henri, followed by Ian and his wolf, stepped inside through the kitchen entrance. Everything around them was quiet as even the servants had already gone to bed.

Without wasting another moment, Henri strode down the hall and up to the first floor, barely aware of Ian's and the wolf's presence behind him. They all moved silently, heading straight toward the bedchambers. If only they knew, which one it was.

Henri prayed that they would not stumble upon Dubois's wife. A shrieking woman was the last thing they needed right now.

"Man," Henri heard Ian mumble under his breath, and as he turned around, he saw the Scotsman giving the wolf a slight pat on its head. "Man," he muttered again, his eyes directed at the large beast before his hand swept up and down the corridor.

As though understanding completely, the wolf lifted its massive head and sniffed the air. It moved a step forward then back before lowering its muzzle to the floor. Again, it sniffed, moving forward and backward before it suddenly paused.

Henri knew very little about his first mate's wolf. Never had the beast caused any stir, but it had simply been there, always by Ian's side.

Neither had Henri ever seen Ian train the beast; however, now it seemed that there was a deep understanding between the two.

Silently, the wolf moved down the corridor until it paused outside a large door. It lifted its head and sniffed again and again before it turned and looked back at Ian, one paw lifted.

Ian nodded, and he and Henri moved forward. When they reached the door, the Scotsman patted the wolf's head and mumbled words of approval. Henri pressed his ear to the door; when all remained quiet, his hand settled upon the handle, slowly pushing it down.

"Wait here," Henri whispered before he slid the door a short way open, enough for him to squeeze through. Then he closed it behind himself, remaining with his back to the door for a moment longer, allowing his eyes to sweep over his new surroundings.

Not surprisingly, it was a bedchamber like many others. Across from him, under two large windows, he spotted a massive bed, and upon that bed, a darkened figure lay sleeping.

Stepping closer, Henri could barely make out Benoît Dubois's features. Yet he knew it was him. This was the man who might lead them to Dubois and from there to Noële's child.

Henri knew he could not hesitate now.

Despite expectations to the contrary, Juliet had fallen asleep the moment her head had settled down upon the pillow. Henri's scent still lingered upon the sheets, and she had curled them around herself, hoping with every fiber of her being that he would return to her soon.

When voices from above echoed to Juliet's ears, her mind slowly began to retreat from the bliss of slumber. She blinked her eyes open and found darkness still thick and almost impenetrable around her.

Turning, she inhaled a deep breath, giving her mind a moment to wake more fully when a shot suddenly rang out above.

Juliet surged upward, her eyes wide and her heart hammering in her chest. Had it been a dream? She wondered before she quickly slid from the bed. Not knowing what might lie ahead, she had not undressed but merely removed her shoes upon lying down. Now, she refastened them quickly; however, the moment she stepped toward the door, thunderous footsteps echoed above her head and then another shot rang out.

Again, Juliet flinched, and her heart felt as though it were tripping over its own feet, unsteady and utterly terrified. What was going on?

Even considering the sheltered life Juliet had lived thus far, she knew that the sounds she was hearing were not good. Clearly, they were not sounds of Henri's return, of joy and satisfaction about a successful mission. No, something had gone wrong. Something *was* going wrong. But what?

Another loud *bang* echoed through the cabin before a shudder seemed to shake the ship around her. Juliet almost lost her footing, her arms spreading out wide to maintain her balance.

Still torn between remaining where she was and heading up on deck to see what was going on, Juliet found her decision made for her when the sound of footsteps echoed closer. Someone was coming! And although Juliet wished to cling to the thought that it was someone she knew, she did not think it to be true.

With her gaze, wide and unblinking, still fixed upon the door, Juliet slowly backed away, step-by-step until she felt the cool glass of the windows in her back. Still, footsteps continued to echo closer, each step more threatening than the one before. Her limbs began to tremble, and she cast a quick glance over her shoulder at the dark waters below. Yet, there was no escape.

And then, the door flew open, revealing not Henri's beloved familiar face, but Captain Dubois's instead.

Juliet almost fainted on the spot as the shock of the reality she suddenly once again found herself in slammed into her. How was this possible? How was he here?

With his hair slightly unkempt, the captain from hell looked at her, and a slow smile began to curl up the corners of his mouth. "What have we here?" he mused in a sickeningly sweet voice, one that echoed across time, reminding Juliet of the night Henri had come to take her from his ship. Back then, Dubois had cornered her as well, and she had been terrified out of her mind. Yes, in the last moment, Henri had come.

Somehow, Juliet felt certain that this time he would not.

Standing pressed against the windowpane, Juliet stared across the small distance of the cabin, her breath coming fast as a reminder to try to make sense of everything. What was she to do now?

Clearly enjoying the terrified look upon her face, Captain Dubois stepped into the cabin, his steps slow and measured as though he was enjoying each and every one of them. His gaze remained upon her, took a moment to study her face before drifting lower.

Juliet felt sickened to her stomach, and she curled her hands into fists, trying her best to hold onto her wits.

"I was hoping to find you here," Captain Dubois mused as he continued to approach, every step of his sending a chill down her back. "You set fire to my ship, and as far as I recall I promised I would make you pay, *n'est-ce pas?*" Despite the accusation falling from his lips, the look upon his face held amusement, enjoyment even.

Juliet shivered. "Wh-what are you doing here?" she stammered, her mind racing with how to respond to the threat he posed. She needed time; time to think, time to plan, time...for Henri to return. But would he? Could he?

An icy chill snaked its way down Juliet's back as a terrible thought entered her mind. "Where's Henri?" she asked almost breathlessly. "What did you do to him?"

Dubois laughed, a dark, sinister laugh that chilled her to her bones. "The man is a fool," Dubois said, a sneer upon his face. "Did he truly think I would ever let such an affront against me go unpunished?" Again, he laughed, something dark in his eyes that had nothing to do with this night's lack of light. "I knew he would return. I knew that little harlot would tell him how she and I knew one another." He chuckled, lifting his brows as he stared at her. "She told you as well, *n'est-ce pas?*"

Knowing that there was no use in denying it, Juliet nodded. "How could you do it?" she heard herself ask, unable to stop the words from pouring from her lips. "Clearly, your brother cares for her. How could you? Is there no one in this world you hold dear?"

Dubois laughed as though the thought itself was preposterous. "You are an amusing little spitfire," he remarked, another two steps bringing him within arm's length. "I knew I would enjoy your company."

Her jaw began to tremble, and she bit down hard to regain control of herself, lifting her chin as she held his gaze. "Why are you here?"

Grinning, Dubois leaned closer, and Juliet forced herself not to drop her gaze as she felt his breath upon her skin. "He took something of mine," he snarled into her face, his voice deathly calm, "and now, I'm taking something of his." Like a snake, his hands shot out and grasped her wrists.

Juliet gasped, urging herself to remain calm, well aware that any struggle would be futile and would only serve to amuse him more. "He will not care," she told him with as much conviction as she could muster in that moment. "I told you before I am no one to him." Even though Juliet knew her words to be false, speaking them felt awful nonetheless.

Dubois scoffed, and his hands upon her tightened painfully. "Do not play me for a fool, *Cherie*! Why would he come for you if indeed you mean nothing to him?"

Juliet swallowed hard, doing her utmost to hold his gaze. "He did not come for me," she replied, hating that tremble in her voice. "He came for Noële. She was his best friend's wife, and he had promised him that he would see to her." Dubois's brows drew together, and she could see doubt flash in his eyes. "He simply brought me along when he found me with her. That is all."

Dubois's teeth ground together, and a muscle in his jaw twitched angrily. "And where is dearest Noële?"

Juliet clamped her lips shut.

Dubois yanked her closer until the tip of his nose almost touched hers. "You might as well tell me, *Cherie*, for this very moment, my men are tearing apart the ship. If she is here, we will find her!"

Juliet closed her eyes, doing her best to think quickly. "She's not here," she finally said, forcing herself to look upon him once more. "He sent her back home. She was injured, as you well know, and she needed a doctor."

"And why did he not send you along then?"

Juliet lifted her chin, forcing a look of wounded pride into her eyes.

"I have no home to return to. After everything that happened, my family in England would never take me back. I am disgraced in their eyes." She bowed her head. "I have nowhere left to go."

"Look at me," Dubois commanded, and when she did not comply, he grasped a fistful of her hair and yanked her head back.

A gasp of pain escaped Juliet, and she drew in a sharp breath as Dubois's dark eyes looked down at her.

"I do not believe you," he snarled quietly as his gaze continued to search her face. "Yet it does not matter." His right arm curled around her waist, pressing her closer against him as a suggestive smile came to his face. "I shall enjoy your *company*, nonetheless."

He grinned, and Juliet wanted to retch.

Then Captain Dubois whipped around and pulled her along, out of the cabin and along the companionway. Juliet stumbled after him, trying hard to keep her feet under her, her wrist throbbing painfully from his tight grip upon it.

And then she felt the chilled night air brush over her face as he pulled her up on deck, yanking her forward. Juliet stumbled a few steps and then lost her balance, crashing down to her knees with a force that sent tears to her eyes. A cry of pain tore from her lips, and she closed her eyes, breathing in deeply a couple of times to regain her wits.

She could not break down now! Not here! Not in front of him!

Slowly, blinking back tears, Juliet pushed herself up onto her feet. Her gaze swept over the deck of the *Voile Noire*, and her heart constricted painfully as she saw injured men lying here and there, moans drifting from their lips and blood gushing from their wounds.

Her stomach clenched, and a sickening sensation rose within her. She clasped her hand over her mouth and then rushed to the side of the ship, bending over the railing as her stomach expelled its contents. She hung there for another moment or two, trying her best to breathe, to stop that shivering from shaking her senseless.

Sounds echoed around her, orders being yelled, mingling with the moans she still could not shut out. And then, a hand seized her once more, spun her around and pushed her back against the railing.

Dubois looked down at her, something contemplative in his gaze. "This is your doing," he snarled, grasping her chin painfully as he lowered his head to hers. "If you had not tried to escape, none of this would've been necessary. Remember that." Then he released her, and Juliet almost crumpled into a heap upon the deck.

Although she did not wish to, Juliet could not help the way her gaze once more swept over the carnage before her. She saw men she knew. She saw Jacques clutching his right arm, blood flowing from a wound upon his head. She saw Pierre, pale-faced and eyes staring into nothing, as he lay in a pool of blood slowly seeping from a wound in his back.

That cold shiver returned with full force, and Juliet knew she would never forget this gruesome sight. Had this truly been her doing? Had her foolish decision brought this on all of them? Indeed, she should never have left England!

"Bring her on board," Dubois ordered, once more seizing Juliet's arm before shoving her toward one of his men, "and lock her up!"

Allowing herself to be pulled along, Juliet spotted Dubois's ship drifting alongside the *Voile Noire*. How had this happened? How had they been able to come upon them unawares?

Juliet turned her head toward the coast. And where was Henri? Was he still alive?

In that moment, Juliet felt utterly exhausted, unsure what to hope for...if anything at all.

Earlier thoughts returned to her in that moment, and she bowed her head in resignation. Yes, it had been a trap but not for Henri. Not in the way she had feared.

If he was still alive, what would he do once he learned what had happened?

The thought brought agony to Juliet's heart.

Chapter Twenty-Seven
THE AFTERMATH

Moving swiftly up the small slope overlooking the coast, Henri jarred to an abrupt halt when his gaze fell upon the *Voile Noire* in the distance. A mere glance was enough to tell him that something was wrong.

Very wrong.

Behind him, his men drew to a halt as well, their breaths coming fast, for they were carrying Dubois's unconscious brother. Indeed, thus far, everything had gone according to plan. The man had not even awakened before Henri had knocked his lights out, and neither had anyone else in the house. On silent feet, they had made their way back to the coast, heading for the small dinghy they had left by a rocky stretch of land.

Glancing down, Henri could still spot where they had left it. Then, however, his gaze moved back to the *Voile Noire*, and his eyes narrowed.

"There!" Ian whispered beside him before his hand shot out and his finger pointed to the distant horizon.

Henri drew in a sharp breath when he spotted the other vessel slowly disappearing from sight; yet, it was still close enough for him to recognize the sails. "Dubois," he gritted out.

"Where did he come from?" one of his men asked, his eyes wide and his shoulders tense.

Henri shook his head, wishing he knew. "We need to return. Now!" Again, his gaze moved to the *Voile Noire*, and this time, it lingered. That feeling of unease crawled down his back yet again, and Henri squinted his eyes, trying to look closer.

Something was wrong; but—?

A jolt of panic swept through him the moment his eyes settled upon the soft orange glow shining out through the windows of the captain's quarters. "Juliette!"

"There's a fire below deck!" one of his men called barely a second later.

The exclamation froze all their limbs but for no more than a second. A moment later, energy surged through their limbs, and they rushed down toward the dinghy.

Quickly, they moved it off the rocky beach and back into the water. Dubois's brother was shoved inside without caution, and a moan drifted from his lips as he hit his head upon the back bench. Then they all settled into their positions, quickly rowing the boat out into the open waters and toward the *Voile Noire*.

Henri kept his gaze fixed upon his ship; his teeth gritted against the nausea that rolled through his middle. What had he done? Clearly, Dubois had expected him to return, and he had played right into the man's hands. How could he not have seen this coming?

Seconds stretched into minutes as they did their best to push the small boat through the water. Closer and closer, they got, their eyes widening and their hearts tensing as the soft orange glow began to grow bigger. Had this been Dubois's doing? Had he attacked the *Voile Noire* and set fire to her? What of his crew? And what of Juliette?

Henri gritted his teeth. He ought to have listened to himself. He ought never have allowed her to come. If any harm had come to her, it would be his fault! His alone!

Upon reaching the ship, the men quickly scrambled on board. The sight that met them turned Henri's stomach and brought anger to his heart. He saw his people bloodied and beaten, perhaps dead, and he did not even dare stop to help them. Instead, they all charged below deck toward the fire. If they did not manage to put it out, they would all be doomed!

A spark of relief came to Henri's heart when he found François rushing down the companionway, a bucket of water in his hands. How the short man had escaped Dubois's attention he did not know; however, he was grateful for it.

"Capt'n!" François called, relief blazing to life in his eyes. "I need to see to the wounded. Will you manage?"

Henri gave a quick nod, glancing at the other men from the dinghy who were already fetching more water. "Go!" he instructed the ship's surgeon, who immediately scrambled up the ladder.

"Where is Juliette?" Henri called after him, his insides tensing as he waited for an answer.

François paused for no more than a second, a look of defeat coming to his eyes. "I don't know, Capt'n." Then he was gone.

Again, it felt as though seconds stretched into minutes and then into hours as they rushed to and fro, fetching more and more water from the galley. The fire blazed in the captain's quarters, reminding Henri of the fire Juliette and Noële had set that night upon Dubois's ship as a distraction in order to escape. Was this a message? he wondered. How could it not be?

By the time the fire was finally out, the first light of dawn already peeked over the horizon. Henri's limbs trembled with exhaustion, and he saw equal looks of fatigue upon his men's faces. Fortunately, the damage to the *Voile Noire* was minimal. The interior of the cabin was destroyed; however, the structural parts of the ship remained intact. What had taken a severe blow, though, was the men's morale as they hurried up onto the deck in order to aid François in tending to the wounded. Fortunately, not a single member of his crew had been killed...

...yet.

While most wounds would eventually heal, François was most concerned with Pierre. The young man looked as though he had been beaten, bruises and cuts everywhere, his skin awfully pale. He had lost a lot of blood, his life force now a large dark stain upon the wooden boards. A shot had hit him in the back and torn through his midsection. Henri knew that a wound such as this was often deadly, bringing with it the danger of infection.

All morning, François still saw to the wounded, settling them down as comfortably as possible. And all the while, Henri kept thinking of Juliette. He tried his utmost not to picture her on Dubois' ship, locked in his quarters, at the bastard's mercy...but the images came unbidden. What if this time Juliette would not be fortunate enough to get away with only the threat of a kiss? What if this time...? Henri's teeth gritted together painfully as a menacing growl rose from his throat.

His muscles twitched with the need to go after her, yet he knew he needed to do right by his men. His heart felt as though it would rip in two at any moment, and he forced himself to turn away from the distant horizon and move below deck to sit beside Jacques.

The man looked as pale and shaken as the others. Still, something fierce burned in his gaze, and Henri knew that the man felt the same outrage and frustration he did.

"What happened last night?" Henri asked, still uncertain how Dubois had been able to surprise them. "Did you not see them coming?"

Shaking his head, Jacques shrugged. "We kept a lookout as you said, Capt'n, but all remained calm and silent." His eyes narrowed as he tried to remember what had happened. "Then a shot shattered the stillness," he closed his eyes and inhaled a deep breath, "and a moment later, Pierre fell out of the rigging."

Henri exhaled a sharp breath, his hand reaching up to rake through his hair. He hardly knew what to do with himself, with the pent-up rage inside him. His jaw clenched painfully as he fought to remain calm.

"I rushed forward," Jacques continued before he heaved a deep sigh, "but they had already been on board." He looked up and met Henri's gaze, his eyes overshadowed. "They were everywhere, dripping wet as they pulled themselves over the railing, knives between their teeth."

"They swam up to the *Voile Noire?*"

Jacques nodded. "We did not see them coming until it was too late." He closed his eyes and rested his head against the wall. "More shots were fired, and more men fell. We tried to fight back, but everything happened too fast and then Dubois' ship was right alongside us."

Henri swallowed hard. "Do you know what happened to Juliette?" He all but held his breath, watching silently as Jacques' eyes opened once more.

The man's gaze fell. "I'm afraid he took her, Capt'n." Anger hardened his voice. "He had her brought on board his ship and then set fire to ours before he sailed away." He shook his head, a deeply apologetic look coming to his eyes. "I'm sorry we failed you, Capt'n."

Fighting to hold onto that last shred of reason that remained, Henri met Jacques' gaze. "You did nothing of the sort. I should've seen this coming. I know the kind of man Dubois is. I should have known that he would find a way to get back at me." Now, Juliette was upon his ship once more.

"You could not have known, Capt'n," Jacques mumbled, fatigue beginning to close his eyes. "For all we could've known, he had sailed away searching for us. You could not have known it was a trap." Jacques' eyes closed for good, his chest rising and falling with evening breaths.

Carefully, Henri eased the man down onto the cot, hoping that he would recover swiftly. They needed to go after Dubois, and yet his crew was not up to it. What was he to do? He could not leave Juliette in the hands of that man. He did not even dare think of what Dubois might do to her. He only too well remembered what the man had done to Noële.

Rubbing his hands over his face, Henri knew that he needed to lie down. With each moment, the exhaustion in his limbs grew, and he found his vision blurred. Gritting his teeth, Henri blinked his eyes quickly, trying to regain focus.

What was he to do? Where was Dubois headed?

His head snapped up as he remembered that they, too, had taken a prisoner.

Benoît Dubois.

Perhaps his brother knew where Dubois was headed or at least could offer a reasonable assumption. Rushing out of the cabin, Henri turned to one of his men who came hastening down the ladder. "Where'd you put Dubois's brother?"

A snarl came to the man's face, disgust open in his eyes. "We put him in the brig, Capt'n."

Henri gave him a quick nod, and the man hurried on. "Then I shall speak to him," Henri mumbled to himself as he stalked down the companionway.

"Sail ho!"

Jarring to a halt, Henri felt his heart thud painfully against his rib cage as the call from the crow's nest continued to echo in his ears. His head snapped around, and his feet immediately turned toward the hatch. Had Dubois returned?

Frowning, Henri rushed up the ladder and up on deck. Why would the man leave and then return a few hours later? It did not make any sense!

Ian met him as he rushed forward, holding out a spyglass. "There!" he exclaimed, his chin nodding toward a tiny dot upon the horizon.

"Dubois?" Henri asked as he extended the spyglass. Then he paused, for the Scotsman's lips seemed to twitch ever so slightly. "Not Dubois?" He quickly fitted the spyglass to his eye.

The moment his gaze fell upon the ship with the billowing sails, Henri felt as though the air was knocked from his lungs. Never in his life had he felt such relief. "Antoine," he breathed as his gaze swept over the *Chevalier Noir*, the Black Knight, his uncle's ship.

Perhaps, now, there was a chance.

Chapter Twenty-Eight
IMPRISONED ONCE MORE

To Juliet, it felt like a bad dream to be back in this cabin that had once been her prison cell. Perhaps *once* was a far from accurate term; after all, only a few days had passed since Henri had come for her.

Still, being back here now, locked in the captain's quarters upon Dubois's ship felt utterly disheartening. Juliet's gaze swept over the familiar surroundings, parts still bearing marks of the fire while others had been replaced, and then lingered upon the cot where Noèle had always lain. Only now, it was empty. At least, Noèle was safe and sound upon Violet's ship, heading home. Had she already arrived? Was she already back in *La Roche-sur-Mer*?

Juliet heaved a deep sigh and sank down to sit in the very spot where she had always sat next to the cot. Tears began to blur her vision as the hopelessness of her situation swept over her. She tried her best not to think of Henri, but her thoughts conjured him no matter how hard she tried to direct them elsewhere.

"Where are you, Henri?" she sobbed, curling her arms around her knees as she hugged them against her chest. "Are you even still al—?" Her voice broke off as a deep pain surged through her.

Allowing her tears to fall as they wished, Juliet rested her forehead on top of her knees, slowly rocking herself from side to side. She knew she ought to keep her wits about her, but here, in this moment, it seemed impossible. What was she to do?

The answer to that question eluded her, and so, for a long while, Juliet allowed herself to break down, to cry and weep as she rarely had before. She allowed herself to fall into that deep dark abyss, hopelessness sweeping over her as she imagined the worst possible scenario that might await her. She imagined most upon the *Voile Noire* dead, and a shiver shook her as images of Pierre, beaten and bloodied, once more rose in her mind. Never would she forget them. Was he dead? Was Henri? Had they succeeded in apprehending Dubois's brother? Or had Dubois foreseen their plan?

If only Juliet knew if Henri was still alive. Not knowing weighed heavily upon her soul, and heart-wrenching sobs tore from her throat again and again. Yet, in the back of her mind she heard a faint echo of Dubois's voice, *He took something of mine, and now, I'm taking something of his.*

Lifting her head, Juliet brushed the tears from her eyes. Indeed, there was no use in stealing something from a dead man, was there? If Dubois truly wanted to repay Henri for what he had done, for stealing her and Noèle away from him, then it was only reasonable to assume that...Henri was still alive, was it not?

A small, hopeful smile tugged upon Juliet's lips. "He's still alive," she whispered again and again, needing to hear the words, needing to believe them. Yes, it made perfect sense. Dubois had taken her to get back at Henri, perhaps even to lure him into a trap once more. From what little Juliet knew of Dubois, she was certain that he was the kind of man who enjoyed seeing others in pain. She could easily imagine Dubois killing her in front of Henri, enjoying the sense of power it would no doubt bring him to see Henri stand idly by, unable to interfere. Was that what Dubois wanted? Was that his way of repaying what he clearly considered an unforgivable affront against him?

Yes, it made sense. But what did that mean for her? What was she to do now? What—?

Juliet flinched when heavy footsteps echoed along the companionway and toward the door she found herself staring at. It was Dubois; she was certain of it.

Scrambling to her feet, Juliet backed away until she felt the cool windowpane behind her. Her eyes were unblinking as she continued to stare, fear sneaking into her heart. What was she to do?

After all, Dubois would not kill her until Henri returned for her. No, the man would not rob himself of the enjoyment of such a moment. However, in the meantime...

The door flew open with a loud crash, and Juliet's head snapped back, colliding painfully with the glass behind her. For a moment, bright spots danced in front of her eyes, and she blinked rapidly, momentarily relieved to find Dubois's outline blurred, the unsettling look in his eyes unfocused.

Perhaps she ought to hit her head more often, Juliet thought, then she would not have to see that terrifying look upon the man's face. If only he could remain blurred for good!

Juliet paused as a distant memory drifted into her mind and...

"I apologize, *Cherie*," Dubois addressed her with a sickeningly sweet grin on his face, "for neglecting you." He chuckled darkly, then he kicked the door closed with his boot. "I hope you did not miss me too much."

Juliet felt close to retching, that sickening feeling once more crawling over her skin. Yet in the back of her mind, she could hear a voice, a voice from long ago.

Annabelle.

Many years had passed since Juliet had last seen her second cousin. She had been a child still; however, for some strange reason, she now found herself drifting back to that warm summer's day, Annabelle's laughing blue eyes looking into hers as she had said, "Any woman can swoon. Yes, it is common practice to awaken the suitor's protective side, to allow for a bit of close contact without the threat of ruination. However, I cannot help but think that gentlemen are no fools. Of course, they must know that it is indeed a common practice. Therefore, I do not believe them to be unaware of our intentions."

Juliet remembered how she had stared at her cousin wide-eyed, her own young heart beating fast at the wisdom that had shown in

Annabelle's eyes. Juliet had been no older than ten or eleven, and Annabelle had seemed like a worldly woman to her, revealing secrets Juliet knew nothing of.

Annabelle had huddled closer then, leaning down and whispering, a secretive gleam in her eyes. "So, if you do not wish for a gentleman to know what you're doing, you simply need to do it better. You need to swoon in a way that truly makes them fear that you are unwell so that you are not found out. Of course, it is still a lie; however, they will not be aware of it." A delighted chuckle, with a mildly wicked hint to it, had drifted from Annabelle's lips as she then had proceeded to demonstrate how a lady ought to swoon...without being found out.

Juliet blinked, her vision clearing as she found herself staring at Dubois. The look upon his face suggested that he had asked her a question or perhaps threatened her, and she had simply failed to respond. She saw displeasure and a touch of confusion in his eyes as he slowly moved toward her, his towering presence making her feel dwarfed and vulnerable.

So very vulnerable.

The terrifying truth was that he could do to her whatever he wished, and she would not be able to stop him. Her thoughts circled back to Noële, to the pain and anguish in the young woman's eyes, and Juliet felt close to fainting.

Again, Annabelle's teasing eyes appeared before her, and she felt a slight frown draw down her brows. Could she?

Dubois's hands snapped forward and seized her by the arms. "Look at me!" he growled, clearly displeased with her distractedness. "Look at me!" He gave her a violent shake, and the back of her head once more collided with the windowpane.

Juliet blinked up at him as Annabelle's voice continued to echo in her head, whispering instructions. "I...I'm t-trying," she stammered, allowing her eyes to close before willing them open once more. "My... My h-head..."

"Are you injured?" Dubois growled, holding her a bit away from him as his eyes swept over her face and then lower. "I see no blood." His voice was rough and rang with annoyance; clearly, he had envisioned this moment to be different.

Juliet did her best to focus on that feeling of detachedness, welcoming the blurry edges of everything she saw. She no longer tried to breathe in deeply in order to calm herself; no, instead she now took quick shallow breaths as Annabelle had instructed her. In an odd way, it felt as though her cousin was standing right beside her, telling her precisely what she needed to do. It felt oddly comforting, and Juliet reached for that straw.

Dubois's hands continued to hold her, his warm breath too close, the smell of spirits and something other, something rather unpleasant upon it. He held her roughly, then he suddenly moved closer, a dark chuckle rumbling in his throat. "Perhaps a kiss will wake you, *Cherie*."

Juliet wanted to push him away from her, but she forced herself not to. Instead, she continued to breathe rapidly, feeling the world around her begin to dim. Her eyes now barely opened, and the blurred outlines of all that she saw began to increase, to thicken. She could barely make out Dubois's face; yet, she could still sense him moving closer, one hand grasping her chin a moment before she felt his mouth close over hers.

The contact sent a shock wave through her, and for a split-second Juliet felt everything within her retreat as her knees buckled, no strength left in her.

And then there was blackness.

Chapter Twenty-Nine
THE DEVIL'S BROTHER

"What do you intend to do now?" Antoine asked, the look in his eyes one of carefully restrained anger.

Henri brought a fist down hard on the table, and it shook with the force of it. "I will go after her! After him!" he snarled, once again beginning to pace the small space of his cabin, the wooden boards now blackened from the fire. Fortunately, only the furnishings had needed replacing. "As soon as the necessary repairs are finished, we will pursue them."

Not saying a word, Antoine nodded, his calm gaze straying back to the map upon the make-shift table. "Where do you think he's headed?"

Henri shrugged. "I do not know," he admitted with a deep huff, feeling his insides twist and turn at the thought that...he might not find her.

Antoine inhaled a deep breath as his eyes flew over the French coastline edged onto the parchment. "He has a plan," his uncle muttered, his forehead slightly creased in thought. "Dubois is not one to improvise. What he does he does with thought." He looked up and met Henri's eyes. "We need to know where he is headed, and why."

Henri nodded. "Then let us go and rouse his brother," he snarled, feeling his hands ball into fists, his body dissatisfied with the immobility forced upon him.

Antoine bowed his head in acquiescence, and a moment later, the two men strode out of the captain's quarters and down the companionway toward the brig.

The dim light down in the ship's belly reflected Henri's mood perfectly, and he could not help but feel a certain measure of disappointment when he found Benoît Dubois awake upon entering the small cell. Indeed, a part of Henri had hoped for the chance to slap the man out of his stupor.

"Where is she?" Benoît demanded the moment they set foot across the threshold. Despite the paleness of his skin as well as the large bump upon his head from being tossed into the dinghy, the man seemed almost livid as he stood before them. "What have you done with her? Where is she?"

Completely caught off guard, Henri pulled to a stop, staring at his prisoner. Indeed, the very questions Benoît had just flung at his face were the ones he himself had meant to ask.

No doubt seeing the look upon Henri's face, Antoine stepped forward. "She?" he asked, crossing his arms over his chest as he regarded Benoît with mild curiosity. "Who do you speak of?"

A somewhat disbelieving laugh left their prisoner's lips as his gaze swerved from one of them to the other. "Noèle Clèrmont, *naturellement*. Who else? What have you done with her? Where is she?"

Henri inhaled a deep breath, remembering what Juliette had told him about the way Benoît Dubois had acted toward Noèle. "I hear you intended to marry her," Henri snarled, linking his hands behind his back lest he should be tempted to strangle the man.

Benoît inhaled a deep breath. "I still intend to do so," he replied, his jaw tense.

Despite his efforts to the contrary, Henri felt his right fist fly forward and toward his prisoner's face. However, in the last moment, Antoine stepped forward, his calm eyes meeting Henri's, his hand placed upon his chest, urging him back.

Benoît staggered backward against the wall, his eyes wide as he clenched his teeth. "What kind of man are you?" he snapped at Henri, a look of deepest disgust in his eyes.

Bowing his head, Henri chuckled, feeling completely at odds with this deeply surreal situation. "What makes you think you have any right to marry her? To speak of her in such a way after what you and your brother have done?" His tone was low and menacing, and he could see the effects of it upon Benoît's face.

"What we have done?" the man echoed Henri's words, a look of deepest confusion slowly etching itself into his face. "We saved her! We saved her after no one lifted a finger to help her." Frowning, he shook his head. "How dare you speak of her as though—?"

Henri shot forward and grasped the man by his shirt front. "You could not take no for an answer, could you?" Henri snarled into Benoît's face, savoring the man's widened gaze and the look of terror that came to his eyes. "You wanted her, and after she refused you, you sent your brother to—" His teeth gritted together, and he could not bring himself to finish the sentence for it conjured images he did not dare look upon.

"I did nothing of the sort," Benoît stammered, his hands trying to push Henri off him. "I never would have—" A frown came to his face. "What are you accusing me of?"

Henri was about to reply when he felt Antoine's hand settle upon his shoulder. "Let us speak calmly," his uncle said in a voice that did not allow for argument. "Henri."

Inhaling a slow breath, Henri forced himself to release Benoît. Then he took a step back and then another until his back came to rest against the opposite wall. Perhaps he truly ought to maintain a certain distance. "Very well."

Antoine looked from one to the other before he opened his mouth to speak. "Do you know where your brother is at present?" he asked Benoît, the look in his eyes as hard and unyielding as Henri remembered it from his childhood days.

Benoît swallowed, the expression upon his face clearly telling them that he did not wish to share any information. However, after a few more moments of silence ticked by, moments in which Antoine fixed

Benoît with a threatening stare, the man's head bowed. "He told me he would retrieve her," Benoît forced out through gritted teeth, reluctance swaying heavily in his voice. "He said he would bring her back to me."

Shaking his head, Henri chuckled. It was a dark sound, a disbelieving sound that spoke to the two very different sides of Bastian Dubois. Was it truly possible that his brother did not know the man's true character? Could he truly be unaware of the evil soul that inhabited Dubois's body?

Henri could not believe it to be so.

"And how did he say he would go about it?" Antoine inquired, nothing in his bearing revealing any sort of agitation. "When he left, where was he headed?"

Benoît shrugged. "He did not say. He merely told me not to worry, to rest and recover and leave all else to him."

"And you did," Henri snarled, doing his best to remain with his back to the wall and not take a step forward. "Like the innocent little brother, you pretend to be, you left this matter in his hands, not once questioning what he would do."

Frowning, Benoît shook his head. "What are you talking about? What did he do?"

"He attacked my ship!" Henri hissed. "He attacked my ship, severely injured my crew and," his teeth ground together painfully, "he took someone from me."

As the look upon Benoît's face darkened in confusion, Antoine added, "A young English woman by the name of Juliette. Do you know her? Do you know where your brother is taking her?"

"Well, that's not possible," Benoît replied without hesitation. "You are mistaken. He has no interest in any Englishwoman. He promised me he would retrieve Noële, free her from you so that—"

"Free her from us?" Antoine inquired. "Do you truly believe we would hold her against her will?" His frown deepened, and he took a step toward Benoît. "Were you there the night of the fire? Did she tell you what happened?"

Henri saw the sinews in his uncle's neck tensing as he spoke of the night that had seen Noële's life shattered yet again. For someone so young, she had lived through countless losses, most of her suffering due to Dubois.

Benoît expelled a sharp breath. "Was I there?" he asked, disbelief in his eyes. Then he pointed down to his bandaged leg. "Yes, I was there. I tried my best to save her, and I am afraid to say that I failed." He swallowed hard. "If my brother had not come along, she would have perished in the flames that night."

"If it weren't for your brother," Henri snarled, his palms pressed against the wooden boards of the wall, "there would not have been a fire."

Benoît was about to reply when he suddenly paused, his wide eyes narrowing as he looked at Henri. Then his gaze shifted back to Antoine, thoughts racing through his head as a deep frown slowly claimed his features. "What are you saying? You're not truly accusing my brother of—"

"I'm accusing your brother of nothing he has not done," Henri hissed in reply, once more tempted to push off the wall and charge toward Benoît. "Did he never tell you what he did to Noële? Did you never ask? Never notice?" He shook his head, his lips curling in disgust. "You're a fool! If you truly know nothing of which I speak, then you are a goddamn fool!"

Benoît exhaled slowly, the look upon his face still whispering of disbelief. Still, Henri could not help but think that a touch of fear now lingered in his eyes, the fear to truly have been mistaken, to have been made a fool.

"As far as we know," Antoine said calmly with a sideways glance at Henri, "it was your brother who caused the fire that night."

Benoît stared at him wide-eyed, but, for once, no words of objection tumbled from his lips.

"That is not all," Henri snapped, inhaling a deep breath at a warning glance from Antoine. "Did you know Noële has a child?"

"A child?" Benoît shook his head, his feet stumbling backward until he hit the wall. "No, you're mistaken. She…" Again, he shook his head, but looked at Henri as though asking for more.

Henri nodded. "A daughter. Ophélie." He briefly closed his eyes.

"Named after her late husband's mother." His gaze once more fixed on Benoît, hard and unwavering, an accusation in it that he saw reflected upon Benoît's face. "Do you know who fathered the girl?" His teeth gritted together so painfully that he barely managed to force out the words.

A brief look of confusion came to Benoît's face before it slowly began to wane, replaced by something that made Henri think that at least a small part of the man was not a fool. "You cannot truly mean to say that...?" He shook his head vehemently like someone knowing the truth but unable to accept it. "No! He would never!"

Pushing himself off the wall, Henri took a step forward, his arms once more linking behind his back. "But he did," he said with a calm he did not feel. "She told us that he came to her after she refused you. He tried to persuade her to change her mind, but when she refused, he lost his temper. He attacked her, forced himself upon her...and told her to reconsider."

For a long, quiet moment, Benoît Dubois stared at him, unblinking. Then, Henri saw tears beginning to collect in his eyes. "It cannot be," he whispered, more to himself than anyone else. "He would never..." He bowed his head, a deep breath rushing from his lungs.

"And then he returned the night of the fire," Henri continued, reminding himself that time was of the essence. If Benoît knew anything of worth, he needed to tell them! Now!

Lifting his head, Benoît looked at him. "Why?"

Henri scoffed. "Do you not know your own brother? Are you not aware that he takes it as a personal insult to be denied anything? Have you never seen how coldhearted and merciless he can be?"

Benoît stared straight ahead. "We had made berth in the harbor a little south of *La Roche-sur-Mer* that night," he mumbled, the look in his eyes distant. "He said that he had some business to see to and that I was to look after unloading the cargo. I promised him, but then..." He blinked, and his gaze settled upon Henri's. "I needed to see her." He shrugged, a helpless expression upon his face. "Almost a year had passed since I had last spoken to her, and...I simply wished to see her." He swallowed. "So, I borrowed a horse and rode north."

"And then?" Henri pressed, uncertain whether or not he truly wished to hear what had happened that night. What Noèle had already told him was enough.

Benoît's eyes closed. "At first, I did not notice anything out of the ordinary. Only when I drew closer did I see the soft orange glow flickering in one of her windows. It seemed to be from a candle, and so, I hurried closer. I peeked in the window and saw her lying on the floor, flames dancing around her." His gaze returned to Henri's, and the anguish in his eyes looked real; Henri had to admit.

"I rushed inside," Benoît continued, tears now silently streaming down his face. "I tried to pull her out, but then one of the ceiling beams collapsed. It pinned me down...and I couldn't move." Absentmindedly, he bent down to touch the bandage upon his lower leg. "I couldn't get to her. I couldn't." He looked from Antoine to Henri. "Then my brother burst in the door. He pulled me out, and I begged him to go back in for her." He inhaled a deep breath. "And he did. He saved her."

Antoine moved to stand in front of Benoît. "Your brother had no business to attend to that night," he said calmly, a certainty in his voice that made Benoît almost nod along to his words. "He went to see Noèle. He learned of the child, and once again, he attacked her. She said when she came to, he was gone and with him her daughter."

"We need to find him!" Henri snapped, striding forward. He came to stand beside his uncle, his hands balled at his sides. "Where would your brother go? Is there another place anywhere that holds meaning for him in any way?"

Benoît's gaze shifted to Henri. "She has a daughter?"

Henri nodded. "She does, and she wants her back." If that were at all possible. After all, Henri would not put it past Dubois to simply dispose of the child. He prayed that the man had not done so.

Benoît nodded. "I...I can try and speak to him. Perhaps he will tell me where..." He swallowed hard, disbelief still clouding his eyes.

Henri surged forward and once more grasped the man by his shirt front. "The child is not the only one we seek," he snarled into Benoît's face. "We believed Noèle dead, and so it was not she we came for that night. Where is Juliette? Where would he take her?"

Benoît blinked, his mind slow and clearly focused on other matters.

"He did not speak of her. He only said he would find a way to get to you." His eyes settled upon Henri. "He said he would save her." A dark chuckle rumbled in his throat. "He said he would save her."

As much as Henri wanted to plant his fist in Benoît's face, he knew in order to gain the man's support he would have to walk down a different path. And so, gritting his teeth against the dangerous impulse simmering in his veins, Henri turned to look at his uncle. "Will you give us a moment, please?"

Antoine's gaze narrowed slightly as he looked at him. "Are you certain?" Concern swung in his voice, and Henri knew that his uncle feared he would lose his temper. Still, when Henri insisted, Antoine took his leave, closing the door behind him.

Stepping back, Henri raked a hand through his hair, trying to collect his thoughts as best as he could. Never had he been one to speak from the heart, and now he needed to do so with one whom he despised.

"You love her, do you not?" he asked, looking at Benoît from the other side of the brig. "Noèle, you love her."

Inhaling a deep breath, the man slowly sank to the floor, his head resting back against the wall. "I do," he whispered, longing warming his voice. "I always have since the first moment I saw her. I knew she was married and happily so, but no matter what I did, I simply could not forget her."

Benoît's words echoed within Henri's chest. "I know that feeling," he willed himself to admit out loud.

The other man's eyes opened, and his gaze moved to meet his. "The Englishwoman? Juliette?"

Henri nodded. "I met her four years ago, and although I knew..." He shook his head, a deep sigh leaving his lips as he remembered the moment he had sailed away from England. "I've never forgotten about her." Seating himself on the opposite side of the cell, Henri looked across the small space at a man not quite as unlike him as he had thought. "Our paths crossed again by sheer happenstance, and..."

"Then she returns your affections?" Benoît asked, the look in his eyes telling Henri that he already knew. It was a mixture of compassion as well as regret because somewhere deep down, Benoît knew that Noële would never love him.

Henri chuckled. "I don't know why, but she does." Once more, raking his hand through his hair, he felt himself smile. "After taking her from your brother's ship, I told her I would see her safely home, but she refused. And when I insisted Violette take her home, she stowed away upon my ship, determined to stay...with me." A part of him could still not believe that she had done so, that she had chosen him.

"And then my brother attacked your ship," Benoît whispered, and it was not a question.

Henri nodded. "I need her back. I need to find her before he can —" He paused until Benoît's gaze met his. "I do not even want to consider the possibility of what he might do to her. There is no time. We need to find him." He gritted his teeth against a wave of despair that washed over him in that moment. "Will you help me...save the woman I love?"

For a long, seemingly endless moment, Benoît Dubois merely looked at him, exhaustion and disillusionment mingling in his eyes. He seemed like a man who no longer possessed the strength to even lift a finger, and Henri feared that all fight had finally left him.

"Please," Henri begged, knowing that there was no limit to how far he would go when it came to Juliette. "I will give you whatever you ask. You can have my ship. You...Anything."

Bowing his head, Benoît sighed deeply. "You're not the man I thought you to be." Then he looked up and finally nodded. "Yes, I will help you...if I can."

A sudden surge of energy chased itself through Henri's veins. "Do you know of a place he would go?"

Again, Benoît nodded. "There is an island," he replied, his voice hardening as the look of fatigue fell from him. "But you have to take me with you. That is all I want."

"Agreed," Henri replied without hesitation, wondering if in another life he and Benoît could have been friends.

Chapter Thirty

LACK OF OPTIONS

The first thing Juliet noticed upon waking was the sun rising in the east. Light streamed in through the windows and cast long shadows across the floor, reminding her that she had to have been sleeping for a long time.

Carefully lifting her head, Juliet glanced around the cabin, relieved to find herself alone. Slowly, she pushed herself up, her hand sinking into the thin mattress of the cot. How had she ended up here?

Squinting her eyes against the bright sunlight, Juliet frowned, trying her best to remember what had happened before she had fallen asleep. Had she fallen asleep? Indeed, the last thing she remembered was Dubois stepping toward her, stepping too close and then...

Her eyes widened when she recalled the feel of his mouth upon hers. A disgusted shudder surged through her, and she felt close to retching. Had he...?

Dimly, Juliet remembered hearing Annabelle's voice. She remembered urging herself to quicken her breaths, to make them shallow and deprive her body of its needed oxygen. Had she truly fainted? Had she truly made herself faint?

Indeed, it would seem so. Juliet could not help but think that her cousin would be strangely proud of her.

Letting her gaze sweep down and over her clothing, Juliet was relieved to find all still in place. No laces or buttons had been undone and re-fastened. Surely, she would know if...

Juliet swallowed, hating the uncertainty that continued to linger. Still, her rational mind argued that Dubois was the kind of man who would want his victim conscious. He would want to see the fear and disgust in her eyes, knowing that he had the power to bend her will to his. No, aside from that brief touch of his mouth upon hers, Juliet doubted that anything more had happened. It seemed he had merely placed her upon the cot when she had lost consciousness.

Relief and pride mingled in Juliet's heart; however, they were only short-lived because she knew that what had worked once would most likely not work a second time. Then what was she to do?

Even if Henri was alive and would eventually come for her, he would need time. She would need to give him time. But what to do about Dubois? Sooner or later, he would surely seek to...claim her once again.

Rising to her feet, Juliet staggered across the cabin, her legs weak and her steps unsure. She poured herself a cup of water and drank it down greedily, feeling its cool freshness reviving her body. She found a crust of bread upon the table and slowly began to eat as she moved back over to the windows. There, she sat down upon the floor, her gaze directed outward at the sea and the rolling waves below.

She needed a plan, something to do when she would next face Dubois. She thought of Violet and the moment she had seen her stand upon the quarterdeck of the *Freedom*, a sword strapped to her hip and pistol within reach. Never had the sight of Violet failed to inspire awe in Juliet. She was strong and dauntless, capable of defending herself and even coming to the aid of others. What did it feel like to possess such strength? Juliet wondered, knowing that these musings would not do her any good. After all, she was not Violet, and she never would be.

No, she was Juliet, a somewhat timid, innocent English lady, who knew very little of the world and even less of men. Still, did that mean she was completely incapable of handling herself? Of finding a solution to such an overwhelming problem?

My little lioness, Henri had called her, and had he not also called her brave?

Juliet heaved a deep sigh as she continued to watch the sun sparkle upon the sea's surface. No, if she was to find any way out of this, she needed to do it her own way. She could not pretend to be someone else. But who was she? What were her strengths? Did she even possess any?

Of course, she could not fight Dubois. He would subdue her in a matter of seconds. She could not even try to sneak off the ship; after all, they were out on the open sea. She was, in essence, trapped here...with him.

What then?

As had happened the day before, Juliet once again heard a mild echo of a familiar voice in the back of her mind. Only this time, it was not Annabelle's, but her mother's. "The art of conversation is a skill taught to any young lady, for in order to secure herself a suitable husband, it is crucial that she know how to speak to such a man. A lady is taught when to speak and when to remain silent, when to ask questions and show interest and when to retreat and rebuff. Conversation truly is an art, for it holds power. Never forget that, Dearest."

Of course, Juliet was not currently seeking a husband, and Dubois was far from a suitor. However, perhaps conversation might serve to distract him. After all, the man was most prideful, thinking highly of himself and demanding others do the same. He had felt insulted when they had fled his ship the night Henri had come for her. It had been the very reason he had lain in wait, stealing her from Henri as a means of retribution.

Yes, Juliet thought. She ought to speak to him, draw him into a conversation, a conversation that might loosen his tongue. Yet, what to speak about? What could she possibly ask him? It was almost impossible to imagine having a civilized conversation with a man like Captain Dubois.

And then it hit her: Noèle!

Indeed, Noèle was the one person who connected the two sides of Dubois, was she not? She had stood against him, and yet, he had triumphed over her. At the same time, she was a threat to him because one word from her lips might forever change the way his brother looked at him. Was that not why Dubois had always hovered close whenever Benoît had come to visit Noèle?

Juliet heaved a deep sigh, knowing that while it was not much of a plan, it was her only option. Perhaps if she managed to draw Dubois into a conversation, she could not only save herself, but perhaps she could also learn something.

Something vital.

About Ophélie...

...and what had happened to her.

Chapter Thirty-One

A LADY'S ASSETS

With her mind occupied, Juliet almost missed the moment Captain Dubois returned to his cabin. She did not hear the heavy boot steps upon the wooden boards nor the sound of the door creaking open. Only when Dubois's presence filled the small space did she look up from her spot in front of the windows, her heart speeding up the moment her eyes beheld him.

"*Bonjour, Cherie*," Dubois greeted her with a devilish grin. "How did you sleep?" He kicked the door closed behind him, his eyes never veering from her as he began to move closer.

Still seated upon the floor, Juliet wondered if she ought to rise. It seemed prudent to be on her feet when a threat moved toward her; however, there was nowhere to run. And so, she remained where she was, her back leaning against the wooden wall, her knees tucked close beneath her skirts. Still, she could feel the pulse in her neck hammering as she tried to breathe in slowly and deeply, the complete opposite of what she had done the day before. Now, however, she needed to remain conscious. More than that, she needed to hold onto her wits.

"Yes, I slept very well," Juliet replied, hearing a slight tremble in her voice, one she knew she ought to banish. "Thank you for asking."

At her reply, Dubois paused halfway across the cabin, his gaze narrowing slightly as he watched her. Juliet could see that her response surprised him. No doubt he had expected her to cower in the corner, to retreat, to hide. He had expected fear and perhaps bargaining, possibly another fainting spell.

Deep down, Juliet wondered if he knew that she had done so on purpose. Was that why he had inquired whether or not she had slept well? Had he tried to rouse her after she had lost consciousness? Short of asking him, Juliet knew she would not receive an answer. Ultimately, it did not matter, though.

"I see you have partaken of a bit of food," Dubois commented with a sideways glance at the table. "I hope it was to your liking." Again, he smiled that devilish smile, one that had deeply unsettled Juliet before. It still did, however, now, she was prepared for it. Her nerves still trembled, and yet, she hoped that her features did not reveal her inner anxiety.

"A bit stale perhaps," Juliet replied, casually arranging her skirts before she lifted her eyes to meet his once more. "However, I suppose one cannot expect a truly delicious meal upon a privateering vessel, now, can one?"

Dubois's brows drew down in confusion while the corners of his mouth quirked upward into an amused smile. "Are you insulting my hospitality, *mademoiselle*?"

Juliet shrugged, willing her fingers not to twist the fabric of her skirts as she fought to remain calm. "Not at all. I am merely pointing out a fact."

For a long while, Dubois simply looked at her, a hint of incredulity in his eyes like one presented with a problem he had not foreseen. Moments ticked by, and then, he did something Juliet would never have expected.

In two large strides, Dubois reached the window front and then sat down on the floor across from her, his back coming to rest against the opposite wall. His dark blue gaze swept over her face, and Juliet felt as though he was trying to look deeper, to unravel the mystery that eluded him. Finally, he asked, "How did a fine English lady come to be on a merchant vessel to India?" His brows drew down even more. "Come to think of it, how precisely are you connected to the Durets?"

Careful to steel her features against any kind of emotion, Juliet waited. She remained still, holding his gaze before slowly allowing a tentative, yet superior smile to show upon her face. She could see a spark of annoyance in Dubois's eyes; yet he held himself back. "Why do you ask?" she inquired, lifting her brows daringly. "Is it mere curiosity? Or do my answers truly hold meaning for you?"

Dubois inhaled a slow breath as he continued to watch her. She could all but see his impression of her altering, changing, adding new facets he had not taken note of before. "I do not know yet," he replied, then lifted his own brows, urging her to answer him.

Sighing, Juliet leaned back against the wall, trying to appear casual and unconcerned. "Well, it does not seem fair that you are the only one to receive answers," she remarked, careful to keep her feet tucked safely under her skirts. "If you must know, I, too, have questions I would like to see answered."

An almost pleasant-looking smile came to Dubois's face. "Then I suggest we take turns asking questions and seeing them answered." His gaze held hers, challenge lighting up his dark eyes. "Honestly, of course."

"Of course," Juliet replied with a gracious nod of her head.

For a moment, she thought Dubois might actually chuckle at her response, amusement showing clearly in his eyes. Fortunately, though, he did not, for she could not help but feel the sound would unnerve her too much. "Very well then." He shifted and settled himself more comfortably, fingers linked and hands resting upon one bent knee. "Tell me then, how did you—?"

Juliet shook her head, smiling sweetly. "No, no. Ladies first."

His mouth opened slightly as though he wished to argue; then, however, he slightly inclined his head and gave in. "As you wish, *mademoiselle*."

Clearing her throat, Juliet put a finger to her lip in a thoughtful gesture, pretending to be considering her question wisely. "Let's see," she mused out loud, her gaze still remained distant and directed out at sea as though she had all but forgotten his presence. "What I would most like to know is," her gaze shifted and moved back to meet his, "how you became the captain of such a magnificent vessel whereas your brother does not call such a one his own?"

This time, Dubois did chuckle, not only amusement but also pride ringing in his voice. She watched him inhale a slow breath, a breath that languidly lifted his shoulders before he exhaled and they sank once more, the look upon his face one of contentment as though he were truly enjoying himself. "It is a matter of ambition, *mademoiselle*," he told her without hesitation, pride mixing with no small amount of derision.

Indeed, it seemed to Juliet that Dubois appreciated his brother even more because in comparison Dubois himself would forever be the one to triumph. No matter what he might lose or fail to accomplish, in comparison to his younger brother, Dubois would always consider himself more successful. It was a constant competition, one he always won.

"Benoît has never longed to elevate himself," Dubois continued without the need for prodding. "He has always been quite satisfied with what he had, never trying to reach for more." His lips curled into a bit of a sneer, and he shook his head. "I, on the other hand, have always known what I wanted."

Without saying a word, Juliet lifted her brows in question.

Dubois chuckled, a wide grin coming to his face as he leaned forward. "More," he said simply, that one word describing him perfectly. Then, his back once more settled against the wall, his eyes fixed upon her. "I believe it is my turn to ask a question."

Juliet nodded her head in acquiescence. "Very well. What would you like to know?"

"Why were you on that merchant vessel?"

Juliet swallowed, trying her best to show unease at his inquiry. She needed him to think that he was gaining something from her that she did not wish to share. "I saw no future for myself in England, and when a friend of mine invited me to join her in India, I thought it might be a chance to start over."

A slight frown came to his face. "And why would you think you have no future in England? A lady such as yourself should have no trouble...procuring herself a husband." He grinned at her, and she felt his gaze sweep over her from head to toe, a suggestive curl coming to his lips that made her shiver. "Would you not agree?"

Trying her best to remain calm, Juliet slowly shook her head, allowing a smile to once again claim her lips. "Oh, no. You've had your one question. Now, it is my turn again."

Dubois's jaw tensed; however, he did not argue, but merely waited for her to continue.

"Do you have a family of your own?"

"I've been recently married," he told her casually, no affection ringing in his voice.

"Children?"

This time, it was Dubois who shook his head. "Is it not my turn again?" he asked with a grin.

Juliet feigned amusement then slowly shook her head. "I inquired after your family, which is a question that does not simply pertain to your marital status, would you not agree?"

Chuckling, he raked a hand through his hair. "No, I have no children as of yet." However, as he spoke, Juliet could not help but think that he was lying. He had a child, and he knew it.

Ophélie.

"How is it," Dubois charged ahead, clearly interested in seeing his own questions answered, "that you and Violette Duret are sisters? Is that not what you said?"

Inhaling a deep breath, Juliet explained how Violet and her mother had fled England many years ago upon Antoine Duret's ship. "After that, Lord Silcox married my mother," she told him, remembering the day she had met the man for the first time, a man not unlike Dubois, who cared very little for anyone else but himself.

He frowned. "According to your tale, the two of you had never met before she and her mother left England. How is it that you know each other now?"

Juliet parted her lips as though she were about to answer; then, however, she closed her mouth again as though suddenly remembering something. "I shall answer your question if you then grant me two." She lowered her brows daringly.

Dubois laughed. "I must say, I find you terribly amusing, *mademoiselle*. Quite frankly, most of the women I do not pay for their company generally cower before me." Again, his gaze swept over her in a most unsettling way. "You, however, are proving to be different." His brows rose teasingly; yet, to Juliet, it felt like a threat. "I find that intriguing."

Although Juliet's plan seemed to be working as well as she had hoped it would, she could not help that sickening feeling in the pit of her stomach. It was clear that Dubois could not be held at bay indefinitely. Eventually, she would run out of questions, as would he, and then...

"Very well. We have a deal, *mademoiselle*. Answer my question, and you shall have two."

Juliet granted him a gracious smile. "I suppose the essence of the story is that my stepfather, Lord Silcox, simply replaced the daughter he thought he had lost with me. You see, Violet had once been engaged to a Lord Dowling, an old friend of her father's. However, once she was believed to be dead, Lord Dowling once again was in need of a wife."

Dubois's brows rose. "You."

Juliet nodded. "You are quite correct."

"Still, that does not explain how you and Violette ever met," he pointed out, the look in his eyes intrigued as he leaned forward, eager to hear the rest of her tale.

"By sheer happenstance, Violet learned that I had taken her place. She felt guilty for having escaped the fate that was now forced on another, and so she came to England and offered me a choice." Heaving a deep sigh, Juliet remembered how she had first laid eyes on her stepsister. Back then, she had not believed a word Violet had told her; over time, though, everything had changed between them. "Ultimately, I chose to end my engagement to Lord Dowling, grateful to receive her support as well as her new husband's." She heaved a deep sigh, remembering the way her life had still changed despite everyone's best intentions.

"And yet, you were considered ruined," Dubois concluded correctly.

Juliet nodded, forcing her thoughts back in line. She held his gaze and once more allowed a smile to show. "My turn," she exclaimed joyfully. "What happened the night of the fire?"

The second the last word left her lips, Dubois's face turned dark. "Why would you ask that?" he snarled, clearly understanding the direction of her inquiry.

Feigning nonchalance, Juliet shrugged. "Well, so far I've heard two recountings of that night; however, they stand in stark contrast to one another. They cannot both be true, can they?"

"What did she tell you?" Dubois hissed, that cold, evil look back in his eyes that had made Juliet shudder before.

Doing her best to remain unaffected, Juliet narrowed her eyes as though in thought, as though she had not yet taken sides. "Well, let me see," she mused. "Noële told me that you came to her house that night in order to once again persuade her to accept your brother's offer of marriage. However, when she refused once more, you lost your temper and attacked her. She said when she fell, she knocked over a candle, which lit the house on fire. Is that not what happened?"

For a long moment, Dubois regarded her carefully, that sneer still upon his face. "Why would I attack her and then save her?"

Juliet shrugged. "I have no idea. It doesn't make any sense, does it? However, your brother said that he was the first one to arrive at the house. He tried to save her but could not. He said that then you came along and saved them both. Is that not true?"

Dubois inhaled a slow breath, and Juliet could see his thoughts circling around what to say. "And what if I had attacked her?" he asked calmly, his eyes fixed upon her face, waiting for her reaction. "What would you think of me then?"

Juliet inhaled a slow breath, knowing that the moment had come. There was no way around it. She would have to push and prod in order to learn something vital. "I do not believe it would change my opinion of you."

His eyes darkened. "And what, pray tell, is your opinion of me?"

Juliet gave a quick laugh. "Come now, you cannot truly be surprised that my opinion of you is quite low, can you? After everything you've done to me, how can I hold you in high esteem? Does this truly surprise you?"

For a moment, Juliet feared that he might surge to his feet and reach for her. Outrage clearly burned in his eyes, for men like Dubois never found fault with themselves. Of course, they always found ways to justify their evil deeds, never once laying blame at their own feet.

However, now, here, in this moment, Dubois remained where he was. "It does not," he growled, and Juliet was surprised to hear a hint of regret in his voice. Did it truly bother him that she did not look upon him favorably?

Again, he regarded her as though indecisive. She could see his jaw tightened with anger before the muscles slackened once more. He looked torn, teetering in one direction and then finding himself jerked back into the other.

"May I remind you, *mademoiselle*," Dubois suddenly continued, "that these are times of war. Men do what they must, what is required of them in order to serve their country." Once more, he leaned forward, his gaze holding onto hers. "The Durets are no different. They plunder and steal and attack." His brows rose. "Are you aware of that, *mademoiselle*?"

Juliet nodded. "Of course, I am not a fool. I am well aware that these are times of war. Make no mistake. However, I, for one, must draw the line at killing innocent, helpless children. What purpose does that serve?"

The look in his eyes was hard, and yet Juliet could not help but think that at least a small part of him regretted that she thought so lowly of him. "I have never killed a child," he defended himself. "Never."

Juliet felt her heart skip a beat as she forced herself not to show the hope that surged through her. "Is that so?" she asked as though they were merely discussing a hypothetical matter. "And what of Noële's child? She told me it was you who took the girl's life."

A snarl twisted up the corners of his mouth. "She lied," he growled, his hands balling into fists. "The harlot lied."

Juliet regarded him curiously. "And yet the child is missing, is she not? From what I understand, Noële has no notion of her whereabouts. If you did not kill her, then what happened? Was she left in the house? Did you save Noële and your brother but left the girl behind?"

Juliet could feel her hands begin to tremble at the notion of seeing a child find its end in such a way.

"Of course not!" Dubois exclaimed, clearly offended by the suggestion. "I merely sought to punish Noële for rejecting my brother. She broke his heart, and thus, she deserved to know what that felt like." A dark chuckle rumbled in his throat. "And so, I told her she would never see the girl again."

Juliet frowned. "And yet you did not kill her?"

A devilish grin came to Dubois's face. "I did not. I did not need to. All I had to do was ensure that she would never discover her daughter's whereabouts, and the result would be the same. Do you not agree?"

Feigning a thoughtful expression, Juliet then nodded. "I suppose that's true. Either way, the girl is lost to her." For a moment, Juliet was tempted to ask how he could speak in such a way of his own child. Was it possible that Dubois truly did not know that he had been the one to father Ophélie?

"Precisely," Dubois hissed, satisfaction lighting up his eyes. "The harlot deserves no less."

"And what of the child?" Juliet inquired, hiding her trembling hands in the folds of her skirts. "Is she not innocent in all of this? How will she grow up, always wondering who her...parents are?"

Dubois shrugged. "That is not my concern."

Juliet pretended to regard him for a long moment before she allowed her features to soften. "I suppose the important thing is that the girl will grow up. Still, I cannot help but wonder what a life she will lead." She let her gaze drift over to the window as though lost in deepest thought.

"She will grow up well enough," Dubois remarked absentmindedly, and Juliet willed herself not to look at him, afraid it might discourage him from sharing more. "The Duvals will see to it. After all, I paid them handsomely."

Juliet clenched her hands to keep herself from drawing in a sharp breath as her heart lurched in her chest. "Why would you do that?" she asked, turning to look upon him once more.

Dubois drew in a measured breath, his dark gaze locking onto hers. "Because she's mine." A slow smile curled up the corners of his mouth, and Juliet felt a cold shiver run down her back. "But you knew that already, didn't you?" His brows rose, daring her to deny it.

Juliet did not trust herself to speak, and so, she simply sat there, doing her best to hold his gaze.

After a while, Dubois unfolded his hands. "I see to my own. I always have and always will."

Juliet swallowed, wondering if she could make him reveal more. "But how can you be certain the Duvals will truly raise her well? Who are they?"

For a moment, Juliet actually thought he would answer. Then, however, something final came to his eyes. "Enough questions," he hissed, then he suddenly pushed to his feet.

Juliet felt the undeniable urge to run. It was an instinct that awoke whenever a predator drew near. Yet she knew there was nowhere to run to. She was aboard a ship, his ship, surrounded by endless water on all sides.

Lifting her chin, Juliet watched him as he slowly stalked closer. "Onto your feet," he commanded, his voice deadly quiet.

Juliet swallowed, then she slowly shook her head.

That amused grin once more returned to his face as he leaned forward, his dark gaze fixed upon her. "It'll be easier on you," he said in that low, almost caring tone, "if you do not fight me."

Fear snaked down Juliet's back. "Did Noèle fight you?"

His grin widened. "She did, and she paid for it dearly. But you already know that." His gaze held hers, once again daring her to resist.

Juliet knew that disobedience would be punished; and yet she could not bring herself to comply. At the very least, she wanted to know that she had done everything within her power to protect herself.

It would be a small mercy, but Juliet wanted it.

"I cannot," she finally said, wondering if she was imagining the spark of respect that flashed in his eyes.

Then, however, Dubois suddenly grasped her arms and jerked her to her feet.

Immediately, all thoughts fled her mind.

With his hands locked upon her upper arms, he shoved her against the wall and her head connected painfully with the wooden boards. "I like you," he whispered, a slow smile curling up the corners of his mouth as he leaned closer, "and I will enjoy your company more than I thought I would."

"What of your wife?" Juliet asked as she felt his body press closer. It was a stupid thought for a man like Dubois would not care about fidelity!

As expected, he laughed. "She will never know," he murmured against her lips. "There are two halves of my life, and I keep them separate at all times." He brushed a curl behind her ear in an almost tender way. "Back home, I'm an honorable and respected man. I obey the law and protect those I am responsible for. Yet out here," his grin widened, "I am a pirate and I take what I want without remorse or guilt." In the next instant, his mouth claimed hers in a plundering kiss that meant to possess and overpower, that told her without a shadow of a doubt what awaited her.

Juliet wished she could simply slip into unconsciousness again. Yet her body would not comply. Her mind remained in the here and now, forcing her to feel Dubois's hands upon her body, his mouth upon hers, forcing her lips apart.

A sickening sensation rolled through her, tensed her muscles and pinched her eyes shut. She could feel every fiber of her being revolt against the contact he forced upon her, and yet she knew she was completely powerless.

Dubois knew she did not want him to touch her, but he did not care. What she wanted did not matter. He held her trapped, her struggles were useless against his strength. It was a feeling of utter despair that claimed Juliet's heart, and she wondered if it would remain with her for the rest of her days.

Never would she forget it.

Never.

"Land ho!"

The echo of those two words drifting down from the crow's nest stunned Juliet as though a bucket of ice-cold water had been dumped upon her head. She tensed...and waited.

With a grunt, Dubois stepped back, annoyance upon his face at the interruption. "I suppose we shall continue this later," he muttered, glancing out the window where nothing but the endless sea was visible.

Releasing her arms, he straightened his clothes, a smug smile upon his lips as he watched her. "With time, you might come to like my attentions." Then he turned away and walked out the door, once again locking it behind himself.

The moment Juliet heard the key turn in the lock, her knees buckled, and she sank down, shivering uncontrollably as she fought against the wave of despair that threatened to pull her under. Still, nothing had changed. If she meant to come out of this alive, she needed to keep her wits about her.

Gritting her teeth against the trembling that shook her, Juliet reminded herself that she *had* distracted Dubois. She *had* made him speak and reveal a name. Duval!

Perhaps eventually it would prove useful in locating Noèle's daughter.

Perhaps.

Hopefully.

"Henri," Juliet whispered, her arms wrapping tightly around herself. "Please, come for me again. Please!" Letting the tears fall, Juliet rested her forehead upon her bent knees, her mind and heart momentarily too distracted to wonder where they had arrived.

Chapter Thirty-Two

A BROTHER'S BETRAYAL

"There."

Frowning at Benoît, Henri lifted the spyglass in his hands and peeked through, pointing it in the direction his prisoner indicated. They stood at the bow of the ship, feet slightly apart, braced against the rolling sea that rocked the *Voile Noire* up and down. "It is an island, you say?"

Benoît nodded. "A string of islands. Small and uninhabited." The man spoke through clenched teeth, and with every word that left his lips, Henri sensed his reluctance to speak at all. Disbelief every so often still flashed in his eyes as though he marveled himself asleep, lost in a nightmare, for he could not truly believe that his brother was the man Henri claimed he was.

Squinting, Henri tried his best to remain as still as possible, his eyes straining to see. Indeed, it seemed like a small speck of land in the far distance. "What is on this island?" He turned to look at Benoît. "Why would he sail there?"

Again, the man's jaw clenched shut, anguish in his eyes.

On some level, Henri understood him well. What Benoît was doing here upon the *Voile Noire*, sharing his brother's secrets with Henri, was betrayal.

Benoît Dubois was in this very moment betraying his brother. It was not an easy feat to accept, let alone make one's peace with.

As the wind continued to whip into their faces, Henri tried his best to remain calm and not push the man by his side beyond his limits. Although he, himself, was far from a patient man, he knew that sometimes it was the only course of action.

Eventually, Benoît's jaw relaxed and he turned to look upon Henri. "My brother has built himself a bit of a hideout there," he explained, reluctance still marking his voice.

"A hideout?" Henri turned his gaze toward the horizon before shifting it back to the man by his side. "Let me guess, it is a place where he stashes stolen goods, goods he ought to turn over to his country. Is that not so?"

Benoît's gaze narrowed, something accusatory sparking to life in his gaze. "He does what he does in protection of *Monpont*. Times are hard, and many people in *Monpont* struggle to make ends meet. My brother..." He swallowed. "He feels responsible, and he does what he can."

Henri fought to suppress a laugh that wanted to burst from his lips. "Is that what he told you? That all he does he does for the greater good of his people?" Sighing, Henri shook his head. "You've been to this island?"

Benoît nodded. "Not often. My brother is the one who sails whereas I mostly remain at home seeing to the other side of the privateering business." He paused, then shifted his gaze to Henri. "You should know what that is like. After all, your uncle and father have divided their business along the same lines, have they not?"

Henri exhaled a slow breath, his gaze again and again straying to that small speck of land upon the horizon. Was Juliette there? In this very moment? A part of him did not dare think of her, and yet he could barely stop himself from doing so. Always did she draw him near whereas the mere thought of Dubois sent him reeling back.

"Did your brother have cargo loaded before he left?"

Again, Benoît nodded. "Yes, he said he would head to the island before heading out to sea once again." He paused, a thoughtful look coming to his eyes. "I cannot think of a reason why he would bring the Lady Juliette along."

Henri could barely stop himself from punching the man in the face. "You cannot?" he growled, allowing utter disbelief to show upon his face. "Then you are either a fool or a liar."

At his words, anger sparked in Benoît's eyes. Of course, Henri had expected that. Still, he also saw no small measure of anguish and remorse. No doubt, the man was thinking of Noële and everything Henri had told him about what had happened to her.

At the hands of his brother.

Henri still was not certain whether or not Benoît believed him. At times, it seemed as though he did while at others, he was most reluctant. That, again, was understandable. Who would like to think of someone they held dear in such a way?

"I suggest we approach the island from the west," Benoît remarked, his gaze directed outward to sea. "It is marked by steep, rocky cliffs, and my brother's dwelling is situated on the eastern shore. There is a cavern nearby where he hides his ship." He swallowed and turned to look at Henri. "He will not see us coming." Again, a look of deep guilt came to the man's face.

Henri paused, torn between tossing the man overboard and offering him his thanks. "What will you do?" he finally asked, watching Benoît carefully. "When you find yourself face to face with your brother once more, what will you do?"

Benoît's eyes closed, and he breathed deeply once, then twice, before meeting Henri's gaze once more. "I do not know."

Henri nodded, well aware that doubt of his brother's guilt remained in Benoît's mind. He had heard all the accusations laid at his feet, and while a part of him knew them to be true, Henri suspected that only hearing a confirmation from his brother's lips would finally convince him. Would Dubois ever admit to what he had done? If his brother questioned him?

Henri did not know, nor did he care. All that mattered was to save Juliette. Yet, to do so, he would need Benoît's help. The question was, could he trust him? Not completely, of course. Yet to a certain degree?

Henri wished he knew; but only time would tell.

Stepping back, Henri moved back up onto the quarterdeck, pulling

Benoît along. Then he signaled to the *Chevalier Noir*, and before long, both ships turned westward.

"Return him to the brig," Henri told his first mate, and Ian immediately stepped forward as Henri took over at the helm.

As the Scotsman pulled Benoît toward the hatch, Benoît suddenly dug in his heels. "You promised to take me along!"

Henri nodded. "And I shall keep my promise. The moment we draw closer, you may return up on deck. You have my word."

Nodding, Benoît bowed his head and then followed Ian below deck. His shoulders remained slumped, and the very look of him never failed to make Henri wonder about the nature of people. How many on this earth loved and trusted someone who neither deserved their love nor the trust?

It was a chilling thought.

Shifting his gaze toward the *Chevalier Noir*, Henri breathed a sigh of relief. Yes, he, too, believed in his family. When hard times were upon them, they always stood together as one.

Always.

He breathed easier knowing that, and he could only hope that they would not be too late. That they would reach the island in time to protect Juliette from Dubois. Yet a part of Henri knew that even a minute alone with that man was one minute too many. Who would she be after suffering through such an ordeal? He remembered the detached and at the same time anguished look in Noële's eyes as she had recounted what Dubois had done to her.

Noële was a different woman now. She barely resembled the cheerful, lighthearted young girl Étienne had brought home. Yes, his loss had changed her, too. But this?

Who would Juliette be after this ordeal was over? Henri did not dare think of it.

Chapter Thirty-Three

A DESERTED ISLAND

With her hands tied behind her back, Juliet was pushed down the gangplank and onto a small pier on the eastern side of what seemed to be a small island; one among many, for Juliet spotted another piece of land sticking out of the ocean nearby. As they had sailed closer, her eyes had swept over dense woods, rocky cliffs and sandy beaches. Then, however, the ship had disappeared inside a large cavern, blocking out the sun and dipping everything into a dim light.

Dubois's right hand remained wrapped around her left arm as he moved her along with him. Her eyes took in the large cavern, seeing stacks of crates and barrels, as Dubois called orders to his crew, his men scrambling to unload even more from the cargo hold of the ship.

"What is this place?" Juliet asked as she lifted her chin, her eyes traveling to the stone ceiling far above. "Why are we here?" Indeed, once she had calmed down from Dubois's assault upon her, Juliet had begun to contemplate the possibility of another escape. She knew her chances would be slim to once again slip through Dubois's grasp; yet it seemed to be her only chance. Now, however, her heart sank when she realized that they had come to an isolated island. "Who lives here?"

Chuckling darkly, Dubois pulled her closer, his dark gaze watchful as it held hers, no doubt wishing to see the fear she felt upon finding herself here, alone with him. "I live here, *Cherie*," he whispered as though his answer would bring her joy. "However, I am willing to share my humble abode with you." Again, a dark laugh rumbled in his chest before he once more pulled her around and shoved her onward.

After a few more bellowed orders, Dubois guided her through a small passage that led out of the cavern. Juliet heard water dripping here and there and the distant sound of rolling waves. She even heard the faint twittering of birds as she moved along on the rocky ground. Before long, though, light shone in from the other side of the narrow tunnel, and after a few more steps, they moved out into bright sunlight.

A dense jungle seemed to surround them, the air warm and humid now at the height of summer. Again, Juliet's eyes swept over green foliage and vegetation of many forms and colors. She spotted rocks that seemed to grow into small mountains as well as endless beaches; however, what she did not spot was any sign of civilization.

Despite the heat, a cold shiver snaked down her back when she realized that Dubois had spoken the truth: they truly were alone on this island.

Once more, panic fluttered into Juliet's heart and she gritted her teeth against the urge to simply sink down into a puddle of misery. Yet Dubois kept his hand upon her arm, urging her onward; and so, she stumbled along, no longer seeing anything around her, her gaze turned inward to a place of her own.

When a voice drifted to her ears, Juliet's head snapped up. Her wide eyes traveled along the path ahead of her and fell upon a manor-sized house built into the side of the mountain. It was made from rock and wood with windowpanes and shutters as well as an iron gate that would keep uninvited guests out...should any ever find their way to this island.

"Does anyone else live here?" Juliet asked as her eyes continued to search for the person who had spoken. Had she misheard? Had someone from his crew called out to him? And yet Juliet could have sworn it had come from the direction of the house. Had it simply been wishful thinking?

Pushing open the gate, Dubois then shoved her up the cobblestone path to the front door. "This house is mine alone," he told her, pride ringing in his voice before another one of those dark, evil chuckles resounded in his chest. "However, under its roof, it houses a few people who see to its upkeep as well as my needs."

At his words, hope surged through Juliet's heart, but died a quick death when Dubois suddenly jerked her around, bringing her face close to his.

"I know what you're thinking," he whispered in a calm but lethal tone. "Everyone on this island is loyal to me. Don't for a second believe that they will assist you in another ill-conceived escape attempt." A broad grin came to his face as he leaned back and swept his free arm outward, indicating not only the house but the island in general. "I am king here, and no one would dare defy me." Again, he moved closer until the tip of his nose almost touched hers. "You'd do well to remember that."

Shock froze Juliet's limbs, and she almost fell as he jerked her toward the front door. Was he mad? It was the one thought that kept reverberating in Juliet's mind, the same way Dubois's words echoed within her head. What delusions of grandeur had the man tried to see realized upon this small speck of land? Had his words simply been forged by boastful pride or did he truly believe himself a king who ruled over his people?

The moment they stepped inside the house, distant voices echoed to Juliet's ears. Again, her heart leapt, and yet it no longer possessed the strength it had before, for Juliet did not doubt his words. Whatever he believed, the truth was that few people would ever dare stand against him. No, she would not find an ally on this island.

She was alone.

Again.

The truth was she had merely traded the ship, surrounded by water, for an island, equally surrounded by water.

Pulling her up the stairs, Dubois led her down the corridor before he kicked open the door to a bedchamber and pulled her inside. It had tall windows overlooking the bay, the view magnificent and breath-taking if it were not for the circumstances under which Juliet found herself in this place. "How long will we remain here?" Juliet asked, her voice breezy and trembling as she found herself facing yet another prison cell.

Dubois chuckled. "You will remain here until I tire of you. But do not worry, I shall return often to keep you company." The look in his eyes told her precisely what kind of company he was thinking of, and a sickening shudder gripped Juliet, almost forcing her to her knees. Hopelessness, the inevitability of something awful heading toward one, was the worst emotion Juliet had ever felt. And although it reminded her of the time her stepfather had forced her into an engagement to his oldest friend, then at least she had not been alone.

Now, here, there was no one to confide in. No one to whisper encouraging words. No one to help her dry her tears and get back up onto her feet.

Never before in her life had Juliet felt so utterly alone.

"I suggest you freshen up a little," Dubois suggested as he stepped toward her, reaching to untie her binds. "Do not worry. I shall lock the door to ensure that you do not...get lost."

Juliet closed her eyes as she felt his hands remove the rope from around her wrists. Her skin felt tender, and the moment she found herself freed of her binds, her hands reached to rub the tender spots. "When will you return?"

Looking down at her, Dubois approached slowly, the corners of his mouth quirking upward into an amused smile. "Are you so eager for my return?"

Squaring her shoulders, Juliet lifted her chin. "Do you want the truth or the lie?"

Standing barely an arm's length apart from one another, she watched Dubois's face still. His eyes continued to linger upon hers, and his lips thinned as though he had truly believed that she would rejoice at the thought of being assaulted yet again. Perhaps the man was truly mad; after all, who in their right mind would ever think such a thing?

Juliet waited for him to growl at her or even slap her in the face; instead, however, he merely inhaled a deep breath and then stepped back. "There is food and water upon the table," he remarked dryly, jerking his chin in the direction of the windows. "I shall return shortly." His brows rose in challenge before he spun on his heel and headed out the door.

Once again, Juliet heard the key turn in the lock, a sound she knew she would not forget for the rest of her life. Not even if by some miracle she were to find herself gone from this place tomorrow.

Stepping up to the window, Juliet looked out to sea, wishing she would see a black sail upon the horizon. Would Henri come? Was he even still alive? And if he was, would he find her? Was there any chance he would discover her whereabouts? Clearly, Dubois kept this island a secret. The stacks of crates and barrels she had seen down in the cavern spoke to illegal dealings, dealings that would get Dubois into trouble if they ever became known. What Juliet would not give to see that happen!

Chapter Thirty-Four
INTO THE LION'S DEN

"If you betray us," Henri hissed, grabbing Benoît by the shirt front the moment the small dinghy touched ground upon the rocky beach, "if any harm comes to her, I will end you. Is that clear?"

Sighing, Benoît nodded, the look in his eyes not showing a whispering of fear but of resignation instead.

Of disillusionment.

Of a life lived in vain.

"Good," was all Henri said in reply before he released Benoît and then turned to the men accompanying him. Of course, there was his first mate Ian as well as the large beast that constantly shadowed him. Since most of the sailors who had remained upon the *Voile Noire* the last time they had gone on land were still injured and not in any condition that would allow them to fight, if necessary, the same four men once more accompanied Henri who had also been with him that night in *Monpont*.

"Keep your eyes and ears open," he instructed with a stern look. "We need to remain out of sight for as long as possible while the *Chevalier Noir* inches closer to the eastern side of the island." His command was met with nods of acknowledgment.

The rocky beach rounded the steep cliff face on the western side of the island. It was a narrow stretch, but it allowed them to keep close to the towering rock, hiding them from view. Everyone remained alert; even the wolf constantly moved its ears as though carefully listening to every sound that drifted closer.

Henri's muscles remained tense as they tried their best to step quietly, which was not an easy feat upon the rocky beach. Pebbles shifted under their boots; fortunately, though, with no one nearby, the sound simply echoed upward on the warm summer breeze.

Once they headed into the woods, Henri felt the back of his neck begin to crawl with anticipation. One hand remained upon the hilt of his sword while the other lingered near the pistol he had strapped to his chest. His eyes swept their surroundings from side to side, every so often drifting ahead, squinting against the bright light. Still, the only sounds they heard were those of nature, of water and animals and plants.

Of the wind.

Henri knew them well and disregarded them quickly. Still, it made him wonder. Was this truly the place? Or had Benoît led them astray? Intentionally or not, had he brought them to the wrong place?

When a hand descended upon his shoulder, Henri snapped around, finding his prisoner right beside him, eyes widened in warning. He looked around their small circle, then he moved a finger to his lips to indicate they should remain silent. Then he nodded his head to the side.

At first, Henri saw nothing of worth, only dense foliage, bushes and ferns. Then, however, his gaze focused, and he spotted a small path leading up to an iron gate in the distance.

Benoît gestured away from the gate and toward the back of the house, indicating that there might be an easier way inside.

Nodding, Henri followed as did the others, stepping quietly as they approached. The closer they came, the more Henri thought to hear mumbled voices. No doubt, Dubois had a number of people serving him here in his hideout. Such a big structure needed upkeep and tending as did a man like Dubois.

Although a tall iron-cast fence surrounded the house, Henri

spotted no windows near the back where it was built into the rock face. Assisting one another, they climbed over and then silently dropped to their feet. Only the wolf remained behind, giving a low whine before Ian patted his head through the fence and told him to keep watch.

Henri could not help but wonder at the odd relationship between man and beast once more; yet he did not doubt that the wolf had understood precisely what Ian had asked of it.

A side door near a small garden allowed them entrance, and they soon found themselves in a darkened room that proved to be the kitchen. Only one window opened to the outside, casting a gloomy atmosphere over the entire work area. Fortunately, it was deserted...

...but not for long.

All of a sudden, a voice echoed through the door.

Someone was speaking or perhaps singing.

A woman.

Immediately, everyone dispersed, trying to make themselves as invisible as possible. Benoît gestured to Henri to remain where he was while he himself stepped into the middle of the room.

Henri gritted his teeth against the urge to jerk the man back, praying that he would not raise the alarm here and now.

And then the door to a storage room flew open, and a rotund woman stepped into the kitchen, her hair almost black and her face round as she hummed under her breath, a large basket filled with vegetables in her hands. The moment her eyes fell on Benoît, she paused before a slow smile came to her face. "*Monsieur* Dubois, I did not know you were here as well. Welcome back."

Benoît returned her smile. "*Merci*, Annette." His gaze briefly moved to the door. "Do you know where my brother is? There's something I need to speak to him about." Henri saw the man's jaw tense, his teeth no doubt grinding together, and he felt relief that Benoît seemed to be a man of his word after all.

At the question, Annette's face darkened, and her gaze fell from Benoît's. A hint of disapproval showed upon her face; however, she shook her head, and it vanished. "I believe he went upstairs," she remarked curtly, then turned and busied herself with the vegetables.

Benoît glanced at Henri over his shoulder, a questioning look in his eyes. Then he jerked his head toward another door that no doubt let out of the kitchen toward other parts of the house.

Quietly, Henri stepped out of his hiding place and slowly approached the woman.

Unfortunately, in that moment, she turned around. The second she beheld him, the basket tumbled from her hands and her eyes went wide.

Drawing his sword, Henri lurched forward. "If you scream, I will slit your throat!" he growled, narrowed eyes fixed upon her.

Instantly, the woman stilled, then her head bobbed up and down rapidly, signaling her acquiescence.

Quietly, Henri re-sheathed his sword, relieved that more often than not the threat alone was enough. He signaled to one of his men, who stepped forward and quickly tied the woman's hands before gagging her as well. Then she was pushed into the storage room, and the door closed and barred.

"We need to be quick," Henri hissed urgently, his thoughts focused on Juliette on one of the upper floors.

Alone...

...with Dubois.

Indeed, the look of disapproval upon the woman's face had told Henri everything he needed to know. *Oui*, they needed to be quick! "Do you know the way?" he asked Benoît, his muscles flexing with the need to move.

Benoît nodded and hurried onward.

~

The moment Juliet heard the key turn in the lock, she knew that her time had run out. Ever since the door had closed behind Dubois, she had lived from moment to moment, washing herself, brushing her hair and putting food in her belly, never daring to think about the next moment.

Now, however, she could not escape the reality that suddenly stood before her.

Stepping over the threshold, Dubois grinned at her. "I see you have taken my advice," he remarked as his gaze swept over her approvingly. He removed his jacket and tossed it aside, sweat running down his temples, which he brushed away with the sleeve of his shirt. "I suppose I could use a bath." His grin broadened. "Perhaps you might like to join me."

Juliet could have retched then and there on the spot. A part of her, wanted this to be over with as quickly as possible while another could not help but continue to look for a way out. "What is in all those crates and barrels down in the cavern?"

Dubois chuckled. "That is none of your concern." Closing the door behind him, he slowly moved toward her. "Undress."

That short, clipped word shocked Juliet to her core, and for a precious moment, she could not even back away, his approach bringing him dangerously close. Yet, where was she to go?

Again, that sense of hopelessness, of being trapped without a way out, washed over her, all but freezing her limbs and making them utterly useless. Perhaps she ought to try and pass out again, she wondered as her trembling legs carried her backward.

Tears rolled down Juliet's cheeks when she finally felt the wall in her back. She had reached the end of her options.

This was it.

Within a heartbeat, Dubois stood in front of her, his right hand grasping her chin to tilt up her head. "I suggest you do as I say," he hissed into her face, a predatory snarl contorting his lips.

Juliet gritted her teeth. "Never," she willed herself to say, her knees close to buckling.

In the next moment, Dubois slapped her hard across the cheek. Her shoulder connected painfully with the hard wall in her back, and her ears began to ring as bright spots started to blur her vision.

Juliet was just contemplating the possibility of baiting Dubois into knocking her unconscious when a voice called out from behind the door. "Bastien!"

After a momentary pause, Juliet felt Dubois turn away from her, her own vision still impaired. She continued to blink her eyes as her gaze tried to focus on the man by the door.

"Benoît?" came Dubois's voice, and she could hear surprise as well as a hint of suspicion. "What-What are you doing here? How did you...?" His words trailed off, and in the next instant, Juliet felt his arms pull her close.

Then something sharp and cold pressed against her throat, urging her to bend back her head until it rested against his shoulder.

"What did you do?" Dubois snarled beside her ear.

In the next moment, the door slammed into the back wall as another man charged into the room. Despite her somewhat unfocused vision, Juliet's gaze strayed to him in particular.

"Henri?" It was no more than a whisper that fell from her lips, and the moment she spoke his name, Juliet tried her best to caution the hope that grew in her heart. He could not be here! He could not! This was a mirage! A hallucina—!

"Juliette!"

At the sound of Henri's voice, her vision began to clear as though it had only waited for him to appear. She blinked, her eyes trailing over his face until she found herself looking into his familiar, dark eyes.

Although Juliet's heart danced with joy, the look upon Henri's face spoke of aggression, and her gaze instantly dropped to the weapons in his hands as he took a step forward. "Release her, Dubois! Now!"

Wrapped in Dubois's tight grip, Juliet stared at Henri, barely noticing the men who came pouring into the room behind him.

"How did you come to be here?" Dubois growled behind her, and she felt the blade dig into her skin as he jerked her closer against his chest. "Benoît, what did you do?"

Chapter Thirty-Five
FOR THE LIFE OF ANOTHER

enri wanted nothing more but to charge across the room and run Dubois through. Unfortunately, the man held a knife pressed to Juliette's throat, making such an endeavor far too risky.

"Benoît, what did you do?" Dubois snarled as his gaze shifted from Henri to his brother, his eyes wide and disbelieving.

Beside him, Henri felt Benoît square his shoulders and stand taller. He no longer held himself like a man wishing to cower in a corner, overwhelmed by guilt for betraying someone who deserved his loyalty. No, it seemed that seeing his brother hold a knife to Juliette's throat reminded him that there was another side to his brother he had thus far been unaware of.

But no more.

"What did *you* do?" Benoît returned the question, a most unfamiliar growl rising from his throat. "What did you do to Noèle?"

For a moment, Henri thought to see a flicker of shock in Dubois's eyes before the man turned his gaze to Henri. "What did you tell him? What lies—?"

"Stop!" Benoît shouted, his hands balled into fists. "Can you truly pretend you're innocent when you're holding a blade to a young woman's throat?" He swallowed hard and then held out his hand. "Release her! Now!"

Henri gritted his teeth as he forced himself to remain still. It was torture to remain where he was and simply watch everything unfold. However, it was worth trying. Perhaps Benoît could reach his brother. Perhaps he could persuade him to—

"You brought them here!" Dubois snarled, a wild look coming to his eyes. "You betrayed me!" Juliette winced as the knife pressed deeper into her skin.

"You betrayed m—!"

Henri placed a warning hand upon Benoît's shoulder. "Do not antagonize him or her blood will be on your hands!" he hissed under his breath unable to look away as Juliette craned her head backward to lessen the pressure of the knife.

Her face was pale and her green eyes so wide with fear and shock that Henri felt the weight of her pain as though it were his own. Her gaze remained upon his, holding on as though she was afraid that he might disappear if she dared blink.

Had she not known that he would come for her? Henri could not help but wonder. Had she truly had doubts?

"Whatever is between us," Benoît continued in a calmer voice, "let us speak about it in private." He nodded toward Juliette. "She has nothing to do with it. Release her."

Henri watched Dubois's face carefully, wanting to believe that all would end well, that Dubois would heed his brother's words. However, deep down, Henri knew it to be a futile wish even before Dubois's eyes once more glazed over with something crazed.

"No!" he snarled, his cold eyes moving back and forth between his brother and Henri. "You brought them here. You betrayed this place. You betrayed me." Inhaling a slow breath, he turned to Henri. "How many of you are here?"

Henri swallowed hard. "Four," he finally replied through clenched teeth, knowing that Dubois would never believe him if he said he had come alone. Still, there was no reason to mention Ian. The Scotsman was stealthy in a way Henri had never seen before. Perhaps...

"In here!" Dubois demanded. "All of them!"

Stepping back from the door, Henri gestured the other four of his crew inside. Everything inside of him rebelled against taking orders from Dubois; still, with Juliette's life on the line, he did not have a choice.

One by one, his men stepped inside, their heads bent in defeat, before they placed their weapons in a heap in one corner of the room as Dubois ordered them to do.

Out of the corner of his eye, Henri saw Ian slip silently down the hallway and far out of sight. "What now?" he demanded from Dubois, afraid to lose Juliette all over again after getting so close to retrieving her.

Dubois stared at his brother. "Tie their hands," he ordered, once more tensing his hold upon the knife when Benoît hesitated.

"Do it!" Henri urged him, his hands balling into fists as he watched Juliette struggle against the blade. She all but stood upon the tips of her toes, trying her utmost to lessen the pressure. Still, Henri saw a drop of blood well up and run along the blade before it slowly wound its way down her throat.

Once Henri and his men were tied up, Dubois ordered them to the opposite side of the room while he retreated toward the door, Juliette still clutched in his grip. "Benoît, come!"

Heaving a deep breath, Benoît looked at Henri, an apologetic look in his eyes. "I'll do what I can to protect her," he whispered, the tone of his voice making it a solemn vow. "You have my word. Please, ensure that he will never get to Noèle again."

Henri nodded, wondering how two men from the same family could be so vastly different. "She is family," he replied with another sideways glance at Juliette. "We will always protect her."

A touch of relief came to Benoît's eyes. "*Merci. Merci beaucoup.*"

"Benoît!" Dubois shouted as he kicked open the door with his boot. "Now!" Bowing his head, Benoît followed his brother out the door and into the hallway. "Close the door and lock it!" Dubois instructed, his hold upon the blade not lessening.

Henri's gaze remained fixed upon Juliette, her wide green eyes looking into his. The hint of a smile played over her lips as though she was grateful for this one precious moment they had been given to see one another...before being pulled apart once more.

"I will come for you!" Henri called out to her, needing her to know that nothing would stop him.

Nothing.

Again, her lips quirked as though she meant to smile. "I know," came a quiet, little croak before the door was slammed shut.

Cursing under his breath, Henri listened to the key turning in the lock, the sound of it so final that he felt it like a stab to the gut.

And then he waited, gesturing to his men to remain quiet. It would not serve them if Dubois heard them make their escape too soon. As hard as it was, they needed to give him a head-start. No doubt, the man would take Juliette and his brother onto his ship and then sail...

...where?

Still, even if Dubois expected the *Voile Noire* to be floating off-shore, Henri doubted he would be expecting the *Chevalier Noir* as well.

Agonizing moments passed, and then Henri heard a sharp *bang* echo to his ears from the other side of the door, the impact of what-ever had caused that sound making it shake upon its hinges.

"Stand back!" Henri instructed a second before the sharp bang came again, a splinter of wood shooting toward them as a hole appeared in the flat surface.

"Almost in!" Ian called from the other side before he brought what Henri suspected to be an ax down upon the door one final time.

As though it were made of paper, it sprang open, revealing the ax-wielding Scot, a determined look in his eyes.

"Did you see them?" Henri asked as Ian rushed into the room. He dropped the ax and reached for the sharp blade upon his belt, then Ian began cutting through the ropes that bound them.

Ian nodded. "He kept the knife upon her throat, looking around wildly as though expecting an ambush." A growl rumbled in his throat. "Otherwise, I woulda snatched her away."

The moment the rope fell away, Henri rushed over to retrieve his weapons while Ian freed his crew. Before long, they were rushing out of the room and down the stairs in pursuit.

"He headed out into the woods," Ian remarked as they rushed out of the house and toward the iron gate, passing a flustered-looking, bald man with a basket in his hands. He stared after them but made no move to interfere.

At the gate, pacing rather impatiently, Henri spotted Ian's wolf. The moment the beast was reunited with its master, a low rumble echoed in his chest. "Find her," Ian whispered in a low voice, his hand flying outward toward the woods.

In an instant, the wolf was off.

Henri could only hope that they would find her in time, that Dubois was not too crazed to realize when he was outnumbered. How did one deal with a madman?

Chapter Thirty-Six

OUT TO SEA

J uliet tried her utmost to dig in her heels, to make progress along the forest path most difficult for Dubois. To her regret, though, the man possessed ample strength, easily shoving her along, her feet tripping here and there as she struggled against him.

"Bastien," Dubois's brother addressed him as he kept pace with their steps, "this is madness. You need to stop. Release her, and we can talk about this."

Dubois laughed almost maniacally, the dark sound rumbling in Juliet's ear for he still held her pressed to his chest, the blade not far from her throat. "You betrayed me," he hissed, and Juliet felt his head turn ever so slightly as he no doubt glared at his brother. "You led them here."

Out of the corner of her eye, Juliet could see Benoît Dubois's gaze narrow. "You attacked Noële," he forced out through gritted teeth, "did you not?" A pleading note swung in his voice as though he still hoped that the truth was simply a lie.

Stopping in his tracks, Dubois whirled around, and Juliet felt the blade press painfully deep into her skin. She gasped, pushing closer against him in order to protect herself from the sharp edge of the knife, her hands clinging to Dubois's arm. "I delivered her to you as you wanted," Dubois snarled, "and this is how you repay me? With accusations?"

Juliet saw Benoît's face pale as he stared at his brother, disillusionment in his eyes. Then Dubois whirled back around and continued down the path through the grove and back toward the cavern. She heard him shout commands to his men when her eyes suddenly caught sight of something.

It was no more than a blur in the underbrush, there one moment and gone the next. She heard no sound as it moved, and for a long moment, Juliet wondered if she was merely imagining things. Then, however, for a split second, her eyes cleared, and she found herself looking into the yellowish eyes of a wolf.

Juliet's heart skipped a beat when she realized that Henri had not been completely truthful with Dubois. Indeed, the four men he had waved inside the chamber were not the only ones who had accompanied him to this island. There was another.

A tall, silent Scotsman.

But where was he?

Juliet clung to Dubois's arm as he pulled her down into the dark cavern, commands still flying from his lips as his men scrambled to see them done. A flurry of activity broke out, voices echoing back and forth, and once again, Juliet found herself dragged aboard Dubois's ship.

"Bastien, where do you intend to go?" Benoît asked, rushing after them. His gaze swept over the busy deck, a look of deepest regret in his eyes. "Do you truly intend to run from this? Is this the kind of man you are?"

Juliet did not see the look Dubois gave his brother; however, she saw Benoît flinch, his shoulders jerking in a way that made him seem utterly small. "I intend to blow his ship out of the water once and for all," Dubois snarled, a satisfied chuckle following his words. "Without a captain, that should be easy to accomplish." His gaze swept upward then across the deck and out to sea. "Fortune smiles upon us. The tide will pull us out and send us on our way." He once more turned to look at his brother. "At least, you betrayed me at an opportune moment." Again, that dark, somewhat maniacal laughter rumbled in his throat.

Juliet met Benoît's gaze, a silent plea in her own. Still, the man's face was pale and his eyes wide, and Juliet knew he was no match for his brother.

Her hopes fell as the waves slowly carried the ship out of the cavern.

Rushing after the large beast, Henri paused when they came upon a narrow tunnel. Dark rock kept out the sunlight, dipping everything into darkness. He blinked his eyes, waiting for his vision to clear before he continued along the stony path. Indeed, it seemed that Dubois had made himself quite at home on this island. He had used the landscape well in order to shield himself from unwanted eyes, caverns, woods and cliffs hiding the fact that the island was inhabited. From far out at sea, nothing of his hideout was visible.

Stepping into a large cavern, Henri ran his eyes across the small pool of water, now empty, the waves slowly rolling outward. "*Merde!*" he cursed under his breath, his hands falling into fists as he moved along the edge of the water to peer out the opening of the cavern. Wide horizon and endless sea met his gaze, Dubois's ship already too far out to reach.

"What now?" one of his men asked, his jaw clenching as he, too, no doubt contemplated their rather hopeless-looking situation. "We left the dinghy on the other side of the island."

Henri ran his hand through his hair, trying his utmost to remain calm and think. His blood was pumping through his veins, urging him onward, and yet he knew that one wrong step might doom them all. "We need a better vantage point," he mumbled as he paced along the water's edge. "At least, the *Chevalier Noir* should be close by now."

Ian nodded. "Before we entered the tunnel, a path snaked off to the side. Perhaps it will grant us a better view."

Giving a quick nod, Henri rushed back out into the tunnel, hearing his men following behind him. The path Ian had referred to was not one frequently traveled, and so, they had to duck often and push branches out of their way as they moved onward. Behind him, Henri heard the occasional gasp of surprise when a branch hit one of his men in the face. Still, they moved without delay, picking their way carefully, but swiftly, as the path curved upward.

And then, the thicket cleared, and Henri found his gaze sweep over blue skies.

Wind blew strong high up on the cliff top, the waves churning below, as he stood there, and his eyes immediately flew to Dubois's ship, heading out to sea.

"They're already too far away!" a member of his crew remarked, defeat in his voice.

Henri gritted his teeth at the sound of it, unwilling to allow it into his heart. No, he could not allow himself to be defeated. Not now. Not here. Not when Juliette's life was at stake.

His gaze swept westward, and there, coming around another cliff face reaching into the ocean was the *Chevalier Noir*.

No doubt, his own ship with only half the crew capable of seeing to their stations would lack somewhat behind. Still, Henri was certain that she too would soon be in pursuit. "Head back down to the beach," he told his men, without removing his eyes from Antoine's ship. "Get the dinghy and row out to the *Voile Noire*. Then follow as swiftly as you can."

"We will never catch them," came a mumbled voice from behind. "They're too far out."

Henri felt Ian step up to him. "Capt'n, what is yer plan?" Suspicion rang in his voice.

Inhaling a deep breath, cherishing the refreshing coolness of the sea air high up here, Henri slowly turned to meet his first mate's gaze. "My uncle's ship has a better chance of catching up," he said simply, the look in Ian's eyes telling him that he agreed. "I need to be on it. I cannot hang back."

Not saying a word, the Scotsman nodded. Then he looked over his shoulder to the other four men and gave a quick nod of his head, sending them along to follow their captain's order.

A few more grumbled words followed as his men turned down the path once more, heading back to the rocky beach and the dinghy they had left behind.

Once they were out of earshot, Ian, the wolf sitting patiently by his side, once more met Henri's eyes. "I shall come with ye."

Henri placed a hand upon his first mate's shoulder. "I thank you for your loyalty, my friend. However, this is something I have to do on my own. I need you to return to the *Voile Noire*, assume command and then follow. We do not know how this will end nor where or when." He swallowed hard. "But whatever happens, someone must remain to ensure that Juliette is safe. Is that clear?"

A muscle in the Scotsman's jaw twitched, and for a moment, Henri thought he might argue the point. Then, however, he gave a quick nod before stepping back. "Good luck, Capt'n."

A moment later, Ian had disappeared down the path, the large beast chasing after him. Henri inhaled a deep breath, then he once more turned around to face the sea.

All his life, he had known that he belonged out there. There had never been doubt or uncertainty. Always had the sea called to him, spoken to him, and he smiled when he felt that familiar tug once more.

Only now, it seemed stronger than ever before, and deep down, Henri knew that it was no longer only the sea calling him.

It was her.

Juliette.

As much as he had tried to ignore that feeling that had taken root in his heart, he had been unable to banish it. Against time and distance, it had remained, and now, Henri knew that it would continue to do so for all the days to come.

The simple truth was that he loved her.

He did.

There was no use arguing about it. And yet, this love had brought her nothing but risk and danger. Who knew how this day would end? As much as he was meant to be out here at sea, Juliette was not.

Although Henri had known that before, it was not until this very day that he realized what he was risking by allowing her to stay by his side.

What *she* was risking.

With his gaze fixed upon the ship in the distance, Henri slowly retraced his steps, his feet carrying him backward toward the thicket.

He felt his muscles tensing, preparing for what lay ahead, his breath going deep, lifting his chest and shoulders before lowering them once more.

Once.

Twice.

And then, with a sharp sprint forward, Henri rushed toward the edge of the cliff.

Chapter Thirty-Seven

BETWEEN BROTHERS

With her hands once again tied, this time in front of her, Juliet stood up on deck, her back resting against a tall mast as she watched the two Dubois brothers.

Outrage and disappointment simmered in Benoît's eyes; yet Juliet could also see a touch of fear as he met his brother's gaze. Despite everything that he felt or simply because of what he had so recently learned, Benoît Dubois seemed to struggle to remain upright and upon his feet. Exhaustion lingered upon his shoulders, and the words he spoke barely drifted to Juliet's ears. "She was terrified of you, was she not? It was not the shock from the fire, but you, the threat of you that had her look so terrified all the time." He shook his head, that look of disbelief still in his eyes. "I cannot believe I never noticed, I never realized..." Again, he shook his head.

Dubois grabbed his brother by the shirt front and yanked him close, his eyes narrowed into slits. "All my life, I've seen to you, protected you. Everything I did I did for you, and now you question me? You question my methods?" His lips curled into a snarl. "You tried for years to win her and you failed, and so I stepped up and—"

"You raped her!" Benoît hissed, a deep sense of menace in his voice that Juliet would not have expected. "You raped the woman I love!

How can you excuse that? How can you even try to think up words that would justify such a vicious deed?" Shoving against his brother, Benoît freed himself of his grip. "You destroyed her! You are the villain in this!" He swallowed, and a look of deepest shame came to his face. "As am I," he mumbled, raking a hand through his hair. "You did what you did because of me. It is my fault as well." He closed his eyes, inhaling a deep breath. "You have no idea how relieved I am to know that she's safe now. From you as well as from me."

A dark sneer came to Dubois's face as he stepped toward his brother. "How dare you aid the Durets? How dare you stand against your own family?"

Gawking at Dubois, Benoît shook his head. "Family? What family?" His arm flew out, and without even looking, Benoît pointed back toward the island. "They are family. They stand with one another. They risk everything to protect their own." He swallowed hard. "Henri told me that they believed Noële dead; otherwise, they would've come for her right away. *Oui*, she will be safe with them, safe from you."

For a long, quiet moment, the two brothers simply stared at one another, both their faces revealing deep emotions ranging from outrage and betrayal to regret and shame.

Juliet had been all but holding her breath watching this moment unfold. Yet, seeing the two men stand head to head, words no longer leaving their lips, she found herself unable to remain quiet. "What about the child?" she asked, squaring her shoulders, fully expecting to draw Dubois's wrath. "What about Ophélie?" Her gaze flitted to Benoît. "Henri told you about her, did he not?"

Closing his eyes, Benoît nodded, and Juliet could see that a part of him had fought to ignore the fact that his brother had fathered a child with the woman he loved.

An angry growl rose from Dubois's throat, and a moment later, he stormed toward her. Juliet shrank back, her shoulders pressing against the rough wood of the mast. The next moment, Dubois's fist connected with her jaw and her head flew back, her feet knocked out from under her.

Even before she hit the deck, Juliet's head felt as though it would explode, the pain radiating from her jaw into her skull and down her neck. Unable to break her fall, she crashed onto her shoulder, another dull pain shooting through her as she pulled up her legs instinctively, curling herself into a tight ball, awaiting Dubois's next attack.

"Stop!" she heard Benoît shout, and the angry footsteps that headed her way abruptly ceased.

Juliet's vision blurred and a dull pain throbbed beneath her temples as she heard the two brothers shouting at one another, hurling accusations. She tried her best to focus her mind as well as her gaze, but it took a long moment before she managed to push herself up. Her legs still felt useless as she sat on deck, her back resting against the mast once more.

"Where is she?" Benoît demanded, fury now darkening his face. It seemed he had abandoned all thoughts of betrayal, now standing in defense of those who had been wronged. "What did you do with the child?"

A dark sneer came to Dubois's face, and for a second, he seemed to glance past his brother to her as though laying blame at her feet.

"Did you...Did you take her life?" Benoît asked outright, his voice now weak. Holding his brother's gaze, he stepped closer, his throat working as he swallowed hard, apprehension and dread in his eyes. "Did you kill a child? A mere babe?"

Dubois clenched his jaw as he stared at his brother. Juliet thought to see the desire to lash out at him, while at the same time a flicker of denial showed in his eyes. Indeed, it seemed that at least on some level, his brother's opinion mattered to him. The loss of it was, indeed, a loss he felt deeply.

Benoît slowly shook his head. "How can you act in such a way? Against Noële? Against...your own child?"

Juliet held her breath, for she had never heard it spoken with such clear precision. So far, everyone had always only hinted at the fact that Ophélie was Dubois's daughter.

"The child lives," Dubois growled as though he were the one who had been wronged by his brother's deeds. "I protect my own. I always have." He leaned down to look at his brother's eyes. "As I have always protected you, and yet you betrayed me."

Juliet could not say that she was surprised to hear Dubois's words.

The man would never lay blame at his own feet. He seemed incapable of recognizing his own wrongdoings, only ever finding fault with others, seeing betrayal in them and their actions, but never in his own.

Some people were like that, were they not? How they had become such people, completely unfeeling when it came to others was beyond Juliet. She barely knew Noèle and had never laid eyes upon her child, and yet her heart ached at the thought of what mother and daughter had suffered. How could Dubois not feel it?

"Where is she?" Benoît demanded. "Tell me now. For once, do the right thing and tell me where the girl is." The look in his eyes had softened, and yet his jaw remained as clenched as ever, whispering of the tension that still held him in its grasp.

A dark chuckle rumbled in Dubois's throat before he threw back his head and laughed. "You will never find her," he hissed. "No matter where you might look for her, she will always be someplace else."

Juliet frowned, confused by Dubois's words. Benoît, too, looked questioningly at his brother. He blinked, his mouth opening to reply, to no doubt ask again when a shout from the crow's nest echoed to their ears. "Sail ho!"

Those two words shot through Juliet as though she had been struck by lightning. Her head flew up, and she struggled to push herself to her feet.

Dubois as well as his brother flew toward the starboard side, grasping the railing as they leaned over, eyes directed toward the bow and all that lay behind their ship. "It's the Durets!" Dubois growled under his breath.

At his words, Juliet's eyes closed in relief, and she all but sagged against the mast. Her body still ached; yet, her heart seemed to dance in her chest.

"They will never catch us!" Dubois growled as he stepped back, then he gestured to his crew and ordered them to turn into the wind. "I do not care where we're headed," he snapped at his brother, casting a sideways glance at Juliet. "But this wind will put a great distance between us. They will never catch us." He cast Juliet one last hateful glare and then headed up onto the quarterdeck.

Feeling that sense of joy fade from her heart, Juliet met Benoît's gaze. He seemed exhausted and haggard as though he had aged more than a decade within the last few days. "I'm sorry," he whispered, his shoulders slumped. "I'm so sorry. I tried." He glanced over his shoulder at his brother. "I never expected..." He shook his head in defeat, a spark of disbelief once more lighting up his eyes.

Juliet hung her head, unwilling to believe that this was it. After everything they had been through, it could not end like this, could it?

A part of her refused to give up; however, it no longer possessed the strength to argue its point. Exhausted, Juliet once more sank down and rested her head against the mast.

Was this truly how this day would end?

Chapter Thirty-Eight

IN PURSUIT

"You look like a drowned rat," Antoine commented with a chuckle as his gaze swept over Henri. "Go and change."

Henri shook his head, brushing the water out of his hair, as he reached for the spyglass. "There is no time," he remarked shortly, his clothes plastered to his body.

Fortunately, upon his jump off the cliff, he had missed the rocks below, his body sinking deep down under the water's surface. His feet had hit the ground below, and he had used that circumstance to push himself off, the momentum propelling him faster back up toward the surface. By the time, he was able to inhale another deep breath, the *Chevalier Noir* had been nearby. The men had cast a line and then dragged him up on board.

Looking through the spyglass, Henri caught sight of Dubois's ship, his insides tensing at the great distance between them.

"What happened?" Antoine asked, his gaze serious once more. "Where are the others?"

Henri quickly explained what had happened, glancing over his shoulder to where the *Voile Noire* drifted near the rocky beach, awaiting the dinghy. "There is no time," he said once more. "We need to pursue them. Now!"

"We are," Antoine replied, reaching for the spyglass and taking it from Henri's hands. He once more looked through, his posture growing rigid. "They are too far ahead," he remarked dryly. "With this wind, we will not catch up." He turned to look at Henri. "Do you know where they are headed?"

Rubbing his hands over his face, Henri heaved a deep breath. "I do not," he gritted out through clenched teeth.

Beside him, he felt Antoine give a quick nod before his uncle turned to his crew, reminding them of what was at stake. Every man around them bore a hardened look, gaze focused and shoulders squared with determination as they saw to their tasks.

Yet not even determination could sway the winds and eat up the distance between the two ships. Henri knew that as he once again found himself forced to stand in one spot, his gaze upon the horizon, unable to do anything.

To make a difference.

～

Juliet watched as Dubois paced along the railing, his gaze going out to the ship in pursuit. She could see the desire to turn and engage them in his eyes, for whatever fault one might rightfully lay at Dubois's feet, the man was not a coward.

"What will happen now?" Juliet asked as she glanced at Benoît.

Dubois's brother stood a few paces away from her, his shoulders slumped, and his head bowed. "I do not know," he whispered under his breath.

With a careful glance in Dubois's direction, Juliet slowly moved closer to Benoît. "You have to do something," she whispered, then she drew in a sharp breath when she felt Dubois's gaze follow her.

"Don't you dare put ideas in his head!" Dubois snarled from the quarterdeck; his gaze narrowed into slits as he glared at her. "All of this is your fault! I should simply throw you overboard and be done with you." An amused snarl came to his face as he contemplated his own words.

Juliet stared at Dubois in shock, her tied hands straining against the rough rope as she pictured herself flung into the sea with nothing to keep her afloat.

Fear clearly showed upon her face, for a large smile spread over Dubois's, and he threw back his head and laughed. "Our choices have a way of catching up with us, do you not agree, *mademois*—?"

A loud bang shattered the still air, and a moment later, something crashed into the waters a small distance from the bowsprit. Spray flew up, and Juliet felt the salty sea water rain down onto her skin in fine droplets.

Instantly, a flurry of activity broke out upon deck, sailors calling to one another as some scrambled up the rigging while others moved toward the gun ports.

Juliet watched as Dubois shot forward, his gaze sweeping over the sea as well as the neighboring islands as he called to the crow's nest, "What do you see?"

A moment later, the words "Sail ho!" echoed down, and Dubois gritted his teeth in anger as his gaze continued to search his surroundings. "Where?"

Standing next to Benoît at the railing, Juliet stared alongside everyone else. And then she saw it.

From behind one of the smaller islands dotting the water like a string of pearls, a tall-masted ship glided slowly out into open sight. Juliet's breath caught in her throat when she beheld it; not because of the British flag flying upon its tallest mast, but because she recognized it.

It was the *Freedom*.

Violet.

$\sim$

As the *Chevalier Noir* cut through the waters in-between two smaller islands, Henri momentarily lost sight of Dubois's ship. He could feel his insides tense and his breath pause, the thought of never spotting it again more than he could bear. What if they were to lose them? What then?

And then a deafening bang echoed to his ears, and Henri's hands clenched around the smooth wood of the railing. "Cannon fire," he muttered, turning to look at his uncle as he came hurrying over, a spyglass in his hand.

Endless seconds ticked by as they waited, their eyes unseeing, their line of sight blocked by a tall cliff reaching far out into the sea.

And then the *Chevalier Noir* moved around the cliff's farthest point and Dubois's ship once more reappeared.

Henri's eyes grew wide as his gaze moved past Dubois's vessel and locked onto the *Freedom*. The ship drew closer swiftly, guns readied, and before he knew it, another cannon ball cut through the air, crashing into the waters near the bowsprit of Dubois's ship.

"A warning shot!" Antoine remarked, his shoulders tense as he watched Dubois's crew ready their own guns, pointing them at his daughter's ship. Then he spun around and yelled orders across the deck. "Ready the guns! Direct warning shots near the stern!"

Henri brought the spyglass to his eye, his gaze sweeping over the deck of Dubois's ship. Where was Juliette? Had Dubois once again locked her in his cabin? Or—?

His breath rushed from his lungs with relief when he suddenly spotted her standing at the rail beside Benoît. He could not make out her features, but her billowing, auburn hair revealed her like a beacon in the dark.

Bowing his head, Henri glanced up at their target, considering what to do. Of course, Dubois would have no qualms firing upon their ships; they, however, would be risking Juliette's life if they tried to destroy his. What to do?

As long as she was on board, their hands were tied.

And then one of Dubois's cannons fired.

Henri watched in horror as the cannon ball cut through the air toward the *Freedom*. It missed the bowsprit by no more than a yard.

Not a warning shot, but a miss.

The next one might hit its target.

What then?

∽

Energy hummed in Juliet's veins as she watched the *Freedom*'s approach; yet, the moment Dubois fired upon her sister's ship, Juliet felt her body turn to ice.

This could not be happening! She had to do something! She had to stop him!

Blindly, Juliet rushed across the main deck, her feet unsteady, before she all but dragged herself up the ladder to the quarterdeck. "Stop!" she yelled, not even turning to look as she heard footsteps following close behind her. "Do not fire!"

Dubois whirled around, outrage in his eyes that she would dare order him around. He opened his mouth to speak when another deafening bang cut him off, the shock of it throwing Juliet to the deck.

Coughing, she looked up to see Dubois glare in the opposite direction, away from the *Freedom*. Juliet turned her head and spotted Antoine's ship. They had finally caught up, and Juliet saw small figures moving around on deck. Was one of them Henri? Where was the *Voile Noire*? Or had it sunk the night Dubois had set fire to it?

If only she knew!

"*Merde!*" Dubois hissed, his face contorted into a grotesque mask as he looked back and forth between the two ships that now flanked his own. His eyes seemed to burn with something dark and unfeeling as though he truly did not possess a heart.

A sensible man would understand that he was outnumbered and outmatched. He would lay down his weapons and surrender. Dubois, however, was far from a sensible man, judging from that wild look in his eyes. Indeed, he seemed mad, utterly and completely mad. What would he do now that he found himself cornered?

Stillness fell over them all as though time had slowed down. For all the activity and noise there had been before, now, everyone seemed almost frozen to the spot, each one of them waiting to see what the other would do. The three ships drifted almost lazily upon the waves; their guns readied...and yet silent.

Juliet watched as Dubois's gaze moved from her to the *Freedom* and then to the *Chevalier Noir*. She wished she knew what went on in his head, concerned about what he might do next. Although she wished he would, Juliet did not for a second believe that Dubois would surrender.

Once more turning to look to the *Chevalier Noir*, Juliet felt the breath catch in her throat when she spotted Henri upon the quarter-deck. The ship had drifted close enough for her to recognize him. Instant relief swept through her, knowing that he was alive, that he was well. But would he remain so?

"Release her!" came Antoine's echoing voice, carried across the waters by a soft breeze. "Release her, and you and your crew will go free!"

Juliet's knees trembled as she stared at Dubois, waiting like all the others for what he would say. She wondered if Antoine truly believed Dubois would surrender, would admit defeat. Deep down, she could not help but hope that it would be so; yet one look into his contorted face told her that she was a fool for entertaining any hope at all.

As though Dubois had not even heard Antoine's demand, his gaze, hard and accusing, remained locked upon Juliet. She could feel it like an icy wind trailing over her skin. It made her shiver, and she backed away until she felt the railing cut off her retreat.

"You," he snarled, his lips thinning as his teeth pressed together, his jaw locked in a way that seemed utterly painful. Yet Dubois appeared unaware, hatred blazing in his eyes. "This is your fault," he hissed so quietly that Juliet barely heard the words he spoke. "If it hadn't been for you, none of this would have happened."

"Release her now!" came Antoine's voice once more. "Or we will fire upon your ship. You are outnumbered. Surrender or die."

Again, Dubois did not even turn his head. A corner of his mouth twitched, and his eyes narrowed into slits. Then his right hand moved, and Juliet watched with wide eyes as the man reached for the pistol on his hip. "You will pay for this," he hissed quietly.

Juliet knew she needed to act, to do...something. Yet everything was happening so quickly that she could not even bring herself to take one step to the side. While before it had seemed that time had slowed, now it appeared to move much too fast. Before she knew it, Juliet found herself staring down the muzzle of a pistol pointed directly at her.

Would this truly be her end? After everything...

Juliet pinched her eyes shut, disbelief filling her.

"I hope he's watching," Dubois snarled, and she heard him cock his weapon. "It'll be a lesson he'll never forget."

"Brother, please stop!" came Benoît's pleading voice; he sounded utterly defeated.

Juliet felt every muscle in her body tense, and for a split second, she wondered if she ought to simply let herself drop overboard and into the sea below.

Then, however, a deafening shot cut through the air, loud and clear...and final.

Chapter Thirty-Nine

A NOBLE SACRIFICE

H enri's heart stopped when he saw Dubois point his pistol at
Juliette. He saw her eyes widen and fear shine clear as day
upon her face. He saw the satisfied snarl upon Dubois's face
and knew that the man was doing this now to get back at him,
Henri.

This was a game for Dubois. Life was a game, and he did not like to
lose or find himself the inferior to another. When Henri had taken
Juliette and Noële from his ship, something in Dubois had snapped in
a way it never had before. It was only too visible in the way the man's
eyes had glazed over with something deeply hateful when he was
surprised by Henri's arrival in his secret hideout.

Because of Benoît's betrayal.

At Henri's behest.

All this had brought them to this very moment, this one heart-
stopping moment. A moment when Henri found himself standing at
the railing and staring, his mind picturing the moments ahead, seeing
Juliette crumple to the floor, her eyes closing as blood flowed from a
wound in her heart. It was a moment that lingered, that Henri knew
would stay with him until the end of his days.

Yet, at the same time, everything seemed to be happening too fast.

In one fluid motion, Dubois reached for his gun, pointing it at Juliette, quiet words leaving his lips, that devious snarl still upon his face.

And then, before Henri had any chance to react, to do something, a shot rang out, shredding his heart into bits and pieces as he stared across the water at Juliette.

Her eyes were pinched shut, her face pale as though she had long since departed this world. And then—all expectations to the contrary —her eyes began to flutter open once more, and she stared down at Benoît Dubois, who slowly crumpled down onto the deck at her feet. Blood stained his white shirt, and his skin seemed to pale a little more with each drop to leave his body.

Relief rocked through Henri like a shockwave. He had been so focused on Juliette that he had not even noticed Benoît's approach. Even now, he could not recall what precisely had happened.

Yet, it did not matter. What mattered was saving Juliette's life. Somehow, he had to get to the other ship—to her—before Dubois could reload and—

Halfway up the rigging, Henri froze when Juliette suddenly vanished from sight, her body disappearing over the ship's railing. Again, fear stopped his heart before his mind could argue that he had heard no shot ring out. Indeed, had she simply...

Henri's eyes widened. "Take the ship out now!" he called down to his uncle before pushing off and jumping down into the sea after her.

"Jump," Benoît's weak voice urged Juliet as he slowly sank down onto the deck. "Now!"

Staring down at the bleeding wound upon his chest, Juliet felt her own heart suddenly beat with renewed strength. Her head snapped up, and her eyes fell upon Dubois's ash-white face as he stared from the pistol in his hand to his dying brother.

"Now," Benoît muttered once again, the effort to speak that one word draining him. "G-Go."

With her hands still tied, Juliet grasped the railing and swung one leg over, her skirts hindering her movements. Still, fear spurred her on as did the certainty that once Dubois recovered from the shock of having shot his own brother, he would come after her.

He would reload his gun, and he would—

The moment Dubois's hard eyes collided with hers, Juliet's hands slipped from the railing and she fell.

Her heart jumped in her chest at the unfamiliar sensation of falling from such a height; yet, the moment passed far too quickly. Juliet barely had time to urge herself to draw in a deep breath when her body plunged into the cold water, sinking fast.

Of course, Juliet knew not how to swim. Even with her hands untied she would not have known what to do, how to keep herself above the water's surface. She had been raised a lady, and ladies did not swim. When safely shielded from prying eyes, a lady might be daring enough to remove her shoes and stockings and wade a few steps into a body of water on a hot day, but...

Kicking her legs against the pull of the deep, Juliet looked up when a dull *bang* drifted to her ears. Looking upward, she saw the heavy hull of Dubois's ship sitting atop the water before it suddenly seemed to shudder. Then splintered wood dropped into the water around her.

Dubois's ship had been hit!

Again, cannon fire echoed to Juliet's ears, the sound dulled by the water surrounding her. Her lungs began to strain for air as she continued to kick her legs, trying her best to reach the surface, to get away, to—

A hand grasped her arm, and Juliet almost opened her mouth to scream; however, in the last second, her instincts kicked in, keeping her lips sealed. Her head spun around, and her eyes fell on...

...Henri!

Despite the pressing concern for air that made her lungs feel as though they were about to burst, Juliet's heart rejoiced at the very sight of him.

Without delay, Henri pulled her toward him, then he pushed her upward, his strong legs kicking hard as they shot toward the surface.

Juliet lifted her head, her eyes seeing the water above her head growing lighter and lighter until her head broke the surface. Her lips parted, and she began to cough as her body fought to draw in air.

Another cannon ball cut across the sky above their heads; this one from the *Freedom*. It hit the starboard side of Dubois's ship, blowing a hole into the hull. Screams drifted to Juliet's ears as her breathing slowly calmed, her body held above the water by Henri's safe embrace.

"Are you all right, *ma petite lionne*?" he whispered in her ear, then he turned her around, his green eyes sweeping over her face. "Are you injured?"

Wishing she could fling herself into his arms, Juliet smiled at him. "No, I'm fine. I'm not hurt." Yet her jaw still ached from Dubois's attack. "Benoît saved me. He—"

"We need to move," Henri told her, urgency in his voice as he glanced over her shoulder. Then he reached for the blade upon his belt and cut through her bonds as though they were nothing. "Hold on to my shoulders," he instructed as another cannon ball from the *Chevalier Noir* cut down the main mast of Dubois's ship.

Doing as he bid her, Juliet watched with wide eyes as Henri swam toward a small island, her neck craned to see Dubois's ship torn to pieces. Wood splintered, ropes tore and sails ripped to shreds. Sailors jumped overboard, their screams and shouts echoing to Juliet's ears. Yet, she never once caught a glimpse of Dubois. Where was he? Was he already dead?

As they drew closer to the island's beach, Henri slowed, then he moved to look at her. "Lower your legs. You can stand here." He reached out to tug a wet strand of hair behind her ear, his gaze sweeping over her face as though he could not believe that she was right here in front of him.

Juliet knew precisely how that felt!

Tears shot to her eyes, and she flung herself into Henri's arms, almost knocking him over. Heaving sobs tore from her throat as relief swept through her, pushing aside the fear that had held her in its talons for the past few days. Once again, she had lived with the sword of Damocles above her head, never knowing if and when it would come down.

"It's all right," Henri murmured in her ear, his arms wrapped around her as he held her tightly against his chest. "You're all right. You're safe. I promise." She felt him swallow before he moved back and looked down into her face, apprehension in his green eyes. "Dubois...he..." Henri gritted his teeth. "What did he do to you?"

Another cannon ball sailed through the air in that moment, making their heads whip around, and Juliet saw that the *Freedom* had been hit as well. Still, the hole seemed small in comparison, and Juliet hoped that her sister and brother-in-law were fine.

Her gaze flickered up to the *Freedom*'s tall mast and came to linger upon the British flag it flew. She heaved a deep breath, then she looked to the French one of the *Chevalier Noir*. Indeed, they were meant to be enemies, but there was something much stronger than one's loyalty to one's country. It was a thought that filled Juliet with warmth. *"Family above all"*, she whispered before her gaze moved to look at Henri. "Is that not the Duret motto?"

Smiling at her, he nodded. "It is." He wrapped an arm around her shoulders, and together, they stood chest-deep in the sea and watched the end of Dubois.

Although Juliet felt saddened by the thought of all those who had lost their lives today, she could not help but be relieved and grateful for how everything had turned out. Only the thought of Benoît, his sacrifice, made her—

Beside her, Henri tensed.

"What is it?" she exclaimed, turning to look at him, surprised to see a slow smile claim his features.

Grinning, Henri met her gaze, then he lifted his left arm and pointed out to sea. "The *Voile Noire*."

From the south, a tall ship with a black sail drew closer, its gun ports readied as the *Voile Noire* joined the fray, a loud shot firing out of the front cannon. It hit the captain's quarters of Dubois's ship, ripping off the wall, and Juliet felt a sense of deep satisfaction to see her old prison cell blown to pieces.

Then she heaved a deep sigh and sank into Henri's arms, burying her face in the crook of his neck. He held her tightly, and she could feel his heart beat against her own. Despite everything that had happened, Juliet felt completely at peace, certain that she would for all the days to come as long as Henri was by her side.

Life had never seemed sweeter!

Chapter Forty

RETURN TO AN OLD LIFE

To Henri, it felt like heaven to stand upon the deck of the *Voile Noire* once more. It was where he belonged, where he had always belonged. His life was out here at sea.

Juliette's was not.

"I'm so relieved you're safe," Violette exclaimed as she hugged her sister tightly.

"But how did you know what happened?" Juliette inquired, gazing at her sister with bright eyes, while her fingers absentmindedly touched her chin where a bruise was beginning to show from Dubois' attack on her. "I still cannot believe you're here."

Smiling, Antoine stepped forward and placed a hand upon Juliette's shoulder. "I left a man behind to point the way for Violette when she returned."

Leaning back against the railing, Henri watched as they all embraced one another again and again. Violette alternately hugged her sister, her husband and her father. Every once in a while, she would even venture over and hug him, Henri.

"You look glum," she remarked on one of these quick trips across the deck. "What is wrong? We saved the day. You should be happy. Don't tell me this is your happy face." She grinned at him, then she slapped him playfully on the shoulder and returned to hug her sister once more.

Dubois's ship as well as the man himself now rested safely upon the bottom of the sea, the only reminder that it had once been there were a few pieces of driftwood as well as a number of sailors locked in the *Chevalier Noir*'s brig. Henri's uncle would return to Paris with the prisoners in order to reveal Dubois's duplicity as well as the location of his secret stash. That ought to ensure that the Durets would not suffer any repercussions from firing upon another French vessel.

After all, Dubois had been a traitor in more ways than one!

"How is Noèle?" Juliette asked her sister, concern in her green eyes. "She's not with you, is she?"

Violette shook her head. "No, she's with Mother in *La Roche-sur-Mer*. I have no doubt that she will recover swiftly. The need to find her daughter will spur her on." Henri saw Violette draw in a shuddering breath as she no doubt thought of little Antoinette, her own precious child.

Henri heaved a deep sigh, then he stepped toward the others. "Unfortunately, we no longer have the option of *persuading* Dubois to reveal the girl's whereabouts." He glanced toward the spot where the man's ship had gone down. "I'm sorry, but there was no other way."

Violette nodded, disappointment in her eyes. "We will find a way. No matter what we will have to do, we will find—"

"I might know something," Juliette interrupted, her green eyes flitting back and forth between all those standing around her.

Feeling himself tense, Henri took a step toward her. "How?"

Her green eyes moved to meet his before she dropped her gaze for a split second, which told him more than he wanted to know. "I...I spoke to him," Juliette finally said, hesitation in her voice as she evaded his gaze and turned back to look at her sister. "I drew him into a conversation." A tense chuckle left her lips. "Perhaps not all skills taught to young ladies are completely useless."

Awe shone in Violette's eyes as she stared at her sister. "And he told you something? Something about Ophélie?"

Juliette nodded. "The way he spoke, I have no doubt that the girl is still alive. He even seemed to take affront when I asked if Ophélie was alive, and he referred to her as his own. He said he always takes care of his own." Henri watched the pulse in her neck speed up as she did her best to calmly repeat the conversation with Dubois; still, the look in her eyes told him about the kind of terror she had lived through on board the man's ship. "He said he paid the Duvals handsomely to ensure that they would see to her. I don't know who they are, but I'm certain that Ophélie is with them." Her brows knit together as she seemed to concentrate, to grasp something almost elusive. "He also said..." Squinting her eyes, she paused. "It does not make sense to me, but he said that *No matter where you might look for her, she will always be someplace else.*" She looked directly at each of them. "I don't know what that means, but I think it is important."

Antoine gently squeezed her shoulder. "Well done, Juliette. *Oui*, I believe we will figure out what it means," his gaze moved to Violette, "and we will find the child. As soon as we return to *La Roche-sur-Mer*, I will make inquiries. We will find her. I promise."

Everyone nodded, hope back in their eyes. Henri turned to Ian, then he spoke under his breath. "Ensure that the *Voile Noire* will be ready to sail at a moment's notice."

A flicker of confusion showed in the Scotsman's eyes; yet he did not ask, but merely nodded and then stepped away.

"Then we return home," Oliver exclaimed, a bit of a questioning expression on his face as he looked from his wife to his father-in-law. "There is nothing left to see to, is there?"

Antoine nodded. "When you say *home...*?" His brows quirked upward.

Oliver chuckled. "I mean *La Roche-sur-Mer*; after all, my daughter is there." He looked down into Violette's eyes. "That is a very good reason to call it home, but it is not the only one."

Henri straightened, doing his best to ignore that cold chill that seemed to linger upon his shoulders. "Before we depart," he said loudly in order to gain everyone's attention, "I need a private word with Juliette." He was well aware of the surprised expressions that came to everyone's faces as they turned to look at him.

"Can you not do that on route?" Oliver challenged with a grin. "You can sail and talk at the same time, can you not?"

Henri ignored the mocking tone in his cousin-in-law's voice, doing his utmost not to meet Juliette's questioning eyes. "I can," he replied through gritted teeth. "However, in this instant, I choose not to."

Violette grinned at Juliette, clearly misunderstanding Henri's wish to speak to Juliette alone. "Then get on with it. I wish to see my daughter."

With a smile, Juliette stepped toward him, her green eyes wide and shining, full of trust and without the slightest hint of suspicion. Henri felt like an ogre; yet there was no way around it.

It was for the best, and one day, she would come to see it.

Stepping into the captain's quarters behind her, Henri closed the door, wondering how he was to begin. Clearly, she suspected nothing, and if she truly felt for him the way he felt for her...

"What is wrong?" Juliette asked as she stepped toward him. "There's a look in your eyes that..." She shook her head as though wishing to throw off the thought.

Running a hand through his hair, Henri cleared his throat. Clearly, she knew him better than he had expected. "I want you to board the *Freedom* and let Violette take you back home."

Juliette's face fell in a way Henri would never have thought possible. It was like sudden frost descending on a hot summer's day. She stared at him with unblinking eyes, and yet the pulse in her neck hammered wildly. "You... You cannot mean that," she whispered as tears collected in her eyes, proof that she believed every word he had spoken. "Why...Why would you—?" Her mouth opened and closed before she slowly started to shake her head from side to side. "No!"

Henri straightened, linking his hands behind his back. "It is not a request," he replied in a hard voice, reminding himself that he had known she would challenge his decision.

Juliette flinched at the unfeeling tone in his voice. "Why are you doing this?" Her tears spilled over and rolled down her cheeks. "I thought..."

Henri forced himself to meet her gaze. "You thought what?"

For a moment, Juliette seemed to retreat, her teeth digging into her lower lip as she bowed her head. Then, however, she suddenly straightened, something fierce blazing in her eyes. "I thought you loved me."

Henri felt his teeth grit together painfully. "That has no bearing upon my decision. It must not." The moment the words left his lips, Henri knew that he had misspoken. He ought to have denied that he cared for her.

He ought to have done so strongly and convincingly.

Now, however, triumph flashed in her green eyes, for she suddenly knew what was on his mind, and perhaps understood him better than he understood himself. "You're doing it again," Juliette remarked, a bitter tone in her voice as she stepped toward him, her eyes unwavering. "You're running away."

Henri knew that she was intentionally baiting him, challenging him. "Say what you wish," he told her with a determined stare of his own, "but it will not affect my decision. You're going home...to England."

Her jaw hardened. "I will not."

Henri loved the defiant look in her eyes, the fierce spirit that shone through; yet he knew that he could not allow her to come out the victor in this battle, for if he did, one day they would both regret it. "You will, and that is final!"

A thoughtful expression came to her eyes as she watched him, her gaze sweeping his face as though looking for something, some kind of clue to make sense of his words. "You referred to me as your bride," she whispered, a small smile tickling her lips. "Why?"

Henri swallowed hard. "How do you—?"

Looking up at him, Juliette reached out and placed her hands on his chest, right above his frantically hammering heart. "Pierre told me the night you went after Dubois's brother. He was surprised to see my confusion. He truly believed me to be your bride, did he not?"

Henri gritted his teeth, cursing silently, vowing that he would end Pierre's life once the lad had fully recovered from his injuries. "I had to tell my men something," Henri echoed the words he had told himself that night. "I had to give them a reason to leave behind their homes and families to chase after an English lady. I had to tell them something."

Juliette's hands moved higher and onto his shoulders. "And you could think of nothing else? No other reason?" Her hands snaked around his neck, pulling her closer against him. "Why did you not simply tell them that I am family? Violet's sister?" She smiled up at him. "I've seen the way they look at her. She is one of them. They would've done this for her as much as for you."

As before, Henri found his resolve waver. She stood so close, her arms wrapped around him, her warmth reaching out. He loved holding her, feeling her heart beat against his own. He loved the way her green eyes looked up into his without hesitation or doubt. As delicate and vulnerable as she sometimes seemed, there were moments when Henri could have sworn that she would have no trouble conquering the world. She was a marvel to him, and he knew that he would never tire looking at her. She drew him in, drew him close, every fiber of his being straining toward her, a deep yearning echoing in his bones.

Around her, Henri felt weak. He felt all else flee his mind, his gaze focused on her alone. His heart urged him closer, whispering of a longing he had borne for four years. When the day he finally gave in came, it had been the best day of his life.

"Kiss me," Juliette whispered, her lips suddenly no more than a hair's breadth away from his own.

And fool that he was, Henri did.

Chapter Forty-One

A MULE-HEADED FRENCHMAN

J uliet knew that Henri did not wish for her to go. Not truly, at least. She could feel it in the way he tried *not* to reach for her. She saw it in the very moment he lost that battle with himself and finally gave in. She felt it the second his mouth claimed hers in an almost desperate kiss.

He longed for her as much as she longed for him, and yet...

As always, thinking became exceedingly difficult once she was in his arms. Her heart soared, and all Juliet was aware of was the feel of him.

His arms held her tightly, clutched to his chest, and his mouth never left hers, kissing her deeply. She felt his left hand curl into her hair and then give a soft tug, tilting her head back. There was something ravenous in him, and Juliet could not help but think that he was kissing her as though...

...as though this was the last moment they had together!

Shock speared her heart, and Juliet abruptly pulled back, staring up into his eyes. "No!" Her eyes searched his, and her heart sank when she saw that unyielding set come to his jaw. Whether he liked it or not, she knew him.

She knew him well.

And right here and now, she knew that he could not be swayed. Still, she could not simply bow her head and allow him to decide for her.

"I will not leave you," Juliet said sternly as she raised her chin and held his gaze. "I will not."

His arms fell away, and his hands linked behind his back once more. "You must return home. It is for the best. You know that as well as I do."

Juliet shook her head. "I know no such thing!" she exclaimed. "I thought..." She swallowed. "I had hoped that..."

Bowing his head, Henri closed his eyes. "So had I," he whispered, then he looked at her once more. "*Non*, we need to face the truth, and the truth is that you do not belong here. This is not a safe place for you, and I will not risk your life because of a selfish desire to have you at my side. I will not!" His eyes were hard, and he took a step back, away from her.

Juliet continued to shake her head, partly in disbelief and partly because some foolish part of her hoped that somehow that simple motion could undo everything, could change his mind. "I cannot go back and—" Indeed, the thought of continuing her old life—without him!—was unbearable! "You cannot make me!"

Holding her gaze, Henri inhaled a slow breath, something torn and almost tortured coming to his eyes. "I will not return to *La Roche-sur-Mer* until you have left, until you are on the *Freedom* on your way back to England."

"I will not!" Juliet almost yelled, the pulse in her neck almost painful.

"Then Noële will have to wait for her daughter that much longer," Henri said calmly, something oddly detached in his voice; yet his eyes held anguish.

Juliet stared at him in shock. "How dare you?" she whispered, stunned and hurt that he would use this against her, that he would do this to force her hand. "Noële has nothing to do with this. You cannot—!"

Grasping her by the shoulders, Henri stared down at her, something fierce blazing in his eyes. "I can, and I will. Life is not fair. Life is not predictable. Life simply is what it is. After everything that happened, how can you not know that? How can you stand here and pretend that there is any chance of...?" His voice trailed off, and although his mouth opened and closed, no words came out.

"I am not pretending," Juliet told him, wishing he would understand how deeply the thought of a life without him pained her. "I do not know what the future will bring, but no matter what that is, I know I want the present right here and now with you."

Henri's lips pressed into a thin line as he slowly shook his head. "I do not," he simply said, then he abruptly released her shoulders and took a step back. "I want you to leave. I want you to return to England where you will be safe."

Fresh tears blurred Juliet's vision. "Safe perhaps, but definitely unhappy."

A muscle in his jaw twitched, yet the look of determination on his face never wavered. "I will not see you taken again or come to harm in any other way," he gritted out, a menacing look in his eyes. "I will not."

His devotion to her touched Juliet's heart, and yet she could not allow him to use it to keep her at bay. "Dubois is dead," she said carefully, her eyes holding his. "He is no longer a threat." She stepped forward, her hand reaching out to touch his face.

Henri grasped her wrist, not allowing her closer, as he slowly shook his head. "He was not the only threat in this world, and you know that. Say what you will," his lips tightened, "but I will not change my mind. You will return with Violette, and that will be it. We will each go back to the lives we were meant to have, lives that were never meant to cross." He released her hand and stepped back toward the door. "This...This was a mistake. We are from two different worlds, and we should never even have learned of the other's existence." He opened the door, but then paused on the threshold. "I'll await you on deck. Goodbye, Juliet." For another heartbeat, Henri's eyes looked into hers before he turned around and walked down the companionway.

Juliet had no notion of how long she simply stood there and stared after him, unable to wrap her mind around what had just happened. Before they had stepped into the cabin, Juliet had been utterly certain of a future shared with Henri. Although he had never said so, she knew that he loved her as much as she loved him. Although she may not have known what their shared future would look like, somehow, she had been completely certain of it. Had that been a foolish notion? Was what she wanted truly something impossible? Something impossible to hold on to?

Sinking down onto one of the two chairs, Juliet stared out the window at the calm sea. She heard footsteps above and wondered what everyone was doing. Had Violet and Oliver already returned to the *Freedom*? Were they aware that Henri meant for them to take her home to England? What would happen now?

Bowing her head, Juliet drew in a deep breath. A part of her wanted to rush up on deck and continue arguing her point. Whether or not she was right to do so did not matter. In the end, all that mattered was that she wanted him. That she wanted a life with him. Was there any point in digging in her heels and standing her ground? Could he be swayed? If not today, then perhaps tomorrow?

Or would it be a futile attempt?

More than that, Juliet realized that after all the risks she had taken —including the risks to her own heart—she did not want to be the only one to fight for this.

This future.

This dream.

This love.

Indeed, Juliet wanted him to take a risk as well, to be willing to do so. For her. Because he loved her. Because...

Henri had come for her, yes. He had done so more than once. He had risked his life to save her, to protect her. And although these deeds spoke loudly of how he felt for her, Juliet knew deep down that risking his own life was something that came easy to Henri.

Risking his heart did not.

The truth was, after all, that he was not sending her back because he feared for her. He was sending her back because he feared for himself. He feared a broken heart, like his father's.

And so, he ran.

From her.

And from himself.

"Will you truly go home?" came Violet's voice from the doorway. "Back to England?"

Juliet sniffled, tears once more blurring her eyes as her sister stepped toward her. "What choice do I have?"

Seating herself across from Juliet, Violet reached for her hands. "You have every choice." Anger curved her lips into a snarl. "Henri is a mule-headed fool! He won't know a good thing unless it hits him in the face." She scoffed. "Perhaps not even then."

Juliet chuckled, despite the tears running down her cheeks. "Whatever his reasons, he has made up his mind."

"And you will accept it?"

Juliet closed her eyes. "I want him to want me. I want him to fight for me. I want him to risk everything he has and everything he is...as I have done." A weak smile came to her face. "When he came for me that first night, I could not believe it. I thought I was dreaming. He was there right in front of me, and yet..." She shook her head, remembering the feeling of utter disbelief that had swept through her. "I will be eternally grateful for everything he did for me, for saving me from Dubois. Twice!" She swallowed hard. "He risked his life for me, and that is no small thing." A shuddering sigh left her lips. "Still, he keeps his heart closed off, unwilling to accept the risk that comes with loving another." She held her sister's gaze. "It needs to be his choice. He needs to want me because I do not want him to bow his head and accept me by his side and in his life simply because he cannot think of a way to rid himself of my presence."

"It is not like that," Violet exclaimed. "You know this. He loves you. We all know that."

Juliet swallowed. "I suppose sometimes love is not enough." Never would she have thought this possible. In all those moments, in all those years, when Juliet had thought of Henri, her head had always argued that they were apart because she had failed to conquer his heart the way he had conquered hers. Not once had she considered that he stayed away *because* he loved her.

It was a twist of fate Juliet had not seen coming, but one that would destroy her life, nonetheless.

Chapter Forty-Two

OUT OF SIGHT

Henri stood up on the quarterdeck as he watched Juliette board the *Freedom*. He held his hands tightly wrapped around the ship's railing; his feet firmly planted upon the wooden boards. Every muscle in his body urged him to move, to go after her, to stop her. Desperate to maintain control over himself, he gritted his teeth against that slow tremble that seemed to move through his limbs. He could feel it in every fiber of his being, and he could not remember a harder moment than watching her sail away right here and now.

As the *Freedom*'s sails unfurled, Juliette stepped up to the railing, her eyes moving to him, that invisible bond once more tugging upon Henri's heart. He could feel it as though she stood right in front of him. Would it ever stop? Would he still feel it when she was back in England? Was this what Antoine had felt fifteen years ago when he had found Alexandra upon a lonely beach in Norfolk?

Henri knew he ought not think these thoughts. They were pointless and torturous. Yet his mind seemed to have a mind of its own. The thoughts came as they wished and stayed until he felt he would go mad.

As the wind caught in its sails, the *Freedom* cut through the water with increasing speed, carrying Juliette farther and farther away. His gaze remained locked upon hers for as long as he could, watching her fall away until the *Freedom* was no more than a small dot upon the horizon.

She was gone.

For good.

"Orders, Capt'n?" came Ian's voice from the helm.

Henri drew in a deep breath and then finally forced his gaze away. He turned toward his first mate, willing his thoughts to focus on what needed to be done. "We will give them a head start," he said with another look over his shoulder toward the horizon, "and then we will sail up the coast toward *La Roche-sur-Mer*."

If his first mate thought it odd that although the *Freedom* and the *Voile Noire* had the same destination, they did not sail together, he did not say so or remark upon it in any way.

"There is something I wish to speak to you about," Henri said to the Scotsman before he turned toward the hatch. Once down in the captain's quarters, Henri addressed his first mate. "You know what we need to do next?"

Ian nodded. "The child." Suppressed emotions swung in the taciturn man's voice, and Henri found himself wondering whether the Scotsman ever had had a child of his own.

"Once we reach *La Roche-sur-Mer*, we will make inquiries about the Duvals, whoever they are. From what we know, it seems that Noële's child was entrusted to them. Since Dubois returned that night to *save*," he all but spat the last word, "his brother and Noële from the flames, I suppose it is safe to say that the Duvals were in the area."

Ian nodded, a stoic expression upon his face.

"However, they might not be anymore," Henri continued, remembering what Juliette had learned from Dubois. Still, he did not know what had happened the second time she had been taken, not precisely. A part of him wished he had asked while another was quite content—if that was indeed the right word to use—with not knowing. "Perhaps they were on a journey of some sort and merely passed through *La Roche-sur-Mer*."

Ian frowned. "Did Dubois plan the child's abduction?"

Henri paused, thinking back to everything Noèle had said. "I don't believe he could have," he murmured as he once again pieced together the events of that night. "Of course, she never told him she had his child, and since none of us knew, I do not believe he could've found out any other way." Henri shook his head, then met Ian's gaze. "No, I believe he did not know. He sought her out that night and that's when he found out."

"If that is the case," Ian surmised, "then the Duvals had to be in the area for other reasons. He couldna have called them to take the child as he was unaware of it at the time. Why then were they there? And how did he know them? How are they connected?"

Henri could not deny that he was somewhat surprised by his first mate's deep interest in the matter. Never before had he heard him speak that many words. "We do not know," Henri replied, frustrated with what little they did know. "My uncle will make inquiries in Paris, and we shall see if he learns anything substantial." He heaved a deep sigh. "Somehow, we need to find her."

Henri met Ian's gaze and saw the Scotsman's lips thin into a determined snarl, something menacing in his guarded eyes. "Aye, we will."

Indeed, it seemed that something about Ophélie's abduction had hit a nerve with him. "Are you a father?" Henri asked, curious to know more about his second-in-command.

For a split second, something blazed to life in the Scotsman's eyes; then, however, his lips thinned even further, all but sealing themselves shut. "Is there anything else you require of me, Capt'n?"

Henri heaved a deep sigh; after all, he had not truly expected the man to reply. "Not at the moment," he told him and gave a quick nod as Ian turned and left.

Left alone in the place he had shared with Juliette, Henri found his thoughts immediately return to her. No matter where his gaze traveled, to the window, the bed or even the table, either sight always conjured images of her. They forced themselves into his mind, and Henri knew, in order to keep his sanity, he would need to ensure that his mind was never idle, to keep it busy at all times. If he had not been concerned about crossing paths with Juliette in *La Roche-sur-Mer*, he would have set sail this very instant.

Now, though, he had a full day ahead of him with nothing to do...
but wait.

Chapter Forty-Three

BACK IN ENGLAND

The moment the *Freedom* docked in England, Juliet felt her heart break in two. Tears collected in her eyes as she slowly stepped off board, one step and then another until her feet were back on English soil.

It was truly over, now, was it not?

Over the past few days, ever since leaving *La Roche-sur-Mer* after a quick stop to pick up Antoinette, Juliet had entertained tentative hopes that perhaps...

Heaving a deep sigh, Juliet shook her head. Indeed, she had been a fool to hope. Never in her life had she met anyone more stubborn than Henri Duret. Whether he had made his decision out of fear or love did not matter, for she knew he would not change his mind. He would not come for her again, and now that she was back in England, he could not even if he wanted to.

The docks were a busy place as always, and Juliet was grateful for the loud hubbub around her. Her heart ached, and she feared the moment a question might be put to her, even one as simple as *How do you do?*

Fortunately, Violet seemed to sense Juliet's fragile hold on her nerves and left her alone, silently directing her steps toward the carriage that awaited them.

Little Antoinette, barely three years of age, prattled along happily, telling her mother and father all about her visit at *La Roche-sur-Mer*. "*Grandmère* made me promise to come back soon, and *Grandpère* did not even get to see me. Why did he not come back with you?"

Violet and Oliver did their best to satisfy their young daughter's curiosity while Juliet stared out the window, her eyes sweeping over familiar sites until the carriage pulled to a halt outside her family's townhouse.

Everything seemed as it always had. Nothing had changed. The world had gone on without her, and although Juliet had not undergone a marked transformation—deep down, she knew she was no longer the same woman who had boarded that ship to India weeks ago—the life that now took her back still fit...at least outwardly. She was still an English lady, expected to marry and provide an heir to her husband. Indeed, that was all that was expected of her. All that ever had been expected of her.

Long ago, Juliet had not found anything odd or upsetting with that notion; now, however, it made her angry. These narrow-minded expectations were the very ones that robbed her of her choices. This was *her* life and no one else's. Should it not be up to her how to live it?

Not as far as society was concerned. Indeed, Juliet was right back where she had started. Nothing had changed.

"Juliet!"

At the sound of her mother's joyous voice, Juliet flinched. Perhaps it was not until this very moment that she truly knew she had returned. Her eyes blinked, and she found the carriage door open and Oliver standing down on the pavement, offering his arm to her.

Reluctantly, Juliet took it and stepped down. She found her mother hasten toward her, joy and relief upon her face before she drew Juliet into her arms, hugging her tightly. "Oh, I was so worried about you," she whispered into Juliet's hair. "I'm so glad to see you well."

Juliet heaved a deep sigh, not knowing what to say. Her gaze moved to her younger brother Jacob, who stood on the doorstep.

When his father—Juliet's stepfather—had died four years ago, young Jake had become the new Viscount Silcox at only eight years of age. Juliet had always worried that this burden would change him, take away the joy of childhood...and it had. Still, every once in a while, she still seemed to glimpse a bit of that familiar, mischievous glimmer in his eyes. He was a sweet boy, forever tempted to seek out adventures that were not meant for him. Juliet could not help but wonder if he, too, would find himself torn one of these days. Torn between duty and desire.

Meeting her gaze, Jake bowed formally, and the severe look upon his face turned Juliet's stomach. Then, however, the corner of his mouth twitched and all of a sudden, he was grinning at her the same way he always had, something devilish lighting up his eyes.

"You must be hungry," her mother exclaimed, then she stood back, her pale eyes sweeping over Juliet's face. "Come. Let's go inside." Her gaze briefly swept up and down the pavement before she turned back to Juliet and leaned close. "Do not worry. As far as everyone knows, you spent the past few weeks with your sister. All will be well."

Of course, her mother feared for her reputation. It was something deeply ingrained, something her mother could not help. Still, even before her departure, Juliet had had little hope of making a good match. She could not imagine that to change anytime soon.

Or at all.

Nor did she want it to. Not even in her wildest dreams could she imagine marrying anyone other than Henri Duret.

And that was the problem, was it not? That was what doomed her. Doomed her to a life not worth living. A wasted life.

Unless she married, Juliet knew she would never have children. After all, one could not be a mother without also being a wife...

...at least, one *should* not.

As her mother turned to Violet and Oliver, thanking them for returning her daughter, Juliet found her gaze staring into the distance as her hand slowly came to rest upon her belly. *Could it be?* A quiet voice deep down wondered. Could she be with child?

Juliet could not help the smile that suddenly claimed her face at the thought of being a mother. The dream of having Henri's child to sweeten her days was the first truly wonderful thought to have found her since bidding him farewell.

"I shall see you soon, sister," Violet told her as she stepped closer, reaching for her hands. "We will remain in England for at least a month or two. Please visit us." She cast a quick glance over her shoulder at Juliet's mother, then she leaned closer and whispered, "And if you ever change your mind about my infuriatingly stubborn cousin..." Her voice trailed off, yet a devilishly wicked smile came to her face. "You know where to find me."

Juliet hugged her sister tightly, wishing they did not have to say goodbye so soon. Still, seeing Violet with her husband and her daughter made Juliet ache for a family of her own, for Henri.

"With the season over, we will soon travel to Silcox Manor," her mother remarked, smiling at Violet and Oliver. "Please, we would love to see you." Her gaze moved to little Antoinette, a longing sigh leaving her lips. "All of you."

Juliet knew that her mother wanted to see her happily married, not only for Juliet's sake but also for her own. She wanted to be a grand-mother with grandchildren to dote upon, a grandchild like Antoinette. But would she also welcome a bastard grandchild? Juliet could not help but think that deep down her mother would not mind; however, she, too, had been raised to fear society's wrath.

After Violet, Oliver and Antoinette had taken their leave, Juliet followed her mother up the stairs and into the house. Her feet felt as though they were weighted down with something heavy, and her legs struggled from step to step. Everything inside of her screamed out against this place, certain that this was not where she belonged.

"Within a week we shall be off," her mother declared joyfully as they sat down to a cup of tea and some biscuits while her brother returned to his studies. "The weather has been fine thus far, and I sent word to have Silcox Manor prepared the moment I learned of your return. There'll be garden parties to attend and neighbors to visit and..." Her mother's voice trailed off, and the forced joy Juliet saw upon her face slowly evaporated into thin air.

For a long moment, her mother simply looked at her. Then she heaved a deep sigh. "He broke your heart, did he not?"

Unable to hold on any longer, Juliet broke down weeping as her mother held her in her arms, mumbling that all would be well. And all the while, Juliet wished she were still a child, capable of believing the impossible.

Chapter Forty-Four

A FATHER'S WORDS

T he moment *La Roche-sur-Mer* came into view, Henri found his thoughts inevitably stray to Juliette. He pictured her walking along the pier or up the hill to his family's home. He pictured her smiling with her auburn tresses billowing behind her. He pictured her...waiting for him with open arms.

A curse flew from his lips at his wayward thoughts, and he turned to his first mate. "Ensure that the *Voile Noire* will be ready to set sail again as soon as possible. See to the crew as well as the necessary provisions."

As always, Ian gave a quick nod.

Leaving the quarterdeck, Henri strode across the main deck to the bowsprit, his gaze fixed upon his hometown. Always had it brought him joy to return here, to see his family. From now on, though, Henri knew that he would forever think of the one who was missing the moment his eyes fell upon *La Roche-sur-Mer*.

Perhaps he would be able to forget about her—at least for a short moment—if he kept himself occupied.

Over the next few days, Henri and his men combed the countryside, speaking to everyone they encountered, asking about the Duvals. Unfortunately, their search led them nowhere, for no one had heard of a family by that name living nearby. Henri forced himself to remember the exact words Juliette had said, the exact words Dubois had said to her. He still felt himself cringe at the thought of her at that man's mercy; yet, it was necessary. He needed to contemplate everything she had told him in order to locate Noèle's child.

To his relief, Noèle was recovering. Alexandra tended to the young woman's wounds diligently, mixing poultices and brewing tea that soothed and healed. Yet, the look in Noèle's eyes was still guarded, a flicker of despair in them far too often. How could it not be? She was still in pain, not only physical pain, but pain, nonetheless. Pain that was in all likelihood far worse than anything that had been done to her body.

And then Antoine returned from Paris and with him a significant piece of information.

It was late at night when they all sat in the library, discussing how to proceed. Henri's grandparents had already gone to bed, and while Antoine and Alexandra had seated themselves on the settee by the fire, Henri's father, Alain, stood with his back to them, his gaze directed outside. Henri stood leaning against the mantel; his gaze fixed upon his uncle. "Well? What did you find out?" Although Antoine possessed the ability of shielding his thoughts, Henri could not help but think that a glimmer of triumph rested in his eyes.

Clearing his throat, Antoine looked from his wife to his nephew. "It is not much," he warned, caution in his voice, "however, I suppose it might be a place to start."

Henri felt his pulse quicken. "What is?"

"In Paris, the men went to a tavern one night," Antoine began, "where they overheard others speak of a traveling circus." His brows rose meaningfully as he paused. "The name Duval was mentioned." He sighed. "Unfortunately, that is all the information they were able to obtain. The man who spoke of the Duvals was too deep in his cups to provide anything more, and the next morning, he could not even recall ever having spoken of them."

Henri exhaled a deep breath. "It truly is not much, but I agree it is a start." Again, he remembered the words Juliette had spoken, the words Dubois had thrown at her head, certain that they would never find the child. "A traveling circus," Henri mused. "Perhaps that is what he meant. Perhaps the Duvals are always on the move, never in one place for too long."

Antoine nodded. "I agree." He glanced over his shoulder at his brother, who still stood with his back to them, not saying a word. "The question is, where do we go from here? How do we proceed?"

Henri shrugged. "Well, we have connections up and down the coastline. I suggest we send word to everyone we know. Perhaps someone will have heard of a traveling circus involving a family named Duval." He straightened. "Someone should also head back down south to Dubois's hometown and make inquiries. It seemed as though he knew the Duvals. Perhaps the name will sound familiar to his widow." He looked from his uncle to his father. "It is worth a try." He heaved a deep sigh. "For Noèle and Ophélie."

Alexandra sat up, her gaze moving from her husband beside her to Henri. "She's almost well enough to travel," she stated carefully, a clear suggestion in her voice. "She will want to come." A knowing smile came to her lips. "After all, she's the girl's mother. Nothing short of death will keep her from her child." Something deeply imploring came to her eyes as she looked at Henri. "You cannot leave her behind."

Henri nodded. "Very well."

Clearing his throat, Alain turned from the window, his gaze moving from his brother seated upon the settee to his son standing by the fireplace. "And who will go?" he asked Henri. "Who will sail down south?"

Henri frowned. "I will," he replied without hesitation, confused about why his father would ask such a question. His gaze then drifted to Antoine, and what he saw there made Henri wonder if perhaps there was something he was not aware of. Had something happened?

Rising from the settee, Antoine held out his hand to his wife. "We bid you a good night," he said with a smile in Henri's direction as Alexandra stood and took his arm. Then they left, closing the door behind them.

Still frowning, Henri turned to look at his father. "What is going on?"

Alain drew in a deep breath, his hands linked behind his back, before he stepped away from the window and moved toward Henri.

"There is something I have been meaning to tell you for a while," he finally said, the look in his eyes an odd mixture of joy and sorrow. "I could never find the right time nor the right words and so...time passed, and I remained silent."

Henri felt a chill travel down his back at the ominous tone in his father's voice. "What is this about?"

His father inhaled a deep breath, his shoulders slowly rising as he gathered his courage to speak. "About your mother."

Henri almost flinched at hearing his father speak those words. For as long as Henri could remember, his father had never once voluntarily spoken of his wife, of Henri's mother. She had been lost to them when Henri had been only six years of age, and it had changed everything.

Swallowing, Henri met his father's gaze. "What of her?" He could not say if he truly wished to know, for the look in his father's eyes made him feel uneasy.

A wistful smile came to his father's face, and the look in his eyes became distant. "I knew she was the one the moment I laid eyes upon her," he whispered, clearly remembering the very moment he spoke of. "She was unlike any other, one-of-a-kind, and I knew that I wanted her, her alone." His eyes closed for a moment, and a deep sigh left his lips.

Henri swallowed, uncertain if he was to say something or not. It almost seemed as though his father had all but forgotten his presence. He wondered if he simply ought to leave, but he could not bring himself to do so, for although he dreaded hearing what his father had to say, part of him wanted to know. He barely remembered the woman who had been his mother. There were still images and feelings of warmth and joy that had stayed with him throughout the years; yet, he could no longer picture her face nor hear the sound of her voice.

"I wanted to court her," his father continued, his eyes open once more and looking into Henri's, "but she sent me away." He sighed. "She was quite adamant."

"Why?" Henri heard himself ask.

His father inhaled a deep breath, and it all but shuddered past his lips when leaving his body, a moment later. "Because she knew she would die."

Whatever Henri had expected his father to say, it had been nowhere near this. Those few little words slammed into Henri like a boulder falling from a high cliff top. He could all but feel its weight upon his chest, slowly crushing his bones. He found himself staring at his father, unable to catch a clear thought let alone ask a question, ask for more.

Yet it seemed his father understood him. He stepped forward and placed a hand upon his son's shoulder. "From the moment she had been born, your mother had been sickly. Even then, the doctor had prepared her parents for the worst." A deep smile came to his face. "And yet she lived on, year after year. She was never well, but she lived."

Henri cleared his throat. "What was it?" Somehow, it was easier to focus on the facts, to ask a question that would have a simple answer.

His father shrugged. "It was a sickness of the lungs. That is all I know."

Henri felt his teeth grit together, for the look in his father's eyes reminded him of the time following his mother's passing, the time when Henri had lost everything, his mother to death and his father to grief. "Why are you telling me this now?"

His father placed both hands upon Henri's shoulders, his eyes holding on to his in a way that Henri knew beyond the shadow of a doubt that whatever he was about to say was the very reason for every word he had spoken that night. "Because you're being a fool."

Henri blinked. "What?"

His father's hands tightened upon his shoulders, and he gave a slight shake. "You're being a fool!" he said a bit louder, a hint of exasperation coming to his face. "You found her, and yet you sent her away." His father shook his head at him in the way Henri remembered from his childhood. "You need to stop running and face your demons."

For a long moment, Henri could do little else but stare at his father. Then he stepped away, shrugging off his hands. "I will not speak to you about her," he growled, then turned and stalked toward the door, determined to escape this conversation.

"Juliette," his father said, and the sound of her name shot through Henri like an arrow. "Can you not even say her name?"

Henri whirled around, glaring at his father. "Why are you bringing this up? She has nothing to do with—"

"Because you're being a fool!"

Henri gritted his teeth. "Yes, you said so, but—"

"When your mother realized that I would not give up," his father replied, the words leaving his lips in a rush as though speaking them was still painful after all these years, "she finally told me the truth. She told me that she would die, perhaps not tomorrow or the day after, but soon. She told me we couldn't have a future, that as much as we might want it, it was simply not possible." Tears misted his father's eyes. "I almost walked away." He closed his eyes and hung his head in shame and regret before he drew in another fortifying breath, his gaze seeking Henri's once more. "I believed her. I believed when she said that we couldn't have a future, but she was wrong."

Stumped, Henri shook his head. "How can you say that? She died, did she not? You should've listened to her. You should have—"

"We had eight years together!" His father shot back, his eyes suddenly blazing with strength as he approached Henri, determination marking his features. "Eight years." He paused, waiting for the hammering pulse in his neck to calm. "Would you call that nothing? We had a son, a wonderful son we both wanted and loved. The day you were born was the happiest in our lives." His father shook his head, the look in his eyes daring Henri to contradict him. "We *had* a future! We *had* eight years! We *had* a child!" His hands shot out and grasped Henri by the shoulders once more. "We were happy, can you not see that?"

"And then you lost her," Henri mumbled, no longer in doubt why his father was suddenly telling him all this.

Alain nodded. "And then I lost her, *oui*, but I never once regretted taking that chance. If we had not, she would have still died, but we would also have lost those precious eight years...and you." His lips pressed into a tight line.

Henri drew in an unsteady breath. "If you hadn't..." He felt his jaw tighten. "You could have found...happiness elsewhere. You—"

His father scoffed. "You truly are a fool, Henri!" Again, his father shook his head at him. "Do you truly believe you get to choose who to give your heart to? Even if I had walked away from your mother, it would not have changed the fact that I loved her. She would've still died, and I would have forever regretted all those moments we had never had."

"It is not the same," Henri gritted out. "Juliette is not dying; quite the contrary, she is far safer where she is now, back home in England."

"Safer, *oui*," his father replied with a shrug. "But happy?"

Henri flinched as his father's words conjured the very ones Juliette had spoken to him before he had sent her away. *Safe perhaps, but definitely unhappy.*

"What worth does a life lived in misery have?" An indulgent smile came to his father's face. "Don't be a fool, Henri. You've never been one. Don't start now. You know that I'm right. You know this to be true. You pushed her away because you're afraid to lose her. You're protecting yourself and no one else." He sighed, squeezing Henri's shoulders. "She loves you just as much as you love her. I saw it in her eyes when she was here with Violette. It broke her heart to leave, and I watched her standing at the stern of the *Freedom*, looking at *La Roche-sur-Mer* until there was nothing to be seen anymore." A frown came to his face. "What did you say to her? I cannot help but think that she did not leave of her own accord. She's a fierce one, your Juliette. Quite honestly, I expected her to stay, with your permission or without. Why then did she leave?"

Henri shrugged and once more stepped away. "How am I to know? Perhaps she had finally come to see that it would be safer for her to—"

"Why did she leave?" his father pressed. "What did you say to her?"

Henri whirled around. "I told her I would not return to *La Roche-sur-Mer* and start looking for Noële's child until she had left," he snarled, disgusted with himself.

His father's jaw dropped. Then anger blazed in his eyes, and he stormed toward Henri, giving him a slap upside the head. "I guess I was wrong! You are a fool!"

Again, Henri felt the urge to leave, to escape this conversation; yet he did not. Instead, he walked up to the window, to the very spot his father had vacated earlier and looked outside at the darkened world. "What do you suggest I do?" he asked quietly, not certain if he wanted to hear his father's answer.

Another scoff left his father's lips. "I suggest you go after her!" He chuckled. "I thought that was obvious."

Henri could feel every fiber of his being yearn to do just that. He felt his muscles tense with the need to move, to rush from the room, not to escape this conversation, but to head down to the docks and set sail. "Even if...I wanted to," Henri began, doing his utmost to fight that deep craving that once more settled in his bones, "she is back in England. We are at war. I could never—"

His father laughed. "That is nonsense! If I recall correctly, you all but strode into England before in order to protect Violette. Do not tell me you cannot do so again!" Quiet footsteps carried his father closer. "You know where she will be. You've heard Violette speak more than once of how the English *ton* retreats to the country after the Season's end."

"Silcox Manor," Henri mumbled under his breath, remembering that lone beach where Antoine had found Alexandra over fifteen years ago. Henri remembered that night well. A storm had been upon them, and they ought to have turned; yet...*something* had made Antoine head toward that beach. *Somehow*...he had known.

"Precisely," his father agreed, grasping Henri's arm and urging him to turn and look at him. "Go, and don't waste another moment." His brows rose imploringly. "Go."

Staring at his father, Henri could barely hold himself back. Every part of him itched to be off, all reasons to the contrary suddenly evaporating into thin air.

"Go!"

The moment Henri made to turn toward the door, he paused, then looked back at his father. "I cannot," he whispered, a deep sense of regret and disappointment flooding him. He shook his head. "I cannot."

His father frowned, exasperation once more blazing in his eyes. "Why ever not? No more excuses, Henri!" he grumbled, lifting a finger in warning.

Henri sighed. "What about Noële? And Ophélie? They cannot wait. I cannot make them wait. They deserve to be reunited before—"

"Send the Scotsman," his father threw in with a shrug of his shoulders. "He is loyal and capable, and quite frankly, the man looks starved for a purpose."

Henri frowned. "Ian? But..." His voice trailed off.

"Do you doubt him? His loyalty or his capabilities?"

Henri shook his head. "Neither, but..." He swallowed, unable to make his peace with such an unexpected suggestion. Never had he been able to hand control to another, to take a step back and place his trust in another. "But...But he would need a ship. If I'm heading to England..." Again, he broke off, a quiet voice in his head whispering, *Are you?*

"He could take your uncle's ship," his father suggested, not the slightest hint of doubt in his voice. "Antoine told me that he's been meaning to take a step back from privateering."

Henri gawked at his father. "He said that? Why?"

His father gave him another one of those indulgent smiles. "To have more time with his wife and his children," he chuckled, shaking his head at Henri. "Is that truly so hard to believe?"

For a long moment, Henri remained quiet, completely stunned by what the past few minutes had brought about. Had he truly agreed to go to England? To...?

"Juliette." Her name left his lips without thought, conjuring her image, her smile, those vivid green eyes. Henri knew that if he did not leave now, he would never find himself looking down into them again. And all of a sudden, that thought frightened him more than any other.

"Go," his father urged him once more, "before she gives up all hope and agrees to marry an Englishman." His brows rose meaningfully, daring Henri to imagine a world where those words were true.

Henri was already halfway out the door before he was even realizing what he was doing. His feet pulled to a sudden halt, and he looked back at his father. "Merci, Papa."

His father smiled at him. "Ah, I'm not doing any of this for you. I'm being selfish because, truth be told, I could do with a grandchild or two." A wide grin came to his face. "Now, go!"

Feeling lighter than he ever had before, Henri rushed down the hall. He knew he could not lose another moment because *truth be told* he had already lost too many.

Chapter Forty-Five
RETURN TO SILCOX MANOR

The garden of Silcox Manor was swamped with guests, their voices echoing through the warm summer air as they promenaded along the meticulously groomed flower beds or sat in the shade on one of many picnic blankets spread across the green, enjoying lemonade and pastries.

It was a beautiful sight, and Juliet wished she could simply join in and allow her heart to be happy. She spotted little Antoinette sitting on a swing as Jake pushed her ever higher, her little hands tightly clutching the ropes as she squealed in delight. "Higher! Higher, Jake!"

"You look miserable," Violet remarked as she came to stand next to Juliet upon the terrace. "Honestly, I have never seen you look so glum. You look almost sickly."

Unfortunately, Violet's words brought back that feeling of nausea Juliet had come to expect as of late. "It is nothing," she mumbled nonetheless; and yet her hands moved involuntarily and settled upon her belly. She quickly removed them, forcing her arms to hang limply by her sides; however, when she looked up into her sister's face, Juliet knew that there was no use in denying it.

Violet's blue eyes were wide as she stared at Juliet. "Are you—?" Her voice broke off as she quickly cast a glance over her shoulder. Then she grasped Juliet by the arm and tugged her along, off the terrace and down the lawn to the edge of the garden where a small path led down to the beach.

Once there, Violet spun around, the strong breeze tugging loose blond curls that swirled around her head. "Are you with child?" she asked, her gaze dropping lower to Juliet's belly.

Closing her eyes, Juliet sighed. "I believe so."

Violet's hand tightened upon Juliet's arm. "Does your mother know? Does anyone? Why did you not tell me?" Her mouth hung open a little in disbelief as well as disappointment that Juliet had not confided in her.

"I have not told anyone yet," Juliet replied, herself still struggling with the notion of becoming a mother.

"Is it...?" Violet paused, hesitation in her eyes before she dropped them for a brief moment. She drew in a deep breath and then forged ahead, "Is it...Henri's? Or...?" A somewhat scrunched up look came to her face. "I mean, you never said...and I wasn't sure if I should ask you or if you would rather not speak about it, but..."

Juliet placed a calm hand upon her sister's fluttery one. "It is Henri's," she replied with a smile. "Dubois never—" She broke off, willing away the memories that sometimes still tortured her at night. She had not been raped, but...

When these moments came, Juliet always forced herself to think of Noèle, willing herself to remember everything the young woman had suffered. It helped her remain strong and count herself among the fortunate ones to have escaped this ordeal with only a handful of dark memories.

"But he needs to know," Violet exclaimed, about to turn on her heel and march back to the house. "Of course, he—"

"No!" Juliet grasped her sister's arm, holding her back. "You cannot tell him. He cannot know. Promise me!"

A deep frown came to Violet's face as she stared at her. "Why? If he only knew, he would—"

"Precisely," Juliet replied, fighting against the urge to allow her sister to do exactly what she wanted. "I do not want him to return out of obligation. I do not want him by my side only because he feels forced to be there. He has made his choice, and this is mine." She straightened, the look in her eyes imploring. "You cannot tell him."

Violet heaved an exasperated sigh. "Can I just say that you two frustrate me to no ends?" She shook her head and then pulled Juliet into her arms, holding her tightly. "What do you need me to do?"

Embracing her sister, Juliet sighed. "I don't know. Please, at least for now, don't say anything to anyone. I don't know yet what I will do. I will need some time to think about it." She stepped back and looked at her sister. "Promise me."

Reaching out to brush an auburn curl back behind Juliet's ear, Violet smiled at her. "Of course. Whatever you need, I'm always here for you. After all, we are sisters."

Juliet smiled with tears in her eyes. "Not by blood..."

"...but by heart's choice," Violet finished the words they always spoke to one another in moments like this one. It never failed to remind Juliet of the Duret motto, *Family above all.*

Juliet heaved a deep sigh. "I know that Mother means well, but," she allowed her gaze to sweep over the many guests attending today's garden party, "I think I could use a little time to myself. Would you mind...?"

"Making excuses?" Violet asked with a grin. "Of course not. Go and...think it through. But know that whatever you decide, I will be right here to stand with you." She gently squeezed Juliet's hand and then stepped away, returning to her husband and child, the happy little family she called her own.

After another envious look at her sister, Juliet turned toward the path that led down to the beach. With each step she took, the guests' voices receded, their echo replaced by a strong breeze blowing in from the sea. It whirled around her, tugging upon her skirts and her hair, undoing the careful hairstyle her mother had praised with such delight earlier this morning. Before long, most of her strands had come tumbling down, and Juliet felt reminded of how she had stood upon the deck of the *Voile Noire*, her eyes gliding over the endless sea.

She had felt at peace then, not only because of the beauty and endlessness of the world before her eyes, but mostly because of the man who had stood by her side.

Only now, whenever she thought of him, tears would sting her eyes and her heart would grow heavy. Again, her hand settled on her belly as she wondered about what to do. Of course, Henri deserved to know; however, knowing would ultimately force his hand. He would do the right thing simply because he was that kind of man, and Juliet was afraid that she would not have the strength to refuse him.

She wanted him, yes, but only for the right reasons, only if he truly wanted her as well. She could not imagine being the one thing in his life he would always regret.

As Juliet strolled along the beach, sand slipped inside her shoes. She continued onward until the soft pinches around her toes and soles became truly uncomfortable. She stopped and looked over her shoulder at Silcox Manor a good distance away, the guests' voices now no longer even an echo. A smile came to her lips, and before she knew it, Juliet had removed her shoes and stockings. Her toes dug into the sand, and her eyes strayed to the water's edge.

Juliet felt her heart skip a beat when she dipped her toes into the water, feeling the cool freshness swirl around her. It was the same sea that carried Henri to his next destination—wherever that was—was it not? Somehow, even in such a small regard, they were still connected. Could he feel her? She wondered. Could he sense that she had stepped into the same waters he called his own?

Shaking her head, Juliet looked out to sea, knowing that her thoughts were foolish. Still, they were comforting as well.

"You look thoughtful."

At the sound of Henri's voice, Juliet froze. Her first instinct was to spin around and look upon him, but she did not. Of course, he was not here. He could not be. It was impossible.

Heaving a deep sigh, Juliet bowed her head. Never before had she heard his voice so clearly in her mind. It had sounded so real as though he stood only a few paces behind her.

If only that could be true. If only he had come for her after all.

"Will you not even look at me?"

Juliet pinched her eyes shut. Yes, there had been a time when she had cherished hearing his voice echo inside her head. Now, however, it simply was no longer enough. It was torture to be reminded of what she had lost, of what would never be. "Go away," she whispered to the wind. "Please, go away and let me be."

Seemingly endless moments ticked by as Juliet waited, hoping the voice would return, hoping it would not. She listened to the sounds of the wind around her, the soft screeches of the seagulls overhead, and slowly her pulse began to calm. She drew in a slow breath, allowing her eyes to glide open, the endless sea once more before her.

Perhaps she ought to have expected this. Always had the sea reminded her of Henri. Perhaps she ought to have seen this coming, standing here upon this very beach. Of course, her thoughts were drawn to him. Perhaps she ought to return to the house.

Heaving another deep breath and cherishing the salty tinge of the sea air, Juliet stepped back from the water's edge. She turned around, her gaze moving over the sand to find the spot where she had left her shoes and stockings, only to pull up short, her breath suddenly caught in her throat as she stared...

...at...at...

With wide eyes, Juliet backed away. "No, you cannot be here." Her head began shaking from side to side as her eyes remained fixed upon Henri. He stood no more than a few paces away from her, the sun lighting up his green eyes as she had seen it do so often. He looked as he had always looked, a simple white shirt with a dark vest, breeches and boots and, of course, a sword strapped to his left hip and a knife to the other.

Again, Juliet could not help but think that he looked like a pirate with his long hair tied in the back and a bit of stubble covering the lower half of his face. He still had that wicked curl to his lips despite the touch of regret that seemed to linger upon his face. Indeed, he looked exactly the way Juliet had always imagined him ever since her feet had returned to English soil. Yet never had she seen him look so lifelike.

Again, her head shook from side to side. "You're not here. You can't be." She pinched her eyes shut, silently counted to three and then opened them abruptly. "Why are you still here?" she mumbled to herself before a curse flew from her lips. "Leave me alone. Please, leave me alone." She backed away another step and felt the cold seawater once more swirl around her feet.

A look of incredulity came to Henri's face as he began moving toward her. "Why is it that you always believe me to be some kind of mirage?" His gaze held hers, and a deeply wicked grin touched his lips. "I remember the last time you thought me to be a dream, and I also remember what cured you of that notion."

Juliet could not move as he strode toward her, one step, then two, then three. She stared and stared, hearing his words, allowing them to draw her back to that moment upon Dubois's ship when she had first laid eyes on him again after four long years. Yes, then, too, she had not believed him to be real.

But he had. He had!

Juliet's heart skipped a beat. "Henri?"

By the time his name flew from her lips in no more than a soft puff of air, Henri's large strides had already eaten up the distance between them. Suddenly, he stood so close...and he did not waste another moment.

He never did.

Before Juliet knew what was happening, she once again lay in his arms, and her heart almost beat out of her chest the second Henri's mouth claimed hers. It was a kiss that spoke of longing and need, but, also, of regret as well as the determination to not feel it again.

Bright spots began to dance in front of Juliet's eyes. She held them closed, and yet she could see them. Her head spun as she clung to him, her fingers digging into his flesh, determined to hold on. Was he truly here? He felt warm and alive, and his kiss reminded her not of all the lonely hours of which there had been so many lately, but instead of the days they had spent together upon the sea.

"There?" Henri whispered against her lips before he slowly pulled back, one hand softly cradling her cheek. "Do you now believe that I am here?"

Another long moment passed as Juliet stared up at him. "You're here," she repeated, a deep frown coming to her face as she fought to make sense of everything. "You're...You're here?"

Henri chuckled, and his hand slipped to the small of her neck, pulling her closer once more. "Can you not feel it?" he whispered, brushing his mouth against hers. A deep sigh shuddered past his lips, and she could feel its warmth against her own. "*Mon Dieu*, I've missed you." Again, his mouth claimed hers as passion and need overwhelmed every other sensation.

As she lay in his arms, Juliet felt the world slip away. It would be so easy to simply give in and forget everything. But she knew she could not. There were questions, countless questions about...

...everything. How was he here? England and France were still at war; he could not simply sail up the coast to Norfolk and...

Yet Antoine had done so, had he not? All those years ago.

Pulling back, Juliet blinked, trying her best to focus her thoughts as well as her vision. "Are you here for me?" she asked, unwilling to let herself believe just yet.

A wide smile came to his face. "*Bien sur*," Henri said, that same conviction in his voice she had heard before. "Why else would I set foot on English soil?" His hands upon her tightened possessively. "I've come for you. I would always come for you. Did I not tell you that once?"

Blinking her eyes against those blasted bright spots, Juliet pulled away, her hands pushing against him to put at least an arm's distance between them. "Yes, I do remember. I also remember that you sent me away." Swallowing, she took another step back until his hands could no longer reach her.

No, she could not go through this again.

And she would not.

Chapter Forty-Six

A LIFE FREELY CHOSEN

J uliette's words cut deep, and yet Henri knew that she had every right to speak them. He had done wrong by her. In order to protect himself, his own heart, he had broken hers. Indeed, he had been a fool, and he whispered a silent thank-you to his father for setting him right before it had been too late. Or was it already?

"If you're here to see Violet," Juliette began, her gaze moving far beyond him toward the manor, "she is up in the gardens as are countless other guests." A note of caution lingered in her voice. "I can send her to you. I—"

"I did not come for Violette," Henri pointed out swiftly, not wishing there to be any doubt. He took a step closer, his gaze holding onto hers. She looked like a frightened creature about to bolt, and although he did not wish to frighten her more, he needed her to understand why he had come. "Not this time. This time, I came for you, and that is the truth."

Her head once more began shaking from side to side before her gaze swept out to sea as though she were looking for something. Perhaps the *Voile Noire*. "You cannot be here," Juliette insisted. "If someone were to find you here..." Her voice trailed off, and she swallowed hard. "No, you need to leave. Now."

"Not without you!"

At the hard tone in his voice, Juliette flinched, her eyes snapping back up to meet his. Her hands were trembling as she lifted them to hug them around herself.

Not wishing her to retreat any farther, Henri quickly closed the distance between them. His hands settled upon her shoulders, and she drew in a sharp breath as though she still was not convinced that he was truly here. "Listen," he mumbled softly, his heart beating as fast as hers if the wildly thudding pulse in her neck was any indication. "I should never have sent you away. I know that now, but it took me a while to realize it." Words had always been difficult for Henri. Never had he gotten into the habit of speaking what was on his mind let alone what was in his heart. Perhaps if his mother had lived, she could have taught him. Whatever the reason, he felt completely inept to accomplish this seemingly simple task.

Yet he knew he had to try.

For her!

"No," Juliette agreed, her chin rising in a bit of a defiant gesture. "You should not have." She swallowed. "Then why did you?"

Henri inhaled a deep breath and then told her of the conversation he had had with his father. All the while, her gaze remained fixed upon his face, watching, observing as she listened, absorbing each word. "I never dared think of her much after that," Henri admitted, remembering the emptiness he had felt after his mother's death. "Back then, my father could not speak of her. He could barely speak to me. He seemed so broken, and for a long time, I feared that I would lose him, too." Henri remembered well how he had done his utmost to distract himself, constantly getting himself into trouble, testing each and every limit, bending each and every rule to the point of breaking it. "Life became...better when Antoine agreed to let me sail with him. I finally had something to do, something worth doing, and I never looked back."

Tears stood in Juliette's eyes as she listened, and Henri could see that her heart could easily grasp the meaning of his words. Something that had taken him a long time to understand came to her with ease.

His hands slid from her shoulders and down her back, urging her closer. "And then I met you, and you turned my life upside down. I think a part of me even knew it that first moment we met in London; only I did not dare admit it to myself then."

Her lips curled up into a warm smile. "I knew it as well," she whispered as a tear rolled down her cheek, "and it frightened me because I thought a man like you could never want—"

"But I did," Henri insisted, and he pulled her closer still, relieved to feel her hands abandon their defiant position upon her arms. "I still do!" he admitted on a growl before claiming yet another kiss.

It would never be enough. Never!

And then her hands reached for him with the same need that hummed in Henri's veins as well. Pushing herself up onto her toes, Juliette leaned into him, her hands sliding up his neck and into his hair as she returned his kiss with equal fervor.

Eventually, their kisses grew softer and slower, and Henri reminded himself that more needed to be said. He pulled back and looked down at her, a lovely glow upon her face he had never noticed before. "I love you, Juliette," he whispered, forcing out the words; after all, not saying them would not make them any less true. "And I do want you to be my wife."

A soft gasp escaped her lips as she stared up at him. "Are you serious?" she whispered, her wide, green eyes flying over his face. "What about...the sea? The *Voile Noire*? How are we—?"

"I don't know," Henri replied shrugging his shoulders. "Honestly, I don't know. I don't know how all of this will work, but we will find a way. Any way is better than a future that keeps us apart." He sighed deeply. "I know that now. It is what I want. *You* are what I want." His hands began to tremble, and he held onto her even tighter than before. "Do you...want that as well? Do you want...me?" A lump settled in Henri's throat as he looked down at her, waiting.

For an agonizingly long moment, Juliette remained silent. Her gaze became distant, and Henri could see that something lingered upon her mind. "Are you certain?" she finally asked again, lifting a finger to stop him before he could make a reply. "No, I need you to be certain. Absolutely certain. I know that you love the life you have chosen, and I don't want you to have any regrets. I don't want to be the reason you lose the very thing that keeps you whole." With tears in her eyes, she shook her head. "I could not bear it. I could not bear what it would do to us." Lifting her chin, she swallowed, blinking back her tears. "So, I need you to be certain. If this is only a moment's infatuation, then allow it to pass and allow us each to move on separately." Her teeth dug into her lower lip as she fought back tears. "Ultimately, it would be for the best."

Henri nodded, uncertain what it was she was saying. Before, she had always seemed so, *oui*, certain. Now, there was doubt and hesitation. "If you no longer want this," he began, feeling his insides twist and turn at the thought that she no longer cared for him the way she once had, "then say so. I will not hold it against you. I will let you go if you want me to...even if it kills me."

Juliette's brows drew down, and an incredulous look came to her eyes before she huffed out a bit of an exasperated breath. "How can you ask me that? I've wanted you from the first moment I met you. I believe I have made that unmistakably clear, have I not?" A hint of anger sneaked into her voice. "Do not turn this around on me. You are the one who could not commit. After everything you've told me, I understand. Yes, I do, but I do not want you to make this choice simply because your father urged you to, because you believe doing as your parents did would make you happy. You need to choose your own path. You need to know what *you* want." She heaved a deep sigh. "That is all I ask."

The tightness that had settled in Henri's chest slowly lessened, and he felt himself breath in with ease. Reaching for Juliette's hands, he pulled them against his chest. "I am not here because I believe I have to be for one reason or another. I am here because I finally realized that although I would like to have a guarantee for endless happy years with you, I know that there are no guarantees. We can only ever do what we believe is right and best for us."

Juliette smiled up at him. "And I am best for you?" she asked with a bit of a raised brow. "What lovely lukewarm sentiment."

Henri laughed. "You always seemed so sweet and innocent and delicate like a true English rose," he remarked as his gaze swept over her, "you're not, are you?"

Juliette's eyes opened wide. "Did you just insult me?"

Laughing, Henri shook his head. "On the contrary, it was the greatest compliment I have ever bestowed on anyone."

Sighing, she bit her lower lip. "Well, what can I say. I suppose those last few weeks out at sea...changed me, revealed sides of me I did not know I had. Perhaps I've always been meant to be this person, and now I finally have the chance to be who I am...with you."

"I like the thought," Henri murmured, releasing her hands and once more sweeping his own over her shoulder and down her back, "of the two of us being who we are together. It seems right, does it not?"

Juliette nodded. "It does." As he lowered his head to kiss her, she pulled back. "Are you truly certain that this is what you want? I cannot risk my heart; I cannot risk my..." She clamped her lips shut, then swallowed. "I need you to be truly certain."

Henri frowned, sensing that she was holding something back. "I am certain," he replied, feeling that ice-cold chill return. "But I cannot help feeling that you...are not. Did something happen? Since you returned to England?" He glanced up to Silcox Manor high up upon the cliff in the distance. "Have you found a new life here?" Henri dreaded her answer, but he needed to know.

To his surprise, that lovely glow returned to her face, and she took a step back before her right hand slipped down and gently settled on her belly. "Sort of," she whispered, and suddenly the corners of her mouth stretched into an enormous smile, one that seemed to light up the world.

Henri stared at her, momentarily confused, a myriad of emotions rolling through him, then disappearing before something in his mind suddenly clicked. "You are with child?" he asked, the shock of it almost rocking him back upon his heels.

Sighing, Juliette nodded. "I believe so." Her gaze held his as she waited, a slight tension in her shoulders as though she worried about his reaction.

The spark of joy that ignited in his heart was cut short when dark memories returned, reminding him of the days they had spent apart, the days she had been upon Dubois's ship. "I never asked you," he said, clearing his throat, his gaze holding hers only with difficulty. "I assure you it will not change anything for me, but I need to know what happened upon Dubois's ship. I know I should have asked before, but I was...afraid of the answer."

To Henri's great surprise and relief, a bit of an exasperated smile came to Juliette's face as she shook her head at him. "Blood related or not, you truly are my sister's cousin, are you not?" Henri frowned. "Yes, only moments ago, Violet asked me the same thing."

Henri swallowed. "And what did you tell her?" He stepped closer, reaching out a hand to gently cup her face. "Are you all right? Did he... Did he hurt you?"

Juliette sighed, and he could see dark clouds passing over her mind. "Not in the way you think," she finally said, stepping into his embrace. "It was a horror to be trapped on that ship with him, never knowing... what he would do." She closed her eyes, and Henri wished that Dubois was still alive so he could kill him all over again. Slowly! "But it seems," she finally said, raising her eyes to his, "that the art of conversation is still of some use. It distracted him, not only for Noèle's sake, but also for my own." She swallowed hard. "He was about to...when a call from the crow's nest called him away. We had arrived, and he was forced to attend to...other matters." A tentative smile came to her lips as her fingers curled into his vest. "And then you came. Again, you came for me."

Henri held her tightly. "Always, my lionhearted Juliette. Always." Indeed, she was stronger than he had thought. To possess the presence of mind to draw Dubois into a conversation when the threat of abuse lingered in the air was not an easy feat. She had shown true courage, and yet Henri wished it had never been necessary. He could not imagine how terrified she had to have been, and he vowed to do everything in his power to erase those memories as much as he possibly could.

Holding her in his arms, Henri felt her breathe in and out as they stood together upon the sand, soft waves washing over her bare feet as well as his boots. He felt as though the sea was calling them back, and as though Juliette, too, had heard her call, she lifted her head and looked at him. "How did you get here? Where is the *Voile Noire*?"

A wide grin came to Henri's face before he looked over her

shoulder toward the cavern he had first seen over fifteen years ago. He had been a young lad then, and he had not known that not only Antoine would find his destiny upon this beach.

"Truly?" Juliette asked after following his gaze. "When did you arrive? Have you been here all day?" She stepped back, looking at him with an incredulous look in her eyes.

"Shortly before dawn," Henri replied with a grin. "I thought it wiser to approach the English coast in the dark. After all, we are still at war."

Juliette nodded, her gaze moving back and forth between the cavern and the manor on the cliff top. "What now?" she asked, looking back at him. Henri inhaled a deep breath, then he held out his hand to her. "Now, we go home, *ma petite lionne*."

"Home?" Juliette asked with a grin as she stepped forward and took his hand. "The *Voile Noire*?"

"The *Voile Noire*," Henri replied with a nod. "Or wherever else we want it to be."

Reaching out, Juliette pressed a quick kiss upon his lips. "I would love that," she whispered, not bothering to pull back. "Let's go." And then she kissed him again as he had hoped she would.

Epilogue

La Roche-sur-Mer, France 1812

Four weeks later

The sun shone brightly upon the small marriage ceremony up on a hill that overlooked the coastline and the village and harbor below. Juliet smiled as her gaze swept over the Duret home, a simple structure made from wood and rock with tall windows and enough space to house the entire family. It was not a place that served as representation, its splendor meant to impress others. No, it was home, a place where a family lived, a large family that loved to sit around the long dining table at the end of each day, chatting and laughing and enjoying each other's company.

Not only Antoine's and Alain's parents, Hubert and Colette, still called this place their home, but it also sheltered Antoine and Alexandra as well as their four young children. Alain also still lived there, as did Henri.

And now, Juliet did as well, as would their little one one day soon.

"Do you think you will feel at home here?" Henri asked as they stood at a little distance to their guests. Alexandra and Colette had outdone themselves decorating the large garden with flowers and ribbons.

Juliet breathed in deeply, savoring the salty sea air. "I already do," she told her new husband, a wide smile coming to her face as she stepped into his embrace. "I love this place and its people." She looked up at him. "Your father keeps hugging me whenever our paths cross."

Henri chuckled. "Yes, I've noticed. Sometimes I cannot help but wonder which one of us is more thrilled to have you here." His fingers grasped her chin, gently tilting up her head. "If it bothers you, I—"

"No, no, no," Juliet assured him quickly. "I love it. Neither my father nor my stepfather have ever shown me this kind of affection. It is wonderful!" Her gaze moved to where Alain stood on the terrace, once again grinning at her in that absolutely charming way of his.

With her husband's arms wrapped around her, Juliet allowed her gaze to sweep over her family, old and new alike. She saw many happy faces. Hubert and Colette were sitting in the shade, speaking to neighbors and friends, while Antoine and Alexandra joined others as they danced upon the terrace. Their four children had joined up with Antoinette and Juliet's brother Jake as well as countless others from the village and were currently chasing each other across the lawn, stealing pastries from large tables, weighted down with inordinate amounts of delicious food. Oliver and Violet were strolling along the cliff top, hand-in-hand, before they stopped and shared a passionate kiss that made Juliet smile and turn to look at her own husband.

"Is it unseemly for a husband to kiss his wife in public?" Juliet asked with a grin.

As expected, Henri's eyes lit up with wicked delight. "I cannot say I've ever cared for what the public thought or deemed seemly," he whispered, bending down to brush his lips against hers. "I generally do what I want without thought for anyone but myself."

Juliet smiled up at him. "And what do you want?"

"A kiss or two," his grin deepened, "or a few more."

"And do I have any say in the matter?" she teased him about his earlier words.

"Always," he whispered, then he lowered his head to steal a kiss.

"Are you not worried that I would refuse you?" Juliet asked as her hand snaked around his neck, pulling herself closer to him.

Henri breathed in deeply. "Not in the slightest," he murmured against her lips, then he claimed her mouth once more in a kiss that took her breath away.

"Henri! Henri! Henri!" came little Antoinette's voice as she came running up the small slope toward them. "You must come! You must come!"

Reluctantly, Henri broke their kiss and stepped away, a heated promise in his eyes to finish what they had begun later. Then, he turned to his little niece. "What is the matter, Toni?"

Her little arms gestured wildly, more or less pointing in the direction of the tall oak tree that stood on the southern edge of the garden. "The swing! The swing!"

Squinting her eyes, Juliet saw that the swing's ropes had wrapped around the branch it was attached to, much too high for any of the children to reach. "I'll come," Henri told her, then he reached out and grasped her little hand, and together, they strolled down the hill.

Juliet heaved a deep sigh as she looked after them, wondering about their own child, her thoughts straying to a day in the near future when she would see her husband and child walking like that hand in hand. Juliet could hardly wait.

"Congratulations, Juliet."

Looking over her shoulder, Juliet found her little brother standing there in his formal attire, looking more grown-up than she liked him to be. At twelve years of age, Jake's childhood was not over yet, and Juliet prayed he would be able to hold onto it for a little bit longer. "Are you enjoying yourself, Jake?"

Her brother nodded, and his gaze swept over the many guests, many of whom were now family. "I like it here," he told her as he watched Henri disentangle the swing from the branch. "Truly, the French are not as bad as everyone says." A bit of a confused frown came to his face. "I cannot help but wonder why we are at war with them."

Chuckling, Juliet nodded. "I feel the same way. Everyone looks so happy, do they not?" Only the look upon her mother's face seemed a bit tense compared to all the other joyous expressions she saw. Yet, it made sense, did it not?

Juliet could not imagine how odd it had to feel for her mother to be here, to see Lord Silcox's first wife, Alexandra, celebrating with them. Indeed, looking more closely, Juliet could not help but think that her mother had taken a great interest in her late husband's first wife. Her pale eyes seemed to follow Alexandra and Antoine as they laughed and danced and kissed. Was there perhaps a touch of envy in her mother's eyes? And longing in her heart for a love like theirs?

"I cannot remember ever seeing Mother that happy," she mused, trying to remember the years before her father had passed away. "She certainly did not love Lord Silcox." Her gaze strayed to her brother. "I'm sorry, Jake."

He shrugged, his gaze lingering upon their mother as well. "It is the truth. Why would you apologize for it?"

Juliet nodded, surprised by the simple wisdom in her brother's words. "I wonder if she's ever been in love." She sighed. "I wonder if she has regrets."

Twice a widow, Elaine Winters, Viscountess Silcox, had always done her duty and married according to her parents' wishes. She had provided for her children as best as she could, always diligent in her responsibility to her title and family. But was that all? Had she ever loved? Certainly not one of her husbands.

"Perhaps it is not too late," Juliet mused aloud as her gaze swept over her mother. A bit of gray had begun to show at her temples, but her hair still shone in a deep chestnut brown. She looked lovely in the pale blue gown she wore today, and only the soft frown upon her face as well as that hint of sadness and regret that lingered in her eyes took away from her beauty.

A chuckle drifted to her ears, and Juliet turned to look at her brother. She was surprised to find a bit of a devilish expression upon his face. "What is it?"

His blue eyes moved to hers, and for a moment, he seemed to

consider whether or not to speak his thoughts. "Very well," he finally said, eagerness to share his secret in his voice, "but you must promise me not to say a word to Mother or anyone else."

Frowning, Juliet nodded, wondering what her brother was up to. "I give you my word."

After once more glancing over his shoulder at their mother as though to ensure that she was truly not within earshot, Jake moved closer, his voice dropping to a whisper. "Ethan and I have it all planned. His father is a widower, you see, and we thought that perhaps the two of them would make a good match."

Juliet stared at her brother. "You're not serious?"

The expression upon Jake's face sobered. "I want to see her happy just as you do, what is wrong with that?"

"Nothing is wrong with that," Juliet hastened to assure him. "However, you cannot simply choose someone for her. What if—?"

"I am not!" Jake exclaimed, a hint of anger in his voice. "Ethan and I discussed it thoroughly. The two of them seem to have a lot in common, and if it turns out we are wrong and they don't like each other, nothing has to come of it." He huffed out a deep breath. "All I want is...to see her smile."

For a long time, Juliet looked at her brother. "Perhaps you're right," she finally replied, wondering if perhaps all her mother needed was a little push. "Is there anything I can do?" she asked with a grin.

Jake's face brightened. "There is no need, sister. Just leave it all to me. Ethan and I know what we're doing."

Juliet frowned. "Ethan? Your friend from school?"

Jake nodded. "The very one."

"I wish you good luck," she told him, wondering if perhaps her little brother's plan would end in a disaster. Still, Juliet knew that her mother's life was one of routine, and even if any hope remained in her heart about one day finding love for herself, she still would never be so bold as to go and seek it out. Perhaps Jake was right. Perhaps this was the way to do it.

Once the swing had been untangled, Jake returned to pushing Antoinette at her behest while Henri quickly strode across the lawn back to Juliet's side. She loved that he never moved away for long or far, seeking her presence, her company as much as she desired his.

"Have you heard from Ian and Noèle?" Juliet asked, suddenly finding herself wondering about others and the love they had never found or lost. "Any news about her daughter?"

Sighing, Henri shook his head. "Not so far, but knowing Ian, he will not give up. He is a determined man, and I believe whatever happened in his own past, it is that which fuels his desire to reunite Noèle with her child."

"Did he ever speak to you about his own family?" Juliet asked, leaning back against her husband as his arms came around her.

Henri shook his head. "You might have noticed that the man never says much." He chuckled.

Settling her hands upon his, Juliet breathed in deeply. "Perhaps he will speak to her, to Noèle. It seems they have both been hurt and suffered losses. Perhaps only someone who knows what that feels like can truly understand."

"Perhaps," Henri agreed before he bent down and kissed the side of her neck. "Please, let us speak of more enjoyable things today."

Turning in his arms, Juliet looked up at him. "What did you have in mind?"

Another one of those devilishly wicked smiles lit up his face, and Juliet knew that she would never tire of seeing them. Indeed, life looked so promising it almost frightened her; but she was done being frightened or scared or terrified. Now, she wanted to live and love and be happy.

And she would be.

Juliet was certain of it.

THE END

Thank you for reading *Scorned & Craved*!

. . .

In case you haven't read *Violet & Oliver's* story yet, you can go back to Condemned & Admired - The Earl's Cunning Wife and read their adventurous love story.

Are you in the mood for a new Christmas romance? In the next installment, Disregarded & Adored - The Widower's Perfect Match, Elaine Winters (Juliet's mother) will get her own happily-ever-after. She married without love. Twice. But they say the third time is the charm, is it not?

Read a Sneak-Peek

Disregarded & Adored
The Widower's Perfect Match

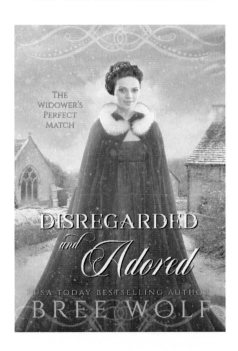

Prologue

La Roche-sur-Mer, France 1812 (or a variation thereof)

A few months earlier

Elaine Winters, Viscountess Silcox, could not recall ever having been happier than when she found herself standing in the lush gardens of the Duret home in France amongst a sea of friends and family, old and new alike, and watched her daughter Juliet marry the man she had loved and longed for for over four years.

Henri Duret.

Happy endings were not impossible, it would seem. They did come to pass...at least for Juliet.

Seeing her daughter's joyous face, Elaine sighed, relieved that after all the tumult that had marked Juliet's life, she was finally happy.

Happy and in love.

Beautiful ribbons decorated the garden and a large table had been set up, heaped with mountains of delicious-smelling food. Children were running around, laughing and giggling, stealing treats and playing catch and pushing each other on the swing that had been tied to a thick branch of an old oak tree. Everyone was dressed in bright, cheerful colors, and merry voices mingled with the soft notes of a small musical ensemble situated on the eastern side of the terrace. Elaine felt a balmy breeze tug on her mostly chestnut brown curls—a few gray hairs were showing—as it blew inland from the sea barely a stone's throw away.

It was a beautiful moment. One Elaine would never forget. Yet she could not help the soft pinch that came to her heart as her eyes swept over the many smiling faces, for most were not simply happy...but in love.

An emotion Elaine had never known herself. Certainly, she had loved her parents. She loved her younger sister and, of course, her children. She knew love, but she had never been *in love*.

A wistful sigh left Elaine's lips as she watched her daughter sink into her new husband's arms. Juliet's eyes glowed in a way that brought joy to Elaine's heart...but it also stirred pangs of envy. If only she could snuff them out!

Even though Elaine's first husband and Juliet's father, Lord Goswick, had been a kind man, he had lost his heart long before she had met him to a habit that had seen them all but ruined. And then he had passed away, his life of gambling and drinking suddenly at an end, leaving Elaine and their young daughter alone to fend off debtors.

In desperate need, Elaine had married for a second time, accepting Lord Silcox's proposal because there simply had been no other way. Unlike her first husband, Lord Silcox had been a rather unfeeling man. An heir had been all he had wanted from her, and once she had given him a son, Jacob—or Jake, as they liked to call him—they had all but lived separate lives.

An arrangement that had suited Elaine just fine.

"Would you like a refreshment?"

Elaine flinched at the sound of her son's voice, her hand flying to her chest as she felt her heart skip a beat before it resumed its normal rhythm. "Jake, oh, you caught me off guard, darling. What did you say?"

Her son's dark eyes seemed to narrow in such a deeply concerned way that he looked far older than his twelve years. "Would you like a refreshment, Mother?"

Brushing a stray curl of his brown hair from his forehead, Elaine smiled at him. "Thank you, dear. I'm perfectly content. Go and enjoy yourself." Her eyes swept over the wedding party. "With England and France still at war, it will be a while before we'll get a chance to come together again."

For a moment longer, Jake's gaze remained upon her, something hesitant in his gaze, before he nodded and then returned to pushing his...?—yes, his step-cousin Antoinette upon the swing.

Indeed, their familial relations were somewhat complicated, which was precisely why Elaine only need turn her head to spot her second husband's first wife, Alexandra Winters, dancing upon the terrace with her second husband, Antoine, another member of the Duret family. Indeed, years ago, Alexandra had faked her death and run away from her husband in the middle of the night, taking their daughter Violet with her. She had been deeply unhappy in her marriage to Lord Silcox —something Elaine could understand—and when Fate had led her into the arms of a French privateer one night, she had given up everything for her chance at love.

And it had ended happily.

Again, Elaine sighed with joy and that familiar pang of envy alike. Alexandra had found a new family and a new home in France while her husband, Lord Silcox, believing her dead, had sought himself a new wife in Elaine.

Of course, the secret had eventually come out as these kinds of things always did. Fortunately, Lord Silcox had been the only one to learn the truth; however, afraid to lose his heir—as his marriage to Elaine was now void—he had done his utmost to eliminate the threat to the continuation of his lineage, namely his first wife and daughter.

With the interference of the Duret family, however, everything had turned out well, with Lord Silcox the only one who had not survived the confrontation.

Elaine had not shed a single tear for her second husband. He had been a cold and unfeeling man, and she was only slightly ashamed to feel relief at the thought of being rid of him.

Now, she was free and safe and master of her own fate for the first time in her life. Her daughter was happily married, and her son would grow up without the harmful influence of the man who had fathered him, but who had never truly been a father to him in all those years.

Life was good again, was it not?

Elaine knew it to be so; yet when her gaze once more wandered from Juliet and Henri to other couples in love—there seemed to be too many to count!—she could not suppress that sigh of longing that made her feel as though something was missing.

"I'm happy," Elaine whispered to the wind as it brushed over her skin. "Truly, I am." And she was in so many ways...but one.

And now, it was too late. Now, she was an old woman, and love was no longer something within reach. It seemed it had never been meant for her. Few married for love. Elaine knew that. She knew that her daughter had found something rare. And yet as Elaine looked around, her eyes seeing signs of love wherever they turned, she could not help but wonder, "What might it feel like?"

Unfortunately, she would never know.

LOVE'S SECOND CHANCE: TALES OF LORDS & LADIES

LOVE'S SECOND CHANCE: TALES OF DAMSELS & KNIGHTS

LOVE'S SECOND CHANCE: HIGHLAND TALES

THE WHICKERTONS IN LOVE

FORBIDDEN LOVE SERIES

SERIES OVERVIEW

For more information visit www.breewolf.com

About Bree

USA Today bestselling and award-winning author, Bree Wolf has always been a language enthusiast (though not a grammarian!) and is rarely found without a book in her hand or her fingers glued to a keyboard. Trying to find her way, she has taught English as a second language, traveled abroad and worked at a translation agency as well as a law firm in Ireland. She also spent loooong years obtaining a BA in English and Education and an MA in Specialized Translation while wishing she could simply be a writer. Although there is nothing simple about being a writer, her dreams have finally come true.

"A big thanks to my fairy godmother!"

Currently, Bree has found her new home in the historical romance genre, writing Regency novels and novellas. Enjoying the mix of fact and fiction, she occasionally feels like a puppet master (or mistress? Although that sounds weird!), forcing her characters into ever-new situations that will put their strength, their beliefs, their love to the test, hoping that in the end they will triumph and get the happily-ever-after we are all looking for.

If you're an avid reader, sign up for Bree's newsletter on **www. breewolf.com** as she has the tendency to simply give books away. Find out about freebies, giveaways as well as occasional advance reader copies and read before the book is even on the shelves!

Connect with Bree and stay up-to-date on new releases:

facebook.com/breewolf.novels

twitter.com/breewolf_author

instagram.com/breewolf_author

bookbub.com/authors/bree-wolf

amazon.com/Bree-Wolf/e/B00FJX27Z4

Made in United States
North Haven, CT
19 October 2022

25619895R00202